THE
BLOOD
KINGDOM

KATE CUNNINGHAM

The Blood Kingdom. Copyright ©2023 by Kate Cunningham. All rights reserved.

Cover Art by MIBLart.

Map by Shepengul.

This book is the intellectual property of the author. This book is licensed for your personal enjoyment only. No part may be copied, reproduced, or transmitted without the written permission of the author. You must not circulate this book in any format. Cover art was obtained legally through MIBLart. This is a work of fiction. All of the characters, organizations, and events portrayed in this novel are either products of the author's imagination or are used fictitiously.

To my husband Thomas, because this book was always for you.

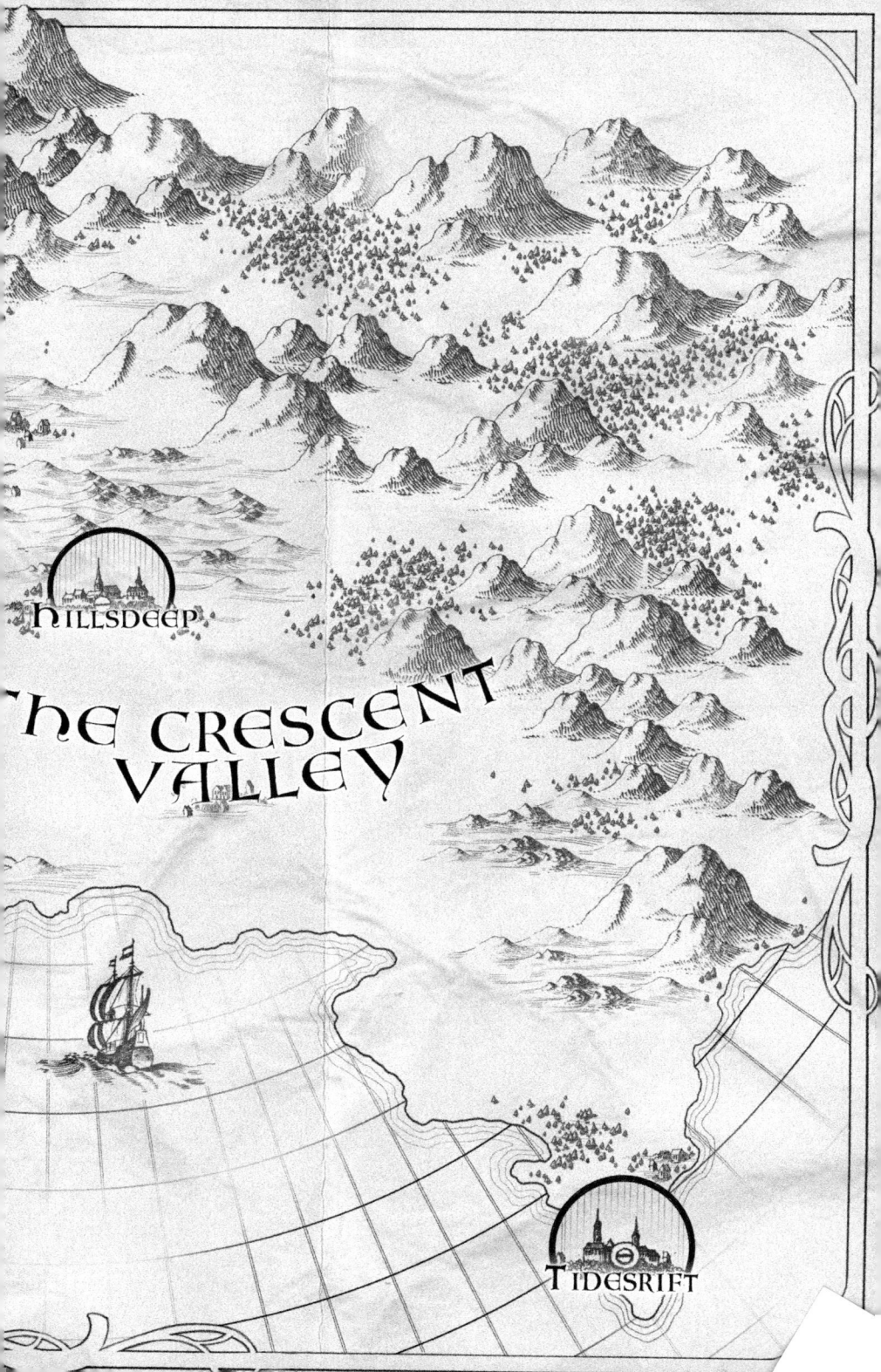

THE
BLOOD
KINGDOM

KATE CUNNINGHAM

Chapter 1

Aurelia found herself walking down the familiar corridor leading to the library. The shadows cast by the flickering torch light along the wall felt like old friends greeting her as she made her way silently through the darkened halls. A path she'd wandered so many nights over the years that she knew every dark alcove, exactly what shadows to blend into to avoid the guards on their nightly patrols.

But something was different this time.

It was too quiet. Too easy.

Not a single blue cloak interrupted her journey this evening. Not even a whisper of footsteps sent her skittering into the shadows tonight. The silence became nearly deafening, everything muted to the point of making her ears ring in an effort to pick up any sound as she walked down the familiar corridor.

She spun on a slippered heel to peer into the darkness flooding the very end. She stared into the shadows for what felt like an eternity, until it began to look like they were bleeding down the corridor, pooling closer and closer to where she stood.

The flame on the very last torch at the end of the corridor guttered out.

Her heart began a slow pounding in her chest, the beat picking up when the shadows stretched further down the hall, impossibly black, as a second torch was snuffed out with a gasp.

She turned to run, but her slippers couldn't find purchase on the gleaming white floors as the darkness behind her yawned wide.

Chapter 2

The images slipped through her fingers like grains of sand the instant she woke up in a cold sweat, no matter how hard she tried to grip onto them, just as they had for the last few months.

Opening her eyes, she convinced herself she was truly awake, silvery light filtering through her window and falling next to her. Clamping her eyelids shut again, she tried in vain to slow her racing heart. Blowing out a breath and shaking off the thick white down blanket atop her, she slid to the edge of the bed, the pads of her toes touching the cold marble floor. Clutching her hands to her knees to stop them from shaking.

Silently padding to the arched doorway that looked out onto her balcony, she opened the door and walked onto the cold polished stone, high above the sleeping Capitol sprawling to the West. Fingertips gripping the white marble balustrade, she filled her lungs with pine scented air. A balmy breeze tangled her dark waves, hinting at the warm summer day ahead.

The scent always came first, cool and whispering as the grey pines concealing the rugged mountains beneath, curling around her like a lover and making the pale skin on her arms pebble. In a few hours the city would open its eyes, and the palace perched at the very edge of the Crescent Valley would come to life. But for now, she still had the dark quiet.

Exhaling, she tried to rid herself of the lightning that crept through her veins. It was the only way to describe the strange sensation that had taken up residence inside her body lately. Always at its worst when she woke from the nightmare that taunted her most nights.

She walked the length of the balcony back through the glass doors that led into her chambers. A depthless black eye stared back from the very edge of the balustrade.

The creature didn't startle her anymore—it had been months now since the bird had taken up a semi-permanent residence on her balcony. The ragged scar across its left eye marking it as the same one that returned day after day to watch her.

The superstitions of old claimed dark wings were a harbinger of dark days. If the legends were to be believed, the ravens had acted as emissaries for the Old Ones centuries ago, and one of them had been seen flying away from the Capitol as first blood was spilled in the war between humankind and the magickal folk. The nurse maids still warned the children that even though the beasts' masters were long dead, they were capable of carrying sighs and whispers into cold graves. But Aurelia wasn't one to believe in superstitions.

The raven's watchful nature never unnerved her. The bird had become her companion of sorts, sharing the quiet of her balcony in the early morning hours, away from the endless chatter and movement of the bustling palace around her. It had a penchant for glittering things—of which she had too many to count, so she had gotten into the habit of leaving small trinkets for the creature. Taking a coin from her vanity, she laid it gently onto the stone threshold just beyond the glass doors, watching as the large bird ruffled its oil slick feathers in delight at the gleaming copper gift.

Throwing a cloak over her shoulders, she slipped out of her chambers and down the corridor. Turning a corner only to stop dead in her tracks at the sight of two blue cloaks.

Pressing her back against the wall, she made her way down the large staircase that led past the original wing of the palace, the only surviving relic from a time before the Republic. The worn grey stones gave way to slick white marble floors ahead, the palace doors thrown open to allow the night breeze in from the gardens.

Aurelia kept close to the walls, but she already knew the muted grey cloth of her cloak hid her well in the watery dawn. The winding path through the gardens was deserted. Aurelia let out a small sigh of relief at seeing she had the lush green to herself, not being as careful with her footsteps now that the soft rumble of the

Kesh drowned them out, the waters of the nearby river slow and lazy this time of year.

She picked up the hem of her skirts, heavy from the morning dew collecting on the grass, past the ever-watchful eyes of the Unnamed, their lifeless marble faces cold and impassive. A tingle ran over her knuckles as she tapped her forehead with practiced fingertips—more habit than reverence. The memory of the Nameless Brother's wooden cane still imprinted on her long-healed skin.

The acolytes that devoted their lives in service to the Unnamed Gods were varying degrees of zealous. But each of them had to give up their birth-names when they pledged their devotion, no longer the individuals that entered the temples, but just a nameless vessel of the Gods. That didn't stop Aurelia and her brothers from coming up with names for them instead, after all, there needed to be *some* way to distinguish the Nameless Brothers.

At a certain age, her eldest brother Wellan had decided he was much too mature to continue referring to their tutor as Brother Bald, or the grumpy Brother that oversaw the archives in the library as Brother Jowls. Her brother Asher, on the other hand, could still make her laugh with the names he whispered as they passed in the hallways. The thought brought a faint smile to her face as she tugged her hood over her dark tresses.

Walking purposefully across the courtyard toward the gate, she noted the handful of blue cloaks posted at the top of the wall dozens of feet above. Every back was turned, looking into the distance for anyone trying to gain entry to the palace, not concerned with someone leaving.

She ducked into the shadow of the gate; only a few more steps and she'd be hidden beneath the pines.

She lived for this. The small escape from her claustrophobic life. The freedoms that had slowly dried up to nothing as she'd approached womanhood. Lowering her hems so that she couldn't climb trees or run without tripping over her skirts. Then came the stiff corsets that forced her to take shallow breaths and restricted her movement. When she turned ten, she'd been banished from practicing with her brothers in the training pit, her behavior deemed unladylike by her mother.

A few years after that she was pulled from her tutoring lessons with Brother Bald and forced into etiquette classes instead. When she'd asked her mother why she couldn't keep learning numbers and history like her brothers, Lady Norrick had simply answered that her time was better spent preparing for her future, and that's when she realized her future looked very different from her brothers'. So instead, she spent her days learning dances and social graces, reciting the names of the families that governed the cities in the Republic; the only knowledge of use for a girl who would be made a gift to one of them at the right time.

The restrictions had been so gradual, so innocuous, that it was like the spotted ivy that grew between the heavy bricks of the garden walls. An inconvenience. An annoyance, until the thick vines had all but covered the stone. Suffocating and inextricable, because to remove them would bring the entire wall tumbling down.

She began doing Asher's math tables for him—not out of any pity for her brother, but for the sheer challenge of it. Just to prove she could. Just to prove that she was every bit as capable as her brothers ... Her small rebellion against the box they'd shoved her into.

She still walked around with that chip on her shoulder; something she hated about herself, but she'd come to terms with her place in life. And she'd found the small glimpses of happiness where she could, learning quickly that if she didn't pilfer them for herself, no one would offer up any pieces.

The rough stone of the palace gate gave way behind her back and the thick green canopy of trees blocked out the dawn as Aurelia made her way into the forest. The soft babble of the Kesh greeted her, the waters low in the late summer exposing the rocky floor of the riverbed. A shadow of the forceful rapids that began somewhere deep within the Shades and tapered off at the edge of the Valley. The wide river split the Capitol in two, the sprawling city on one side, and the palace on the other.

Picking carefully across the broad flat stones that broke the surface of the water, she made her way to the expanse of trees on the opposite bank, where the Grey Wood melted away into the blue mist of the Shades, so dark they were nearly black.

There had once been magick here, or so they'd been told. The tales of the Old Ones passed from generation to generation, in the nursery rhymes mothers sang to their babes, in the stories told around campfires in the rural villages.

The Nameless Brothers would have them believe that the demons of old still walked the rugged mountains, searching for lost souls to bring their king. The nurse maids liked to tell the children it was fairies and wood nymphs who would steal them away as a gift for their witch queen in her jeweled forest realm. The boys whispered that it was vampyres, luring virgins to their eternal death to convince the girls to slip away into dark corners with them.

The stories of the ancient war to save humanity were told and retold so often that most of the details were lost to time. And though they had won, extinguishing the evil that threatened them, there was something ancient that remained in the pines. Something with watchful eyes.

Despite the Nameless Brothers' best efforts to assure the people that the Unnamed Gods kept their borders safe, the people of the Valley still clung to the old superstitions; delicate silver chains hanging around maidens' necks and heavy iron coins clanking on the men's belts. Wrought iron fences still guarded homes, and cut glass was strung up in every window to reflect the sunlight.

The Grey Wood had earned its dark reputation, seeming to keep those who were too bold or stupid to turn back before the mists swallowed them up. Whether they were unable to find their way home in the disorienting fog, or if something found them first, no one knew for certain.

The warnings had been spoken so often, in so many different ways, that no one ventured too far under the sprawling expanse of dense green. But that never stopped Aurelia and her brothers from making bets on who could stay underneath the trees the longest without losing their nerve.

The three of them would sit in a circle, taking turns telling the old tales they'd heard from their nursemaid Galina. Then they'd push each other just over the border of the Valley onto the carpet of pine needles that covered the Shades, shrieking and running back into the sunlight of the river bank.

Aurelia had gone dashing into the mists of the Grey Wood as a girl, after Asher had dared her. Her brothers never thought she'd do it, but they usually underestimated her. She outlasted them by an hour that day, until they reluctantly charged into the pines to drag her back out, making empty threats if she ever spoke a word of it to their mother. But she could never shake the feeling she had standing beneath those behemoth pines. Wondering what secrets they kept for the thousands of years they stood vigil. It was why she came back over and over. Sneaking out in the early hours of the morning long after she'd been forbidden to leave the palace grounds.

She hadn't felt fear—no. It was recognition. It was a calling. Like the mountains beneath her feet could feel her, too. And while she stood awestruck, looking up at them, they were silently taking her measure as well.

Chapter 3

Exhaling the pine air from her lungs, Aurelia ducked back under the large archway of the gate just as an arm snaked around her waist, pulling her into the quiet stables. Her gasp quickly dissolved into laughter as a familiar weight pressed her against the wall.

"A little early to be out, don't you think, Lady Norrick?" Bastien said with raised eyebrows. "Did you really think you could slip back into the palace without anyone noticing?"

"Clearly not." Aurelia rolled her eyes, her lips curving in invitation.

Bastien's brows furrowed in exasperation. "The Shades aren't safe—how many times have I told you? And I know if I double it, that's probably how many times Asher has told you." His words were chiding, but his tone was playful as he bent to kiss her.

"Good thing I have a blue cloak who haunts my steps," she whispered against his lips.

"I'm serious, Aurelia," he replied, placing a hand on her shoulder and forcing her to meet his blue eyes. "There have been strange reports from the villages at the Valley's edge—" But before he could launch into a lecture, she'd raised herself up onto her toes to cover his mouth with hers. A shameless distraction as she felt his body melt against hers in response. He pulled away at last, running his thumb across her cheek. "You're too wild."

"And will the bold Captain Veron be the one to tame me?" she asked, tangling her fingers in the soft waves of his tawny hair, pulling him into her again.

"I'm not sure anyone is capable of that," he answered, "Least of all me."

These stolen minutes were the only thing they had, and Aurelia was ravenous for them. But Bastien, ever the voice of reason, reminded her of the dawn light that was beginning to spill into the Valley.

"Before I forget." Bastien's hand slipped inside the cerulean cloak that marked him as a member of the Blue Guard, a thin black book in his grasp when he removed it.

"You found it," Aurelia exclaimed breathlessly.

"I did," he answered with a tight expression as he handed the journal to her, still holding a firm grip on the edge as Aurelia tried to pry it from his fingers. "If Wellan notices this is gone—"

"He won't," she interrupted, tearing it from his grasp. "I doubt he even knows it exists," she mumbled distractedly as she flipped through the first few pages. Her father's familiar scrawl on the paper sending an ache through her chest.

"We did everything we could, Aurelia. I don't know what else you could hope to find in there," Bastien said gently.

With a huff of breath, she answered, "If nothing else ... closure."

Bastien looked like he'd been about to give her another lecture on staying inside the palace walls, but both of them turned their heads at the whinny of the horses. All of them rousing from their slumber and nervously stomping the ground. A dark blot had appeared over the open door. The proud outline of the large raven, motionless as it left everything around it unsettled.

Bastien let out a shrill whistle, piercing the quiet morning.

"What are you doing?" Aurelia hissed.

"Calling for Ned, so he can finally shoot the damn thing," he answered, placing two fingers in his mouth to whistle again.

"Don't!" Aurelia shouted, yanking his hand away.

"That beast has been startling the horses for weeks now! Every time it comes around, they get agitated." He gestured to where the raven had been moments ago, but the space was empty now, its dark occupant gone. Bastien swore under his breath as Aurelia heard Ned's heavy footsteps. And she slipped away again into the early morning with her father's journal safely tucked into the pocket of her cloak.

Peering into the glass mirror above her wash basin, Aurelia raked her fingers through her dark brown hair, tangled from the breeze and still tumbled from her restless night. Some errant strands gilded in the early morning sunlight, others glinting fire.

The woman staring back in the mirror was almost unrecognizable from that strong, wild girl she'd once been. The same heart shaped face was there, the same eyes looked back at her, amber bursting into gold at the center. But there was a sharp edge to her gaze now, something she had tried, in vain, to soften at the behest of her mother. She'd been repeatedly reminded that the men at court would be too intimidated by her stare alone that they'd never work up the nerve to speak to her, much less marry her. She didn't mind.

She didn't want a man who was afraid of her.

Bunching up her mud-stained cloak, she buried it in the bottom drawer of her dresser. If any of the lady's maids her mother employed found the evidence of her morning excursions, they'd be sure to pass it along to Lady Norrick.

She'd pleaded and begged her mother to let their nurse-maid Galina continue to see to her needs, but Lady Norrick had insisted that a proper young lady should be surrounded by her peers. What Lady Norrick had left unsaid was that she thought the older woman that Aurelia loved like a second mother was a bad influence, turning a blind eye to her daughter's unladylike behavior and indulging Aurelia's love of wild tales.

It indeed was Galina who sparked Aurelia's passion for storytelling. Her voice was rough with age. Husky and soft when she told stories of the creatures that used to rule the world. Lilting and smooth when she sang the old rhymes of warning and protection.

Aurelia had been hungry for more of the stories. Ravenous for the world outside of the palace walls inked onto the age-worn maps hanging in her father's study. And that's when she'd started sneaking into the library at night. Voracious for a glimpse outside of the small existence she knew, even if it was only through ink on paper.

But even that small pleasure had dried up, the faces of her lady's maids ever-changing, but their eyes always watchful. Whispering behind delicate hands. Being a member of the Norrick family came with its own "bag of shit" as Asher would say.

Of course, the family had prestige, power, and wealth ... But everything came at a price. Aurelia had grown up watching what she said, because everything could be used as leverage. Any secret, no matter how dull, could be fuel for a scandal. The perpetual feeling that everyone was waiting for her to stumble and fall from grace, hungry for it, haunted her steps.

Throwing on a dressing gown, Aurelia slipped her father's journal into the narrow drawer of her vanity before going into her bathing chamber and splashing water onto her face. A few moments later, a faint knock against her door was the only warning before lady's maids poured into the room to begin the tedious process of making Aurelia presentable for the day.

One of them dug a hand into the wardrobe, tugging out a bright magenta gown while the others scraped and combed her hair into submission. It took all three of them to wrestle the skirts of the gown and lace the corset, but when she took a final look in the mirror, the lady's maids seemed pleased with themselves.

She had to admit the color *was* beautiful on her, setting off her pale skin and dark hair. The neckline cut to follow the curve of her breasts without being immodest. The sheer fabric of the sleeves gathered at her shoulders and billowed out to brush against her arms, collecting at the wrists in delicate cuffs. The bodice was beaded with small pearls and cinched in until she could barely breath. Flowing magenta and burgundy chiffon skirts draped elegantly along her curves and pooled to the floor.

She huffed out a breath, or as much as the rigid corset would allow. At least her mother would be pleased.

Chapter 4

Her bright skirts whispered with each step down the white marble floor, looking like a fallen rose petal on fresh snow. Aurelia's dark hair threatened to escape the elaborately pinned hairstyle balanced on top of her head, leaving her scalp and neck aching already as she turned to look out the windows lining the hallway. Ornate carriages already lined the drive. A steady stream of visiting delegations had begun arriving early this morning.

The governors from the larger cities within the Valley had descended on the Capitol, the reason for this particular visit unclear, but a frenetic energy had blown into the palace with them. When her father had been a Councilor, he'd spent much of his time entertaining the various governors, usually trying to negotiate new trade agreements for their cities or handling disputes between the regions. And while the men talked business, the women traded gossip.

Lady Norrick's tastefully appointed sitting room was already full to bursting. Nearly every lilac-colored sofa and chair was occupied, a handful of the ladies taking in the fresh air on the generous balcony. Golden afternoon light fell through the large windows, and while usually these social engagements were grating, today Aurelia fought to ignore the dull headache forming behind her eyes.

The last few months she hadn't had a full night's rest, and it was finally catching up to her. The headaches had become more frequent, too. Starting a few weeks ago as a dull throbbing ache that never really left, always showing up at the most inopportune times.

She tried desperately to follow the thread of conversation around her, the young ladies exuberant about the ball this evening, pressing her for the details. It was in celebration of her twenty-fifth birthday, after all, but nothing about tonight was of her choosing.

Her mother had requested a large celebration, and she hadn't fought back on it; if only to lighten the pain of her father's absence. It would be a welcomed distraction for her entire family after the difficult months they'd endured after his death. She still dreaded it, knowing the absence of his laughter and his quiet presence would plague her all evening.

Sitting next to her was the pretty young wife of Bastien's uncle. Lady Jane Veron was a stunning woman. Her pale blonde hair shining like spun gold in the afternoon light as she smiled graciously at one of the young ladies across from her. Aurelia had always envied her of that—her ability to effortlessly blend in. The epitome of elegance and grace.

Jane had come from a wealthy family in Hillsdeep looking to gain titled connections. She'd arrived at court with every eye turned on her. The young woman's beauty was unmatched, much to Lady Norrick's dismay. Jane was always ready with a witty response, her sparkling smile contagious and warm, easily pulling everyone into her orbit. And while the other young women at court had always smiled at Aurelia while whispering behind their hands as soon as her back was turned, Jane had only ever been kind and genuine. Maybe not quite a friend, but something close to it.

When Jane caught Councilor Veron's eye, it was the best her family could have hoped for. The Verons were one of the original seven families that formed the High Council in the aftermath of the war, holding a seat for centuries. Bastien's uncle currently held the position, though the two men were so unalike in disposition and appearance that no one ever assumed they shared blood. The title would never fall to Bastien either, if his uncle had any say in the matter. And if half the rumors were true, Councilor Veron took his duty to sire an heir quite seriously, diligently fucking every woman within the Capitol who would let him into her bed.

Lovely Jane was the answer to Councilor Veron's need of a legitimate heir, and he was her family's answer to a powerful connection. Little did they know they were handing their daughter over to a monster ... And if they did, would it have changed anything?

Aurelia realized she'd let her gaze linger for a little too long when Lady Veron discretely tugged the sleeve of her gown back into place. Her slender fingers hiding a fresh set of bruises beneath the dark fabric. Somehow everyone else failed to notice the covered dresses she wore in the stifling heat, the tear-stained cheeks when she thought no one else was looking.

Aurelia pitied the woman. No—pity wasn't the right word. Admiration wasn't quite it, either, but there was steel in the young Lady Veron's eye that whispered of strength Aurelia could never hope to possess. Something in the way she held her head high and regal that spoke of duty before all else. At the expense of everything else. And it made Aurelia wonder what it must feel like to have that sense of purpose governing your life. What was it like to willingly accept your lot? She wasn't sure she'd ever know contentment, but she envied those around her who settled into their places without a fight.

The constant chatter was like nails on stone. It was impossible to drown out the conversations in her mother's sitting room, the volume rising to an unbearable level until Aurelia felt like she was suffocating in the noise. The blaring sunlight coming through the glass feeling like it was burning a hole through her pupils.

Excusing herself, she made her way back to her chambers, ignoring the pointed look from her mother as she left. She'd get an earful about her abrupt exit later.

Pinching the bridge of her nose between her thumb and forefinger, she closed her eyes for a second, basking in the small relief from the pressure building in her head as every patch of light set off a flare of pain in her temples.

Closing the heavy drapes in her room, the pain subsided slightly in the dark. Tugging open the small drawer of her vanity, Aurelia looked for the headache tonic Galina had given her. It didn't get rid of them entirely, but she'd drink anything to take the edge off the stabbing pain—

The black leather journal slid to the front of the drawer.

She rubbed her fingers across her father's diary. Her headache forgotten for a moment, she opened the first few pages with shaky hands, savoring the familiar writing. The simple notes her father made during his days. Reminders to send correspondence, items to discuss at Council meetings, all of it so ... ordinary.

Leafing through to the final pages, dread pooled in her gut as her father's elegant handwriting descended into frantic scratches. The crack forming in her chest splitting a little wider with each word she read, until at last she closed the journal. Afraid that if she read any further her heart might split in two.

She woke to a flurry of activity in her chambers, her lady's maids arriving with a tower of sparkling fabric and velvet boxes balanced precariously on top.

Her birthday, she remembered with a grumble as she rolled out of bed and stumbled into her bathing chamber. Gods, what she truly needed was about thirty-six hours of uninterrupted sleep, she thought, splashing a handful of cold water onto her face.

The ladies worked efficiently, helping her step into the dress her mother had selected. It was easily the most eye-catching garment Lady Norrick had commissioned for her yet. The satiny cream fabric shone with thousands upon thousands of tiny crystals sewn into the bodice, gently fading down into luscious skirts that swished and sighed. The neckline dipped ever so slightly to show the swell of her breasts, and the sleeves were made of delicate strings of glass beads that began just below her shoulder and draped around her arm to the back of her bodice. A little more daring than the gowns her mother usually preferred.

Opening one of the small velvet boxes that had arrived with the gown, Aurelia sighed at the glittering diamond encrusted hair pins inside. One of the ladies collected her pile of dark waves at the nape of her neck into an elegant twist of curls. And after a few minutes, the silky strands were pinned into place, forming a glittering crown along her head.

She was still smoothing out the skirts of her dress when she heard a knock on her door. Asher stood just outside, clothed in the cerulean uniform of the Blue Guard that set off the dark red of his hair, extending an arm to her.

"You know it's ridiculous that mother won't let me walk the palace alone after dark anymore," she muttered, rolling her eyes as she looped her arm through his.

Asher chuckled, but his tone quickly grew somber as they started down the corridor, "She's still ... unsettled after what happened to Father. It's only been a few months. Just let her have this. It gives her peace of mind."

"I suppose you're right," she sighed. "Though I've given in to every ridiculous detail she requested for this evening. It's a little over the top, even for her."

The corner of Asher's mouth twitched ever so slightly. It was the same tell he'd always had when he was hiding something, even when they'd been children. When he'd tried to convince her that if she played too close to the Grey Wood the evil witch queen would send her demons to come drag her away, or if she ate the berries that grew at the edge of the Valley she'd sprout blue wings and be able to fly, when really they just made her stomach cramp horribly and gave her the shits for an afternoon.

She elbowed Asher in the ribs. "I know when you're hiding something ... Out with it."

"Just remember not to kill the messenger?" He rolled his green eyes up to the blue crescent moon sigils hanging from the ceiling with a sigh. "Mother has invited every eligible bachelor in the Republic to your party tonight."

Her steps faltered, but Asher's arm steadied her as she gave a hard swallow.

"I don't know why she bothered with a party when we both know she and Wellan will make the choice for me," she uttered under her breath, tugging at the rigid corset digging into her ribs. Asher didn't reply, only offering a sympathetic sigh as he gave her hand a squeeze.

Deep down, she'd known. She'd picked up on all the heavy-handed hints their mother had been giving her about her age, rattling off every detail of the visiting parties.

It wasn't the first time Aurelia had been dangled like a carrot in front of powerful men. Men visiting the Capitol on official business, negotiating new trade agreements, overseeing the selection of ministry members for the larger cities in the Republic. Her family always made certain that they would catch a glimpse of the young Lady Norrick. Put just a kernel of a thought that she might be theirs if they played by the rules her family laid out. But so far, she'd dodged every proposal.

Their footsteps echoed loudly down the marble corridor, approaching the large wooden doors leading into the Great Hall. Asher glanced down at her, but she refused to meet his stare. He would try to soften her anger and would most likely be successful. So, she continued ignoring him, staring straight ahead.

"Ready?" he whispered.

She squeezed his arm back in silent confirmation, bowing her head to shake off the fire burning in her eyes, schooling her features into a gracious smile as they prepared to enter the Great Hall. The blue cloaked guards flanking either side of the corridor gave a dip of their chins to Asher, opening the doors.

Chapter 5

The cavernous hall was full of smiling faces that turned to watch their entrance, awash in golden light from the sparkling chandeliers high above their heads. Blue sigils hung from every wall, the silver thread catching the light, illuminating the crescent moon and seven linked circles embroidered into the heavy fabric.

Every surface glittered with delicate dishes, silver serving platters, and glass champagne flutes reflecting the light from hundreds of lit candles. Even the softly bubbling wine in everyone's glasses added to the glowing ambiance Lady Norrick had created. Aurelia's breath caught at the beautiful sight, but soon her anger simmered back to the surface. Asher hadn't been exaggerating when he said their mother had invited every eligible bachelor in the Valley.

But, *why*? Why was her mother putting on this ridiculous show? If her fate had already been decided, they could have told her and been done with it. She had no power to refuse. No authority of her own to argue the decision.

Her eldest brother silently took his place beside her as Asher stepped away with an apologetic glance. Wellan's tall figure loomed over her shoulder as he welcomed the visiting parties and made introductions. She was certain that he'd been a part of their mother's scheme, but he didn't bother to offer an explanation, and she hadn't been expecting one.

No less than a dozen suitors left chaste kisses on her hand. She smiled politely and accepted their compliments graciously, but she knew them for the hollow tokens that they were. As the only daughter of the Norrick family, a marriage to her would come with a great deal of political sway, including a brother-in-law on the High Council.

The music had picked up in the ballroom, and soon she was swept away onto the dancefloor in a never-ending line of men. A blur of faces and names, titles and lands that she wouldn't remember come tomorrow, and it didn't matter anyway, there was only one man here that she wanted.

Standing next to Asher in a matching Blue Guard uniform was Bastien. He'd been studiously avoiding her all night, just as they'd agreed. His ice blue eyes landed briefly on her before he went back to his conversation and she was whirled away again.

She finally had a chance to excuse herself, thanking the gods that her mother always kept the sparkling wine in healthy supply as she plucked a glittering glass from the neat row on the table. Only gulping down one sip before a beautiful woman with upswept auburn hair approached.

Still a renowned beauty within the Republic, age had done nothing to dull the charm of Lady Norrick. If anything, time had taught her how to wield her stunning smile, laughing green eyes, and ethereal grace like a cudgel to bend others to her will, and she'd honed it like a weapon.

Aurelia gulped down the rest of her champagne—she wasn't nearly drunk enough for this. "I hear I'll be leaving with a husband tonight?" she hissed, with enough bite to elicit a shocked look in her mother's green eyes, her usually cheerful expression turning serious.

"Ari... It's time. You're twenty-five," Lady Norrick whispered. "Our world is not kind to women without the protection of a powerful husband."

The world wasn't kind to women with powerful husbands either, Aurelia thought with a glance toward where Lady Veron stood across the room. The gossamer sleeves of Jane's gown covered her arms to the wrists. Her smile as radiant as ever, never hinting at the hell that she lived through behind closed doors.

"Trust me, Aurelia." Her mother tucked a stray strand of hair behind her ear, gently dropping Aurelia's hand from her own. Putting a well-trained smile back onto her face, Lady Norrick walked into the crowd.

All evening, Aurelia was passed from man to man—each of them boasting of their titles, their homes, their fortunes. Governors and noblemen. The nephews and sons of Councilors. Even a few of the wealthier merchants from the port cities. Their ages spanning from nineteen-year-old boys to seventy-year-old men. And she danced with them all, a practiced smile etched onto her face, counting down the minutes until the evening would be over.

Aurelia nodded distractedly as the aging Governor of Hillsdeep regaled her with his family's lineage. "And my mother's uncle was a Fost, you know. He held a seat on the Council for fifty years—"

"May I cut in?" a deep voice rumbled from behind them.

And though the Governor looked ready to protest, his eyes widened, graciously giving Aurelia's hand to the man.

A newcomer to the Capitol—she was certain of it, because he was easily the most beautiful man she'd ever laid eyes on.

Jet black hair fell in dark waves just below the sharp line of his jaw, and dark eyes the color of... well, she couldn't be certain. Every detail seemed to be swallowed up by the shadows in the hall. Even in his relaxed posture, she guessed he must have stood at least a few inches taller than anyone else in the room, though his build could never be confused for lanky with the way his broad shoulders filled out the sharply tailored jacket he wore.

His eyes met hers briefly before she glanced away again, knowing a blush was creeping into her face as he led her across the dance floor. All of her usual manners were nowhere to be found; every topic of polite conversation escaping her in the strange daze that had fallen over her until the song ended and he brushed a kiss across her knuckles, disappearing into the crowd once more.

"And may I have a dance? Or have they all been spoken for?"

The familiar voice startled her from the stupor she'd been in, and Aurelia's face lit up when she turned to see the Governor of Tellus. She sent up a silent thanks to the Unnamed that her friend was here tonight. At least there was one man she could relax around in the middle of this spectacle her mother had created.

"Of course, as long as you don't step on my toes like you did the entire night at the last ball, Governor Caspane," she drawled.

Christian's face broke into an infectious smile, his boisterous laugh filling the hall. "To you—I'm still just Christian," he replied, extending his hand. He'd filled out since the last time she'd seen him, but she would recognize her childhood friend anywhere—even if the better part of a decade had passed since she'd seen him.

The queue of suitors cast envious looks Christian's way as he led her onto the dance floor. "Do you think this is how the prized stallions feel at the spring auctions?" she asked sarcastically.

"Oh, come now," he chided. "At least your mother always serves the finest wine." He grinned, getting a laugh out of her. "And which of these lucky men will win the heart of the young Lady Norrick this evening?" Christian teased as she glanced up again to take one more look at the handsome stranger across the room—only to find he was gone.

"Are you volunteering?" She smiled, trying to shake off the strange sensation that had taken up residence in her chest. "You've sent the entire Capitol into an uproar over your arrival. Every unmarried woman at court has been lighting candles to the Unnamed that they might be the one to catch Governor Caspane's eye." The handsome new Governor of Tellus may have been the coveted bachelor, but to Aurelia he would always be the lanky teenager that had become fast friends with her brothers.

"Me? Oh, I could never allow you to stoop so low." His dark brows knitted together with mock severity. "What about the Governor of Hillsdeep?" Christian teased with a nod in the direction of the Governor hunched over his dinner, looking like he was on the verge of falling asleep.

"In want of a nap, I'd guess," Aurelia whispered as the Governor nodded off.

"You'd be tired, too, if you'd been a governor for half a century and outlived three wives," Christian laughed.

"I don't intend to be number four," Aurelia joked. Gods—she hoped Wellan wouldn't do that to her.

Christian bent his head toward hers. "Though, I must admit, I think my greatest competition here tonight is the dashing Captain Veron," he whispered conspiratorially.

Looking over Christian's shoulder, she saw a small crowd of young ladies had surrounded Bastien and Asher across the hall. An unbidden pang of jealousy stabbed at her chest.

"He looks occupied at the moment," she replied more bitterly than she intended.

"It's not any of them he's staring at," Christian muttered with a hint of a smile at seeing Aurelia's eyes snap back in Bastien's direction.

Sure enough, Bastien's gaze was focused on her as he began walking across the dance floor.

Christian quietly excused himself, his timing impeccable as always, as she turned to see Bastien only a few steps away, his tawny hair in its usual mess of curls. He held out his broad hand to her, his eyes glittering like chips of ice in the candlelight as he gracefully swept her away.

It was impossible to ignore the way her heart pounded when he whispered in her ear. Gazed down at her with those eyes, the color of cloudless summer days. Like the frozen Kesh in the winter. She'd gotten too comfortable looking into those eyes. Too familiar with his touch.

For months, years, she'd told herself that it didn't mean anything. That he was another small rebellion. But they'd both uttered words to each other in the dark of night that couldn't be taken back. Words that would make it that much harder to end things.

Aurelia hadn't been able to touch anything all evening. Her stomach had been in knots since she'd left her chambers this morning, and she'd been twirled around and around the dancefloor so many times that she might vomit if she had to make one more spin. She just needed one moment alone to drop the smile that had been plastered to her face for the last two hours. And the Unnamed knew there were plenty of other single women here tonight to keep all of the men her mother had invited occupied.

Walking past the impressive tower of champagne flutes, she smiled politely at the other guests, dodging anyone who looked like they might try to stop her with small talk. Past the quiet alcoves, where more than a few couples had snuck away to find a dark corner.

A streak of copper hair ducked into the last dimly lit alcove, and immediately she knew it was Asher. He'd recently picked up a bad habit of entangling himself with the married women at court. She rolled her eyes and stifled a groan.

A hand reached out and wrapped around her waist, dragging her into one of the darkened spaces. But before she could protest, Bastien's laughter filled the small area.

His bronze curls tumbled over his forehead and his blue eyes glittered with mischief as he bent to cup his hands around her face and kiss her. "You have no idea how much I've wanted to do that," he whispered.

"Then why did it take you so long?" she playfully asked, stretching up on her toes to kiss him again.

"Because I'm an idiot." His chuckle rumbled through her chest as he slowly, torturously pulled away from her. "And your brother would kill me if he knew how many nights I've spent in your chambers."

"Which one?"

"Both," he answered, before tugging her against him.

What had begun as stolen kisses in the darkened corners of the palace as teenagers had turned into late night trysts in the gardens as they'd grown older. Each of them knowing that there was no future where they could be together. Aurelia would be given to whichever man possessed the alliance her family required. Bastien would continue to move up the ranks of the Blue Guard, though his title would never be enough to secure a marriage with her.

And they'd never said the words aloud, but they both knew their time together was limited. It was the unspoken rule between them. But these small acts of rebellion were the only fleeting moments when Aurelia felt in control of her caged existence, so she took them greedily.

"Aurelia." Bastien's breath was warm down the side of her neck when he spoke her name, his voice husky now. He lifted her chin with a finger to meet his gaze, then pressed his lips to her mouth. Gentle at first, then harder with longing and possession.

She kissed him back, rougher than she intended, biting his lower lip hard enough to draw blood. Shocked at her own aggression, she pulled away, but when he leaned in to kiss her again, she found herself licking away the small drop of red. Tangling her fingers through his hair.

Bastien's tall frame pressed into her body, driving her against the cold wall behind them, his hips meeting hers in dangerous invitation. His fingers wove through her dark silken waves so that she couldn't move her head from his grip, even to catch her breath.

A fire had ignited inside her. The relentless headache muted and the incessant nausea receding in the wake of the delicious warmth that spread through her body at Bastien's touch. She kissed him, savoring the taste of him. Like every nerve had awakened.

Bastien's voice was low, whispering sweet words into her ear as his hand made a steady sweep up her thigh. His thumb making torturous circles, edging closer to where she wanted it. He pressed his mouth to hers again, brushing kisses down her neck as a breathless gasp escaped her. That now familiar heat under her skin burned its way down her arms as Bastien wedged his hips against hers.

She kissed him again, catching a hint of copper as her tongue swept in his mouth. Opening her eyes, she saw the satisfied grin on his face as he pushed himself away from her with a final chaste kiss on her cheek. A silent understanding passed between them. It was too risky to stay here any longer.

He brushed a thumb across her cheek, and the pounding in her skull that had ebbed for a few blissful minutes came rushing back as she watched him leave.

Chapter 6

Large oak doors loomed before her. Swinging open silently on freshly oiled hinges as she checked for any sign of the Brothers working late into the evening. No lantern light greeted her. Only the dim light of the moon filtering through the large window inside.

Maybe it was the mysterious history of the place that drew her back over and over again, the pock-marked stone such a stark contrast to the gleaming white marble that surrounded her everywhere else. Or the fact that her favorite place was housed in this otherwise unremarkable stretch of corridors, but her feet always led her back here.

The first time she'd been caught sneaking into the library, one of the grouchy old Brothers had pulled her by the ear to her father; she'd been thirteen and shadeberry red from embarrassment. And even as her father made a promise of punishing her, he'd given her a wink from behind the Brother's back. That night when she'd expected a lashing, or at the very least a scolding, he'd simply said, *Next time—don't get caught.*

And she hadn't.

The faint scent of musty paper and old leather always called her back. She loved reading too much to stay away from the library entirely. She'd just gotten better at sneaking into the stacks in the dead of night and quietly removing one book at a time, replacing it with the last she had borrowed. She was quickly running out of the books she loved to read. Legends. Tales of the kingdoms overseas. One of the few ways she could escape her planned, predictable life, even if it was only in her mind.

Her father seemed to be the only one who understood her restlessness. Her discontent. And now that he was gone ... Those feelings only seemed amplified without a kindred spirit.

She remembered hiding from her dance instructor in her father's study, looking at the maps on his wall of all the places outside the palace walls. Begging him to tell her every detail of the trips he made to the faraway cities, knowing he would always indulge her curiosity.

Running a finger down the spines of each book, Aurelia stopped when she found one of her favorites. A collection of the kinds of stories her nursemaid used to tell her at bedtime, tales of the dangerous creatures that ruled their world before the High Council was formed.

"The histories are a favorite of mine as well," a deep voice said from the dark, startling Aurelia so much that she nearly dropped the book in her hands.

Whirling around, she caught the profile of a man, outlined in the dim moonlight leaking through the windows. Full lips curved up slightly in a conspiratorial smirk, his silhouette giving him away as the same stranger who'd danced with her.

Dark waves fell just below his sharp jaw, a straight nose like the ones chiseled onto the marble faces of the Unnamed Gods. Full lips that seemed to be holding back laughter as he said, "I won't mention seeing you here if you don't mention seeing me either."

She relaxed a little at his casual tone, testing the weight of the book in her hands. "I'd hardly call them histories—folklore might be more appropriate," she said, the darkness making her bolder than she should have been with a stranger.

"And what does your 'folklore' tell you?" he asked, his words polished and rounded, betraying a noble birth. Or at the very least a wealthy one.

"Do the Nameless Brothers not pound it into your skull where you're from?" she hedged, her curiosity piqued as she tried to get a better look at him, though somehow he always managed to stay just in the shadows.

"I grew up in a more ... rural area."

Pacing the stacks in front of her, she ran a finger across the cracked leather spines, pausing in front of one particularly large volume. "Centuries ago, beings who wielded magick ruled the world, threatening to wipe out the human race." Taking the book into her hand, she let it fall open at random, the binding splitting open to reveal a frightening drawing of the Old Ones, "But the Unnamed Gods intervened on our behalf—pressing a righteous thumb on the scales of victory."

She snapped the book shut again, returning it once more to its home as she spoke the words she knew by rote, reciting them in the same intonation the Nameless Brothers used. "The Unnamed protect us still, within the borders of the Valley, their wisdom passed through the First Brother to the original seven families who were chosen to govern on the High Council," she finished with mocking reverence.

She didn't bother to hide her disregard for the Nameless Brotherhood. None of the Brothers who'd had the unfortunate task of tutoring her had given her much faith in their divine duty. And the aging First Brother who'd served as advisor to the High Council since she could remember never struck her as anything other than another man at court hungry for more power, his sermons at the palace temple usually a mixture of fear mongering and shameless guilt trips.

It was easy for him to speak to the citizens of the Valley about tithing when he lived in luxurious quarters here in the palace, all his needs met without a single thought to how they were provided. He condemned the old superstitions with righteous indignation, chastising the women for the silver that hung around their necks, and shaming the commoners for the iron fences that surrounded their homes. But it was easy to believe in the protection of the Unnamed when the thick walls of the palace surrounded him.

The stranger gave an irreverent tilt of his head. A lank of silky black hair falling over his face and further obscuring the handsome features hidden in the shadows. "There's a seed of truth in every story. Though, the passing of time and the fallibility of human memory distorts the real history."

She slowly scanned the row of books, her finger landing lightly on one detailing the supposed dark creatures that roamed the Shades long ago, each page more ridiculous than the last. Even when she'd first laid eyes on it at the age of seven she'd thought it preposterous. "And what truth has been distorted in here?" she laughed, holding up the book.

A grin tugged at the corner of his mouth. "I, for one, don't care to deal in absolutes. To think that every person who possessed magick wielded it for evil," he gave a slight shrug of his broad shoulders, "just as likely as every human being inherently good."

"I don't know if I believe any of it," she laughed, glancing up to see his dark eyes studying her. "Blasphemous, I know," she added, pushing the book back onto the shelf.

"And yet here you are, pilfering books about the very thing," he chided with a click of his tongue, raising his dark brows.

Turning to look at him again, wishing so desperately that he would take just one step into the moonlight, she couldn't help smiling at the playful accusation. She liked the way he bantered with her. It was—*real*. Not the polite, rigid conversations she'd suffered through the entire evening.

"I never could resist a good story," she replied.

He gave her a knowing smirk in return, and though she couldn't make out the color of his eyes in the dark library—they were fixed on her in a way that made her blood heat. And she was thankful for the cover of darkness as she felt a blush creep into her face.

She cleared her throat. "Are you here with one of the delegations? I don't think I've made your acquaintance before."

"It's my first visit to the Capitol." A smirk curved his lips, like there was some joke she'd missed.

"And are you going to make me guess where you're from?" He sketched a mocking bow, the movement graceful despite his height. "Hmm ... not Hillsdeep," she murmured. He didn't have the lilting accent that their people possessed. The vowels that rolled like their green hills.

He shook his head, his grin egging her on in their game.

"Not Tellus."

"No?" he taunted.

The truth was, she didn't care to guess right. She'd rather waste the time clinging to a few more moments here in the quiet library with him than return to the party. *Her* party. She shook her head, "Christian would never allow someone in his company that might outshine him," she added with a laugh. "And unless you're some noble's nephew or distant cousin invited recently to court ... You must be with the Tidesrift delegation."

He raised a dark brow at the comment, giving a small nod in confirmation.

"I'm sorry the party was such a dull affair that you left," she added.

"I could say the same to you," he replied, pushing off of the shelves he'd been leaning against to stand to his full height, "Seeing that we both ended up here." He tucked the errant lock of his dark hair behind his ear and grinned, "Except—I'm not sorry."

"No?" she whispered, her heart pounding against her ribs at the sound of his voice, wishing that she could make him keep speaking to her.

"Until we meet again," he said with a dip of his chin.

It wasn't until he left that she realized she never asked his name.

Chapter 7

A parade of messengers delivering flower arrangements and gifts flooded Aurelia's chambers the following morning. Only a handful of the names attached to them jostling her memory enough to remember the men who sent them.

One man was firmly imprinted in her mind, and though she'd barely made out his profile in the darkened library last night; the sharp edge of his jaw, the straight slope of his nose, the dark brows raised in amusement—those features were etched into her memory.

Asher's copper colored hair shone brightly in the afternoon light of Aurelia's chambers. He sat across from her, sipping coffee and taking liberties with the fruit and chocolate arrangements that had been sent to her. At least someone was enjoying them; one look at the fruit was making her stomach turn. She was too distracted to eat, anyway.

Throwing herself onto the divan, she pressed the cold cloth to her eyes trying to rid herself of another splitting headache.

"You should let Galina make her special tonic for you."

"I'm *certain* that Galina's hangover cure would only make me sicker."

"That's the magic of it," Asher replied gleefully, "Gets the alcohol out of your system expediently."

Aurelia gave a groan in reply.

"Who are the lucky contenders for my sister's heart?" Asher asked, absentmindedly lifting a note attached to the bouquet next to him. "Oh! The Governor of Hillsdeep! What a lucky lady you are. And if you're *really* lucky, he might even live long enough to make it to the wedding!"

Aurelia chuckled, rolling her eyes as he continued to read out the ludicrously simpering notes. These men had spent only a handful of minutes with her all evening before declaring their undying love for her.

Every time she turned, there was another pungent floral arrangement reminding her that an hourglass had been turned on her freedom, the grains of sand steadily pouring out minute by minute.

"And ... Bastien?" Asher asked.

Aurelia huffed out a breath, caught off guard by Asher's sudden seriousness. Standing up to get a glass of water, she purposely turned her face away to hide the blush that was creeping up her neck.

"Aurelia ... I'm not blind. Everyone can see the way he looks at you," Asher pressed when she didn't respond, "He's been my best friend since we were children. You know you have my blessing if that's what this is about. I can't think of anyone better to hand my sister off to."

"I'm not a possession to be handed off," she bit off. But she knew better than to hope for any say in the matter. Bastien's position as a Captain in the Blue Guard had nowhere near the reach Wellan hoped to achieve with his little sister's match.

"You know what I mean, Ari," Asher said apologetically. "He'll take good care of you. He's kind, he's well respected at court ... It's plain to see you like each other well enough." Asher took a gentler tone, "Those are better circumstances than most of us can hope for. I don't say that to be cruel, I just want the best for you. Becoming Bastien's wife, having his children—that would be a good life for you."

A good life for a *woman*, is what he left unsaid.

A hint of sadness passed over Asher's face when she looked at him again, but the last thing she wanted to talk about was her impending engagement, especially when it would serve no purpose other than to make her wish for something that would never be.

The weight of her father's journal pressed into her side as Aurelia walked down the hallway later that afternoon. Wellan usually took his tea around this time, and if she was lucky, his study would be unlocked, and she could replace the journal before he noticed its absence.

She paused outside the door, rapping her knuckles on the oiled wood. Her pulse jumping a little as Wellan's gruff voice answered, "Come in."

"Wellan—" she began, hoping she'd find an excuse for seeing him, but as the door opened wider, she saw Asher in one of the high-backed wooden chairs, their mother seated next to him.

"It's good you're here." Wellan gestured to an empty seat in the study. She glanced toward Asher for some explanation, but his eyes were trained on the floor, color high in his cheeks like he'd been arguing as Wellan added, "I've accepted a proposal on your behalf."

Her stomach went into her throat. "Who?" was all she could muster as she found her voice again.

"Governor Westeron of Tidesrift," Wellan answered.

"There were *other* proposals—" Asher cut in, his knuckles turning white as he gripped the arm of his chair.

"None worth considering given what Tidesrift can provide for us. A union with that man could guarantee us unlimited access to the markets overseas. Not to mention the benefit of his sizable armada," Wellan seethed.

Clearly, they'd been arguing the point for a while now. Would they have bothered to tell her at all if she hadn't happened to come down here?

"Or detrimental," Asher interrupted, "Think of the power he could use against us if he had our little sister as leverage hidden away in his city, far from her family," his voice rose in challenge.

Wellan waved an impatient hand through the air. "He's been going on about Tidesrift leaving the Republic for years now. It's only talk."

"But with the right bargaining chip, it may become more than talk, brother," Asher replied. "Not to mention, the man has a reputation."

"And you're one to talk, *brother*. Do you know how many scandals I've had to quash on your behalf? Do me a favor and stick your cock in *unmarried* women from now on," Wellan barked.

And both of her brothers seemed to remember themselves at the same moment, muttering, "Sorry, Mother," as Asher cleared his throat.

"And what of Aurelia's happiness?" he asked.

"Aurelia has a duty to perform—just like the rest of us." Wellan's voice was tinged with frustration, "We need to strengthen our hold within the reaches of the Republic—"

It wasn't the lack of choice that bit her so harshly, it was that they'd kept her ignorant to their plans. They'd maneuvered her as they'd needed to. A pawn in their game of chess.

She looked around at the walls that had once been covered with her father's maps. The ones that had been sun-bleached from the window overlooking the Kesh and yellowed from her fingerprints.

In their place were pristine, glass-covered maps. Free from the scribbles and notes in her father's writing, the details that he would add after making a journey to visit one of the rural towns. Every trace of him gone from this place.

Asher was still arguing with Wellan, but she could tell from his tone that he'd already made up his mind. She'd known for years now that she'd be given away to the highest bidder, that her marriage would be a strategic play for her family's political gain. But something about overhearing them talk about her life as if she wasn't an active participant in it...

"When?"

Her brothers' raised voices quieted immediately. Asher shook his head in frustration, his green eyes flecked with sadness as he glanced over to her.

Wellan's mouth was a thin line as he answered, "A month's time."

"Very well." She stood up from her seat. There was no reason to waste any more of her time. Asher could argue with Wellan on her behalf for hours longer—she loved him fiercely for the fact that he would—but it wouldn't change anything.

"I would have played my part, brother. And you could have avoided all the theatrics," she said, glancing up to where Wellan sat across from her. "Do you still think me an errant child?" She tried to keep the bitterness from her voice, but it leaked through her words anyway as her blood heated under her skin. "That if I'd known your plans, I would have raged against them and spoiled the future you've so carefully laid out for me?"

Wellan let out an exasperated sigh, "He is a shrewd man. If I'd told you—if you'd shown any kind of manufactured interest in him, he would have seen through it. It was better this way." He waved a hand dismissively.

"For him to see the multitude of suitors vying for ties to our family," she replied with a mirthless laugh as she now understood why they'd bothered with the lavish party.

"Don't sell yourself short, sister," Wellan added dryly.

She excused herself from the study—a far cry from the escape it had once been for her as a child. The door opened behind her, but she didn't turn around. Only stopping at the sound of her mother's voice.

"Aurelia—"

Her eyes were still trained ahead, there was nothing for her to say to any of them. Nothing that could change what they'd already decided for her.

"He's a good man," her mother offered.

Aurelia let out a humorless laugh as she finally turned to face her mother. Surprised that she'd bothered to follow her out of that room at all.

Her mother let out a sigh. "I'm not ignorant to the rumors about him—the women he has ... It's not ideal, I'll admit. But he treats them well, offers them a good life."

"I guess it's a good thing he's the wealthiest man in the Republic if he's going to support a wife now, as well," Aurelia bit out.

"Wellan is anxious to reaffirm ties with the major families in the Republic, as are the rest of the Councilors." Her mother wasn't one for handwringing, but the hesitation in her voice caught Aurelia by surprise. "I had hoped—I *still* hope that you'll find a love match."

Emboldened now that her fate had been sealed, Aurelia replied, "I have—I did … Or did your eyes and ears not discover that as well?" There was nothing more for them to take from her, so how could the truth possibly harm her now?

Lady Norrick's mouth tightened into a thin line of disapproval, taking a step closer. "A life together cannot survive on infatuation alone, Aurelia," she whispered fervently, "It takes a sturdier foundation than some empty promises and sweet words … It takes security. Stability. You will have neither of those things if you marry a man beneath your rank."

The harsh words cut like a knife.

So her mother *did* know. She had found out about Aurelia and Bastien through whatever whispers had been carried to her. She knew her daughter had already found love—and it didn't change anything.

Her mother took a few more steps forward until she was only an arm's length away. "It's important that you see this through before Wellan accepts a better offer from a worse man."

Tears pricked at the corners of Aurelia's eyes, but she'd be damned if she let them fall out here.

Chapter 8

The royal blue gown was cinched so tightly that Aurelia let out a gasp as she braced herself against her bedframe. If the maid's objective had been to push her breasts to her chin, she'd succeeded.

The cut of her gown tonight was on the verge of scandalous, but no doubt that's what her mother had intended.

So be it.

Looking in the mirror, Aurelia swore her face had a green tinge. Tamping down the nausea that now accompanied her headache, she couldn't decide if she was ill or just dreading tonight. The gradual pressure behind her eyelids was growing by the minute, every caress of lace and satin like claws on her skin.

She might have been worried about being pregnant if it weren't for the contraceptive tea Galina regularly smuggled into her chambers, and the fact that she'd finally started bleeding after months of not having her courses. She'd long since learned not to panic about its unpredictable appearance. Never confessing to her mother when her cycle went from monthly, to every two months, to now every four or so, knowing it would only have made Lady Norrick worry about having to hide an infertile daughter.

It didn't matter now. Her fate would be sealed soon enough.

Her blood was humming under her skin with restless energy despite feeling unwell. Her mind circled over and over again to the stranger from the night before. Something about him felt so familiar that it nagged at the back of her mind. He was intriguing—though she chalked that up to the mystery of him, but it made the thought of tonight's dinner a little more bearable.

Most of the seats were already taken around the large dining table in Wellan's chambers when she and Asher arrived at dinner. The silverware was set to perfection. Delicately handwritten place cards waiting at every seat. Not a single detail left to chance, just as her mother preferred.

Wellan sat at the head of the table, already engaged in conversation with the Governor of Tidesrift. The Governor of Hillsdeep sat on his other side, looking like he might doze off any second as Councilor Fost and his wife were in a heated discussion with the rest of his party.

Asher took the open seat next to Christian, much to the dismay of some of the other young ladies, though both her brother and his friend didn't seem to notice. Aurelia found her place at the very center of the table, scattered with familiar faces from the night before. But as she scanned the guests, her heart sunk a little at one missing person in particular.

The older man to her left introduced himself as the Trade Minister of Tidesrift, nodding to three other men as they made their introductions. Aurelia made polite conversation, waiting for the arrival of their companion without being obvious. But minutes ticked by, slowly bleeding into hours before she lost hope that she might see the stranger again.

The Governor didn't lift his gaze as the first few courses of dinner were served, he and Wellan still deep in conversation where they sat further down the table. No doubt working out the trade agreements Wellan so desperately wanted before he'd agree to offer up his sister.

The evening passed uneventfully and Minister Gorn turned out to be an easy conversationalist, which was just as well. Her future husband barely spared a glance her way, too busy discussing business with Wellan and the other Councilors.

He was handsome enough, though one glance to where Councilor Veron and his wife sat across the table reminded her that looks could always be deceiving. Her mother had confirmed the rumors that her future husband enjoyed multiple mistresses scattered throughout the major cities in the Crescent Valley. But she'd expected as much. There were worse things than having a husband who found his pleasure elsewhere.

She'd been told since she'd been old enough to understand that she would be the one to ensure peace, prosperity, and the continuation of support for the council. A chess piece to be played at the correct time.

She wasn't important. Not who she was as a person. Her opinions, her character, and her motivations. No—simply her existence as a daughter of the Norrick family. And nothing felt more true at this very moment, sitting four seats away from the man that she would marry in a month's time. She didn't even know his first name.

She had never been idealistic enough to think she'd find a love match. Her life was too calculated for that, thanks to her family's title in the Republic. But she had to admit that her own parents found love within their arrangement. Not at the beginning, or so her mother claimed, but they found it along the way in building a life together. And the adoration in her father's eyes when he looked at her mother had been undeniable.

There was one person who seemed to see her—seemed to notice her for more than her last name. Her family's position here at court. And even though she'd never believed Wellan would let her marry Bastien, she didn't realize until today that she'd been holding onto a small shred of hope that they might find a way to be together.

In one month, she'd have a new last name, live in an unfamiliar city, and wouldn't know a single soul there. Well, there was one person...

She looked around the table again, trying not to let the disappointment leak into her voice as she turned to Minister Gorn. "And where is your other companion? I had the pleasure of meeting him at the ball but didn't get his name."

The Minister's bushy eyebrows furrowed in thought. "Our other companion? There are only the five of us who made the journey, Lady Norrick." He gave a nod toward where the Governor sat. "Including Alaster, of course."

Something hitched in Aurelia's chest.

Marking each of the faces at the table once more, certain that the stranger she'd met last night was not among them, she leaned toward Christian. "Do you remember the gentleman that danced with me before you?" she whispered.

A look of confusion clouded his dark features. "You were standing alone, it's why I came over to ask for a dance—I thought it odd, given the line of men waiting for your attention..." he trailed off, but only white noise filled her ears as her stomach sank.

Her future husband had parted with a lukewarm kiss on her hand—the only attention he'd spared her all evening. Dinner had ended with the men taking drinks in Wellan's chambers and the women heading off to bed, but Aurelia knew sleep would evade her for at least another few hours, so she'd drifted into the gardens.

The scent of jasmine mingled with the citrus trees around her, hanging in the air without the usual breeze from the Shades. Taking a seat on the bench, she tilted her head back, breathing in the familiar scent.

She had never really considered what it might feel like to leave this place. And the irony was not lost on her that her heart had yearned for adventure, for something *more*—for as long as she could remember, and yet she only felt dread at the prospect of leaving. Away from the mountains. The pines. Away from Bastien.

Her family may have never allowed her to marry him, but she could have been happy loving him in secret. Not a full life, but enough for her.

He'd been her first and only love. A childhood crush on her brother's best friend that had slowly developed into something deeper. The first man that had seen her as a woman, not just the daughter of Councilor Norrick. The first one who saw her as more than a trophy. More than a prize to be collected.

She still remembered the first time she realized she was in love with him. She'd been ten and he was a lanky twelve-year old. Some Governor's son had been visiting the Capitol with his family, training in the pit with her brothers and Ned.

As one of her father's dearest friends, Ned had always had a soft spot for her, turning a blind eye when she snuck onto the sand to practice in the shadows. But the Governor's son took offense at her appearance, squawking that *girls weren't meant to train. Girls were meant to have tea parties and play dress up*—and of course she liked those things, too, but she wasn't about to let some little prick tell her what she could and couldn't do.

Asher just rolled his eyes and muttered under his breath as a fire lit inside Aurelia. Wellan looked mortified, of course, as he usually was by his little sister's antics. But Bastien had been quietly watching from the balcony above.

He called out to the boy, saying that if he wanted Aurelia to leave, he should make her. Then with a shrug, Bastien waited, baiting the boy even further.

The boy had taken the challenge with Ned's hesitant blessing. And as Aurelia passed the older man on her way to the center of the pit, Ned whispered, *Don't leave any visible bruises, aye?* as he handed her a wooden practice sword.

She'd gotten the boy flat on his back in under a minute, leveling the wooden blade at his chest as he sputtered and turned shadeberry red.

He'd gone running straight to his father after that, but as Aurelia glanced up at the balcony, Bastien had given her a small nod and a smirk and she'd been in love with him ever since.

It took another five years before he worked up the nerve to kiss her, but there had been no one else for either of them since that moment. And even now, she couldn't bring herself to feel guilty for the way she felt about Bastien while knowing she'd be married to another man within a month.

The veiled eyes of the Unnamed towered motionless above her. Their likenesses carved out of gleaming white marble, just like everything else around her. If they did indeed exist, they certainly had a dark sense of humor. And as Aurelia stared into their cold, expressionless faces, she heard it—

Or rather—the absence of sound. Like a wave of silence had washed over the gardens, hushing every bird, every leaf, every creak of branches in its wake.

A cold fear seeped under her skin, telling her not to breath. When the hairs on her neck raised even in the warm humid air of late summer, she risked glancing around her for the source. And as her mind screamed at her to run, her body couldn't obey. Wouldn't obey.

A loud caw shook her from the trance she'd fallen in, and finally able to move her frozen limbs, Aurelia looked to find the one-eyed raven perched on the branch above her. It's loud calls shattering the silence that had encased the gardens. Leaping to her feet, she scanned every direction. To see... Nothing. Only night seeping in over the high walls.

Wings fluttered behind her, the rush of air finally giving her feet momentum as she sprinted through the open doors of the palace and slammed them shut behind her so hard the glass panes rattled in their frames, drawing the attention of the pair of blue cloaks nearby. And as Aurelia gave an embarrassed smile, she quickly began the walk back to her chambers, trying to convince herself that it had been her imagination.

And she wondered if this is how it felt to lose your mind.

Chapter 9

Her heart thudded in her chest as she made her way through the darkened halls, the words scrawled onto the final pages of her father's journals churning in her mind.

A familiar stretch of worn grey stone appeared in front of her. This wing was the only surviving part of the original palace. Built so long ago that the architects had been forgotten, any record of who had ordered its construction lost to time.

The ceiling in the abandoned wing was low, dimly lit by torches in iron brackets lining the walls. It was rumored to have been lined with iron, the bricks embedded with salt to ward off the creatures of old. Lining the center of the stone floor were lapis blue tiles aged nearly black. The silver crescent sigil of the Republic was embedded into each of them, some still shining dully in the torchlight—others tarnished by time.

There were exactly thirteen.

An unbidden memory shoved into her thoughts—

The look on Asher's face that night ... He'd been the one to find her. Tell her the awful news.

In some ways, it had been a blessing. A relief from witnessing their father slip further into madness. A man who should have been at his peak, brought crashing down into the depths of insanity in the blink of an eye.

One day, Guardian Norrick was his usual quiet self, his warm demeanor the steady comfort Aurelia had come to rely on, the next—a paranoid, secretive man, convinced someone was trying to harm him and his family.

That, unfortunately, had come to pass. But whether it was a foreboding or coincidence, Aurelia would never know.

Her family had cut the investigation short—something she still hadn't forgiven them for. But she suspected Wellan and her mother didn't want anyone digging too deeply into her father's final weeks. Preferring to bury the paranoia that had plagued his every waking moment, leading up to his death. They'd tried to shield her from it, but she wasn't blind.

Recalling those dark days, she ran her fingertips along the cool stone walls, ancient and worn smooth with time. This part of the palace was such a contrast to the one she knew, with its polished floors, lofty ceilings, and unblemished surfaces. Here, shadows danced in every corner from the flickering of the torch light. So quiet, it felt like the very stones were holding their breath as she passed. The sound of her footsteps nearly swallowed up in the dark.

Her brothers had tried to keep her from seeing their father's body, but she fought them until they released her. She'd watched, struck silent and frozen with horror, as his blood had been wiped from the thirteenth tile. All trace of their father's murder washed away.

She couldn't be certain if the crescent at the center of that tile had always been black, or if somehow her father's murder had irrevocably stained it. But just like a moth to a flame, she found herself pausing to study it every time she passed. As if somehow—it would tell her what happened here.

And maybe that's why she'd ended up here of all places. Always left wondering what delusion chased him down here in the dead of night. A fresh wave of grief took root in her chest at the thought that he had died alone and scared.

There was something that always pricked at her senses when she ventured down to this wing, but she refused to let it stop her from coming back. Morbid fascination forced her to return again and again. A stubborn refusal to give in to fear, ignoring the way the hair on the back of her neck stood on end—or maybe defying it—

Movement drew her attention to the very end of the hall where the flames of the torchlight didn't quite reach.

Peering into the shadows, she squinted, her eyes fixed on the inky darkness. Shaking her head, she turned away—this was folly to come down here expecting to find anything other than terrible memories.

A flicker in her periphery stopped her again. And this time, when she looked into the darkness—she saw him.

A man. Standing so still, he seemed to be made of shadows himself.

Aurelia froze, not daring to breathe as she watched the Shadow detach himself from the darkness seeping around him and take one long stride through a doorway at the end of the hall.

Fear coiled around her stomach, but a surge of adrenaline forced her feet forward. A moment later she was racing toward the end of the corridor, her footsteps echoing loudly in the dark silence.

She burst through the open door, her chest heaving from the exertion, color rising to her cheeks as she caught her breath standing just beyond the threshold.

No one. Absolutely no one was in this room.

She whirled around, thinking the shadow must be hiding behind the open door. But as she yanked it shut, ready to … Ready to do what, she didn't know.

Her golden eyes slowly swept the room. There was nowhere for a person to hide in here. The room only contained a musty bed, covered in a thick layer of dust, and a mirror in the far corner, half hidden with a cloth.

Ripping off the white shroud covering the glass, a nervous laugh escaped her mouth.

Only her wide-eyed reflection stared back at her. Her face still pink from running down the hall after ... Shadows—she had run after shadows and a conjuring of her imagination.

Is this how it had begun with her father, too?

What had started off as adrenaline rushes catching her off guard for months now had slowly turned into a simmering heat under her skin that pounded its way up to her temples until she saw strange auras from the blinding pain. And now? Now she'd imagined...

Shaking her head, she ran a finger along the intricate pattern in the gilded edge of the mirror. A shocked breath escaping her at the bite of the cold metal, making her quickly withdraw her hand. It was odd that the mirror didn't seem to have any dust collecting on it when the bed had decades worth, she thought, rubbing her forefinger and thumb together to ease the icy numbness. Her own strikingly clear reflection stared back at her. Only—

A white light radiated from her hands, like a halo reflected back in the mirror.

With a disbelieving gasp, she tore her eyes away from the glass and looked down.

Her hands were their usual pale color. Completely unremarkable. An exhausted breath escaped her lips before she finally made her way back to her chambers.

The silvery gleam of dawn woke Aurelia. Stretching, she rolled over onto her side, tucking an arm under her head as she closed her eyes again, trying to get a few more minutes of rest. The sunlight was persistent, the glare coming through the window permeating her eyelids even though she'd turned away.

She fluffed the pillow next to her, something heavy sliding down the silk pillowcase and landing on the comforter beside her fingertips.

Cracking her eyes open, she realized the glare had been coming from the object next to her.

A slash of gleaming metal.

A dagger.

Chapter 10

The blade pulled loose with a wet hiss, grazing bone. Upon its release, the bloodied demon turned to ash and softly blew away into the perpetual mist of the Shades.

Ven stood, drawing ragged breaths in the dark quiet of the grey pines. The silence was always jarring after a kill. Every sense on high alert, bombarded with smell and taste and sound. And then … nothing.

Sending out a flicker of shadows into the silvery light of dawn, he tested his power. He could make it back to Ravenstone by casting. His magick would be depleted, but it would be a hell of a lot faster than walking through the Shades. He'd made that walk enough times after his power had been completely spent to know how tedious it was. More often as of late with these damn demons slipping through cracks they had yet to locate.

He shouldn't have gone back.

The female had almost caught him, and he'd almost *let* her catch him. But as she rounded the corner, he couldn't help himself from staying just a second longer in that corridor. Watching the torchlight turn the dark strands of her hair into red and spun gold, the amber of her eyes catching him off guard.

How long had it been since he'd seen eyes that color? Centuries, at least. And just when she'd caught sight of him and he expected her to run away in terror, she'd chased after him. A dark chuckle escaped him at the female's boldness. The frustration that was palpable in her expression when he'd slipped through her fingers.

Risking the journey back through the portal in the deep black of night was foolish, but he couldn't stop himself. Couldn't resist that tug he felt toward her. Odd that the trail he'd followed had led him here of all places. To the human realm. And if he had so easily slipped through the broken wards, who knows what else might have? He couldn't leave her unprotected, not when the beings of this realm seemed so naïve to what creatures lurked just beyond their borders. But returning through the portal had cost him.

Stalking down the black tourmaline halls of Ravenstone, Ven wiped the blade of his dagger onto the sleeve of his gear under the flickering torchlight. Demon blood had a particularly revolting smell. Like putrid sulfur poured over the acidic tang of copper. He had killed hundreds, maybe thousands over the centuries, but he never got used to it. He wanted to peel the blood-soaked shadowskin from his body and step into a scalding bath to rid himself of the layer of grime caking his skin, but duty came first.

He pushed open the set of heavy wooden doors, revealing a large oval slab of moonstone surrounded by his Wraith lieutenants. The heated discussion that had bled through the thick doors stopped abruptly at his entrance, every face looking up to where he stood in the doorway. Eight fists rose up to press against their hearts, a reverent dip of their chins before their discourse resumed. Ven was grateful for the efficient acknowledgement. He'd take being outnumbered by enemies any day over lingering attention.

The translucent veins in the rock shimmered with the fire reflected from the torches lining the chamber walls. The milky stone had the power to wring the truth from anyone in its presence. More tradition than anything else, most council chamber tables among the kingdoms were still made of the large cuts of opalescent rock.

At the far end of the smooth stone sat a statuesque female with a dark sheet of hair cut bluntly above her shoulders, the sleeves of her black gear a stark contrast to the pale stone table where they rested. Next to her, a raven sat on the back of his empty chair, watching the room like a black feathered gargoyle.

"Enough," Nira said, barely above a whisper.

Even though the conversation had reached a frenzied volume, the chamber was instantly quiet at the sound of her voice. Placing both of her hands on the pale grey surface of the table before them, she stood. The rest of the Wraiths did the same, reading the unspoken sign of dismissal and quickly exiting the room.

Nira turned her dark gaze to the corner of the room where Ven stood, still as shadow. Her sweeping stare caught on the blood crusted in his black tangle of hair and speckled across his forehead. The concerned line between her brow relaxing when she scented that it wasn't his.

She slid a glass toward him. "You encountered another one." Not a question.

"It was waiting for me," he answered, swirling the red liquid as he lifted the glass.

It had been millennia since the Blood Folk had been reliant on actual blood for their magick—their survival. And though the properties were the same—the Allokin were meticulous in their development— the flavor was never *quite* as satisfying as the real thing.

It had been a long time since he'd tasted actual blood. Over the last few centuries, he hadn't missed it. It wasn't worth the intimacy that usually came along with it, and he'd grown tired of the short-lived trysts of his younger years. But lately, he'd been craving it.

Craving *her*.

"The surge has woken up creatures that have long slumbered. At least it was only a demon and not something worse," Nira said, stalking towards the roaring hearth at the end of the room. "You could have sent someone else, you know."

"I needed to do this myself," Ven answered, not leaving room for discussion.

Nira turned abruptly at his tone, but only gave a slight raise of her dark brows. "And should we tell our friends in the North?" she asked.

"Tell them what they need to know—nothing more," he responded. "Someone has been watching my movements. Though between the Wraiths and Cog, I don't know how we haven't found them yet," he muttered, draining the glass and setting it on the table.

Nira began writing out a concise note, the pen poised between her fingers coming to a halt. "The other court?" she wondered aloud, picking up the paper and folding it in half.

She turned toward the fire and cast the slip of paper into the flames. They both watched as the fire flared violent blue, consuming the note, and returned to red-orange embers.

"The wards have been severed. I stepped right through their portal, who knows what other things found the weakness before we did. And if something else is coming through into their realm, they are fatally unprepared for it." He let out a frustrated huff of breath. "Not like the humans we fought beside once."

"It is no mere coincidence that ancient things are awakening at the same moment you felt a surge of power," she murmured.

Ven turned to leave, looking down at the bit of copper in his hand. Flipping it between his fingers, he examined the circle of seven links on one side, the crescent on the other.

Chapter 11

Bolting upright, Aurelia put distance between herself and the dagger as she scanned her quiet bedchamber. Nothing else was amiss. Not a single thing out of place.

She stumbled from her bed, tripping on the comforter that had tangled around her legs in her haste to check the bathing chamber. But the only reflection was her own as she carefully peered around the door.

Tiptoeing back through her room, she flung the wardrobe doors open. Rifling a hand through the gossamer pastel fabrics, she angled her body toward the door in case she needed to bolt. But there was nothing. No one.

Crouching down onto the floor, she looked under her bed. Empty.

When she stood up again—there it was. The gleaming weapon perfectly placed in the center of her bed as if it had been conjured out of thin air.

She cautiously approached it. "Don't be a fucking coward," she whispered to herself.

Finally exhaling the breath she'd been holding, she stared down at the slash of metal. Just a blade. Nothing more. Beautiful, certainly—but it wasn't as if it could do any harm on its own. Gingerly picking up the dagger, she examined it.

It was unlike any blade she'd ever seen. More lethally beautiful than any of the polished weapons Bastien and Asher strapped to their uniforms. The hilt was heavier in her palm than she expected, embedded with smooth black stones that seemed to swallow up the light in her room. The dagger was made of a deep black metal, the variation in the color seeming to ripple like water under the smooth surface. It must have cost a small fortune, and she was trying to decide if it was a gift or a threat...

The merchants that visited the Capitol liked to display their wealth with similarly made weapons, bejeweled daggers and knives that dangled from their belts. A signal to the common folk that they had money—a signal to the nobility that they were not to be taken lightly.

But none of them looked like *this*.

It hadn't been on her bed when she'd crawled into it late last night, and the resulting conclusion sent a fresh waves of goosebumps over her skin.

Someone had entered her chambers while she slept.

A loud knock sounded at the door, sending her heart leaping through her chest. Throwing the dagger under her pillow, she tried to compose herself before answering. She blew out a breath, squaring her shoulders as she walked to the door. The heavy metal latch was still in place, exactly as she'd left it last night.

A maid stood outside with a tray of breakfast, and Aurelia made her apologies about feeling ill before sending her away. Discarding the meal with a clatter onto her table, she stalked across the room to her vanity. Rifling through the drawer, a spark of anxiety flared in her chest as her hands grasped the age-worn leather of her father's journal. Cracking the spine open with shaky hands, she read and reread the last pages. The words barely forming sentences for how short and chopped they were.

Being followed. Darkness.

Who to trust?

She closed the journal again, her eyes landing on the dark dagger that she had dug out from under her pillow. The black metal glinted threateningly, as if to say, *I'm still here.*

There was no longer any doubt in Aurelia's mind that her father's fears had been valid—just not the source.

Wellan had quickly put the investigation to rest under the advisement of the other Councilors. Admitting a murderer was loose in the Capitol would only cause panic. Her eldest brother had been tight-lipped about whatever small amount of evidence they'd found, brushing off Aurelia's questions.

Her mother refused to discuss their father's final days as grief overtook her. And even in Aurelia's frustration, she had to admit that they did everything they could. The palace had been locked down, every inch searched for whoever had been responsible, but it was as if they'd simply vanished.

Her father's delusions had come on so suddenly that it had crossed her mind he might have been poisoned, a thought that didn't emerge until after his death when it no longer mattered. Aurelia's mother refused to speak of it with her children, and if her brothers knew anything about his illness, they had never spoken a word of it to her. And even if they *would* tell her, she didn't want to dredge up the grief they were all so desperately trying to bury.

Her parents were private people, given that her father's title left little room for airing dirty laundry. But her mother had always held a firm belief in the unfaltering wisdom of the Unnamed. Lady Norrick claimed her piety was merely expected as the wife of a Councilor, but Aurelia knew she regularly lit prayer candles for each of her children in the temple.

Only one other person might have been privy to the true extent of her father's madness during his final days. Only one other person that her mother might have confided in when her father was at his worst—

And that was why, in the fading afternoon light, Aurelia found herself in the least likely of places.

Nearly as grand as her father's study had been, the First Brother's chambers were outfitted with a heavy teak desk and bookshelves spanning every wall. A large painting in front of her depicted the righteousness of the Unnamed Gods. Battle scenes and the anointing of the seven Councilors spanned the others, all of them gilded and gleaming. Decidedly opulent taste for a man who had signed away his identity in service to the Unnamed.

Across from her sat a rather unremarkable looking man. He had a wiry build and the distinctly pinched features of a rodent. When they'd been children, Asher had called him Brother Weasel under his breath for the better part of a year until finally one day their mother overheard it and boxed his ears.

The First Brother tapped his heavy ring impatiently on the desk between them before stretching out his hand in front of her. She bowed her head and bent to kiss the large red stone that sat on his finger. The heavy sleeves of his dark blue robes sighed as he settled back into the large chair behind the desk, more throne than seat.

"Lady Norrick, your visit is a surprise," the First Brother said with a warm smile.

"It's ... well. It's a rather sensitive subject." Aurelia hated the way she forced her voice to sound. Hesitant. Uncertain. Like a child asking for permission. But the Brother seemed to enjoy his position of authority, and she had a feeling that playing this part might get her the answers she needed. "I was hoping you might be able to tell me about my father."

"Ah." The First Brother tapped his forefinger thoughtfully against his chin. "Well, I'm not sure what questions I could possibly answer for you ... His loss was a shock to us all. I assure you, Lady Norrick, if I had any helpful information about his death, I would have shared it." He lifted his hands apologetically.

"My father was ... not himself at the end," she said carefully.

The First Brother tilted his head in an invitation to speak freely.

"My mother is still grieving, as are my brothers ... I don't want to sound morbid, but if I could just know *why* my father was afraid—*what* made him so fearful in his final days ... maybe it would offer me some peace." And the tear that slipped from her eye was not an act. She'd come here with her own motives, but what she told the First Brother was the truth.

His eyebrows knitted together in pity. "I would expect you to seek out some closure given the nature of your father's passing." The Brother sat in silence for a moment before letting out a weary sigh, his eyes cast down in thought. "Your father believed that dark magick had returned."

A shocked laugh escaped her lips.

"Lady Norrick—I do not say this to discredit his memory. Your father truly believed that he had witnessed the demons of old creeping through the halls at night."

It was worse than she'd been expecting. Her father had been even more delusional than she'd realized. It was plain enough from his last few journal entries that he thought he was being stalked—but this? This was pure madness.

She pushed herself to her feet, offering an apologetic smile to the First Brother. "I'm sorry to have wasted your time, but thank you for indulging me."

The First Brother took a long pause, seeming to weigh his words. "I am inclined to believe him." Aurelia turned to look at him, not bothering to hide her shock. "Though I can't say I have witnessed the things your father did. There has been a change in the air," he whispered gravely. "People from the villages near the border of the Shades are traveling the Capitol with harrowing tales—frightening stories, indeed."

She had heard the rumors, too. Asher and Bastien had come back from their patrols with strange tales from the rural villages. People claiming that their children had gone missing, lured into the Shades. Sightings of strange creatures that sounded more lore than truth.

As a result, the First Brother's lectures had become increasingly zealous, warning the noblemen and commonfolk of the dangers that lurked outside the Valley. But even for him, this theory seemed far-fetched. He had been the only stone left for her to turn, but it was clear the man didn't have any *real* information to offer her.

With a polite nod she turned back toward the door. "Thank you—I won't take any more of your time." She excused herself before he had a chance to corner her with the same weekly sermons she was subjected to in the temple.

There was a small amount of relief in knowing at least one other person in the Capitol hadn't completely written her father off as insane. But the true threat remained elusive, and her own strange experiences were too insubstantial to speak about with anyone else.

How could she begin to explain that she'd met a man no one else remembered? That she felt in her very core he had been hiding in the shadows of the palace. She was certain it was the same person who had left the dagger for her, but speaking any of it aloud would make her sound just as crazy as her father.

She needed tangible evidence, something more than just a threat left in her room. But all of it felt like trying to catch wisps of smoke between her fingers.

———⊙———

Days passed, but the feeling of being watched never left her. She armed herself with the dagger, it's heavy weight against her thigh during the day and gripped in her hand under her pillow at night. And she couldn't be certain if it was her heightened vigilance or something else, but the headaches had become crippling. Creeping up suddenly and violently, leaving her in a fog for hours at a time.

Another one had taken root in her skull as she made her way back to her chambers, turning into a stabbing pain the further down the corridor she went. Every patch of sunlight was blinding, every passing conversation unbearably loud. But she was too restless to lay down, turning over every detail of the stranger she had met the night of her birthday.

She'd seen someone in the old wing of the palace—and she was almost certain it was the same man. But why he'd been there and how he had gotten away remained a mystery.

The dagger, however, was a clear message.

If he'd been the one to kill her father months ago, what was he doing back in the palace? He'd had the chance to kill her, too ... but he'd left a warning instead. Someone hired him, but who would have paid an assassin to kill her father? He had been one of the most senior members of the Council, well-respected and well-liked.

The few occasions when she'd gone with him to visit the outskirts of the Capitol, he had always received a warm welcome from the commoners. They invited him into their homes, and he always accepted graciously, taking tea with the families and listening to their concerns. It had been the part of the job that wore him down the most—fighting for a better life for the commonfolk. The other Councilors were less concerned with the people in the Valley than their own political ties, but even so, her father had seemed to find a way to reach a hand between them and find common ground.

Aurelia's head pounded with the thought that she didn't know who to trust. She had nearly made it back to her rooms when a warm breeze whipped through the open doors of the palace, bringing the scent of sweat and dirt.

Slowing her steps, she took a moment to catch her breath. And as heavy thuds and grunts filled the air, she realized where she'd wandered.

The balcony overlooking the training pit was just a few short feet in front of her, and while her mind lagged behind on what her body had already decided, she crossed the distance in a moment. The intoxicating scent growing stronger with each step. Something in the air calling to her like a siren song. The coppery tang of blood forcing her closer, circling like a vulture. Like a reaper on a battlefield.

And it hadn't been the first time.

The mounting violence in the pit when training was at its peak always seemed to send a current roiling under her skin, aching to get out. Though she couldn't understand *what* was aching to get out, what this feeling was. Never quite being able to rid herself of that cresting wave of charged energy that followed in its wake.

She only knew that when she was here, the nausea, the headaches—they disappeared. And she'd take this strange feeling over the lingering illness any day.

The proximity to the fighting chased away her symptoms, just as it always did. A dizzying elation that made her forget how she'd found herself here in the first place.

A clash of metal brought her attention back to the pit. A handful of men crowded the far corner, but Aurelia's golden eyes snapped to Bastien's tall figure, his tumble of bronze curls setting him apart from the others. Sweat gleamed as it beaded down from the damp strands at his forehead onto the bridge of his straight nose. His frost blue eyes moved from the men in front of him up to the space on the balcony that she occupied.

The way he looked at her sent a pang of longing through her chest. Unbearable sadness that threatened to break her for a moment. He still didn't know—she'd been such a fucking coward that she still hadn't told him about her engagement. He deserved to know. He deserved a clean break from her ... But finally saying the words out loud to him would mean having to admit them to herself, too.

Bastien barked instructions at his men before striding under the balcony, shaking out the sweat from his dark blonde hair. He gave her no more than a passing glance from under the damp curls clinging to his brow as he left the pit.

The headache was only a dull throb at the back of her skull as she left the balcony, walking in the direction of Bastien's chambers. Glancing behind her, she made sure she wouldn't be seen. They'd done this so many times that it was second nature now as she ducked into the fifth alcove on the right.

Her eyes had barely adjusted to the dimly lit space before Bastien pressed into her, his body meeting hers until they were molded to each other. Gently kissing his way from the corner of her mouth down to the soft skin of her throat, until she thought she might burst into flame from wanting him.

The heat under her skin was building to a boil, threatening to torch them both as Bastien tore his mouth away from hers. "Aurelia. What are you doing here?"

She'd come here for a reason but damn her—she couldn't remember why.

"Will you come to my chambers later tonight?" he whispered as Aurelia tried to catch her breath, and it was like she'd been doused with cold water, her head clearing from the fog she'd been in.

The proposal from the Governor—

She meant to tell him that their time was limited. That they needed to end things for both their sakes. Because soon—too soon, she'd be leaving.

And she meant to tell him about the ominous gift she'd received the night before, the strange things she'd been seeing. But those thoughts fled from her mind, too, as his hand slowly pushed up her skirts, gliding up the side of her thigh. Instead, every thought funneled into savoring the feeling of his hand and how it relieved the pressure in her head ever so slightly, giving her dizzying, delicious relief from the headaches that hounded her night and day.

"Shit." Bastien yanked his hand away.

She smelled the cut before he even lifted his hand from where it had been buried under her skirts. He held it in front of him, blood beading at the small nick in his finger.

The dagger. She'd completely forgotten about the dagger.

"Aurelia, what the hell are you doing with that thing?" Bastien asked incredulously, his eyes darting to the sharp blade strapped to her thigh.

And she should have told him everything. She should have told him about the stranger she'd met the night of her birthday—the presence that she'd felt watching her, haunting her steps. That she thought it might be the same man that killed her father.

But instead, she answered, "It was a gift from my father."

"He was always too lax with you," Bastien uttered, shaking his head as he looked around for something to staunch the bleeding.

She might have been annoyed at the words had she not been so relieved that he didn't press her about it. The metallic scent hit her again. Sending her pulse pounding through her veins with a sensation she couldn't quite place.

Glistening crimson blood slowly ran down his finger, and before she knew what she was doing, she brought it to her mouth, licking the ruby drops as they trailed down into his palm. Unable to stop herself from savoring the taste of his blood on her lips, even as she realized what she'd done.

Bastien studied her with confusion and mild disgust written on his face, and she reluctantly released his hand. A voice in her head screaming *more, more, more*. Her skin feeling too tight and the blood underneath near boiling as her heart threatened to burst out of her chest. She closed her eyes trying to make it go away. Trying to steady her breathing. Her heartbeat.

She pressed her body against his, driving him into the wall behind them, a look of surprise crossing Bastien's face quickly giving way to desire as she reached for the loose pants around his hips, one hand splayed across his chest, still gleaming with sweat from training.

Something else drove her. Something darker than desire for him as she let him lift her skirts and take her against the wall. His breath heavy against her neck as she chased a hunger that evaded her until she pushed him to the hard floor, climbing on top of him and riding him until they both fell over the edge.

Chapter 12

More drugar. It was always fucking drugar. There shouldn't be any left with the amount of them he'd killed over the centuries, and yet somehow there always were.

Karro was at his back, three demons circling them. Their tongues flicked out to scent blood or fear; he wasn't sure. He glanced quickly to his right, spotting the twins a dozen feet away dealing with the other two. Knowing Nira and Seth would dispatch the demons quickly, he snapped his attention back to the three in front of him.

"Any preference?" he asked Karro, as he casually flipped the dagger in his hand.

"I'll take the ugly one, I guess," Karro replied from behind him.

"They're all ugly, that doesn't narrow it down," Ven muttered.

Two of the drugar lunged forward.

"I guess they're smarter than they look," grunted Karro, as he swung his sword into the gut of the first demon that charged them. He yanked the blade out, turning the drugar into a fine grey dust that blew away in the breeze.

Ven coughed, unable to dodge the cloud of ash in time, his vision blurring through the haze of dead demon. His thrust was messier than he intended, his eyes still burning as demon blood splattered across his neck and fighting gear, caking him in a fine layer of dust.

The last drugar had the sense to run.

Ven flipped the short black blade in his hand. The sharp point was only in his fingertips for a second before it was twisting through the air and hitting its target with a dull thud.

The demon disintegrated as Ven retrieved the dagger lodged in its back. Wiping his blade onto his sleeve, he glanced to where Nira and Seth were standing under the pines, brushing away the thin film of ash coating their shadowskins. Seth had that glazed-over look in his eyes like he always did when they had to face off with the drugar.

They'd all been people once—humans, or Blood Folk, or others. It's what made these demons harder to kill than the rest. Most of them had been trapped in the Void for so long that they barely resembled what they'd once been, but it still hurt Seth to dispatch them. Even when he knew he was offering a cleaner death than they'd had when they lived.

Heavy wings burst through the trees overhead, and a moment later Cog landed on Ven's shoulder. The beast's familiar weight rested for only a moment before the raven took off again to the West with a loud croak.

Ven broke into a sprint, reaching out for his magick. Shadows answered his call, slithering along the forest floor and wrapping around his body as he ran.

Chapter 13

Aurelia sat in the scalding water trying to wash off the lingering oily revulsion from her skin. Swirling tendrils of steam engulfed her in the deep marble tub. She felt *good*. Physically, at least.

She'd been feeling ill now for weeks, but whatever had happened tonight with Bastien ... the desire had come on so suddenly—so instinctually, that she hadn't quite felt in control of herself. And not just the sex...

Her appetite had come back with a vengeance, and she'd devoured the biscuits left for her with the tea that had gone cold on her table. No headache. No nausea. Her belly was finally full again. But what the hell was happening to her?

She slipped under the surface of the water, and that's when she felt it ... A sudden prickling along the back of her neck.

A summer storm was approaching. Outside her windows, flashes of lightning lit up the Valley followed by the muted rumble of thunder. Rain slashed against the glass, wind rattling her balcony doors in large gusts.

Wrapping herself in a silk robe, she stalked into her bedroom, heading straight for the arched glass doors of her balcony. Throwing them open, she dashed into the wind whipping a storm over the Capitol. Unbothered by the lightning breaking open the sky overhead, she leaned dangerously over the white stone balustrade.

No one—absolutely no one, could make the forty-foot climb between the edge of the palace courtyard to her balcony. Or make the drop and survive. But the feeling remained. The feeling of being watched.

Standing in the charged air, the warm summer rain soaking through her robe until it melted against her body, she finally uttered a curse in defeat and turned on her heel to walk back inside.

Ven peered through the clear glass doors into her room.

Even before, he had found it difficult to stay away, but now ... Impossible.

It was easy enough to walk back through the mirror, partly why he had come back so soon. Wanting to make sure nothing else walked through as well.

His shadows concealed him from the patrolling guards, past lovers in darkened alcoves, through the sleeping palace. Casting him from the worn stone corridors to the white marble balcony jutting out into the darkened sky. The storm outside hid him from view, his shadows surrounding him to cover what was not already hidden by night, yet somehow, she sensed his presence even though she couldn't see him.

The female had steel in her spine. He'd seen a glimmer of that when he'd encountered her before, but it was a glorious thing to witness when she came charging out of her chambers onto the balcony. And he could have sworn the lightning that cracked overhead lit her eyes at the same moment. A bright white-hot flame surging in her pupils.

When she marched out to the edge of the balcony, his speed and strength were the only things that saved him from coming face to face with her—he had a feeling even his shadows wouldn't be able to conceal him from those eyes.

Flinging himself over the marble balustrade, he dug his fingertips into the thin stone ledge and dangled precariously over the dark courtyard far below. The rain-soaked stone was slippery beneath the pads of his fingers, but it wouldn't have mattered if he fell. He'd leapt from further heights without so much as stumbling when he made contact with the ground, but the movement would have drawn her attention.

Her footsteps stalked back into her chambers just as he caught the heady scent of her. Golden light and citrus. Ven's breath caught at that, his mouth watering. But centuries of control kept him from edging any closer until she had closed the balcony doors behind her.

Taking up his vigil outside of her chambers once more, safely wreathed within his shadows, he watched her full lips tighten into a line as she pulled something out from under the thick mattress. Her brown-gold eyes examined the item in her hands, widening with appreciation.

The dagger.

Yanking the leather sheath from where she kept it hidden in the chest of drawers, she moved with purposeful strides. It had been easy enough to ask the tanner to fashion one for her; she'd told him it was a gift for her brother, and he hadn't asked any more questions.

Buckling the strap around her thigh and sliding the dagger against her skin, a ritual she had performed since the morning it appeared, she threw a cloak over her soaked robe. She didn't have time for one of her lady's maids to fuss over lacing a gown at this hour, and she didn't care to explain herself.

It was foolish to go alone. Reckless. But something told her that if she found Bastien and explained everything, it would be too late.

She made her way to the old wing of the palace. If only because something deep in her gut was urging her footsteps in that direction, maybe because that was the last place she'd seen the

Shadow. Or thought she saw him ... She couldn't trust her instincts anymore.

Rounding the corner, she halted—

Torchlight illuminated the familiar silhouette. And as she stood frozen in place, not daring to breathe, Aurelia knew the Shadow was looking straight at her.

His face was hidden beneath the stretching night, but she felt his gaze all the same. There was no doubt in her mind that this was the same man she had met the night of her birthday. The sharp line of his jaw, his broad shoulders, the way he carried himself—it was unmistakable.

Her eyes dropped to the dark heap on the floor. She glanced back up to where the Shadow stood, but his form was shifting, already turning hazy as if he were fading into something not entirely solid.

She broke into a run, sprinting toward whoever lay on the cold marble floor ahead of her.

The Shadow's form seemed to dissolve right in front of her, disappearing with every step closer.

She skidded to a halt where he should have been standing, only wisps of smoke left in his wake. Aurelia looked down at the person rasping wetly, but before the breath could leave her lungs to call for help, she saw who it was.

Councilor Veron's coldly handsome face was contorted in pain. The ragged gashes across his chest stained his shirt as blood poured from his wounds. His eyes focused on her, wide with fear and urgency as he clutched at his chest. His lips moved soundlessly, pleading for her to do something.

She should have called for help—one shout and a handful of blue cloaks would have been there in an instant. But the assassin was gone. They'd never hunt him down—how could they possibly find someone who disappeared into smoke.

Bastien's uncle writhed on the floor beneath her. He was so much worse at hiding pain than his lovely young wife. Interesting how the ones who usually doled it out couldn't handle it.

A year ago, she'd found Lady Veron with tear-stained cheeks in the garden. A set of fingerprints along her collarbone that she'd quickly tried to cover with her cloak. Aurelia had seen the evidence of Councilor Veron's temper long before then, but she hadn't been close enough to Jane to intervene. Aurelia let her anger get the better of her that day, imploring Jane to find a way out of the Capitol. But Lady Veron had been adamant that it was impossible, that the Councilor would ruin her if she left, would kill her if he managed to find her.

It was hard to imagine this man being a threat to anyone right now, laying on the floor in a puddle of his own blood and piss. Weak.

She watched with sick satisfaction at the pain written across his features. Enjoyed the confusion in his eyes as she stood silently over him.

And as Aurelia knelt beside him, close enough that she knew he would hear every word, she uttered, "How does it feel?" watching with dark pleasure as his eyes widened in understanding.

And she waited. Counting the minutes as the Councilor's face grew pale, the blood draining slowly. A minute for every bruise she'd seen on his pretty young wife's arms ... For every mark hidden beneath carefully chosen gowns. For every woman he'd recklessly used because his power and his title made him untouchable—well, almost.

And only when his chest stopped rising; the rattling breathes ceasing altogether, did she find her voice again, shouting for a guard.

Chapter 14

There should have been guilt—maybe some remorse. But no matter how deeply Aurelia dredged her soul, there was none. She hadn't killed Councilor Veron, but she certainly hadn't saved him either.

She'd been inches away from her father's murderer in that damned library and didn't have a clue. She'd even found the bastard charming. Nausea roiled in her stomach at the thought that she'd been so blindsided. So close.

Asher and Wellan had questioned her relentlessly about every detail of the night before, until she'd recited what she'd seen at least a dozen times to the Blue Guard commanders and the Councilors. Telling them of the man she saw standing over Councilor Veron's body, even admitting that the Shadow had seemed to disappear. But she knew well enough that to say he disappeared in a puff of smoke would not only earn laughter from the blue cloaks, but would discredit everything else she'd said, too.

No—the entire truth of what she'd seen was something she would keep to herself.

She splashed her face with cold water after the sleepless night. The first rays of dawn were breaking through her windows when a knock sounded on the door. She prepared to recount the evening again, surprised when she opened her door and Bastien was standing outside.

The look on his face bordered exhaustion and disbelief as he wordlessly stepped into her chambers.

"Bastien—"

One hand wrapped firmly around her waist, the other tangled in her dark hair as Bastien's mouth covered hers. She gasped at the indiscrete display of affection, turning to shut the door, and when she faced him again, his ice blue eyes were focused, serious.

"They've appointed me as the new Councilor," he uttered flatly.

"What?" Aurelia stammered, still trying to catch her breath.

Bastien scrubbed a hand over his face, seeming to be as stunned by the news as she was. "My uncle died without an heir."

In the chaos of the previous night the last thing on her mind had been who would take Councilor Veron's seat, but now—

"I took my oath not more than an hour ago," Bastien whispered. "And now—I'll go to Wellan to ask for your hand."

The breath left Aurelia's lungs. "Wellan's already accepted the proposal from the Governor of Tidesrift. He'll never let me out of that arrangement, Bastien—"

"He will. I'll make sure of it," Bastien answered with a cold resolve that seemed unlike him.

She wanted to believe him, but he didn't know Wellan like she did ... Even with Bastien's new title, Wellan would never threaten the new relationship he'd formed with the most powerful man outside of the Capitol. But all of it felt trivial compared to the real threat...

"I was the one who found your uncle ... I saw the man that killed him," she uttered.

"It's being handled, Aurelia. You don't need to worry. The entire palace is locked down—no one is allowed to leave the grounds, and whoever did this won't be able to hide for long."

"You don't understand," she pleaded, "He *vanished*. I don't know if it was some illusion, some trick—but I watched him disappear in a wisp of smoke."

Bastien took her hand into his own, gently stroking a thumb over her skin. "Aurelia, you know that's not possible." He bent slightly so that his blue eyes were level with hers. "He's just some man, and I promise you that we'll find him and bring him to justice—not just for my uncle, but for your father, too," he said the words gently, slowly.

No—she knew that tone. That look. It was the same one Wellan and her mother had used around her father in his final weeks. When his delusions had become more and more paranoid. More impossible. And if Bastien didn't believe her ... who would?

As Bastien left her chambers, she glanced behind her, unable to shake the feeling of being watched even now. Shafts of sunlight streamed into her room, but they did nothing to chase away the fear that skittered across her skin.

The feeling never left her, even when daylight bled into evening. Like a nagging thread being tugged at the back of her spine. It was why she feigned sleep, one arm tucked under her head, the other underneath her pillow, holding the beautiful blade in her hand, waiting.

The very one *he* had placed by her head while she slept.

She'd given the perfect performance, readying herself for bed and dousing every candle in her chambers knowing all the while she was being watched. Stalked. Hunted. And though she never heard him. Not so much as a click of the glass doors or a creak of his weight shifting on the floorboards, she knew he was in her room. Waiting.

She felt his presence like a flame, warmth flooding her body as he drew closer.

Ripping the blankets away, she bolted upright, leveling the blade where the Shadow stood at the side of her bed.

He took a single stride into a shaft of moonlight shining through her balcony doors.

He was beautiful. So beautiful it nearly took her breath away, just like the first time she'd seen him. The sharp angles of his face were cast into stark relief against the silvery light. All hard, lean muscle from the look of his broad shoulders and the way his body filled out the strange clothing he wore. Not armor exactly, like fitted leather molded to him. His dark hair fell in waves down to his ears, his gaze tearing through her.

"If you're here to kill me, it was stupid of you to give me a weapon," she said quietly into the darkness.

The sound of his voice was like the rumble of a mountain stream over stone. Deep and velvet smooth when he finally spoke. "If I had come here to kill you, we wouldn't be discussing it." His tone wasn't condescending. A mere statement of fact.

"You killed Councilor Veron." She swallowed hard. "You killed my fa—" She couldn't finish the thought, the words catching in her throat. Confusion passed over his gaze, but he only gave a slow shake of his head in response.

"Liar," she hissed. "You've been creeping around the palace. Hiding in the shadows ... watching." Her voice steadied as she found her resolve again. "Tell me. Who weighted your pockets with gold crescents to kill them."

His eyes flashed dangerously, like she'd insulted him. He took another step, his chest only inches away from her chin, and it was then she realized how tall he was. She had danced with him at the ball, spoken with him in the library—but for some reason those memories felt hazy, mercurial. Nothing like the solid man in front of her.

She held the dagger firmly between them, the sharp point of it digging into his jacket. And slowly reaching his hand out, his long, elegant fingers gripped the sharp metal and easily twisted it from her grasp. As if the bite of the blade's edge felt like nothing. As if she had barely been holding it.

She stumbled back a step and watched in awed horror as he rubbed caked blood from his palm, where the blade had sliced him deeply—revealing perfectly unmarred skin.

His deep voice rumbled again like the distant thunder outside, "Let me be perfectly clear, Love. I have plenty of blood on my hands—but none of it human. And none of it in exchange for *your* *metal*." He said the words with clear distain.

Wiping the blade clean on his sleeve, his eyes never left her face as he offered the jeweled hilt to her.

Against her better judgment, she snatching the gleaming blade back from him, trying to make sense of what she just witnessed.

Some kind of charlatan. An illusionist as well as an assassin.

"What *are* you?" she whispered.

Dark laughter reverberated through the chamber. "I am something long forgotten by the people of this realm." He smirked, stalking toward her with a predatory grace, forcing her to back up against her bed to keep some distance between them. "And when you close your eyes tonight, you'll forget about me, too," he whispered, with just a hint of sadness tinging his voice, foreign words rolling off his tongue.

The dagger felt limp in her hand as his gaze focused on her, edging close enough now that she could have sworn his dark eyes were blood red.

She blinked, and he was gone. Only curling tendrils of shadow left in his wake.

Chapter 15

A constellation of small red drops speckled the white floor.

Definitely not a dream.

After the Shadow vanished from her chambers, she'd gone running out onto the balcony hoping to finally see how he'd managed to sneak into her locked room. But it was as if he had disappeared into thin air right before her eyes. Again.

Impossible. But she had no other explanation for it.

Pacing her chambers for the remainder of the night, dagger in hand, she stewed over his words. Replaying them again and again. Another headache was pounding its way into her temples, that same strange white aura forming around her fingertips as she paced. Squeezing her eyes shut, she blew out a slow breath, relieved that when she opened them again the haze was gone.

That was twice now he could have killed her, and he hadn't. In fact, she'd drawn first blood, and instead of retaliating, he wiped the blade clean and handed it back to her.

The arrogant prick.

Illusionists from Kostris had circulated the Capitol when she was a child. Men that could vanish in a whirlwind of smoke before the eyes of huge crowds, skilled at deception and misdirection. One had even performed at the palace for the Summer Solstice festival years ago, but it was nothing like what she'd seen the Shadow do. And as for the foreign words she heard him speak, she knew for certain it wasn't the tongue of the Kostrians. She wasn't fluent, of course, but she'd picked up enough phrases from the merchants that visited the Capitol to recognize the sharp r's, the staccato consonants.

No—his words had been fluid like water. Soft and caressing like the Kesh in the early Autumn tumbling over smooth stones. A sound that triggered some nagging thread in the back of her mind. And though she expected him to deny killing her father, she hadn't expected the sincerity in his eyes. No hint of deception. And in a place like the Capitol, where every spoken word had a double meaning, it was ... undeniable.

It didn't change what he was.

Dangerous.

The polished floors glistened in the torchlight. Aurelia stuck close to the wall, trying to avoid the blue cloaks on their nightly patrol, but with their increased presence it was almost impossible. So instead, she nodded her head in greeting, walking with purpose and praying to the Unnamed that none of them would offer to escort her to her destination.

No flicker of candlelight greeted her tonight in the library. Her eyes swept between the rows of bookshelves as she crossed the cavernous first floor. The scrawled writing in her father's journals echoing in her mind as her hand brushed across a book she'd read at least a dozen times.

It seemed silly now, as she flipped through the worn pages. Descriptions of the creatures that had walked the Shades so many centuries ago. Beasts so gruesome they couldn't possibly have existed. Ones that were green like spring leaves and could control nature. And then she stopped, the next illustration catching her attention, sharp fangs and barely human features, blood dripping from its mouth—

"A rather unflattering portrayal," rumbled a deep voice from behind her.

Aurelia's stomach dropped. She whirled around so quickly; the book fell from her hands with a loud thud onto the floor. Her eyes slowly traveled up from where the book landed, to the graceful hands that now grasped it.

A dark lock of hair fell over the Shadow's lethally beautiful face as he idly leafed through the pages. "Demons are much uglier than that, trust me," he said with a click of his tongue. He continued flipping through the book, not bothering to look up to where she stood plastered against the bookshelves.

That all too familiar heat started building under her skin. Flooding her veins as panic started taking hold, just as the Shadow let out a whoosh of breath.

"Oof. The Green Folk would not be pleased to hear they're referred to as 'wood nymphs' here in the human realm." His dark brows knitted together. He looked up, flashing a feral grin and winking at her. "Best keep that to ourselves."

"You keep saying human as though you're—not," she murmured. She didn't flinch as his gaze met hers again. She'd be damned if she showed an ounce of fear in front of him, but her heart threatened to betray her with every staccato beat in her chest.

The Shadow shifted, his face mostly hidden by the dark lock of hair that fell across his forehead before he tucked the errant ebony strands behind his ear. A movement too graceful for a man his size. Too beautiful.

"Our existence has been long forgotten by human memory, relegated to the lore in their books."

The stories she'd been told growing up were etched into her brain. The Old Stories. The myths. She knew them all, only half believing them. Thinking that if indeed these creatures had existed, they were long gone. Much like the absent gods her mother still clung to.

The Shadow took a single step toward her, closing the distance between them as he shut the book and pushed the spine back onto the shelf behind her. And it was only then that he was close enough she could see the color of his eyes—

Crimson.

Her spine ached from pressing even further into the bookshelves. Trying to get any scrap of distance between herself and this...

"What are you?" she hissed. "You vanish into shadow, you bleed but you heal instantly..." she murmured in disbelief.

"You remember me," he uttered, a stifled look of shock on his face. "You are not as you appear either, if you could block me from your mind," he drawled, idly crossing his arms behind his back, giving her the same look she guessed a Shadecat did as it sized up a meal.

And now the pieces of the conversation she'd had with him in the library began to fall into place...

There's a seed of truth in every story.

"You're one of them," she breathed.

Heat licked down her palm and radiated into her hands. Glancing down, she saw the strange white haze crackling around her fingertips, and uttering a curse she pinched her eyes shut. Not now—

When she opened them again, the Shadow was directly in front of her. She followed his gaze down to her hands, still wreathed in a white halo—shocked that he seemed to be seeing what she did. And when she looked back up at him, the strangest expression was on his face.

Awe.

His chest brushed against hers, hinting at the hard muscle beneath his jacket. He was so close now that she could feel the soft caress of his breath as he uttered more of the strange foreign words he'd spoken in her room the night before. A language she didn't understand, but the soft lilt of the accent felt familiar to her ears. Like a scent from childhood she couldn't place. Like the bridge of a song she couldn't remember.

His crimson eyes glittered with fascination as he whispered, "I think the better question, is *what* are *you*?"

He was trying to unnerve her, she knew, but he looked slightly unsettled too, even though he seemed to be trying to hide it. Questions were still forming in her mind as his body suddenly went taught around her, his arms braced on the bookshelf behind her like a rigid cage.

"Do you trust me?" he whispered urgently.

"Of course not," she hissed incredulously.

"Good."

And before she could speak another word of protest, something black skittered across the floor toward them. Dark wisps approached in every direction and started pooling along the worn stone, slithering softly to where they stood.

Impossible. What she was seeing was ... Impossible.

But the dark tendrils of mist continued to gather at their feet, sweeping up their legs, unconcerned with her faith in their existence as they curled around her like a thin veil. The darkness felt softer than silk, lighter than air, as it draped around her body. Cool like the mists of the Grey Wood when they kissed her skin. Just then, barely audible footsteps circled closer to where they stood.

Sense poured into her head again. She opened her mouth to scream. To alert whoever was nearby that there was a monster in their midst, but her voice was snuffed out by the shadows that had wrapped around them.

The footsteps grew louder, and the lean silhouette of a man stepped in front of them. His footsteps unhurried, like he was browsing the books at leisure here in the dark. He didn't carry a lamp with him, which seemed odd to be searching in the library in pitch black.

The man took one step down the row of shelves, into a small shaft of moonlight that fell from the window high above, his blandly handsome face unrecognizable in the dim light. But something about his demeanor; the aura around him, like the moonlight flinched from touching his skin, told Aurelia that remaining hidden was the best course of action. He stared right at them. Right *through* them. And then continued his quiet steps to the other side of the library, as if he hadn't seen them only ten feet away.

The Shadow detached himself from where he had pinned Aurelia against the shelves, to stalk closer to where the other man paced the rows of desks.

Aurelia tugged at the wisps of shadow that circled her wrists, trying to slip away while the Shadow was distracted, silently straining against the silken restraints. Somehow completely unforgiving, not yielding an inch, and yet leaving her skin unharmed as they held her fast against the shelves.

A voice spoke from the darkness, and her head snapped up instantly at the sound—

"I thought I smelled the stench of Wraith," the man said, as he swiped a slender finger across the wooden tabletop. A smooth, cultured accent clipped his words. His voice was young and old all at once. Beautiful and terrifying as it made the hair on her neck stand on end.

She turned to look across the library to where the man and the Shadow faced each other.

"And what, may I ask, brings a Prince of the Void to the human realm?" the Shadow retorted with equal disgust.

"I could ask you the same," the prince responded, putting both hands in the pockets of his white jacket, and spinning on a heel to face the Shadow.

She sucked in a sharp breath—under perfectly manicured brows were only pure white eyes, seeming to radiate their own light in the darkness of the library.

There were more of them.

There was something so grotesque about not being able to tell where his eyes were focused. And she struggled against the shadows that bound her—stopped her from fleeing like her body was begging her to.

"Seems your creatures have been wandering where they aren't supposed to be," the Shadow purred.

"With the door wide open," the prince gave a shrug of his shoulders, "How could you expect them not to? They've grown restless. As have we all." The prince cocked his head to the side in a way that was more predator than human, and with a slow smile he fixed those dead white eyes on the Shadow. "I'd expect to receive a little gratitude from you—I'm sure you've gotten bored as well. A hunter with nothing to hunt." He gave a click of his tongue. "A sad existence, indeed—*Ven*," he spat out the name like a curse.

Ven.

At least now she knew the Shadow's name. Whatever he was. Whatever *they* were.

"And here I was about to call you by your title, but how could I forget that you gave that up." The prince gave a hollow laugh. "So noble."

The shadows that bound Aurelia's arms suddenly released her, slithering away in a stream that seemed to make a path for her to follow. A cold sweat broke out over Aurelia's skin, fighting to look away from the depthless white eyes of the prince, but she didn't hesitate. And one step onto the blanket of inky black told her that she was still hidden.

The Shadow slowly circled the white prince, his broad back mirroring her movements as she edged closer to the door. "I enjoyed the exercise the last few gave me. But it seems I remembered them being," The Shadow gave an insolent shrug. "More formidable." The glint of metal in his hand was the only sign that he'd removed a blade from somewhere on his body. Lazily twirling it between his index and middle fingers before he began cleaning his nails with it. His gaze flicked to where she skirted the perimeter of the library before landing back on the prince. "It seems your pets have gone a bit—soft."

Aurelia soundlessly slipped through the open door, finally daring to breathe.

She needed to alert someone—anyone. Bastien's chambers were the closest, but hopefully there would be blue cloaks on patrol nearby.

She dashed out into the darkened hallway, chest heaving as she spun on a slippered heel to peer into the darkness flooding the very end. She stared into the shadows for what felt like an eternity, until it began to look like they were bleeding down the corridor, pooling closer and closer to where she stood.

The flame on the very last torch at the end of the corridor guttered out.

The nightmare.

The nightmare that had given her restless nights for so long now that she couldn't remember when they'd started.

Her heart began a slow pounding in her chest, the beat picking up when the shadows stretched further down the hall, impossibly black, as a second torch was snuffed out with a gasp.

Shit.

The darkness behind her yawned wide. She ran.

Past where the torchlight ended, to the very last room, slamming the door shut and wrenching the rusted latch down into place. This dusty old room. A dead end. And now she was trapped in here, those creatures out there—how long had they been biding their time? Only to come back now, wreaking havoc on her home.

She needed to make her way back—find guards on patrol and alert them, tell them to send up an alarm that the Old Ones had returned.

Braced against the door, she listened in the dark silence for any sound. She slowly exhaled the breath she'd been holding, just as something heavy scraped against the wooden floor behind her.

Another scrape.

A low snarl ripped the shroud of silence from the dark room.

Chapter 16

Asmodeus loved to talk about himself.

A trait that, at this moment, Ven was grateful for. The longer he could keep the prince talking, the more time she had to hide. It didn't matter that she was scared of him, too. It was better that way.

The amber torchlight from the hall had been extinguished, leaving the two males staring at each other in the pitch black of the cavernous room. Ven felt it before he heard it—

A deep reverberation through his chest. A slow, methodical, prowling rumble.

He looked into the white depthless pits on the prince's grotesquely beautiful face before going back to idly picking at his nails in a way that he knew made the comically prideful male breathe fire. Asmodeus hated when he lost his audience.

"I see you brought another one. How many are you down to now?" Ven asked, never lifting his eyes from his cuticles and the sharply honed point of his blade.

"It doesn't matter." The white prince shrugged. A satisfied look on his face. "I wonder—why were you trying to hide that pretty little thing?" Ven held his breath as anger flooded the prince's pupilless white eyes. "Your little wisps of smoke conceal *nothing* from a Prince of the Void," Asmodeus breathed. His voice betraying the fragile ego beneath a flawless, pale façade.

And that's when Ven struck—just a smooth flick of his wrist, sending the dagger straight into the prince's chest. The prince looked down in disbelief, his perfectly tailored white jacket slowly staining black with oily blood. "You dare—" he uttered, before falling to his knees.

Ven took a single step that brought him inches away from the prince's kneeling form. Slipping the heavy metal from his pocket, he placed the iron coin between Asmodeus's maggot white eyes. Watching the prince go up in flame and ash as he sprinted from the room.

Her back firmly planted against the door; Aurelia forced herself to look in the direction of the sound.

Two eyes, glowing like phosphorous in the darkness, drew closer to where she stood. She couldn't make out any details, only the flash of sharp teeth and a body bigger than any hound's, closer to the size of a horse. Another low rumble reverberated across the floorboards to her feet.

She hiked up the heavy fabric of her cloak, silently cursing the extra layer between her and the blade strapped to her thigh. Fumbling with the dagger, she ripped it from the leather strap and brandished the weapon just as the beast drew closer.

Then the animal lunged, and she saw its canine shape in the dim moonlight filtering in through the room.

It's head and body were almost skeletal, dark leathery skin where there should have been soft fur. The claws that protruded from its paws scraped the floor, tearing long gashes into the stone as it propelled its heavy body toward her.

With a crash, it knocked the breath from her lungs as she hit the unforgiving stone floor. She wildly swiped with the dagger, but the beast was so large it hardly seemed to feel the blade. Its claws pinned her cloak to the floor, and as she tried to roll out from under it, she heard a loud tear as it finally ripped.

Stumbling back to her feet, she braced for the next attack. Looking at the monstrous animal, she held the pitifully small blade in front of her. And lightning fast, the beast lunged again. This time it's claws bit into the bare skin on her leg.

Searing pain lanced through her as its massive claws swiped her thigh, and she looked down to see a stream of dark blood pouring down her leg onto the grey stone. She pushed against the heavily muscled body, but the leathery beast had her pinned under its weight. And the more she struggled, the weaker she felt.

The dagger-like teeth in its opened jaw were poised to snap around the delicate skin of her neck, but just as its hot rank breath reached her face, the beast screamed. Not the whimper of a dog, but a bone-chilling shriek that rattled the room.

A death knell.

Silence enveloped the space again. The only sound, the wet scrape of her dagger as it left the beast's enormous ribs. Shoving against the leathery hide, she prepared for another attack—but it never came.

A rancid smell filled the room, the scent burning her nostrils as she frantically tried to get out from underneath the suffocating weight of the creature. But just when her lungs began to burn, the pressure released. Slowly at first, just enough that she gasped for air. And right before her very eyes, the beast started disintegrating into a fine grey dust. Until it was sifting onto the floor, like dark grains of sand.

Gasping as adrenaline flooded through her veins, her hand shook, gripping the hilt of the dagger so hard it hurt. She'd seen enough impossible things tonight to linger in this room any longer...

Stumbling to her feet, she edged around the pile of dark powder on the floor, wondering if somehow, she'd imagined the creature entirely. But the blinding flare of pain in her leg reminded her it had been all too real.

She pressed her hand to the ragged slashes tearing open her thigh, still pouring blood. She would need to bind these, but ... later. She could do that later. Right now, she needed to find a way out, but the only way out of this room would lead her right past the white-eyed prince and the Shadow.

A wave of dizziness hit her, and she stumbled into the mirror, her palm hitting the glass as another flare of pain shot through her leg.

A cool, wet sensation kissed her palm.

Peeling her hand from the glass, she touched it to the surface again, her breath catching at the strange feeling—like skimming her hand over water.

The searing pain was forgotten for a blissful second as she tapped the mirror with her finger and the glass rippled like a pebble breaking the surface of a still pond.

Taking a deep breath, Aurelia plunged through.

Chapter 17

Her knees hit soft ground.

It took Aurelia a moment to get her bearings and shake off the sensation of walking through the mirror. Like icy fingers gripping her forehead, neck, and shoulders trying to pull her back into that room.

There was only black as her eyes adjusted to the darkness that surrounded her. But the scent hit her immediately, her other senses seemingly heightened with the loss of her vision. Pine. She must be somewhere in the Grey Wood. Deep enough into the Shades that she couldn't see any light from the palace or the Capitol as she glanced around from where she knelt in the dirt.

Damp seeped into her burning skin through the fabric of her cloak, and she spread out her hands, clawing her fingers into soft dirt and pine needles. She tried to stand, but the blinding pain from the wound in her leg sent her knees buckling to the ground again. That's when she realized the wet seeping through her cloak wasn't just from the earth. It was blood...

Her head screamed at her body to stay upright as she slumped to the cool ground, giving in to the weariness that seeped into her bones like the damp.

The moonlight filtered through the canopy of grey pines towering high above her as her vision lost focus. Somewhere far away, she heard the sound of wings as she closed her eyes, the rustle of pine needles. Deep down she knew that she needed to stay awake. Needed to stay conscious. Alert. But she was so damn tired. And the darkness beckoned like a sweet lullaby.

A loud caw sounded from behind her, and she used the last scrap of strength she possessed to turn her head and crack her eyelids open.

A dark eye stared back, oil slick feathers ruffling in recognition. The raven sharply turned its head, and she saw the familiar scar on the other half of its black iridescent face, a faint smile touching her lips as she plunged into unconsciousness.

In that dark quiet place, she could have sworn she felt cool silk wrapping around her.

Aurelia woke to the silvery glow of dawn falling onto the soft pillow next to her. The thick comforter on top of her was heavy and luxurious, beckoning her back to sleep even though she felt—rested. The first deep dreamless slumber she'd had in months.

High above were soaring black stone arches, soft light splintering through a domed web of windows spanning between them.

This wasn't the Capitol.

The richly appointed chambers weren't opulent, but comfortable. The walls and floor were made of beautiful ebony stone veined with gold and bronze, illuminated by the embers glowing in the large fireplace. Her eyes trailed down to the thickly piled rug and set of overstuffed leather armchairs sitting before the hearth. A pair of crimson eyes stared back at her.

Scrambling back against the headboard, the breath punched out of her lungs, pain shooting down her leg. Between the moment she tried to sit up and her sharp inhale, the Shadow had crossed the distance between them, only a blur of movement.

"I'm not going to hurt you," his deep voice rumbled. He slowly reached out, like a man trying to tame a wild dog, placing a warm callused hand under her arm. "Your ribs are cracked, by the way," he added, helping her sit up against the massive headboard. Close enough that she could feel the warmth radiating from his body. His scent, the same pine and citrus that filled her lungs when she had fallen into that dark oblivion.

The events of the previous night came flooding back. Monsters had indeed been lurking through the palace … And now she was here with one of them.

Looking down, she self-consciously pulled at the hem of the silky nightshirt and pants that covered her body, the material sinfully smooth against her skin—not wanting to consider how she'd come by them. How many hours had passed, days?

"Did you bring me here to kill me or keep me?" she uttered, as her mind dredged up every awful detail from the tales she'd read about his kind. Little more than beasts. Delighting in violence and blood and torture.

"If it weren't for me, you'd be lying dead in the Shades," he answered, the hint of a smile tugging at the corner of his mouth, like this was some game to him.

The arrogant bastard was right, of course. She should be dead, but given her present company—she would be soon enough.

He gave a dark chuckle, revealing the tip of a too-sharp canine. "You are not my captive. You are here as my guest."

He sat down in the chair again, his movements slow and deliberate like he was making an effort not to scare her. It was only now that she noticed the purple smudges under his eyes as if he hadn't slept—*If* these creatures slept.

"Your guest," she scoffed. "You lied to me about who you were—why should I trust you now?" she spat.

"*You* weren't supposed to remember meeting me. Or that night when I came to check on you in your chambers."

"I think the word you're looking for is 'Stalked'."

He gave a shrug, that infuriatingly smug look on his face never leaving. "And you think it would have gone over well if I'd told you who I really am?"

"You mean, *what* you really are," she bit out.

He flashed her a grin, reminding her exactly how close she was to death. But glancing out of the large window next to the bed, her stomach plummeted even further.

The blue green expanse of pines fell away sharply below them, somewhere high above in the mountains. Not a hovel ... Not a ramshackle outpost—a fortress. And by the look of the beautifully crafted stone chamber around her, one that had remained hidden for a very long time.

"Where am I?" she uttered, half expecting him not to answer.

"Ravenstone."

With an elegantly dismissive wave of his hand, Aurelia flinched as a small feast appeared on the table between them. Roasted chicken, fluffy potatoes, buttery greens. Aurelia's stomach lurched at the sight, rumbling from hunger. Was this some trick? Some sleight of hand to tempt her into submission?

Filling a plate, he leisurely walked around the table to where she was stranded in the bed. She suppressed the urge to bolt as his footsteps halted a few inches away, placing the offering in front of her. But she knew it would make her sick—just like everything had for the last few weeks. And she didn't trust him not to poison the food anyway, so she didn't acknowledge the gesture, didn't intend to give any reaction—but her stomach betrayed her, roiling at the scent. It was enough to make her push back further into the headboard even though she couldn't remember the last time she'd eaten.

"Not to your liking?" he asked, striding back toward his own seat.

"What kind of trickery is this?"

"It's magick," he answered succinctly. "Basic magick, really. Just a matter of bringing something from one place to another." He gave a dismissive wave of his hand as though it was something he'd grown bored of being able to do. Another snap of his fingers had two crystal glasses of wine thunking down onto the table between them.

"I hope you didn't prepare the food on my account. I thought your kind preferred ... something with a pulse." She slid the plate away, trying to rid herself of the nauseating smell. If he hoped to win her over with a little food, he'd be sorely mistaken.

"I've no doubt the stories have made you believe we only drink the blood of virgins. But we enjoy food as much as anyone else." A feral smirk was on his face now, and he made no effort to hide the pointed fangs on either side of his mouth as he began piling food onto his own plate.

"But you do drink blood—to be clear," she said, giving him a saccharine smile. If she was going to die today, she wouldn't go out of this world mincing her words.

"Our magick demands we consume it, but we prefer blood from our own kind—much stronger." He winked, tucking into the food on his plate with surprising eagerness.

"Why am I here?" she asked impatiently.

"You are here to heal and to rest," he answered with a nonchalance that made her see red. "Now eat," he ordered, stabbing a fork toward her heaping plate.

"I could heal and rest in the Capitol. In my home," she ground out with only the barest hint of civility. If he intended to kill her, why was he wasting his time? What kind of game was he playing?

"Your wounds required powerful healing magick. You would have died very slowly and very painfully if I hadn't brought you here," he stated with infuriating calm.

"If your intentions are as innocent as you claim—"

"I never claimed they were innocent," he interrupted with a smile that sent a lick of fire down her spine and a flare of irritation through her chest.

"—then you'll let me go," she finished, trying to tamp down the heat flooding her face.

It was impossible to ignore his beauty, even though she knew what he was. She couldn't help the response she had to him. The same one she remembered from that very first night she'd met him—when she'd thought he was some noble's son. Looking at him now, she cursed herself for not seeing what he truly was from the start. But the monsters she'd been warned about as a child weren't supposed to look like him. Act like him.

"As I said, you are not a captive here," he replied with an irritated glance toward her untouched plate, "But it will take a few more days for your leg to fully heal, and there are worse things than Shadecats and Mist Wolves that prowl the mountains at night."

"Things like you?" Aurelia uttered with contempt, meeting his gaze and watching his eyes grow darker. Dangerously flashing as her insult landed. Good.

"Things much, much worse than me," he replied, cutting into the meat with lethal precision before taking a bite, his table manners impeccable—her mother would have swooned.

"There's no creature worse than a vampyre," she uttered. Fangs, dark magick, a glass of what was probably blood in front of him; it was an educated guess.

"Vampyre, demon, nightwalker..." He put his knife down, picking up his glass and swirling the contents. "My people have been called many things. Crude terms humans devised long ago when they no longer remembered our *true* name." He drank deeply, his eyes never leaving hers.

"Which is?"

He set the empty glass down. "The Blood Folk."

A fresh wave of goosebumps pebbled her skin at the name. Ancient and imperious.

Fighting the warning that crept across her shoulders, she gave him an insolent look. "A noble name does not change what you are." She knew how careless it was to anger him. But her sharp tongue was all she had right now.

"That may be true." He shrugged. "But either way, you should eat something." He pushed her plate toward her again.

She shoved it away once more. "If you're hoping to use me as some *pawn* in whatever it is you're plotting, I promise you I know nothing of consequence. I am no one." She'd given up any pretense of civility, letting her anger leak through. Dignity be damned.

"I have no hidden motives, Aurelia. Other than to see you safe and well."

She bristled at the sound of her name on his lips, ignoring the fact that the tingle creeping up her spine wasn't altogether unpleasant. He was hiding something from her. There was a reason he was keeping her here.

"You've been sneaking around the palace for weeks. I saw you kill Councilor Veron—"

"I didn't kill him; I was just the first to find him—and he was still breathing when I left." His eyes sharpened on her. "I can't say the same for you."

Her face paled, something that wasn't quite guilt pressing down on her chest. Had he watched her stand over Bastien's uncle as the life drained out of him? Was this some kind of thinly veiled threat? He could use the knowledge against her—but only if he returned her to the Capitol.

He gave her a pointed look. "I'm sure you had your reasons," he drawled. "Regardless, he was a dead man. It's rare for a human to survive a demon attack."

Her breath caught in her throat.

A demon.

He nodded to her bandaged leg. "It was probably the same one that gave you that nasty little cut."

Demons and vampyres ... What other creatures of old weren't just bedtime stories?

Swallowing her disbelief, she replied, "You still haven't told me why you were in the Capitol, so you'll have to forgive me for being reluctant to believe you don't have any *hidden motives*."

He reached across the table to pour himself another glass of red wine, or maybe it was blood, she still couldn't be sure. "There was a surge in magick. One powerful enough to break the wards that have held for centuries."

Hating to appear ignorant in front of him, she bit back the urge to ask what the word meant.

"Magickal barriers," he clarified. "They protect the border of every kingdom. The ones guarding the human realm were shattered, and that's when the demons began slipping through. I've been tracking them ever since, hunting them down."

The memory of the leathery beast flashed in her mind. "How long have you been tracking them into the Capitol?" she uttered with dawning horror.

"Months," he answered darkly.

Months. They'd been entering the human realm for months.

She ripped at the bandage covering her leg, and peeling the white cloth away, she braced herself to look at the wounds that creature had inflicted—

They weren't nearly as severe as they should have been ... It had been less than a day ago that she'd fought for her life, bleeding out onto the forest floor. But they were already knitting themselves back together, the ragged gashes across her pale skin only angry red lines. Whatever sorcery they possessed here had sped up her recovery by weeks. But it was the size of them, the pattern of four distinct claw marks that dredged up the awful memory etched into her mind.

She'd seen these exact marks on her father's body. Her family had passed off her father's ramblings as those of a man falling into madness, but he knew someone had been stalking him—some*thing* had been stalking him. He'd been trying to warn his family, and he must have felt the way she did—like he was losing his mind. Like he couldn't quite put into words the danger that he sensed. Until finally...

She moved to stand up from the bed but buckled under the pain that shot through her leg. The Shadow rushed to her side once more, his brow creased in concern as she looked up into his unnatural eyes, hating the desperation that tinged her voice as she begged, "Please—if you truly mean what you say ... I need to warn them—" she cut herself off. Any weakness could be used against her here, especially the people she loved.

"Your loved ones are safe. I promise it on my life," he answered, seeming to read her mind. The reverence in his tone made her almost believe him, but the color of his eyes reminded her that he was a something *other*.

A creature of old—one of *them*.

But she wasn't in a position to do anything about it now, she just had to hope that her family was safe for the moment, until she could find a way to warn them. Swallowing her fear, she sat back against the pillows.

With a sweep of the Shadow's hand, the plate of food in front of her vanished and the glass of deep burgundy wine took its place directly in front of her. But she didn't make a move to drink it; not trusting the contents.

"It's not poisoned," he grumbled, grasping the cup and taking a healthy swig of the wine. "Besides, tradition demands that once food is offered, no harm may come to you inside the host's walls." He pushed the cup toward her again.

"And is that the lie your ancestors told mine before they tried to eradicate us?"

"Our people have never been enemies to the humans."

A disbelieving laugh escaped her lips at the bold-faced lie. Cut off at once by the raw, primal anger that blazed like liquid fire in the Shadow's eyes.

"Do you really think the human realm would be safe if we didn't wish it to be? Truly?" he asked. His deep voice was midnight silk, making her wonder what kind of discipline was required to keep his true nature in check.

Swallowing back her indignance, she was confronted with an ugly truth.

The Nameless Brothers were always performing ridiculous ceremonies. A sprinkle of powder, some muttered words. She'd never really believed they protected the Valley against anything—but then again, she never really believed things like *him* still existed.

Her trust was in Asher, in Bastien—in the loyal, worthy men that wore the cloaks of the Blue Guard and protected the Valley with their lives. But she'd seen how easily the Shadow slipped past a palace full of them—what it would be like fighting an entire army of creatures like him?

The Shadow swirled the wine in his glass. "Human memory is fickle—fleeting. Just like their lifespans. And what their books *forgot* to mention is that many kingdoms of the Folk fought to protect the humans long ago. It was *my* people that fought and died by their sides. *Our* blood that was spilled alongside the humans on the Valley floor," he growled, taking another sip of his drink and leashing his temper.

She picked up the cup in front of her, buying herself time to think.

If he was lying and it was poisoned, better to die a quick death. If it was drugged—she was in a sorry enough state as it was, what difference could it make.

Bringing the cup to her lips, she drank. And damn it—it was delicious. She gulped the thing down before she could think better of it, the Shadow making no effort to hide his self-satisfied smirk. Putting the drained glass down, she spun the stem between her fingertips. Maybe if she played nicely, put all those courtly manners to use that her mother had beaten into her...

"And when I am well, will you return me to my home?" she asked, trying to soften the edge in her voice.

He dabbed the corners of his mouth with his napkin and stood up from the table. "Rest, Aurelia. If there is anything you require while you're here, you only need ask."

Her empty glass of wine refilled itself as he left the room.

She listened for a latch to fall into place, waiting for evidence that she was trapped here—a prisoner. But it never came.

Peeling away the thick blanket, she gingerly lifted her leg to assess the damage. It was still sore, but the searing pain from the night before was gone. Picking up the clean white bandages that she'd ripped away earlier, she carefully re-wrapped her leg, wincing as the cloth tightly bound her wounds. Putting her toes onto the floor, she let out a quiet exhale of triumph as she tested her weight on her injured leg. Sore, certainly. But not immobile.

Stiffly hobbling from the bed, she made a slow progression across the room, the soreness leaching away with every step. And holding her breath, she pressed an ear against the heavy wooden door.

Silence. Well—that wasn't quite true, but as she steeled her will and cracked the door open, she realized the low sigh in the corridors was the sound of the air whipping against the windows. The quiet rustle, the sound of the leaves outside the thick stone walls, already turning brittle and golden this high up in the Shades.

Throwing the heavy iron latch into place, she slumped back against the door, the fight leaking out of her in the echoing silence of the room. Not a dank cell. Not a dungeon. In fact, far more comfortable than even her own chambers back home.

The room itself was tidy, but clearly well-loved and regularly used. One large window arched gracefully to the domed ceiling above, violet light pouring into the room around her. A softly piled rug took up most of the floor, and the furniture was made of a deep red wood, oiled and shining in the cozy light of the large fireplace. Bookshelves spanned the wall across from her, filled with neat rows of leather-bound books.

Not what she expected from a race of bloodthirsty creatures. But it was the view from the large window that caught her attention again. The steep drop into the Shades below meant she must be at least three or four stories up. The deep blues and greens of the pines stretching endlessly below the fortress.

She hated to admit that she found herself believing him—that he hadn't been responsible for her father's death or the Councilor's. After all, it seemed she had come face-to-face with that monster herself, but it didn't mean these creatures weren't enemies all the same.

And if the other things the Shadow said were true—that he'd been hunting stray demons, that the magickal barrier protecting the human realm was severed—it meant more of *them* could enter freely.

What she knew for certain was that her family, Bastien, Galina ... They were all in danger. The Old Ones had returned, and she needed to find a way to warn them. A way out of this place and back home.

Think. Aurelia begged her memory for any detail that might be helpful to her now. Anything that would save her. How did that damned nursery rhyme go?

Safe we stay in the golden light of day,
And when shadows fall, iron keeps the beasts at bay.
Iron and sunlight—

Late afternoon light spilled through the tall windows in the bedroom. The urge to run was tempting. Every sense in her body screaming to find a way out of this place. But she was no match for him even in perfect health, and with an injured leg—she'd never stand a chance. With only a few hours of daylight left, she'd barely make it into the Shades before he would come looking for her.

The smarter play was to get her bearings in this place. And hopefully avoid being a meal or a plaything for these monsters until she had her chance to escape.

Aurelia's ears prickled with every noise, every sigh of wind setting her teeth on edge as she searched the room to find anything—anything, that might be made of iron. Her eyes fell to the bookshelves again, and she scolded herself for getting distracted. But there—in a haphazard stack, was a leather-bound book with an iron latch.

Snatching up the book, she tore the soft cover with a small amount of guilt, ripping away the latch and stuffing it into the small pocket sewn into the pants she wore. She didn't know exactly what to do with it, but she felt better simply having the small piece of iron against her.

A loud pop from the fireplace sent her whirling around, the heavy book falling to the floor with a loud thud as the amber flames turned an impossible shade of blue.

Something fluttered out from the fire, twirling in the air for just a second before it softly landed on the rug in front of the hearth. The flames quickly died down, returning to their usual color. And cautiously approaching the small piece of paper, she picked it up, unfolding the note and reading the precise, neat handwriting inside, already knowing who it belonged to.

Join me for dinner.

And she let out a yelp as the note went up into flame, disintegrating in her hand as soon as she'd finished reading it. Muttering a curse at the sneaking feeling that the Shadow knew exactly how much he'd startled her with this little trick.

She turned toward the bed, stopping short when she saw a puddle of dark fabric that hadn't been there only seconds before.

A gown.

Picking up the dress, she let the smooth fabric slip across her fingers. Fine. She'd play whatever game he wanted. Be obedient. Bide her time. And when she found her chance—she'd escape.

Chapter 18

Sheer black sleeves kissed her skin down to her wrists. Draped layers of midnight blue and ebony fabric sighed along the floor as she moved. Some kind of material akin to leather wrapped around her waist and breasts, supple enough that she didn't feel that familiar ache in her lungs from the corsets she normally wore.

She inhaled a deep breath, expanding her diaphragm to its fullest, a smile lighting her face when she felt no restriction, only a slight soreness left in her ribs. The gown had been easy to put on—which was well enough since she couldn't remember the last time she'd dressed herself without assistance from a lady's maid and there didn't seem to be a surplus of them here.

A slit peaked at the curve of her hip, and though only a sliver of her leg was bare, just the edge of the bandage on her thigh visible, she might as well have been naked for how exposed she felt. Like she was wearing a costume, dressing up in someone else's clothes. But at the very least, it made her *feel* dangerous. And she needed all the confidence she could get.

Her hair was loose and wild, and she combed her fingers through the tangled waves trying to tame it, straightening her spine as she looked at her reflection. She was trapped with this beast—let him see that she was a little feral.

Glancing in the mirror with one final turn, a flash of metal caught her eye.

A desk was tucked into the corner of the room that she hadn't noticed before—covered with newly oiled blades.

The arrogant asshole hadn't even bothered to remove the weapons from her chambers.

She snatched up one of the daggers, its jeweled hilt a twin to the one she'd lost somewhere in the Shades. Not too heavy, but large enough to inflict damage even in her untrained hands. It wouldn't kill him if the tales were true, but it might be enough to slow him down. Easy to access with the cut of this dress, she thought with a smile. No layers of fabric between her hand and the weapon.

As she was cinching the dagger to her thigh, decisive raps sounded on the door.

Lifting the heavy latch, Aurelia cautiously opened it.

"Your presence has been requested," the hooded figure outside said without preamble. But it wasn't fear that made Aurelia step back, it was shock at the rich feminine voice that spoke from beneath the hood.

An exquisite face was revealed beneath. Sharp cheekbones and arched black brows above beautiful almond shaped eyes. Her dark crimson irises briefly landed on Aurelia before they narrowed again with impatience.

"Come," the dark female uttered, leading Aurelia down the corridor.

Beautifully arched ceilings yawned above them, lit by large torches suspended in the recesses of the stone ribcages vaulting up into shadow. Tall windows cast pools of light down the lengthy hall, the dark rock stretching down the corridor beneath her feet like the belly of a mighty black beast.

The soft rumble of conversation echoed in the hallways, dying away as pairs of ruby and garnet-colored eyes trailed Aurelia's steps as she struggled to keep up with the female's long stride. Strong, slender hands removed the hood from her head without breaking their brisk pace.

The female's hair was cropped to the same short length as the Shadow's, making her face even more strikingly beautiful. She wore the same dark gear, too. Lean, hard-won muscle underneath the form-fitting outfit.

Aurelia swallowed hard, following silently behind the female's lithe form as they passed through the maze of tunnels and stone bridges that spanned the caverns within the mountain. The Blood Folk were all dark beauties, it seemed. Black sheets of hair and various unnerving shades of red eyes. An entire kingdom of them lurking just outside the human realm, right under their noses. But here she was, in the midst of this place that shouldn't exist.

While she stood out like a beacon with her cinnamon-colored hair and honey-gold eyes, at least the dress didn't feel out of place. They passed females in gowns much more revealing than the one she wore, others wearing the same black gear the female ahead of her seemed to prefer.

Tense silence stretched, her escort not seeming concerned in the slightest if she kept up with her pace, never bothering to look back and see if Aurelia was still behind her. Or maybe it was that she just knew with her heightened senses that Aurelia trailed after her like a lost puppy.

They approached a set of towering doors, and without another word, the female pushed them open to reveal a cavern that stretched so high up Aurelia couldn't see where the walls ended in the darkness. The swell of voices was so sudden that she had to force her feet to follow the path the dark female cut through the massive room, echoing with the sounds of lively music and raucous laughter, the din of conversation and clink of dishes stopping abruptly at their entrance.

A sea of crimson eyes watched her progression through the hall, metal glinting at every hip and arm, rows of daggers strapped across chests. Gods ... There were so many of them. All of those unnatural eyes staring at her as she trained her gaze straight ahead—not daring to breath too loudly.

The Shadow stood at the front of the hall, a crowded table around him, his gaze landing on her as he pulled the empty chair out beside him.

It was a show—bringing her here to wade through hundreds of these beasts. A kingdom of blood-thirsty creatures who would kill her at the first chance, and *he* was the only thing standing between her and certain death.

The female led her to the table, depositing her in front of the Shadow before turning on her heel and leaving, the soft rumble of conversation resuming throughout the hall. Another glass of the dark red wine appeared in front of her before she could even take a seat. She needed to keep her wits, so fighting against the urge to gulp the thing down, she took a small sip, trying not to flinch as the Shadow stepped behind her, helping her into the seat.

"Nira's not one for small talk—but in a fight, there's no one better," the Shadow said, taking the chair next to her.

"And were you expecting one?" she asked demurely. Her mocking tone drowned out by the voice of the male seated at the Shadow's other side.

Ruggedly handsome, his stature was so impossibly large that no one could ever mistake him for human. Bronzed skin just a shade darker than the Shadow's, and jet-black hair cropped short above his deep-set eyes. He wore the same black gear as the rest of them, wicked blades strapped to his arms and a beautiful female lounging across his lap, completely wrapped up in whatever story he was telling.

"So then I removed its head the most efficient way I could." He shrugged. "With the talon it had lodged in my calf," he finished with a feral grin. The female sitting on his lap looked a little green. Nira, who had occupied a seat further down, only rolled her eyes before polishing off the glass of wine in front of her and snapping her fingers to refill it instantly.

The male turned, his vermillion eyes pinning Aurelia in her seat, a predatory gleam in his eyes; she'd watched Asher throw that look at enough women to know it was the look of a male who was devastatingly charming and well aware of it.

"Karro," he said, reaching across the Shadow's seat to capture Aurelia's hand in his own and brush a kiss across her knuckles. His sharpened canines on display in a way that seemed more invitation than threat.

It was all too clear how the tales had been spun over centuries—of these creatures luring virgins to their eternal damnation. Especially if any of the humans had met Karro.

A low growl rumbled from the Shadow, and whatever passed unspoken between him and Karro had the other males averting their eyes and finding anywhere else to look. Karro's wide grin fell into a smirk at the corner of his mouth as he lifted his cup to Aurelia before turning his attention back to the female on his lap.

"You'll have to excuse our manners—" The Shadow cleared his throat. "We've lived in relative isolation for the last few centuries."

"Is that why you and your—*friend* found yourselves in the human realm. In my *home*?" she asked, stifling a shudder at the memory of the pale prince with the milky white eyes.

"The prince is no longer a threat," he answered curtly, taking another bite of food. "As I said, your loved ones are safe."

"How can you be sure?"

"Because I killed him," he stated dryly, his eyes lingering on her as he took a sip of the dark wine. There wasn't even a hint of remorse in his voice. He didn't even seem concerned that it might frighten her. But truthfully—she was glad. Something in her liked his brutal honesty. At least this creature didn't handle her like porcelain, which was more than she could say for everyone else in her life.

"Unfortunately, it's not permanent ... But he'll have to claw his way back out from the lower levels of his own realm, and that will take a while," he added with a grim smile.

She raised her cup to him, "To one less monster roaming freely." And with a faint smile tugging at the corner of his mouth, the Shadow raised his glass in return, the watchful eyes of the Blood Folk in the hall seeming to find their way back to the food and drink in front of them.

For a fortress this size, she'd expected more of them. The dining hall alone could have accommodated double, and she suspected this was only one wing of the sprawling mountain keep. But it made her wonder where the rest of them were.

"What, exactly are you trying to prove with all this?" she bit out, her frustration with the charade finally getting the better of her.

"I'm not trying to prove anything."

Bullshit. Was he trying to intimidate her? Show her exactly how unprepared the humans were for an attack against their home?

"You're not in danger here," his voice rumbled softly.

"I think this room would prove otherwise," she answered tightly. If he was trying to put her at ease, it would take a lot more convincing than some empty words.

"The Wraiths are not a threat to you—"

She scoffed, "Is that what you call yourselves?"

Two hundred pairs of red eyes narrowed in her direction, and she took a gulp from her cup to hide the nervous bob of her throat. Too far—she'd gone too far. And she could only hope now that what he'd told her in the room about their tradition held true as she drank deeply from her wine.

"It was the name given to us by the first Blood Queen. Elite warriors tasked with protecting her kingdom from threats—and now, tasked with ensuring that creatures of the Void don't find themselves where they don't belong."

"And yet somehow ... these creatures that shouldn't exist have been finding their way into the Capitol ... Into my home. That wolf—" she stumbled over its true name, not quite able to admit to herself that demons were real—that she'd encountered one, "likely killed my father—How many more will have to die before you'll let me return to warn them?"

Surprise flashed across his crimson eyes, "I want to find out how they've been escaping the Void as much as you do," he uttered, his gaze never leaving hers as she searched for even a hint of deception.

"Then take me back," she whispered urgently, hoping maybe this was the opening she'd been looking for—a way to convince him that she should return. "Let me warn them of the dangers, help me find a way to protect the borders of the Valley from those creatures."

"I can't do that," he answered somberly, as if he had no choice in the matter.

"Why not?" she demanded. "You said yourself that we want the same thing—we share the same enemy. If I'm not a captive here—prove it!" she hissed, her frustration bleeding into her voice as her temper rose. "Prove you're not a monster!"

The murmur of conversation around them had gone quiet as the Shadow toyed with the glass of wine in front of him. Swirling the red liquid and taking another drink instead of answering her.

A buzzing swarmed her head. Every thought eddying out of her mind as ragged breaths filled her lungs. Why did he refuse to let her leave? Why was he preventing her from going home and warning them of whatever was coming?

The heavy weight of the cup in her hand made her suicidal, clearly, because without thinking—she threw it as hard as she could at him.

He caught it easily before it could hit him squarely in his straight, elegant nose, smirking in a way that made her wish she'd left it broken and bloodied.

Instantly, hands were at their blades. Some of the Wraiths already out of their seats, watching the Shadow with unnerving stillness ... Waiting for an order, she realized, as dread pooled in her gut.

Without taking his burning ember eyes from hers, he lowered his hand toward them. And she swallowed hard as every Wraith in the hall sat back down at once, going back to their meals; eyes warily watching her, as if *she* were the threat.

It was so silent in the hall that she could hear her own heartbeat pounding with pathetic mortality. She stood abruptly, nearly knocking over the chair as she moved to leave the table. Not a single Wraith blocked her path as she left, and the Shadow didn't make a move to stop her. But as she turned away, she could have sworn she saw Karro's shoulders shaking with barely controlled laughter.

It wasn't until Aurelia was in the echoing silence of the corridor that she realized she didn't know the way back to her chambers. And she sure as hell wasn't going back into that vipers' nest to ask. She was lucky they'd let her leave unscathed. So instead, she squared her shoulders and tried to remember the twists and turns she'd taken when she'd been led down here.

It seemed the Shadow had told her one truth at least—she wasn't a captive here. No guards haunted her steps or barred her way through the fortress as she wandered the empty corridors for the better part of an hour. Turning down a darkened hallway, she realized she'd walked in a circle. Again.

A figure up ahead detached itself from the wall, and she stood frozen in place, her heartbeat thudding into her throat.

Nira's fiercely beautiful face emerged in the torchlight, doing nothing to calm Aurelia's panic as the dark female's clipped steps stopped abruptly in front of her.

"Need help finding your way?" Nira asked, her voice laced with ice.

With a shallow nod, Aurelia followed behind the terrifying female, struggling to match her pace with Nira's long strides. They walked in silence through the maze of corridors, finally turning down one that looked a little more familiar than the rest, Nira stopping rigidly in front of the door to her chambers.

"Thank you." Aurelia uttered a bit begrudgingly, turning to go into the room.

Slender fingers shot out to grasp her arm, the callused hand stronger than she expected as Nira forced her to turn around and face her.

"Don't you understand what he's offered you?" Nira asked coldly, narrowing her eyes at Aurelia in a way that reminded her of the golden feathered hawks the blue cloaks used atop the wall. "He's our Commander. The—" Nira stopped short, cutting off whatever she'd been about to say. Her ruby eyes blazed with irritation. "He just made certain that every Wraith in this kingdom knew you were under his protection."

Aurelia's stomach sank. She'd guessed that he was some kind of leader here with the way they all seemed to revere him ... But their fucking commander.

She scoffed, "He claimed his prize, you mean." The Shadow wanted to show her exactly how quickly she would be dead if it weren't for his intervention, and he'd succeeded.

Aurelia removed her arm from Nira's grasp, surprised when the female dropped it, but none of the fury left her expression.

"Stupid girl," Nira spat, making Aurelia's face flush in embarrassment. "You come from comfort."

It was a statement, not a question. And she didn't have the energy to deny the truth.

"You reek of it," Nira sneered, her nostrils flaring as she drew closer. "But your noble birth means nothing here. We do not take kindly to outsiders—he's made sure no one will question why you're here and whether you deserve to remain."

But that's where Nira was wrong. Her noble birth had taught her how to play the game. Everyone wanted something. It was just a matter of discovering what. But she didn't intend to stay here long enough to find out what the Shadow wanted from her.

"And do *you* know why I'm here?" Aurelia prodded. Maybe she'd find a reluctant ally in Nira. After all, the female seemed to want her here just as little as she wanted to *be* here. If nothing else maybe she'd get more information out of her.

"I trust him," was all Nira said before turning on her heel and disappearing again, leaving Aurelia alone once more.

What did creatures like this know of trust. Of loyalty or love. They might look human. Act human. But it would never be enough to replace the souls they'd never possessed. But that was none of her concern now—she'd accomplished what she'd set out to do.

She found a way out.

Opening the large wardrobe in one corner of the room, she grabbed the first few items she found. Shrugging on a loose shirt, she hastily buttoned it. Stepping into the pair of pants, she laced the front and rolled the hem about five inches. The boots inside looked to be easily twice the size of her own feet, but they were better than nothing.

Raiding a drawer of leather straps, she cinched one around her uninjured thigh and another around her waist, sheathing the black dagger she'd taken from the desk earlier and returning for a smaller knife she'd seen. And then she waited.

And waited. Thanking the Unnamed that no one had come looking for her.

Never in her life had dawn felt so reluctant to appear. But as the first signs of periwinkle and violet crept over the mountains, she slipped quietly from the room. Every minute of sunlight would be crucial to her survival, and she wouldn't waste a second of it.

Opening the door wide enough now to fully see the corridor beyond—her breath was taken away at the sight.

Soaring arches spilled down from the cavernous ceilings high above. Appearing to have been etched entirely from the mountain surrounding her. The hallway she padded down might be better described as a bridge. One side encased by floor to ceiling windows, elegantly curving up, up, up to reveal the expanse of the Shades just beyond the fortress walls. The other side contained only by a stone balustrade, dropping away into a lower level below. She glanced around, pressing her back against the stone wall, listening for any footsteps in the corridor.

Nothing.

Not at all like the ones at home; always teeming with noise and life. But as she picked her way through empty corridor after empty corridor—the absence of sound was unnerving. Either they kept their victims locked deep in the mountain where their screams couldn't be heard ... or she was the only fresh blood in these halls.

The gold and bronze veins running through the dark stone were set aflame by the dawn light pouring in through the windows. And a level below, a large cavern yawned wide, ripping the mountainside open, exposing it to the elements. Aurelia leaned over the edge, looking down into the cavern, and a cool breeze rushed past as if in answer. A ledge of stone jutted out into thin air, the pines and rocky terrain of the Shades tumbling hundreds of feet below the sharp outline.

Finding her way through the corridors, she kept note of every turn she made. The halls were silent, spurring her faster, breathing through the pain that lanced up her leg with every other step. Her mind was so wholly consumed with the single purpose of escape that she gritted her teeth against all sensation pounding through her body. Her ribs were screaming now, sending a flare of pain through her chest with every breath, reminding her that she was achingly, pathetically human in this mountain keep full of immortal creatures.

The entrance to a large chamber yawned wide in front of her. And through the gloom of the murky dark, the tangles of vines and knotted brambles—she saw it.

Her escape.

The windows that framed one side of the chamber illuminated the crack in the decaying wall. A mess of broken stone where the exterior had given way, allowing nature to reclaim a small piece of the sprawling fortress.

She tore at the crumbling stone with her fingers, cursing her own weakness as she struggled to lift the heavier stones away. Thankful for the overgrowth of vines and moss that muffled the noise she was making. Who knew how much time she had before he noticed she was missing? But as soft morning light started pouring through the opening, she gave a stifled sob of triumph.

Shoving away the remaining stone and bits of gravel until her palms bled, she ducked through the space, the fabric of the pants tearing as they snagged on the rough edges of the wall. She took a lungful of air and staggered outside. But the relief only lasted a second as she looked at the descent.

The wall had been hewn from the peak of the mountain, and the only natural ledge to follow was so narrow that she'd have to press her back against the fortress to keep from diving headfirst over the sheer drop down the cliffs.

Blind determination moved her feet forward. This was her chance. Her only chance at survival, and she wouldn't waste the daylight.

The wind whipping the mountainside pulled at her, clawing her face, and threatening to pull her over. But she closed her eyes, feeling her way along, pressing her back into the hard stone and searching for a foothold with every step.

The path grew just a little wider as she made her way down the mountain, growing darker as she neared the pines crowding the fortress wall. Ahead of her was the iron gate leading out of this damned place. But between...

A narrow bridge. Cleaved from the mountainside itself. Wide enough for three people to stand side-by-side without toppling over into the abyss waiting on either edge, a small relief from the treacherous path she'd just walked, but completely exposed. And it was all that stood between her and freedom.

Swallowing her fear, Aurelia placed one foot onto the bridge. She didn't have the energy to turn around and make sure she wasn't being followed. She'd never outrun them, anyway. But she let her eyes skirt the periphery as she edged across.

No one.

Not much of a fortress if the guards couldn't man the wall in broad daylight without threat of bursting into flame. She let out a satisfied laugh, slightly manic from the pure disbelief that she'd made it this far. The dark green expanse was so close that just a few more steps would bring her to freedom.

Her foot landed on soft pine needles. The canopy of trees was thick enough now to blot out the light, but she couldn't stop here. The afternoon sun was still high in the early autumn skies, and she needed to put as much distance as possible between herself and this place before nightfall. No sign of the Valley in sight, but *down* would get her there eventually.

She walked for hours, winding her way through the pines until she finally allowed herself to slow her pace a little, the adrenaline subsiding enough that she couldn't ignore the ache in her leg. The sharp pain with every inhale.

Down, down, down. Her footsteps were much slower now as she stumbled through thickets and brambles, roots catching her feet and threatening to twist her ankles. And finally, when the afternoon sun was high above her, she allowed herself to stop.

The Shades were still thick around her—a small comfort that she would be well hidden. A large rock jutted out of the forest floor ahead, and that seemed as good a place as any to rest and catch her breath.

Hobbling over to it, she slumped down against the cold stone. The pain in her leg was relentlessly throbbing now, a pounding ache that she felt in her bones, but she needed to close her eyes. Rest. And then she'd continue her way down the mountain, she'd be able to orient herself once she reached the valley floor, however long that took.

Her eyes were heavy, but she only needed a moment—just a moment to rest ... and then...

Chapter 19

The crunch of leaves and dry pine needles startled her awake. Aurelia held her breath behind the boulder. Waiting. Praying to the Unnamed more fervently than she had since she'd been a child and still believed they existed. Or cared.

Flattening her back against the boulder, she glanced up—the sun was hanging low in the sky now. She was running out of daylight.

Without thinking, she pushed herself off the boulder, stumbling and limping further down the mountain as her traitorous leg protested with every step. Her damned heartbeat thudding so loudly in her chest that she couldn't hear anything else around her. Glancing over her shoulder, she saw ... nothing.

Her footsteps slowed, her heartbeat still pounding wildly as panicked laughter escaped her. Leaves—it was only leaves, she reassured herself as the sunset bled over the mountainside and she continued her slow progression.

The trickle of water up ahead gave her renewed energy and she hobbled closer to the rocky bank of a small creek, picking her way across the boulders until she was close enough that she dipped her hand into the cool, clear water and drank.

The sunlight filtering through the treetops had faded into the bruised purple of dusk. It was only then she noticed how quiet the forest had become. No chatter from the birds. No rustling of small animals. Even the pines seemed to be holding their breath.

The sandy riverbed sucked at her boots, seeming to try to pull her back as she fought to climb up the embankment to higher ground. She'd be exposed if she stayed by the river, she needed to look for cover—

Slipping the dagger from where it had been strapped to her thigh, she brandished the weapon. Crackling energy radiated down her arms and into her fingertips, and with it was another spear of pain that sliced through her temples, making her lose focus for a precious moment. But when she shook her head, trying to clear the fog, that hazy white glow was seeping through her clenched fists.

Fuck. Not now—

An acrid stench burned her throat, taking her back to that night in the old wing of the palace, to that dusty unused room.

Sulfur.

A low clicking reverberated across the mountainside, sending icy fear into her chest. And as she spun in the direction of the sound, acid green eyes glowed from the shadows nearby; dozens of them fixed on where she stood.

Her mind was screaming at her to move, but she was frozen in place by those hypnotizing eyes. The same luminescent green fire that had burned behind the irises of the creature she'd encountered in the palace ... But this one was worse.

Prowling into the clearing, the hulking body of the demon blotted out the last of the fading sunlight as it drew closer. A sharp clicking sound coming from the concentric rows of teeth in its mouth—if you could call it a mouth. A dozen wickedly sharp legs descended from its bulbous body, giving it the appearance of an overgrown spider.

It moved with unnatural speed toward her. She braced herself for death, the dagger held out in front of her.

Four black plumes of shadow hit the ground with such force that the mountain shook.

Dark figures emerged, metal glinting across their chests, and she wasn't sure who the larger threat was—either way, she was dead.

The demon lunged for her—its circle of gnashing teeth so close that she felt the hot stench of its breath against her face. But just as quickly, an inhuman scream of frustration ripped through the night.

The demon reared back on six of its legs, swiveling its eyes to look at the gleaming blade protruding from its body. It shook the dagger loose, chittering in agitation as it snapped its mouth at the black-clad figure nearby. The beautiful male from the dining hall had stepped into the clearing, the final threads of sunlight illuminating his face...

Sunlight.

How many other things had the tales gotten wrong about their kind?

The demons' rows of teeth missed Karro by only a hair as its legs were taken out from beneath it by coils of shadow. Nira was at the other side of the clearing, casting black tendrils toward the demon as Karro and another male leapt on top of the creature.

A callused hand reached out and grabbed Aurelia's arm as she saw the flash of dark blades. The ground around her feet darkened in the moonlight. The deep indigo and jades of the forest floor turning black as shadows slithered across the ground to wrap around her legs.It only took a matter of moments, but Aurelia felt like she watched the shadows wrap around her body for an eternity. Stunned by their beauty. And as they caressed her skin, her stomach plummeted. The feeling of weightlessness so sudden that she was completely disoriented.

She landed on solid ground again a few moments later. A strong grip still holding onto her while her equilibrium caught up. When her vision stopped spinning, her stomach sank.

As the dark wisps of shadow slithered back into the forest, the Shadow's face appeared above her, a cold mask she couldn't read. The landing had jarred her body, and the pain in her leg came rushing back with a vengeance, but she gritted her teeth—determined not to let it show.

The same curved stone wall that she'd followed down the mountain now loomed in front of them. A few short hours ago she'd hobbled and stumbled her way down the path. Only to wind up right back here.

Ravenstone.

"That thing..." she bit off as another flare of pain racked her body.

"A vorak," the Shadow supplied with cold indifference.

"You gave them *names*?" she gritted out through clenched teeth.

"They had different names once. All his demons were something else before—something alive. Until he got a hold of them," he answered bitterly.

The adrenaline that kept the pain at bay had subsided, every breath agony as she tried to remain standing.

"The fortress is warded from anyone entering its gates by magick. So, we'll have to take the long way up," he uttered, catching her before she could crumple to the ground. And hooking her arm over his broad shoulders, he easily lifted her into his arms. She didn't have the breath to protest, worried she might grind her teeth to dust from the pain.

He gently carried her across the narrow stone bridge leading into the torchlit halls of the mountain keep. And once inside, his shadows swallowed them again, spitting them out into the chamber where she'd awoken a day ago.

Laying her onto the bed, he seemed to be aware of every wince she tried to hide, every hiss she swallowed back.

She was a fool. To think she could leave this place and find her way back home. Injured. Nauseous. Dizzy. With those *things* creeping through the forest at night. And it clicked into place; how easily she'd managed to escape the fortress.

"You son of a bitch—" she hissed.

"The lady has a tongue after all," he replied with venomous calm.

"You *let* me escape."

"You already believed me a monster—I didn't think I'd help my case by keeping you locked up here." He gestured to the room around them.

"You said I'm not—your—captive," she gasped out, gritting her teeth through another stab of pain, but this one was pounding through her temples. So sharp that it blotted out every thought from her mind.

He crossed his arms over his broad chest, his crimson eyes studiously trained on her. "And I meant every word. But I have no intention of allowing you to die out there," he responded flatly.

"Then take me back!" She fought to get the words out as the pain finally subsided.

"I can't do that, Aurelia," he answered darkly, turning away from her.

"Tell me why I'm here! Why won't you bring me back?" she pleaded, hating the desperation in her voice as she crawled from the bed to stand in front of him—forcing him to look at her.

His gaze searched hers. "How long have the headaches been plaguing you?" he murmured quietly.

She ignored him, gritting her teeth and dropping her hands from where they'd been rubbing her temples.

"*How long*, Aurelia," he pressed, a hint of concern hiding under his careful mask of indifference.

"Weeks … Months," she answered. What difference did it make? Why did he care?

"And the last time you were able to keep any food down?" A lock of dark hair fell across his eye as he turned to look at her.

She didn't bother responding, turning on a heel to look out the window at the darkened Shades. Maybe if she made enough suicidal attempts to return on her own, he'd finally take her back.

He let out a heavy breath behind her. "The sensitivity to light, the illness … That's how it starts."

The color drained from her face as she finally turned to meet his crimson eyes.

"You cannot go back, Aurelia, for a few reasons—" he said, taking a step toward her. "But chiefly, because you're not human."

Chapter 20

"What kind of game is this?" she hissed with barely controlled rage.

"This is no game to me, Aurelia." He leveled his gaze at her. Those immortal red eyes reminding her exactly how little power she had. "You have magick in your blood, and if you aren't careful, you'll be dangerous when it fully wakes. Your power called to mine in the human realm—had I not found you..." the Shadow whispered, his voice hushed with some urgency she didn't understand. "You are here— because you belong here."

And it was his tone that made her swallow back her anger. Not even a hint of the fiery temper from a moment ago. It was the gravity in his deep voice that made it worse somehow.

Pain collided into her skull so suddenly that she had to brace herself against the table. The Shadow reached out a hand to steady her, but she slapped it away angrily.

With a snap of his fingers, a glass of wine appeared before her and before she could think better of it, she greedily took it—one sip making the agony recede. She stared at the deep red liquid with dawning clarity. How could she have been so fucking stupid...

Blood.

The wine was laced with blood.

A cold sweat broke out over her skin as she considered how many glasses of the stuff she'd consumed since she'd awoken here, and she threw the glass across the room with a strength she didn't realize she possessed, watching as the crystal shattered against the wall.

"What have you done to me..." she uttered, lead filling her gut as she tore at her clothes—looking for bite marks, some sign that he'd tried to turn her into one of his creatures. Or maybe he'd poisoned her with his blood long before now. Had he bitten her that night that he'd left the dagger on her bed?

"It doesn't work like that—magick is something you're born with. Not something you can *infect* people with," he bit out, snapping his fingers once more and cleaning up the smashed glass and red-stained floor in an instant.

Magick. It was all so ridiculous. So impossible.

Taking two strides toward where he stood, she slipped the dagger from where it had been strapped to her thigh, bringing the black metal just under the sharp line of his jaw. It was futile—he was faster and stronger. Invincible—immortal most likely.

"I'm not like *you*. I don't belong *here*," she raged, cursing that infernal heat that was building behind her shoulder blades.

"You are. Regardless of whether you claim it or not," he answered, unmoving as she pressed the blade into his skin.

"No—you have me mistaken for someone else. *Something* else." Her voice betrayed the panic rising up in her chest. "And you've been letting me drink—" She spat onto the floor, unable to say the word aloud, wiping her mouth as if it would undo everything that had happened.

"Would you have drank it if I'd told you?" he drawled.

"Of course not!" she protested, watching a bead of his red blood well against the sharp edge of the dagger.

"It's the only thing that will keep the headaches and the nausea at bay," he said matter-of-factly, as if it had only been wine that he'd offered her and not ... *someone*. "It's synthetic, if that puts your mind at ease," he continued, standing still as granite.

She didn't know what the word meant, but she wouldn't give him the satisfaction of asking. She dropped the blade and tried to step around him. But suddenly his large body was in front of hers again, blocking her path.

"That rush through your body, that feeling under your skin. The way your emotions feel volatile. Violent. The craving for blood—those things will only get stronger," he whispered. So close to her now that she could feel the caress of his breath against her skin, sending traitorous shivers down her spine.

"Get out of my way!" she demanded, her frustration turning into boiling rage—then panic, as she tried not to think about the strange white haze that had appeared just before the demon found her. Trying to convince herself that she hadn't savored every sip of the rich wine here.

Shoving against the wall of vampyre in front of her, she might as well have been trying to move a boulder for all it did. She glanced up, seeing wry amusement on the Shadow's face that only made anger flare in her chest.

Heat flooded her palms, and she shoved him again. A vicious rage taking root in her gut that he *wouldn't. Fucking. Move*—

Stumbling back, a shocked expression clouded his eyes for a moment.

She'd pushed him—she'd actually managed to move him.

The smell of singed fabric filled the room, and she glanced down to the front of his shirt. Scorch marks marred the fabric that had been perfectly white only a moment ago ... Two burned imprints—the exact shape of her hands.

Choking back a stifled gasp, she stumbled back, hitting the windowpane. She turned her hands over. Her ordinary, pale palms.

"A curious thing—to summon fire at will," the Shadow said.

His hand gracefully flicked out, a small flame hovering just above his upturned palm. The black fire flickering over his smooth skin, not seeming to burn him in the slightest as the small flare danced in his hand.

And realization dawned.

Recognition.

She stood dumbstruck, disbelief still clouding what she'd just witnessed. What *she* had done. "What's happening to me..." she whispered.

The Shadow stalked across the room, unbuttoning his ruined shirt, and tossing it into the fire. Hard cuts of muscle layered his body. His bare skin broken by lines and whorls of black ink. "You're going into stasis," he answered, opening the doors of the wardrobe. "Or you will be soon." He shrugged on black gear just as the heavy wooden door burst open behind them.

Two dark figures emerged into the dim light of the chambers.

The Shadow's posture changed instantly as he rushed over to where Karro was leaning heavily against Nira, who cleared the table with a sweep of her arm.

"Who else—" the Shadow demanded.

"Seth. A few others." Nira's voice caught ever so slightly before she continued, "They'll be alright, but they need the healers' full attention. This asshole on the other hand—" she grunted, before unceremoniously dumping Karro onto the table.

"Go help Embra with the others," the Shadow ordered as Nira gave him a slight bow before stalking back through the door.

Karro's torso was a bloody mess. The Shadow had stripped off Karro's shirt, revealing mangled flesh across his ribs. He winced with every movement but didn't make a sound save for the breath he hissed out of his lungs. Aurelia didn't have much experience with tending wounds. She'd seen men injured; the aftermath of a routine patrol gone bad. A botched uprising or a gang of boys trying to prove themselves men. Always watching from far away. A bystander. Inconsequential.

It was because of her own stupidity that Karro—this stranger, was injured. He'd fought off that creature to keep her safe, even when she hadn't deserved it.

"Tell me what to do," she said, the pain of her own injuries forgotten.

The Shadow glanced to where she stood while he lifted Karro's legs onto the table, then moved to the desk, rummaging through the drawers just as she had a few hours before. Another pang of guilt hit her in the gut at the thought she might be slowing down whatever help he was looking for.

"Tell me what to do!" she shouted. A singular focus sharpening her tone as the Shadow lifted his gaze to meet hers again.

"Keep Karro distracted," he answered. "I need to find something to help burn out the venom. Don't do anything stupid while I'm gone, brother," the Shadow muttered, leaving the room.

Karro's labored breathing made her look down to where he sprawled across the table.

"And what, exactly, did you do to deserve that?" she asked, forcing levity into her voice, trying to take both of their minds off how much blood was pooling underneath him—trying to keep him conscious. If the healers were occupied with worse...

"Went in for the kill when I should have let that demon go crawling back to whatever hole it came from," Karro answered with a lopsided grin.

"Looks like it got the better of you," she chuckled, relieved that he was well enough to smile—saying anything to keep the grimace of pain from returning to his face.

The Shadow called him brother. They looked similar enough for that to make sense, the same sharp jaw and dark red eyes. But it was impossible to tell with the Blood Folk all seeming to possess this dark beauty.

"And what about you?" he asked, nodding to her bandaged leg, now exposed thanks to the tear in her stolen pants. That disarming smile on his handsome face again, a conspiratorial gleam in his eyes. She cracked a smile too, already feeling at ease with him. His mischievous grin reminding her so much of Asher that it made her heart ache.

Shit.

Asher. Bastien. Gods, they must be worried sick about her. Bastien would turn the Capitol inside out to find her, and Asher would be right there next to him...

She tried to tamp down the surge of emotions that rose in her throat. The awful reality that she might never see them again, or her mother. It would probably take Wellan weeks to realize she was gone. Only once his bartering chip didn't show up to the wedding would he notice her absence—

"A demon, from the look of those cuts," Karro said a little hesitantly, noticing the look on her face.

"Not just any demon," a deep voice rumbled. Aurelia looked up to see the Shadow emerging from the doorway. "One of the Fengul," he added with a grim smile. Karro exhaled a curse, the two males sharing some silent understanding.

"The Fengul are particularly vicious," the Shadow clarified as he crossed the room. "I've seen them take down highly experienced warriors who had much more at their disposal than a small dagger."

A shiver of fear swept down Aurelia's spine at the sheer luck she'd had. She shouldn't be alive.

"Right—hold him down," the Shadow ordered. "He'll heal quickly, but this is going to hurt like a bitch," he added, giving Karro a hearty slap on the chest, making him grimace.

Aurelia stood at Karro's head, bracing her palms on each of his massive shoulders, trying not to let her eyes linger on the broad swathes of black ink etched into his bronze skin. Elegant lines and swirls across his chest and torso cut apart by the ragged skin across his ribs. Unbroken as they carved around the swells of hard muscle in his arms to continue down his back.

"Enjoying the view?" Karro asked, his roguish grin nearly hiding the pain knitting his brows together, his shamelessness making Aurelia laugh despite herself.

"Karro—" the Shadow growled in warning, uncorking a small vial in his hand filled with shimmering liquid.

"What? If I can't look good while I'm bleeding out, what's all the training been for?" Karro asked, trying to mask his grimace.

"If you hadn't tried to be a fucking hero, you wouldn't be bleeding out in the first place," the Shadow calmly stated as he poured the vial's contents into the gash, making Karro grit his teeth.

Karro clamped his eyes shut against the pain, gasping out, "There is no valor in unmarred skin, brother."

"And there is no glory to claim if you are dead," the Shadow answered roughly.

"Don't tell me you're—getting sentimental," Karro ground out through his teeth as the liquid sputtered and burned its way through the hole torn into his chest.

"I will not light your pyre nor sing a lament for you this night, brother," the Shadow responded.

Karro coughed out a laugh, but the line etched between the Shadow's brows only deepened as they both struggled to keep Karro's shoulders pinned to the table.

She knew he wasn't trying to fight her, but the fact that she could keep the monstrous male pinned at all meant he must have been seriously weakened by the venom. She knew first-hand the scorching pain it caused, and whatever was still left from the scratches in her leg must have only been a fraction of what the elixir was burning out from Karro. He was gritting his teeth so hard she wondered how they didn't shatter as it foamed and fizzed into his wounds, pumping putrid black bile from the bite.

Finally, the line between Karro's brows smoothed over with relief, his breathing evening out. And as his eyes grew heavy, the Shadow braced an arm behind his broad back.

Helping Karro sit up, the Shadow jerked his chin toward a cut crystal decanter of dark red wine on the desk. "A glass of that will help," he said, looking to her.

She crossed the room, pouring out a glass. Karro grasped it with shaky hands, gulping it down like a man dying of thirst. With every swallow, the whorls of black ink across his chest knitted themselves back together, as if they'd never been disturbed.

The Shadow helped Karro down from the table, the two males making their way back to the door of the chambers and stepping into the darkened room across the hall. It was only then that everything hit her at once—the demon, the blood-laced wine, the male in front of her at death's doorstep only to be completely healed in moments…

She stumbled back into one of the chairs, worried that her legs would give out from beneath her at any moment.

The Shadow came back into the room, his eyes darting to where she sat, concern creasing his brow again.

"I'm fine," she choked out. A lie. A knee-jerk response because she needed a moment to think. To wrap her head around tonight.

His eyes studied her for a moment before he gave a nod of his head, seemingly satisfied that she was alright for the time being. "I need to go kill a demon," he growled, jerking his chin towards the desk. "If you plan to run off again, at least take a few more of my blades with you."

Shadows slithered across the floor from every corner of the room, gathering at his command. His shoulders tense as he flexed his hands absentmindedly, the crack of each knuckle like thunder warning of a coming storm as he vanished.

Chapter 21

A thousand questions rattled around in Aurelia's mind as she waited. She couldn't deny that something was happening to her. The illness that had become a constant companion over the past few weeks, the strange white haze, the burn marks she'd left—

And as much as she wanted to blame the Shadow, wanted to convince herself that he had poisoned her, that *he* had been the one to do this to her—she knew the restless feeling under her skin had been there long before she'd met him. It had been simmering for weeks before her father had been killed. Before the first demon had made its way into her home.

Not her home. Not anymore...

But how was any of this possible? Her parents were completely, irrevocably ... human. The evidence was plain in the fact that her father died—and she hadn't. Her mother? No, that hardly seemed likely.

A dull ache spread through her leg. Her borrowed pants had torn sometime while she'd been lost in the Shades, and the bandage around her injury was caked with dirt and grime.

What if the Shadow was wrong about her? What if she wasn't one of *them* after all?

But deep in her gut, some instinct buried inside her had answered to his magick. That small, beautiful flame that he'd conjured in his palm felt ... familiar, in a way she couldn't put into words.

She turned her hands over again, but whatever evidence she was hoping to find there was gone. And she let out a strangled scream of rage. The anger dissolving into something else as she beat her fists against the table and anguished tears rolled down her cheeks.

If only she'd never left her chambers that night.

Fucking *fool*.

She'd been so close—so close to something like happiness. Contentment. And instead, she'd gone searching for answers that shattered any chance of that.

Hysterical laughter escaped her lips, only because the alternative was sobbing, and she already hated herself enough.

Maybe she'd be lucky, and the Shadow would change his mind—decide she wasn't worth the trouble and leave her in the Shades for one of those horrifying creatures to find and this nightmare she'd stumbled into would end.

The heavy door creaked opened, and even in the dim light, Aurelia recognized the Shadow's silhouette immediately. She choked back the rest of her tears, hastily wiping her cheeks.

There was a heaviness to his footsteps as he entered the room. He shucked off the leather bandolier from across his chest. Unbuckling every strap on his arms and legs, he removed the glinting black metal daggers with such practiced fingers that it was clear he'd done it countless times. The weight of every jeweled hilt making a dull thunk on the desk as he deposited them.

It was only then that she caught the faint stench of sulfur on him. A constellation of black specks were scattered across his face and hands, the only skin exposed on his otherwise leather clad body.

His jacket was the next to go, and as he peeled it away from his torso, the hints of black ink she'd seen before were completely exposed now. Elegant whorls and symbols like the ones she'd seen on Karro were sprawled across the broad planes of his chest, wrapping around to his back. A band of small dashes spiraling up the entire length of his arm.

For a moment, she wondered if he'd forgotten she was here—and she turned away, a blush coming into her cheeks. She was no stranger to the male form. She'd spent countless days watching Bastien train in the pit, countless nights with her body entangled in his, but somehow, this felt more intimate. She swallowed hard, looking back as he walked into the bathing chamber.

The crack of the faucet and the rush of water were the only sounds before plumes of steam billowed out into the room. He emerged a few moments later, the dark strands of his hair clinging to his neck in waves from the humidity as he wiped away the blood and grime with a cloth.

Shrugging on a fresh shirt, he jerked his chin toward the open bathroom door. "Come," he said roughly. "Your wounds won't heal properly with half the Shades lodged in them." He nodded to her leg.

"But what about the others?" she asked with a pang of guilt.

"The others are fine. But I won't be able to sleep until I see that bandage replaced." He finished buttoning his shirt, leaving the last two undone, the dark ink spiraling up his chest left on display. "Consider it a favor to me."

Suspicious of the offer, she fixed him with a challenging stare from where she still stood across the room. He didn't wait for a reply as he began to walk back into the bathing chamber.

With a glance over his shoulder he added, "I promise I won't bite."

A large basin of steaming water sat on the floor of the bathing chamber. An awkward silence settled around them in the tight space as the Shadow wrung out a clean white cloth. He reached for her arm, gently beginning to rub away the caked blood and dirt from her skin, letting the warm water soothe away the sting of her cuts and scrapes.

She hissed as he reached a deep scratch on her arm, and he paused his ministrations for a moment. Gritting her teeth, she nodded for him to continue.

There were deep cuts on his hands, too, and she wondered what manner of dark creature had given them to him in the short span of time between when he'd left her and now. But as he dipped the cloth back into the clean water, his cuts faded, the blood washing away to reveal perfectly smooth skin beneath.

She glanced down at her own fingers, still raw and bloodied from where she'd ripped away the crumbing stone of the fortress to escape hours ago. "If I'm one of you ... why don't I heal like you do?"

"Your body will become more durable after you go into stasis—you'll heal quickly and be harder to injure. You'll be stronger, faster. But it's a grueling process," the Shadow answered. "The flood of magick requires a significant amount of blood. And without the proper precautions ... It can be unpredictable. Unwieldy. Dangerous—for you and for others. The tales humans whisper of *vampyres* are because of who we become during that change. *What* we become."

"How is this possible?" she asked. "My family—my home..." She shook her head, at a loss for words. Still in denial that magick, and vampyres, and demons were real.

"I don't know," he answered roughly.

"But I don't look like you—*any* of you." All of them were impossibly beautiful. Terrifying and mesmerizing. The onyx hair, the bronze skin, the garnet eyes...

"Your eyes will change color once you go into stasis—the rest," he glanced up at her, "I'm not sure," he said with a shake of his head. "But we don't come into our power until we near our twenty-fifth year. Until then, we're almost indistinguishable from humans."

The nightmares, the white auras shimmering around her fingertips—they'd started the night her father died. She'd woken up in a cold sweat only seconds before Asher had come bursting into her room—that look of utter anguish on his face. And all of it had been just a few months before the night of her birthday ... When she'd first met him.

"You said my magick called to yours—" she began, sifting through the bits and pieces of information he'd given her since she'd arrived.

"I didn't realize it at first..." he said, his voice hushed and ragged. "It's been centuries since the last fire-wielder went into stasis—I didn't see you for what you were. Your scent was so mercurial." Sadness tinged his voice as he glanced to the window in the bathing chamber—to the darkened Shades beyond, and she wondered what he saw with his heightened vision that she was still blind to. "It was Fate that brought me to the human realm."

Silence enveloped the room again as she tried to piece together this new understanding of her world—*their* world, and the creatures that prowled it. Her place within it.

He rinsed the cloth again, the water clouding with blood and dirt. "I would take you back if I could," he whispered, his crimson eyes meeting hers. "I would take you back to the people you love." His choice of words hit her with jarring clarity. *The people you love*—not family. "But if you return to the human realm ... You will do things you will live to regret for a very, very long time."

She swallowed hard. After what she'd done to his shirt in a fit of anger ... she could only imagine what she might be capable of in a realm of people much more fragile than him. The faint smell of sulfur still clung to the Shadow, and another wave of guilt smothered her that he was sitting here cleaning up her injuries, cleaning up her mess.

He moved onto her leg next, ripping away the shredded fabric of her pants like it was nothing more than paper and tearing away the grimy bandage to examine her cuts.

She reached out her hand to touch the raised red slashes on her leg, finding it difficult to believe she'd almost died from these wounds less than a day ago. If the demon claws had sliced any deeper, she wouldn't have left that room alive.

"I need to know that they'll be safe," she whispered.

"I've stationed some of my most trusted Wraiths to watch the portal, but nothing else has tried to come through the mirror, if anything does—they'll handle it," he answered solemnly as he washed away the grime and dirt, finally dropping the cloth into the basin. "You have my word."

The mirror. It explained how she'd taken a single step that brought her from inside the palace walls into the very heart of the Shades. A journey that should have taken days, maybe weeks by foot given how high up in the mountains they were.

"And is that one thing the tales got right?" she asked, repeating the words she'd heard time and again about their kind. "A bargain struck cannot be broken?"

He reached for a small glass jar nearby, unscrewing the lid and scooping out a kind of balm. He began to apply it to her injuries, his touch gentle despite his rough calluses.

"Our word is our bond—when you live as long as we do, vows are sacred, and broken bonds are not easily forgotten," he answered, his crimson eyes briefly meeting hers. Long enough for her to see the promise there, and something loosened in her chest just a little.

A fire was softly glowing in the corner of the room as they left the bathing chamber. The Shadow threw his gear over his shoulder, picking up the discarded blades from the table.

"Why did you save me?" she whispered.

He turned toward her, and with a small shrug, he answered, "Because you're one of us."

Shouldering his gear again, he made to leave the room. As if that simple answer was enough to explain risking their lives for her. A stranger. A nobody here in their world.

"Thank you—Ven," she called after him. And as it left her lips, she realized that was the first time she'd called him by his name.

He stopped in the doorway, with his broad back still towards her—his sharp profile cast in relief by the firelight.

"We are not monsters, at least not all of us." He said quietly.

Chapter 22

She locked herself in the chambers. Not so much out of fear, but because the thought of being here— whatever it was that was happening to her, it was too much. And confining herself to the space of this room made her feel a little less like she was spiraling into oblivion.

The torches and candles had slowly dimmed of their own accord as the hour grew late. At first, she thought her eyes were playing tricks on her. But she watched the flicker of amber light grow smaller and smaller, until the torches along the wall doused themselves completely and she was left alone in the darkness, with only her thoughts to keep her company.

Exhaustion took over as she laid down on the soft bed. A weariness that seeped into her very bones. The ache in her ribs had eased so that she could take a breath without gasping. The pain in her leg dulled to an annoying throb, but at least it gave her something else to focus on. Something *other* than the daunting thoughts of the life she'd left behind ... The people she'd left behind.

Sleep evaded her for hours. A throbbing ache formed behind her eyelids that made her grit her teeth, and as she cracked open her eyes—the decanter of ruby red wine sat in invitation. Exactly where Ven had left it.

She didn't want it. Didn't need it … Because she wasn't one of *them*.

You have magick in your blood.

She scoffed, shaking her head and rolling over. It was impossible that she could be something like him. Pain shot through her temples, making her clamp her eyes shut. Seconds or minutes passed before the searing torture ebbed away. She took a breath. She was fine … She didn't need it—what she needed was sleep. Just a night of uninterrupted—

It felt like an ice pick was piercing the back of her skull. A stabbing pain so relentless that she stumbled from the bed, nearly falling to her knees as she gritted her teeth against the assault.

The next one blurred her vision so badly that she found herself on the floor, crawling her way across the black stone toward the table, finally giving in and shakily pouring herself a knuckle of the red liquid, gripping the crystal tumbler so hard she wondered how it didn't shatter in her hand.

The viscous wine glowed like the facets of a ruby, a reminder of what the glass contained. For a fleeting moment, she hoped disgust might win out—that she wouldn't be able to drink it after all.

But the scent—the scent cleared her vision for just a split-second, dissipating the haze of pain. Her body acting of its own accord as her hand lifted the glass to her lips.

The instant it hit her tongue, the pressure behind her eyelids ebbed away with whatever conviction had been left in her. And she would have cursed herself had it not been such a blessed relief from the pain.

A soft knock roused Aurelia from her fitful sleep, and she woke to find it was already late morning, bright sunlight streaming through the window into the room. The door opened quietly, and she expected another hooded figure, another being wreathed in shadows, clad in black gear. But certainly not the beautiful female that let herself into the room.

Something familiar about the female's appearance nagged at her memory, drawings of water sprites and wood nymphs not quite matching up to who was in front of her—but the ethereal female must be what these crude depictions were failing so desperately to describe.

Her hair was deep green. Shades of emerald, seafoam, and teal as the light shifted along the thick braid trailing over one shoulder, swaying with every graceful movement. Everything about her was so flawless, from the gently pointed tips of her ears to the smooth green skin of her face. So pale that it might have been a trick of the morning light, so perfect that no one could ever mistake her for anything but immortal.

A goddess incarnate.

Such a stark contrast to the black stone walls that surrounded them that it took a moment for Aurelia to remember to breathe. She tried to keep herself from staring, but even with her mother's words branded into her skull; it was rude to stare, brazen to meet someone's gaze for more than a heartbeat, she couldn't look away from the deep brown eyes that met hers.

"Hello, I'm Embra," the female said with a reassuring smile, breaking the trance Aurelia found herself in. "I've come to check on you."

The female was tall, willowy. Her elegant movements reminded Aurelia of the traveling company of dancers that would perform at court every few years. Embra's silvery green robes were whisper soft against the stone floors, making her appear to glide across the room before she came to a stop, hovering over Aurelia's outstretched leg.

"May I?" she asked.

The female began to remove the bandage with practiced fingers. Bending slightly, she placed a warm slender hand over Aurelia's skin, pausing as a hiss escaped her mouth.

"I'm fine," Aurelia gritted through her teeth, bracing for Embra to continue her examination.

Her skin heated beneath the female's touch. A pleasant warmth that eased the throbbing ache in her leg almost instantly. And glancing down, she was shocked to see that the wounds were only faint pink lines across her skin.

And maybe it was the blissful relief she'd given her from that hounding pain, but Aurelia felt comfortable enough that she finally said, "You don't—look like them."

Embra gave a small laugh, the bright sound like tinkling wind chimes. "I hail from a different kingdom. My skills were needed here during the war, and I found more than a few reasons to stay." She glanced up at Aurelia with a smile.

But that was ... Centuries ago—and yet the beautiful female before Aurelia looked ageless. Embra appeared no more than ten years older than herself. Or maybe younger—it was impossible to say. But there was something ancient that bloomed behind the female's rich brown eyes, the only hint of the centuries she'd witnessed.

There were so many questions she wanted to ask, but she bit back each of them, watching Embra use whatever strange magick she possessed, radiating deep comforting heat into the tissue and muscle beneath. Embra turned her attention to Aurelia's bruised ribs next, every breath a little easier as she worked.

"You're healing quickly—that's a good sign," Embra said, gently patting Aurelia's leg as she helped her out of the bed.

Aurelia took the first step cautiously, then another. She paused, taking in a large breath, expanding her lungs to their fullest, expecting a sharp ache in her ribs that never came. A wide grin splitting across her face as she realized there was no more pain.

"Thank you," she said in awe.

"Of course," Embra replied, "You may feel a little tired, but rest will help the magick draw out the last of the venom."

She swept across the room with a whisper of robes and Aurelia heard the crack of the faucet in the bathing chamber a moment later. She followed Embra, watching as the healer poured an iridescent powder into the steaming water filling the stone tub, the water turning pearly white before her eyes.

"Soak in this for at least an hour. The longer you can stand it, the faster you'll heal," Embra ordered, and with a small bow, she glided across the floor to leave Aurelia alone once more.

Gritting her teeth as she eased into the scalding water, she'd expected pain, but somehow this was worse. The scrapes and cuts on her arms, the healing gashes across her thigh—they itched worse than anything she'd ever experienced. The unbearable sensation dredging up the memory of one summer when she'd played hide and seek with her brothers at the edge of the valley and accidentally hid in a patch of poison milkthistle. The rash had lasted for weeks, every blister making her want to itch her skin raw; her mother fretting that she'd have permanent scars on her arms and legs—but it was no match for what she felt now.

Digging her fingers into the side of the tub, she counted every breath and prayed to the Unnamed that at least ten minutes had passed. And just when she thought she couldn't take it anymore, the itching subsided, a blessed relief as she sunk beneath the warm water.

Emerging, Aurelia lifted her arm, turning it to see that every scrape, every cut, had disappeared. Her fingertips were soft and healed again. Lifting her leg out of the milky water, the large claw-marks had turned a faded pink. So faint now that they looked like the decades old scar she had on her knee from stumbling on a slick rock in the Kesh as a child.

She soaked in the tub until the water went tepid, trying to enjoy this small, familiar pleasure. The first time in days that she felt thoroughly clean. But before long, guilt tightly coiled around her stomach again, a permanent nagging pit since she'd woken up to find herself here. Safe. Alive.

Her mother was probably frantic; her fears of Aurelia wandering the halls at night alone proven true after all. Thinking her daughter had fallen to the same fate as her late husband. And Asher; he was probably losing sleep trying to find her. She needed to send word to them—but what she could possibly say that would stop her family from worrying about her ... What words would ever convince them to stop searching for her?

Bastien. She tried to remember the exact color of his eyes. The feeling of his fingertips trailing across her skin in the early mornings before he would slip back to his own chambers. The way his voice rumbled through her chest when he would whisper promises that both of them knew he could never keep.

She slipped completely under the warm water. Letting bubbles slowly escape her lips in a tidy column back to the surface. Her fingers ran over the skin of her thigh, tracing the three long lines that were now nearly smoothed over.

As she toweled off her damp hair, the throbbing ache returned to her temples with a vengeance. The headaches had come on more suddenly, more fiercely since last night. And she tried to fight back the urge to pour herself another glass of the wine from the decanter Ven had left on the table for her, but the pain had become hounding now.

She gave in, pouring herself a tumblers' worth and taking a large swallow that gave her blissful relief. Slumping down into one of the overstuffed leather armchairs, she savored the rest of the glass—hoping it would buy her an hours' worth of freedom from the torment.

Another speck of white fluttered out from the hearth with a snap of embers and her gaze slid to the rug where it landed as she considered ignoring the summons. Nursing the contents of her glass, she finally pushed herself from the chair and glanced at the note, tossing it into the air as it went up into a lick of fire.

There weren't many things her father had been superstitious about; he left that to her mother, but one thing Councilor Norrick had instilled in each of his children was that a life debt was not something you wanted to owe.

She still wasn't certain she could trust any of them, but it was twice now that Ven had saved her when he could have left her for dead. And accepting a dinner invitation seemed like a small start at chipping away at her repayment.

Chapter 23

Nira's garnet eyes narrowed as Aurelia opened the door, and the dark female pushed herself from the wall she'd been leaning against. "Just wanted to make sure you didn't get lost again," she muttered, before falling into step with Aurelia.

She deserved that. Running away into the Shades had been a half-cocked plan at best, and the Wraiths were the only reason she'd come back alive. Still, the prospect of being *here*, surrounded by these cold, cunning warriors, was not a happy one. If she had just one ally, one person she might count as a friend.

"Thank you—for coming to find me last night. I'm sorry that Karro was injured because of me," she stumbled over the apology. What could she possibly say to all of them for risking their lives for her? A complete stranger, an interloper. *Sorry* wasn't close to adequate.

"Karro knows better than to go rushing after a Vorak without backup—he deserved to get bloodied," Nira replied darkly.

So much for making friends.

Another apology had formed on Aurelia's lips, but before she had the chance to speak, a large set of doors loomed in front of them—not the ones to the dining hall, she thought with a small amount of surprise.

Tendrils of dark shadow curled out from the bottom of the doors as they opened into the room on a phantom wind. Ven sat at a large oval slab of stone, papers and books strewn in front of him, the light from the roaring hearth picking out the strands of his ebony hair and turning them indigo and midnight blue.

He pushed his chair back as she entered, snapping his fingers and making the books and papers vanish, replacing them with two glasses of dark red wine. And damn her, but she salivated at the mere thought of taking another sip—hating the response her body already had to the blood-laced wine. She glanced behind her to see the door closing, no sign of Nira.

Her eyes flicked to Ven. He stood unnervingly still as he waited for her, his dark hair tied back at the nape of his neck and his simple white shirt and black trousers making him look nearly ... human. But a human could never be that lethally flawless.

The thought of being alone with him made the room feel too small—but the idea of going back into the massive dining hall with the Wraiths was worse, so she took a step forward.

"How are you feeling?" he asked, handing one of the glasses to her.

"Much better, thanks to Embra ... and you," she admitted a little sheepishly. "Though I don't think I'll make a particularly good dinner companion."

"I don't mind—consider it a favor so I don't have to eat alone," he added, taking a sip of his wine.

She suspected he was doing this more for her benefit than loneliness. She'd noticed the looks of reverence he received from the Blood Folk even when his back was turned, there was no doubt in her mind that Ven would be welcomed at any table.

He was watching her carefully. Keeping a distance between them that didn't seem to matter with the searing brand of his undivided attention. Taking a sip of her drink to cover the heat that crept into her face, she asked, "And how are Karro and the others doing?"

"Karro—" Ven cleared his throat, "is doing well enough to ignore Embra's advice to keep resting, and the others are making a speedy recovery as well."

Something in her chest loosened a little. She didn't know any of them well enough to call it relief, but she was glad all the same that Karro and the others were healing.

"Is he your brother?"

"My uncle. Though he might as well be my brother," he added. Aurelia's eyebrows lifted in surprise. "My grandsire died when Karro was young, so my mother raised him alongside me. We ate, slept, studied, and trained together our entire lives. Nearly inseparable," he explained, a grin tugging at the corner of his mouth.

"You sound like my brother and Bast—" She cut herself off before saying his name, taking another sip of wine.

"There's no one else I trust more than Karro to fight by my side." His mischievous grin faded into a sad smile. "He was next to me when my mother fell on the battlefield ... His mother in a way, too."

The emotion in his voice caught her off guard. "I'm sorry. To lose a parent is ... it's like losing a piece of your heart," she said, trying not to dwell on her own memories with her father—a deep ache of homesickness settling in her gut.

She walked toward the row of windows encircling them before the feeling could pull her down and drown her. The Shades dropped away steeply into deep violets and sapphires, the highest peaks curving away as they faded into the starlight. Ven came to stand next to her, the muscles of his shoulders flexing under his shirt as he placed his hands behind his back and stared out at the night-darkened expanse.

"Would you tell me about him? Your father?" he asked with a small amount of hesitation, as if she might refuse.

Sudden emotion flooded her throat. She hadn't been expecting the question, or the genuine compassion that accompanied it.

"He was kind. Warm," she said softly. "He loved learning, reading." A faint smile came to her lips at the memory of hiding away under his desk to read. The countless afternoons she'd stowed away in his study when she should have been in her etiquette lessons or with her dance instructor. Pouring over the maps on his walls, demanding he tell her of everything he saw on his trips to the other cities. The landscape, the people, the dialect. He'd laughingly oblige, never one to be able to tell her no.

She'd been hungry for knowledge for as long as she could remember. Ravenous for tales of the faraway cities in the Republic, the kingdoms overseas, the places she could only ever conjure in her mind. Her father had seen her curiosity and did not condemn her for it—did not treat it as a burden, a defect. He'd always indulged her. Nurtured her love of learning.

And she wondered now, if he let her engage in the small transgression of sneaking books from the library because he knew that her existence as a woman would always be limited. It was the only freedom that he could offer her, even as one of the most powerful men in the Republic.

She turned, finally, taking another sip from her glass and glancing at the large oval slab of milky white stone that ate up most of the space in the chamber. At least a dozen empty seats surrounded it. Stepping closer, she noticed there were lines and curves etched into the otherwise flawless plane.

"What is this?" she asked.

"Take a closer look," Ven answered over his shoulder, his eyes never leaving the night-darkened peaks of the Shades.

Leaning over the table, she traced the grooves with her fingers. A map, but nothing like the maps littering the walls of her father's study. Large mountain ranges and swathes of hills followed the gentle curves of a river. The Blood Kingdom sprawled across the center, cut in half by an etched line so jagged it looked like an open wound. The Court of Shadow on one side, a Raven marking the fortress beneath their feet. The Court of Flame marked the other half with a bleeding fist clutched around a dagger.

A swath of the rugged terrain marked as the Allokin Kingdom sat far to the North. Three overlapping stars labeled a large city named Eisenea. There were more, so many more—but her eyes snapped to the bottom corner of the map. The Crescent Valley's footprint remained the same, but it was almost unrecognizable amidst the land that surrounded it.

The kingdoms labeled in front of her were all unfamiliar. Their vast territories dwarfing the tiny sliver of land that had been her home.

Was she truly so ignorant? Never aware of the land that stretched so far from the center of everything she knew. Her tiny, miniscule world. Her small, inconsequential life.

Another truth he'd told her ... The humans never would have won the war on their own. Not against kingdoms of this size. Even without the magick and the immortal strength and speed they possessed, their sheer numbers alone would have overwhelmed the human realm.

"There are so many," she whispered in disbelief. It was one thing to realize that an entire civilization had remained hidden for centuries, but an entire *world* had been hidden. "The first night I met you ... You said human memory had gotten things wrong about our shared history."

Ven walked over to where she gazed down at the moonstone table, flattening a broad hand over a pit that had been etched away. "There are seven princes who rule the Void. You had the misfortune of meeting one of them the night you left the human realm."

A shiver crept down her spine at the memory of the prince's milky white eyes. It was a small comfort to know Ven had killed him.

"The cruelest among them was not content to stay within his own kingdom. He grew greedy, lustful for power, and his brothers were more than happy to join him." He nodded toward the small crescent of land next to her fingertips. "Humans were the easiest target."

His eyes darkened, looking back at some distant memory. "The King and Queen of the human realm resisted—knowing it was suicide, but willing to die defending their people." He walked around the table, coming to stand beside her. His long fingers trailed the edges of the Blood Kingdom to rest atop where the very fortress around them stood. The only thing standing between the jagged edges of the Void and the Human realm. "Many kingdoms came to their aid, including ours. We were allies once. Friends," he said sadly.

She noticed now that patches of the gleaming moonstone slab were marred and blackened with scorch marks, rendering the kingdoms beneath unrecognizable.

"A ... Flare of my temper when I was younger," Ven whispered quietly when he saw where her gaze landed.

"And the Unnamed Gods?"

He didn't scoff at the question. "If they exist, they were nowhere to be found that day when the final battle came to a head. They did nothing to save this world when entire races were wiped out fighting the Princes of the Void—they did not pay the price for this world's freedom," Ven whispered.

"How is it possible the human realm has remained completely unaware of the kingdoms surrounding it?" she asked.

"After years of bloodshed, the Princes of the Void were contained, unable to reach any realm but their own. The kingdoms of the Folk agreed to have no contact with the humans after the war was over, allowing them to exist without interference. Their border was protected with wards, so there was no chance of magickal beings entering without permission."

Ven crossed his arms over his chest. "And magick began to die out. We lost many of our people during the war, but even those of us that were left possess a mere shadow of what we had 300 years ago. A gradual decline, over decades, centuries ... So small, that over the years the changes have been almost undetectable. That is, until recently."

She looked up from the map to see he was staring at her. Those immortal eyes looking at her like she was the answer to some long-forgotten question.

A flare of pain in her temples came on so suddenly that she doubled over the moonstone table, her fingers digging into the sides of her head.

The splitting pain snuffed out every sense except for the comforting warmth of a large hand gripping her elbow to help her into a chair. A loud buzzing in her head drowned out every other sound.

After what could have been minutes or hours, the ringing in her ears dulled to a faint echo. Somewhere in the distance she heard Ven's muffled voice, but she couldn't make out a damn thing he was saying to her.

Her blurry vision cleared to reveal his face in front of hers. His eyes dark with concern as she shook out the last of the bells chiming in her head.

Aurelia.

And she realized he'd been saying her name. "I'm fine," she managed to say. But it did nothing to ease the crease that formed between his brows. "Truly." But she barely got the word out before the pain speared through her temples again. A surge of heat rolled through her so powerfully and so suddenly that her knees buckled.

"Aurelia?" Ven crouched next to her on the floor, wrapping an arm around her back to hold her upright. The loud buzzing filled her head once more as heat formed at the base of her neck. Her skin becoming so blisteringly hot that she wanted to tear it from her body.

"Aurelia—I need you to look at me," Ven's deep voice commanded. "Look at me!" Her body obeyed out of some primal instinct even as her eyes were fighting to stay open. "You're entering into stasis. I need you to keep focusing on me."

A flare of white-hot pain ripped down her spine, sending her doubling over again as strong hands gripped her shoulders. She'd felt this same heat wending its way through her body for months now, but never this intense.

Ven ushered her towards the door as a cold sweat broke out along her brow. "What will happen?" she gritted out between clenched teeth, carefully choosing which words were worth the breathless pain.

"It will be quick. You'll feel fevered—then it'll feel like you've been thrown into a furnace," he uttered under his breath. She threw him a scathing look, just before she crumpled under another burst of heat searing its way through her veins, thankful for the steady arm that was hooked around her waist.

Ven held her upright as they made their way down the corridor. The blood-red sunset leaked through the windows, and the sharp sensation was akin to knives stabbing into her retinas even though she knew Ven was purposely guiding them through the shadows.

"Breathe," he ordered. "Inhale through your nose, exhale through your mouth. Breathe through the pain."

Aurelia closed her eyes, letting him guide her through the fortress; their destination unknown to her. Every ounce of focus spent on remaining conscious. Trying to fight back the heat threatening to make her combust.

Ven shouted to someone, his words a jumble of syllables to her ears as at last they entered a space that was blessedly dark. The fire inside Aurelia banked for a blissful moment as he closed a thick stone door behind them, shutting out any remainder of light from the corridor beyond.

She cracked open an eyelid, her vision quickly adjusting to the darkness. The chamber was carved deep within the mountain. A large domed ceiling followed the curve of a naturally formed cavern. And sunk into the center of it was a pool of clear blue water, so still that the surface looked like liquid glass.

The next wave of fire seared through her body and she collapsed again. But at least the stone floor of the cavern was cool. Arms were suddenly wrapping around her, lifting her as if she were weightless. And cool water kissed her fevered skin a moment later.

She could feel Ven tugging off the dress she wore, and she mumbled an incoherent string of sounds, but her capacity to give a shit about modesty right now was beyond reach. Especially once the cool water lapped at her naked body like silk, soothing away the scorching heat.

But the relief was short-lived as the next onslaught came.

Her skin was burning away from her bones—it had to be. The heat was nearly unbearable as the beads of water pooled and sizzled against her arms, her throat, her legs, evaporating instantly. Ven waded them further into the water until they were nearly both submerged, but it was no use. Relief evaded her as every drop hissed and steamed against her skin.

It might have been ten minutes or ten hours as the blistering fire surged through her body. Wave after wave receding for a few moments, only to return again threatening to incinerate her. She felt Ven moving again, the water receding as he walked toward the cavern floor. Her naked body was still curled into his chest as he laid her gently onto the cold black stone, and another wave overtook her.

Through the haze of pain she heard him say, "You need to feed."

Willing her eyes open, she watched him remove a black dagger from wherever he had strapped it to his body. He brought the blade to his golden skin, cutting across his wrist in one fluid motion. Ruby drops welled up at the vulgar gash.

A second later the scent hit her. She salivated, that same instinctual response she'd had when Bastien had cut his finger.

Her body raged with white hot fire, burning away the moisture instantly.

Ven brought his wrist to her lips, and as the first drop of his blood touched her tongue, she closed her eyes in ecstasy, his blood a sweet relief on her scorched throat. A lifeline showing her that she might survive this.

Her lips latched onto his wrist, and as she opened her mouth wider to greedily take more of his blood, he only leaned in closer, never flinching from her hunger. "You will make it through this, Aurelia," he whispered into her ear, a sweet caress in the midst of this brutality.

Her fingers wrapped around his arm, gripping his wrist to her mouth. The thirst overtaking every other thought. His blood was pure vitality rushing through her. She gasped for air, releasing him for a moment, but the pause was enough to send pain thundering back through her body. Enough to make her bite her tongue from clenching her jaw so tightly. She lifted a finger to the corner of her lips—and found a razor-sharp edge.

Another flare of pain jolted down her spine. Strong hands gripped her shoulders, and she felt the hard muscle of Ven's chest beneath her. A quiet rhythmic thudding drowning out the fire inside of her, like all her senses had singularly focused on the sound.

His heartbeat...

The sound of his blood rushing just under the pale skin of his neck.

"Take what you need from me," he whispered, with enough dark invitation that she didn't hesitate.

Her teeth were on the smooth skin of his neck in an instant. His blood so rich, so delicious that she'd never crave anything else as long as she lived. A hard impact jarred them both, and she realized she'd driven his much larger body against the wall of the chamber.

The force was enough to bring her back to her senses, and she released him, looking into his face again for any sign of fear, of pain. But he only shook his head and uttered, "I promise, Love, it will take much more than that to hurt me."

Lifting his chin, Ven offered his neck again, the blood barely dried from where she had already punctured it. She was on him again in a moment.

Drawing more and more from his open vein, she greedily drank. Her appetite was ravenous, euphoria like she'd never known as every sense awakened. Only blissful relief from the pain she'd been in. But too soon that pain rushed back, the searing heat no longer kept at bay by his blood. She knew it was the only thing keeping her from combusting entirely.

Heat engulfed her body, flooding her veins and spilling out through her fingertips in white flame. Bursting out in an unending rush that filled the cavern surrounding them with pure light. A cleansing fire that burned away any semblance of who she'd been before. Her body forged and reborn as she let the heat course through her veins.

The sheer force of it was so powerful that she released Ven from her grip with a gasping breath. No longer able to see him as the blinding light enveloped her. Every sense gone in the flash of white.

Chapter 24

There was no more pain. The scorching heat was gone, but so was everything else.

She saw nothing, felt nothing—

Was this death? If so, it was much kinder than she'd expected.

But then coolness seeped into her skin again. She moved her fingertips, trailing them over the smooth, hard surface beneath her.

A cave—Ven had taken her into a cave.

Her body finally obeyed her demands, her eyes opening. Quicksilver puddles of pure white light eddied and swirled like mist around her, gathering in slow tendrils and caressing their way through her fingertips.

The heat was no longer a searing, torturous pain, but a soft healing warmth licking its way back into her veins. Back to wherever this power stayed hidden within her.

Aurelia blinked slowly, the aura underneath her eyelids still blinding white. But in the washed-out haze, she saw him.

His outline hunched over her body. As if he could protect her from the blast of power. From herself.

Her heartbeat slowed again, her breath returning to a quiet, steady rhythm—and that's when Ven's eyes finally opened. And she thought her heart might break at the relief she saw there.

"Your eyes—" he whispered reverently. Confusion clouded his expression. "They're still amber."

Her vision cleared, and whatever relief she felt shriveled up.

Deep purple bruises covered Ven's wrists, fingerprints marring his skin to where his shirtsleeves were rolled. His neck was worse—covered in bruised bite marks, dried blood leaking down onto the collar of his shirt.

And the burns ... Angry red blisters were raised in patches along his perfect skin. Parts of his shirt were singed away entirely.

What had she done?

A choked sob escaped her, and Ven looked down to where her gaze had landed.

"I'm fine—" he whispered into the quiet darkness of the chamber. "Look." He rubbed away the caked blood from his wrist and his neck. The bite marks vanishing before he wiped the dried blood away completely.

"I—I'm sorry. I didn't mean to hurt you."

"I told you it would take a lot more than that." He lifted his arm, the bruises already fading into a faint yellow; the blisters vanishing even though his shirt showed the evidence of what she'd done.

Aurelia blew out a shaky breath. The fire in her body was finally gone, but in its place was such utter exhaustion that she couldn't fight it any longer. And as her eyelids grew heavy, she felt the room tilt, dropping away until a warmth settled around her chilled body, and she gave in to sleep.

Chapter 25

When she awoke, she was back in her chambers, Ven sitting in the chair next to her. He'd changed into fresh clothing, but the sight of his torn blood-soaked shirt had haunted her dreams. His posture so similar to that first morning when she'd awoken here that she felt a pang of guilt remembering how she'd treated him.

A smile tugged at the corner of his mouth when he noticed she was awake, his fingers twirling a small bit of metal that he idly tucked into his shirt pocket before standing up. He walked to the table underneath the large arched window where rain lashed against the darkened mountainside beyond.

Flickering light from the fireplace reflected in the facets of a tray of exquisitely cut crystal glasses. Pulling one from the sparkling row of them, he unsheathed one of the black blades strapped against his arm; the jeweled hilt a twin to the one she'd lost somewhere deep in the Shades. In one smooth stroke, he sliced his palm, clenching his fist over the rim.

Aurelia took a sharp inhale, about to protest, but the scent made her close her mouth again, clamping it shut against her body's betrayal as she salivated. Unable to tear her eyes away as the bright ruby drops fell into the bottom of the glass.

Taking two long strides back to the bed, he silently extended the glass to her. He looked at her, eyebrows raised.

An invitation.

A damnation.

She took the cup with a shaking hand. It was one thing to drink the blood-laced wine he'd offered her before. But this—

She knew from the scent alone that this would be the only thing to quench her thirst. A thirst she hadn't realized had been gnawing at her for months now, leaving her nauseous and dizzy. One that was undeniable now. She tried to convince herself she didn't crave it. Didn't want it. But before she could think twice, she lifted the glass to her lips and drank.

The flavor of him was rich and satiating, somehow just as she remembered from her fevered state locked in the stone chamber with him ... Nothing like the wine she'd been drinking before. Not even a comparison to the small taste of Bastien's blood that she'd had weeks ago, months? She couldn't be certain anymore.

This—This was the best thing she'd ever tasted, smooth and warm down her throat. Sending a hum through her veins, chanting *more, more, more.*

This is what she'd been craving.

Her senses awakened. Like a haze around her had been lifted and she could see, hear, taste *everything* around her. Like her existence before this moment had been muted and muddied. Like she'd been living underwater.

There was no going back after this. Whatever small sliver of hope she'd held onto that somehow she could go home—that somehow he'd been mistaken about her, had evaporated.

Heat flooded her face as she set down the drained glass. But Ven only cut his palm over and over again, never saying a word—saving her the embarrassment of having to ask. Because, gods damn her, she would have begged.

Now she understood.

How the legends had been spun. The tales she'd been told of vampyres draining the blood from humans who wandered too far into the Shades. And at once she understood his motivation for keeping her here. The marks she'd left on his body, the amount of his blood she'd taken with that gnawing thirst. She didn't want to consider the destruction she would have caused had she gone back home.

Home.

The word felt foreign now. Abstract. The only life she knew was in the Capitol, but it wasn't a place for something like her. With beings so fragile. So breakable. Ven had stumbled on her in the human realm and somehow found her before she'd had a chance to hurt everyone she loved.

"Why did you save me..." The words were out of her mouth before she could stop them.

"I told you—you're one of us." He leaned against the window, rain pattering the glass behind him. Crossing his arms over his chest, he looked down at the floor. "But selfishly ... because it's been a long time since I've met another fire wielder."

"What about the others?" she asked, surprised by the loneliness that tinged his words.

"They're shadow casters."

"I've seen you control shadows, too."

"My mother's side," he answered, the ghost of a smile on his face.

She turned her hands over as if somehow that would reveal the truth to her. "But what does that make you and I?" she finally asked.

He turned, looking out into the darkened Shades. "I—am a half-breed. And you? Well ... I'm not exactly sure," he answered, all cockiness gone from his tone. "But I know you belong here."

"My family—is there a way for me to let them know that I'm..." she trailed off. *Safe? Alive?* How could she explain anything that had happened to her ... And what could she possibly say anyway that would keep them from searching for her?

"In a few weeks, the bloodlust will lessen—you could go back briefly," he said quietly.

"It would be safe for me to do that?" she whispered in disbelief.

He turned to face her again. "I'll make it safe," he answered decisively, his crimson eyes meeting hers.

Return. The thought of seeing Bastien again, seeing Asher, her mother...

But the anticipation died away instantly. And say what? Tell them she loved them one last time? To make her apologies? How could she possibly explain why she'd left, why she couldn't stay. And if the wards would be sealed again soon, was there any reason for her to warn them of the danger that surrounded them?

Bastien was probably devastated that she was gone. Little did he know it was for everyone's safety. And her family...

Gods, she was selfish. She didn't want to go back because the thought of looking them in the eyes and telling them she couldn't stay was too much to bear. But if she were in their place—if Asher had gone missing one night, never to be seen or heard from again; it would consume her every thought until the day she died.

Studying her hands, she finally glanced up to see Ven's eyes wholly focused on her, patiently waiting for her answer.

The deep puncture marks on his neck from hours before were gone. No trace of the ugly purple bruises that ringed his wrists, as if they never existed on his smooth unmarred skin. But she saw them. Burned into her memory like the angry blisters that no longer covered his arms.

She shook her head, dropping her eyes to the floor as she swallowed back the emotion making her throat feel thick. "I don't trust myself—I barely know myself anymore ... I—I can't," she whispered sadly. Hating that she couldn't accept what he offered.

"Is there something that you wish them to believe?" he murmured. Her eyes found his again, trying to read the meaning behind his stoic expression. "I could—convince them that you're safe. Cared for. Something vague that would ease their worry," he said softly, his tone measured and level as if he'd admitted an indiscretion.

That night in her chambers—his parting words had stuck with her because of how strange they'd been.

And tomorrow, you won't remember me either.

As if somehow, it would have been possible to forget him. And yet he'd seemed surprised that she'd remembered him when he'd found her again in the library...

"How?" she asked, her voice barely a whisper.

He let out a heavy breath, leaning back against the window again and hooking a booted heel over his ankle. "It's a rare gift for our kind," he answered. "Compulsion." He shrugged. "With a few well-placed thoughts in your loved ones' minds..."

Fear widened her eyes—had he been suggesting things to her while she was here? How could she know what thoughts were hers alone and which ones had been planted there—

"I haven't attempted to use it on you since you left the human realm," he said tightly, reading her expression. "It's not a gift I enjoy using, but if it can avoid bloodshed—" he added quietly, his dark brows lifting.

She tamped down the small amount of guilt she felt at assuming the worst in him.

"One of the reasons I suspected you were one of us," he said. "I—tried to make you forget me. I thought if I contained the threat of the demons quietly, the wards could be rebuilt, and the human realm would remain unaware." He shrugged. "But then you remembered me ... And I realized that *thing*. That pull that I felt to come back over and over again ... It wasn't just to track down the demons. It was because your magick called to mine."

It was the most vulnerable she'd seen him. No hint of the arrogant smirk that usually occupied his face. No clever remarks or polished words... And something frozen in her chest thawed just slightly toward him.

"Could you—" She was at a loss for words, trying to think of anything that would keep her family from trying to search for her...

And it came to her. The very plan she'd laid out to Bastien almost a year ago when she'd seen the deep purple bruises on his uncle's wife's arms for the first time. Bastien had scoffed at the idea, getting angry when she'd become adamant that they find a way out for the woman.

"There's a temple—far away on the southern coast. Women go there to give themselves to the Faceless Sisters. Sometimes to escape an indiscretion ... Or if they no longer have a family, no marriage prospects," she uttered. She'd nearly taken the young Lady Veron there herself, but Bastien had threatened to tell her family of her plot if she so much as left the palace grounds.

"Tell them I've given myself into their service." It would be plausible. Young women had been known to give themselves over to avoid being married off, and with the marriage that had been pushed on her just a few days before she disappeared, it would explain why she'd left. It would buy her time, at least. Weeks or months maybe. "Tell them—tell them not to come looking for me," she added as an afterthought.

Ven gave a shallow dip of his chin in acknowledgement. "You have my word."

If any of her family members ever went to retrieve her only to find she wasn't there ... Maybe they'd think she was dead. It was better than the truth.

"I'm sorry," she whispered. And it wasn't just for the physical harm she'd caused. It was for the harsh words she'd spoken in her ignorance. For not recognizing the safe haven he'd given her when the world she knew would have rejected her. Would have feared her for being the kind of monster she'd accused him of being.

A warm callused hand lifted her chin, and she looked up into Ven's beautiful face. His sheet of black hair falling forward, enclosing the space between them. "I'll accept no more apologies from you, Love. Certainly not for things outside of your control." And his crimson eyes were so fixed on her that she couldn't breathe. Couldn't move.

When she finally found her voice again, she needed to change the subject. Anything to stop the deluge of heat that wound through her body at his touch. His proximity.

"Then ... Thank you," she whispered again.

"Well, I couldn't have you incinerating my book collection. I'm quite partial to it and I suspect you already have enough misplaced guilt on your conscience." He grinned, a small amount of that playful arrogance seeping back into his tone, though the emotion in his eyes was deeper than the lighthearted words.

She swallowed hard as an unexpected onslaught of remorse hit her. And Ven was kneeling on the floor in front of her in an instant. His hands on either side of her face.

"It wasn't your fault," he whispered.

And the tight leash she'd had on her emotions, everything she'd bottled up since she'd walked through that damned mirror and her old life had gone up in flames, finally snapped. Great racking sobs tore through her chest. Ven reached out a hand to her, stopping himself short as she flinched.

"Please," she begged. "Please, I just need to be alone."

And with a reluctant nod, he stood up again. He left the room without another word, something like sadness flickering across his features.

When she was finally, completely alone, she let her tears fall freely, drowning in the whirlpool of emotions and letting them rip her under until she was spent and drained and fell into a fitful sleep.

Chapter 26

The gnawing thirst had been relentless through the night, waking her every few hours with her throat on fire, an itch underneath her skin that was unbearable. Ven had returned sometime after she'd fallen asleep, staying with her through it all.

She suspected he hadn't slept, because every time she would open her eyes, he was there—sitting beside the bed and reading a book in one of the leather armchairs as if he had nothing better to do. Ready to open a vein for her without hesitation.

When the thirst finally subsided, he reluctantly left her alone again, but food began to appear at regular intervals in his wake. The aroma was mouthwatering, but her appetite was still nowhere to be found. Tight coils of dread and guilt and disbelief still wrapped around her gut.

For a while, she had abstained from the decanter of deep red wine that sat invitingly on the table next to her, finally giving in when her throat burned from denying herself. And then she swigged down glass after glass of the stuff, hating herself more with every taste of it. The denial warping into self-loathing.

How could she possibly have hoped to return?

Gods ... If she'd actually managed to make it back—she didn't want to think of the consequences as the torturous thirst wracked her body again. Setting every nerve aflame until she would take another drink. Realizing quickly that it was mostly blood—*his* blood. Definitely not what he'd called *the synthetic stuff.* Now she could *taste* the difference.

Never before in her life had she been able to tell the difference between red wines, much to her mother's disappointment. Lady Norrick only ever stocked her parties and her private chambers with the expensive stuff—bottles that were fifty copper crescents apiece. But Aurelia could never distinguish those from the cheap bottles that she and Bastien stole as teenagers out of the palace kitchens.

But now—she could taste every subtle hint of Ven's blood as she finished off the last drops in her glass.

Curled up under the heavy comforter, she finally willed herself to crawl out of the bed and pad toward the bathing chamber. Her newer, stronger body devoid of any aches or soreness. Her movements somehow felt ... effortless now. Fluid.

Pulling up the hem of her robe, the reflection in the mirror only showed completely smooth, healed skin where her injuries had been. Even her old scars from childhood had faded; replaced with new, supple skin. Any evidence of her life before, the woman she'd been before—completely gone.

It was grey outside the windows, but candlelight flooded the bathing chamber as she leaned in to look at her reflection. Her amber eyes still looked back at her. But she wished, not for the first time, that she'd gotten her mother's eyes.

But it made sense now—why she didn't favor her mother the way both of her brothers did. Those sparkling green eyes the shade of new leaves in spring. She'd always guessed she'd taken after her father's side, but now...

Her skin had taken on a luminous quality, like every blemish had been polished away, every faded scar, every sun-kissed freckle—gone. There wasn't any one thing in particular that had changed—well, that wasn't true.

She lifted the edge of her lip, feeling the sharp point of a fang against her fingertip. And when she stood still—in that same unnerving way Ven did—she felt a hum just under the surface of her skin. A constant, thrumming heat that had become inextricably bound to her.

And she finally came to grips with what this meant.

She really was one of *them* ... Untethered to her old life, but not rooted in this new one either.

And when that familiar warmth flooded into her arms—she didn't stop it. Couldn't stop it. The tears formed in her eyes but evaporated instantly with the heat coursing through her veins. And the light burned its way into her palms, now outstretched before her, a release of emotion that blasted through her like a lightning strike. And just as quickly, it was spent. Leaving her gasping and slicked with cold sweat.

The next morning as she was splashing a few handfuls of water over her face, avoiding her reflection—a knock sounded at the door.

Ven stood outside, extending a pile of garments in his large hands. "Until clothing can be made for you."

"You—didn't have to do that." she replied.

The Wraith commander was delivering clothes to her chambers—there must have been a hundred other people in this place who could have done it, a hundred other things that he should have been doing, but instead, he was here. Just as he had been throughout the night. Just as he'd been holding her when she'd gone into stasis—completely out of her mind with pain. Dangerous … Exactly as he'd warned her when she'd made her pathetic attempt to return to the Capitol.

"Your new garments should be ready by tomorrow—but in the meantime." He gave a shrug of his broad shoulders before turning away again. "Right, well. Let me know if there's anything else you need."

He was trying to make her feel comfortable, welcome. And she didn't want to appear ungrateful, but her insides felt wrung out. Not a single drop of … anything. Not even the energy to offer a polite smile in return as she finally said, "What am I—what am I to do here?"

He glanced over his shoulder. "Do as you wish," he said simply as he turned to walk away.

The next few days were quiet. Only occasional knocks on the door to see if she needed anything or to invite her to meals. Usually Ven or Embra, occasionally Karro.

She'd gone back to the dining hall once more, bracing herself for wary glances and hostile looks. But, as she passed the dozens of tables, dark heads only raised to glance at her—giving a dip of their chins in her direction before returning to their meals.

The Blood Folk weren't what she'd expected—a deadly, half-feral kingdom. But she was finding with every passing day that the stories had gotten many things wrong. This place they inhabited; though on the face of it was a stone fortress hidden deep in the mountains—it was also a home. They laughed and sang. They ate and drank. They were friends, they were family. They were ... not completely unlike the people back home.

Not home.

And somehow the similarities made the feeling of homesickness worse. So even as she found herself restless, she politely refused every offer—though she suspected Ven was responsible for the small feasts that appeared on the table in her room three times a day. Seeming to change ever so slightly based on what she'd picked at previously, until they were tailored to her favorite dishes.

It was roasted chicken and potatoes today. She tore off another bite of the thick slice of bread on her plate as she read one of the history books she'd plucked from the shelves. The fully stocked bookshelves in the room had proved to be a useful distraction. But there was only so much she could read before her thoughts would inevitably turn back to what had happened. How her life had completely dissolved. There hadn't been a day in recent memory where her every waking moment wasn't scheduled for her. And now there was—nothing.

She didn't miss the teas and dinners and glittering parties. She'd never enjoyed being wrapped up like a gift in the corsets that made her ribs ache and left scars along her hips. But they'd become such an expected part of her life that she wasn't quite sure what to do with herself now. In the silence. With nothing but time.

Do as you wish.

What did that even *mean*?

Reaching for the fresh set of clothing that had been left for her, she pulled on the soft pants, feeling the fabric mold to her body in a way that had been foreign the first few times. The act of dressing herself had been clumsy initially, but her fingers now deftly buttoned the crisp white oversized shirt. She raked through the tangles of her dark hair, feeling a little strange to be leaving without every wave smoothed, and tamed, and perfectly pinned into place.

A pair of boots her size had appeared one day, too. And she'd come to like the way they felt when she pulled the laces tight. Substantial. Durable. So unlike the slips of silk she had worn for most of her life. Ruined if she so much as walked through the damp grass of the gardens.

She would probably never see the gardens again, she thought with a twinge of sadness, but before the feeling could fester, she was already moving again. Deciding she'd had enough of staring at the same four walls, she cracked the heavy door open and stood on the threshold of the chamber leading into the corridor beyond.

An entire world beyond.

The last time she'd ventured out of these rooms, it had been to escape. Not just this place ... but the inevitability of what she was. And now that she was seeing the fortress in a different light—she was stunned by the beauty surrounding her.

Painstakingly detailed architecture was hewn from the heart of the mountain, every arch, every buttress, every beam thoughtfully and richly carved from the black stone. This was not just a fortress for the Blood Folk—It was a sanctuary.

Her footsteps echoed loudly down the broad causeway that ran the length of the cavern, but this time she felt no need to muffle them. Her fingers traced every design carved into the railing, her golden gaze following the stone balustrade as it spilled down into a waterfall of staircases leading into the lower levels.

Turning to face the arched windows that lined the wall, she watched the rain fall in fat drops, pattering against the glass in dull thuds. In the reflection of the window, she saw the outline of a large bird perched on the stone balustrade behind her. So still, it looked to be carved from the same dark stone that surrounded her. But as she turned, the raven shifted—tilting its head to look at her, revealing a familiar ragged scar across its face, ruffling its oil-slick feathers in recognition.

"Well, hello there," she crooned, as the bird hopped down the length of railing to where she stood.

She held out a hand to him. He cocked his head towards her in invitation and she hesitantly glided her palm down the silky feathers of his back. With a loud croak, he glided down the corridor in front of her, swiveling his head to look at her with his remaining eye as if to say, *Come on, then.*

So, she followed the beast. Past caverns and massive halls. Through the dark corridors of Ravenstone until at last he soared to the end of a hallway, fluttering to a stop.

Perching on Ven's shoulder, the raven hopped down again and began to clean himself, seemingly satisfied that he'd done his duty as Aurelia made her way to meet them.

"Cog's the reason I found you that night in the Shades," Ven said, studying her with those unnerving garnet eyes as she approached.

"I suppose I owe you a thank you as well, then," she murmured to the bird who ruffled his feathers with a self-satisfied look and continued preening himself. "Yes, you're very handsome," she added with another pat as she glanced back to Ven.

"You must be well acquainted already if you know flattery is his weakness." Ven smirked.

Cog gave a disgruntled croak in response before going back to cleaning his iridescent wings.

Aurelia reached out a hand to touch the lustrous black feathers. "If I didn't know better, I'd think you were following me."

Ven lifted his large shoulders in a shrug. "Just making sure you're settling in all right. I thought seeing a familiar face might help." He nodded toward Cog—who was now purring, if it was possible, as she scratched his head.

The cascade of rain was now a gentle roar outside the thick walls of the fortress. "It's so quiet here," she whispered, not wanting to interrupt the tranquil rumble of distant thunder.

"This wing is for the Wraiths use. Where we sleep, eat, train—it's quiet compared to the rest of the fortress," he said, leading her to the towering double doors across the hall.

She glanced over and Ven's garnet eyes glittered with excitement as he put one large hand on the carved wood and pushed the doors open.

Chapter 27

The scent of worn leather, ink, and paper greeted her like an old friend in an unexpected place.

Aurelia stood frozen in awe. She'd thought the library at the palace was beautiful—but it was nothing compared to this.

The sprawling lower level yawned wide into a vaulted ceiling. A spiral staircase stretched up to the second story. Shelf after shelf lined with books.

Thousands upon thousands of books.

Arched windows spanned one side of the library, nearly from the floor to the cavern ceiling high above them, making the entire place feel like a floating castle as the deep emeralds and indigos of the Shades fell away beneath them. The dark velvet of evening stretched endlessly outside, but dozens of candles floated above their heads, lending a soft glow to the space. Some of them captured in lanterns—others suspended by magick.

Something about this place was so ... alive.

The atmosphere was hushed, but lively with activity. A handful of dark heads bowed over their work or between the stacks. But there were others, she noticed now. Shades of bright red scattered amongst the ebony. When she finally tore her eyes away from the beautiful sight, she threw an appreciative glance at Ven who stood silently next to her, a self-satisfied grin on his face.

Her breath caught with an ache in her chest, "But am I allowed to be in here?"

Ven looked taken aback at the question. "Allowed?"

His eyes darkened, the line of his jaw tightening as if he were gritting his teeth. And she wondered if she'd insulted him. Of course, she was allowed in here with *him* by her side, he was the Commander of the Wraiths—no doors were closed to him. And she silently cursed herself for letting the stupid question escape her.

When he finally spoke again, it was with deadly calm. "We would never restrict knowledge, it is the greatest weapon a warrior can wield. And any book within this kingdom is yours should you want it," he uttered, those crimson eyes pinning her in place with every word. "No door is closed to you here."

She swallowed hard as Ven left her standing at the threshold of what might have been the most beautiful place she'd ever seen. She looked around at all the books within her grasp. What histories and records they might contain. The kind of knowledge they housed of the old kingdoms that had been hidden from memory in the human realm.

What must it be like to have access to all of them? To have so many words at her fingertips anytime she wanted. No sneaking down dark corridors and tiptoeing into the stacks to return books before they were missed.

Haltering steps brought her further into the space, still half-expecting that she'd be asked to leave without Ven by her side, but no one so much as lifted their eyes at her presence here. And before long she was swallowed up by the towering stacks. Piling books into her hands about everything from the history of the Blood Kingdom to records of the War. A streak of red hair passed the end of the shelves and for a moment she felt a pang in her chest.

Not Asher, she chided herself as she turned the corner.

The fiery red hair came into view again. The male reshelving a stack of leather-bound books had hair something akin to the shade of rust and sunsets and the flesh of a blood orange. But it was his skin that made her gawk. So pale that she swore it was blue in the warm glow of the candlelight. His robes were a swirl of muted grey blue. And there were females too, wearing the same attire as they sat reading at the desks or walking through the stacks.

She might have been lost in the books for minutes or hours—all sense of time completely gone.

The rainy morning had cleared, and the only indication of how long she'd been between the shelves was the sunset that bled over the mountains through the windows.

With a stack of books in hand, she made her way up the spiral staircase to the second story. Passing row after row of bookshelves, she found herself at the very edges of the upper level. Shelves had even been cut into the rough-hewn walls of the mountain. Their curves unpredictable and wild, smoothed over with time.

Following a soft glow at one of the back corners, she found a fireplace crackling cozily. Some comfortably squashed reading chairs scattered in front of the glowing hearth. Ven's sheet of dark hair had fallen forward over one of his eyes as he studied a book in his lap. His long legs and broad shoulders eating up the space between the large chair and the low table in front of him.

He looked up, a faint smile on his face like he'd been expecting her. And without a word, he snapped his fingers and a small feast appeared on the table along with two glasses of dark red wine—the sight of them making her realize how thirsty she'd become. The rumble of her stomach a much quieter instinct than the first.

Ven gestured for her to take a seat as she took a sip of the wine that immediately extinguished the fire building in her throat. She had no more than settled into the chair when a loud thump startled her out of it again.

A neat stack of books had appeared on the low table between them, and she glanced to where Ven sat across from her, a grin tugging at the corner of his mouth. His crimson eyes were playful as handed her the book on top of the pile. "Books on the histories of the realms, some of them are just dry records ... But, I thought you might be interested."

And so they sat in companionable silence. She piled a plate of food for herself, noticing that all her favorite dishes were present.

Roasted chicken, mashed potatoes swimming in gravy, more of the thick hearty brown bread that she'd come to love. Another flash of startling red hair drew her attention to the male that passed through the stacks closest to them.

Seeing where her gaze had landed, Ven said, "They hail from high up in the mountain peaks, far North of here. Their power is in weaving spells, fabrication—imbuing objects with their magick. They're the ones who created synthetic blood and made it possible for us to exist without taking life," he added, raising his glass of wine. "A few of them came here during the War and never left."

"What are they doing in the library?" she whispered.

"The Allokin are lovers of knowledge. The largest center of learning is housed in Eisenea, the seat of their kingdom." The name snagged in her memory, and she recalled seeing the city carved into the moonstone table that he'd shown her. Three overlapping stars marking its place within the large kingdom high in the peaks of the mountains. "They enjoy trying to understand the world around them. But anyone is welcome as a custodian of the books here." Ven refilled her glass, handing it back to her as she settled into her chair.

If she'd had a choice in life, that's what she would have done. As a child, she'd pleaded with her father to let her study to become a Nameless Brother, wanting nothing more than to spend her days inside the library's walls like they did. Asher and Wellan had teased her mercilessly as her father patiently explained that to become a Nameless Brother, you needed to be a man.

Scholarly pursuits were only offered to men in the human realm. Even the Faceless Sisters weren't given access to the libraries located within the larger temples of the Unnamed. They had given up their lives in service to the Gods, but they were still barred from any knowledge of them that didn't come directly from the Brotherhood.

It was late into the night when Aurelia finally looked up from her reading. The candles throughout the library had doused themselves, only the small corner still glowed with firelight and a dozen candles hovering high above her head.

Ven had left hours ago, but anxiety no longer coiled tightly around her stomach like it had when she'd first walked through the bottom level. Loosening its grip on her with every passing minute. The Allokin and the Blood Folk alike left the library, peeling off one by one. But none of them asked her to leave or questioned why she was still here, until she was utterly and completely alone.

The realization on its own was enough to make her stay late into the night. She was ravenous in this place. All these books at her fingertips, and she could read them here, at her leisure, in a comfortable chair next to a roaring fireplace. No slinking around in the dark, snatching the closest book she could find before the fear of being caught forced her to creep back to her chambers.

Chapter 28

A cool breeze whipped through the corridor as she left her rooms the next morning. Bringing with it the scent of rain and leaves and earth.

The cavern mouth below yawned open into the Shades beyond, a curtain of rain cascaded outside of the fortress, pattering against the shelf of rock that jutted out beyond the walls. She took a step closer to peer down into the cavern below.

A rugged shelf of rock jutted out precariously over the Shades far below. The first time she'd laid eyes on it, it had been completely empty, but now it was full of movement. Familiar sounds greeted her ears as she drew closer and looked down into the training pit.

She'd watched the blue cloaks train countless times at the palace, but the speed and strength of these males seemed impossible. So fast they were nearly a blur. A few of them had stripped off their shirts, revealing hard-earned muscle twining with whorls of dark ink to varying degrees. She couldn't look away from the beautiful designs etched into their skin, only catching herself staring when a warmth spread over her shoulders, and she turned to see Ven had appeared, bracing his forearms against the railing as he took up the place beside her.

"We are marked at our induction into the Wraiths." He nodded to the males below, answering her unspoken question. "Our prayer to the Goddess of Death," he added, as her eyes caught sight of a foreign language tattooed down their spines. One perfect line of script in an ancient tongue.

"What does it mean?" she asked.

"Light my pyre and sing a lament for me." He smirked. "It rolls off the tongue a little nicer in the old language."

She looked over to where he leaned against the stone, his large hands wrapping around the curved balustrade. Inked dashes spiraled up his arm, disappearing under his rolled sleeves. His mouth tilted up as he noted where her gaze had fallen.

"These—" He lifted his forearm, "are for every enemy we kill."

There must have been hundreds—no, thousands of those small dashes that made up the complex pattern on his arm. And as she looked up, his crimson eyes met hers, searching for something ... If he was looking for fear or disgust, he would not find it. There was something visceral in Aurelia that responded to his blunt admission. The same response she'd had when he told her he had killed the White Prince.

Understanding. Admiration.

Because had she been capable, she would have done the same. But she'd been relegated to the sidelines because of her sex her entire life. Forced time and time again to be weak, submissive. If she'd had the choice to protect the people she loved, fight for them, she would have.

She thought back to that night she'd found Councilor Veron. His death never haunted her dreams, because she knew if she'd been capable of killing him herself, she would have done it long before the demon found him. It was the same searing vengeance that kept her awake at night for the weeks following her father's death. But it had been there just under her skin far longer than that.

Before she could think better of it, she reached out, her fingertips grazing the black lines across Ven's golden skin. An act that she knew was brazen even as she was doing it—but he remained impossibly still, his eyelids fluttering shut for just a moment.

Her pulse was in her throat as her hand fell back to her side. An apology was on her lips, but before she could say it, Ven opened his eyes once more—unflinchingly meeting her gaze.

"There's somewhere else I'd like to take you before you hide away in the library for the day." He said roughly. She opened her mouth to protest, but he held up a hand. "It will only take a few minutes, and I promise you can spend the rest of eternity in the library if you choose."

She let out a defeated sigh.

"Consider it a—"

"Favor?" she finished, her lips tugging up into a faint smile that surprised even her. "Any more favors and you'll owe me something large in return," she said dryly.

"I'm counting on it," he replied.

There was no getting used to the beauty that surrounded her at Ravenstone. Underground waterfalls trickled through some of the larger caverns in the fortress and narrow paths cut tunnels through the black stone only to emerge in the emerald green canopy of the grey pines.

"Black Tourmaline," Ven said from beside her, gesturing to the black rock that surrounded them. "The bands of iron trapped in the stone act as a second layer of protection should the wards outside the fortress fail."

She craned her neck, her eyes following the arches that curved above them like the ribcage of an enormous beast. "What would happen if a demon entered the fortress?"

Ven snapped his fingers, conjuring a wisp of shadow that lazily dissipated in the air.

Her eyes followed the metallic ripples with a greater appreciation now. Scattered light cascaded onto the floor, illuminating the gold and bronze veins of the stone and setting them aflame under their feet.

"Beautiful," she whispered reverently.

"Yes," Ven agreed.

She smiled, glancing over to see that his eyes were locked on her, looking away quickly as footsteps sounded from behind them, echoing in the passageway. Aurelia ducked her head, trying to hide the rush of heat to her face as a large silhouette ate up the hallway.

"Were you extolling my many virtues again, brother?"

"Your timing is impeccable as always, Karro," Ven grumbled.

"Aurelia, you're looking well," Karro winked. The same swaggering bravado he'd had even when he'd been torn to pieces the first night she'd met him. How many times had that been enough to get a female into his bed?

"Careful, she's strong enough now to hand you your ass if she wishes," Ven warned.

"Am I?" She grinned.

"Who says that's not exactly what I'm hoping for?" Karro replied with a wolfish smile as Aurelia rolled her eyes, laughter escaping her.

"Didn't I send you to attend a meeting in my place?" Ven interrupted with a tinge of irritation.

"You did. Finished early," Karro answered brightly. "So where are we headed?"

Ven sighed loudly as he waved them forward.

The outline of a dark stone tower jutted into the sky through the windows of the fortress. It glowed with warm light even in the gloomy weather. She lost sight of it as they rounded a corner, but soon a set of wide stairs emerged ahead of them, flanked by a set of glass doors. Even from a dozen feet away, the shadows of plants and outlines of leaves were visible through the frosted glass.

A lush oasis greeted them as Ven opened the doors. Thick emerald vines trailed from the domed ceiling at the top of the tower all the way down to where they stood. Long rectangular boxes sat snugly against the edge of the room, bursting with plants of every kind.

Jars lined neatly organized shelves, filled to the brim with dried burgundy flowers and crushed cerulean petals. Magenta berries, the size of a copper crescent, and citrine-colored ones smaller than a pea. Iridescent liquids bubbled and boiled over small blue flames on slabs of wooden desks that perforated the otherwise open space.

A riot of color crowded the row of windows. Sprays of light purple flowers the size of her pinkie nail, stalks of large violent red and orange petals that towered above even Ven. Deep blues and vibrant pinks.

Row after row of small glass vials spouted with little green leaves, every shape and size. Broad flat leaves that were bottle green, frilly ones the color of lace and seafoam, fat succulents dripping with strings of pearl shaped leaves. And in the midst of it all, a familiar rope of dark green hair fell down the back of the female hunched over one of the desks.

Nearly blending into all the greenery that surrounded her, she reluctantly lifted her eyes from her work to where the three of them stood.

Embra's brown eyes narrowed menacingly.

"No!" she shouted sternly from across the room.

Aurelia started at Embra's tone. She looked to where Ven stood, his arms crossed over his powerful chest, only a smirk on his face and his dark brows raised in amusement.

Looking back at Embra, anger glittered in her russet eyes, and for a second Aurelia wondered if this was indeed the same female who had carefully and gently tended to her wounds just a few days ago. It was only then that Aurelia caught the blanched look on Karro's face. All of his usual bluster draining away as the slight female approached them, her robes swirling in an outraged flurry as she crossed the room.

"No," she said again, her brown eyes ablaze as she stopped just in front of where Karro stood.

His broad shoulders caved in slightly as he backed up. *Backed up*—Aurelia thought with no small amount of shock—from the much smaller female in front of him.

"He's not allowed in here." Embra shoved a finger into Karro's large chest while she looked pointedly at Ven.

Ven only raised his brows, putting both of his hands up to recuse himself from the battle.

"It was an accident!" Karro pleaded, his eyes looking to Ven for back up.

"I don't care if it was an accident. You don't—mess—with my—plants!" Embra said, emphasizing each word with a jab of her finger into Karro's thick chest that made the large male wince. "This ass—"

Karro's eyes widened in affront. "*Ass?*"

Embra's eyes narrowed at the interruption. "Isn't allowed near any of my fragile, beautiful, expensive," Karro rolled his eyes. "*essential—*" Embra threw him a scathing look, "equipment."

"How many times do I have to apologize?" Karro raised his hands in surrender.

"As many as you wish," Embra fumed. "You're still not allowed back in here!"

Aurelia failed to catch the squeak of laughter that slipped out of her mouth at watching the mountain of a male humbled by Embra. The only female in the fortress that seemed immune to his charms.

"Fine!" Karro put up his large hands in defeat, knocking a jar from the shelf with the back of his hand and sending it twirling through the air.

Ven's arm whipped out and caught the glass before it had the chance to shatter across the pristine floors. And without another word, Embra pointed a slender finger at the door as Karro huffed out a defeated sigh.

"Yeah, yeah," he said, his large shadow filling the doorway as he turned around and left.

"Aurelia." Embra's tone snapped back instantly to the gentle lilt Aurelia was familiar with. "Good to see you again." She smiled warmly. "Are you feeling well?"

Aurelia turned to look at Ven, who shook his head, silently mouthing "Don't ask," with a chuckle as Embra showed Aurelia her overflowing greenhouse and the laboratory attached to it.

Somehow Embra was even more beautiful when she talked about her work, her face lighting up as she rattled off every plant's name and its purpose. Aurelia swore the vines were stretching to follow the slender female's trail as she guided them through the tower.

Thanking Embra as they left, she felt a warm squeeze in her chest when the female took her hand and said she was welcome back any time.

Following Ven back down the stone steps into the corridor, she was a little sad to be leaving the warm glow of Embra's domain. She was easy to like, and she made Aurelia feel like maybe, just maybe, she had a friend here in this unfamiliar place.

Karro's large shadow detached from the wall outside the tower doors, falling into step beside them.

"What could you possibly have done to warrant *that*?" Aurelia asked once they were safely out of earshot.

"This was just the latest in a string of offenses," Ven whispered, "He didn't get back into her good graces from the last one until about fifty years ago."

The reminder of their long lives jolted her again—the way they spoke of decades as if they were weeks.

"I don't know why she's still mad," Karro muttered. "She would have forgiven *you* weeks ago." He threw a glare at Ven, and something unexpected caught in Aurelia's chest. Was there something between the beautiful Embra and Ven?

"How long did she ban you from the greenhouse then?" Aurelia asked, trying to distract herself.

"Ten years..."

She gasped, her jaw dropping. "Ten years?"

"Give or take," Karro muttered.

"Maybe because you raided her beloved plants to try to make yourself a hangover cure?" Ven suggested.

"Only because she refused to give me one!" Karro grumbled.

"Because you'd been trying to get Nira into your bed the previous night." Ven pinched the bridge of his nose. "What, exactly, did you think would happen?" he drawled.

Karro pressed both of his hands into his temples, "I didn't know they were together!" Emphasizing the words as if he'd made the defense quite a few times in the past.

It was hard for Aurelia to picture anyone working up enough courage to proposition the dark female, but even more shocking to know that Embra and Nira were together.

There had been rumors of women who preferred the company of their own sex, but they usually ended up married off quickly and quietly or sent away to the Faceless Sisters. Women who went against the expectation of marrying and having a family were not tolerated in the Republic. A fact that had always prickled at Aurelia's senses. You couldn't help who you loved. And anyone who was lucky enough to find love in their lifetime should never be deprived of it.

The vice that had clamped around her chest loosened a little, a smile tugging at her lips, and not the polite ones that she'd been forcing. That shell of numbness that had settled over her since she'd become something else finally cracking just a little.

"Every fifty years or so, Karro likes to get rip-roaring drunk and make an ass of himself," Ven whispered to Aurelia.

And genuine laughter burst from her, the first in—she couldn't remember how long. And it felt so damned good. She wasn't sure which was making her laugh harder; the image of Karro trying to convince that fearsome female to sleep with him or Embra passive-aggressively withholding a headache remedy in retaliation.

Ven inclined his dark head towards her. "Anyway, we've all taken wagers on how long he's banned from Embra's lab this time. My bet is fifty years."

She gave a sidelong glance toward Karro. "Well, I'd need to know what he did to make an informed decision," she hedged.

"Karro?" Ven drawled.

"The things she keeps in there are nightmare fuel, brother," Karro responded, skirting the question. "You really should be more concerned with what she's doing in that laboratory of hers."

"I leave Embra to do what she does best. She's highly skilled, and I'd be stupid to interfere with her work," Ven chuckled.

Aurelia's face hurt from smiling so much, but damn, did it feel good to laugh like this. And when she finally stopped laughing long enough to wipe away the tears, she glanced over to Ven and saw the strangest expression on his face before he looked away again. Before she could give it any more thought, they came to a stop.

"As promised," Ven said, sweeping his hand toward the library doors in front of them.

Karro had already made his way inside. Pulling up a chair at one of the long tables occupied by a dark-haired stranger, clapping the male on the shoulder as he took a seat. She realized it was the other male who had helped save her from the Vorak so many nights ago.

"Aurelia, this is Seth," Ven said, ushering her over to the table and pulling out a chair for her.

She thought she'd gotten used to the immortal beauty of the Blood Folk, but Seth was so impossibly flawless that it was difficult to look directly at him.

Karro and Ven were handsome, too. But in a rugged, masculine way. Seth had a face made for sculptures, painters. His sharp features angular and angelic. His movements fluid as he took her hand and pressed a kiss lightly to her knuckles. The words completely gone from her head as she took a seat at the table.

Ven smirked from where he sat next to her. "Don't let Seth's polished manners fool you, Karro still hasn't bested him on the Ledge."

"And what's even more insulting is that he won't even crow about it, the humble bastard," Karro added. Seth didn't deny it as a small smile formed on his lips.

The three males fell into an easy banter around her, but Aurelia didn't hear a word as her gaze drifted back to the bookshelves surrounding them. One night of exploring the library here hadn't been nearly enough.

Ven leaned toward her. "You don't have to pretend to be polite, you know."

She looked up, startled from her thoughts, realizing she hadn't put on a good show of listening.

"Go," Ven chuckled, "Get lost in the books, I'll find you later."

Chapter 29

A tidy stack of books was already in front of Aurelia by the time Ven made his way to the chairs in front of the roaring fireplace. He plopped down into the seat across from her without invitation, throwing his booted feet up onto the low table between them as he thumbed open a book. With a snap of his fingers, another small feast appeared, accompanied by two glasses of red wine.

Aurelia chewed on the inside of her cheek, finishing a chapter in one of the books Ven had given her the day before. "There were queens once—" she murmured disbelievingly, "They ruled the human realm before the council was formed."

"Fierce women indeed." Ven smiled fondly, glancing up from the page.

Aurelia dropped the book into her lap and sat up. "You knew them?"

"Some—others I only knew by reputation, but the one that fought beside us during the war was an incredible female. She and the King were some of the bravest people I've met to this day," he replied, sadness darkening his eyes.

"She must have been the last..." Her voice was hushed with reverence.

He nodded, "The last two rulers of the human realm gave their lives for their people's freedom. They didn't leave an heir to claim the throne, so their advisors formed the council after the war was over."

So the myth surrounding how the seven guardians had been chosen by the Gods ... It was all a lie. She'd never really believed it, but still, to be confronted with the truth stung even more.

She shook her head thinking of all the power the Nameless brothers possessed within the Capitol. The First Brother always had a seat on the Council. Always advised with the will and guidance of the Unnamed Gods. And to know that it was all constructed from the rubble of the war—it was all bullshit.

Sitting back in her chair again, Aurelia buried her nose once more in the lengthy volume. She sipped the wine and took bites of food as she comfortably lounged in the chair near the fire in a position her mother would have absolutely deemed unladylike.

She was devouring any record she could find about the early history of their world, reading the truth for the first time. Finding accounts and records that were more than vague warnings or exaggerated allegories.

"This record keeps mentioning the four relics," she murmured.

"They were objects the Dark King used to harness an excess of power." Ven looked up from his book, his eyes darkening slightly as he set it down on the table and picked up his glass. "Magick always seeks a balance, and every vessel has a limit."

He waved a hand to his body. "Some of us have a deeper well of power to draw from before it needs to be replenished, but there is *always* a limit. It's why our kind requires blood to replenish our magick. For the other kingdoms, it's amplified through elements, nature ... Without each of these basic sources of power, our magick would diminish entirely. But hoarding it, overfilling the vessel and channeling an excess of power will demand equilibrium."

He'd told her that their power was only a shadow of what it had once been ... And she wondered what kind of magick they'd once possessed if this was a mere fraction of it.

"The princes of the Void are not capable of creating magick, only consuming it ... Corrupting it. It's why they're constantly seeking footholds in the other realms. Constantly ravenous for sources of magick to devour." He swirled the wine in his glass. "But the Dark King's appetite began to take a toll, and magick exacted its price ... Until he found that he could use objects as extensions of his power—a way to control an excess of magick without it leeching the immortality from him."

He leaned forward, his forearms braced on his lean legs. "For a time, it made him nearly unstoppable. An infinite well of magick that didn't draw on his own reserves." He shook his head, propping his chin on his palm, his gaze falling to the red wine he swirled in his glass, lost in bitter memories.

She'd been so quick to label him a beast—and he'd let her. Unimaginable loss seemed to weigh heavily on his brow and she wondered how many of his loved ones he'd outlived. The war had raged on for years. Years that the humans and the Blood Folk had fought in a seemingly unwinnable war. Suicide.

But was it better or worse to have survived when so many didn't?

"You defeated him," she said quietly, reminding herself of the fact, too. Trying to shake the chill that had skittered down her spine.

"We finally realized how he was doing it. And we used the only weapon against him that remained." His eyes snagged on hers. "His pride."

"The commanders of every army knelt before him under the guise of surrender. Guise might be too noble a word—last ditch effort, perhaps. And as he stretched out his hand to accept our offer, the human queen cut the ring from his finger. A distraction. A sacrifice, to disrupt his power so that the rest of us could remove the other objects. Without them, he was weak, his body unable to control the kind of magick he was siphoning off of the battlefield."

The last human queen had given her life for a chance … Had sacrificed herself so that her people—the other kingdoms, might have a future.

"And were the relics destroyed?" she breathed.

He gave a humorless laugh. "We did everything we could to try and destroy them ... But it was impossible." He shook his head, leaning back in his seat again with a weary sigh.

The sound of someone that had lived too long. Seen too much. And she wondered if maybe immortality was not a gift after all...

"We separated the relics, safely hid them away so that he could not rise to his full power again."

"And are they dangerous?" she asked, a part of her wishing she'd remained ignorant to their existence.

"They're conduits. Harmless on their own, but better left undisturbed," he answered vaguely, and while she suspected he would answer any question she asked of him, a weariness had seeped into his expression, and she didn't care to dredge up any other memories for him.

Discarding the book on the table, she reached for her glass of Red—the shorthand they'd given the blood-laced wine here. "I think I'd like to know more about the last human queen," she said, standing up from her chair and bolstering her nerves to track down one of the grey-skinned Allokin librarians.

Ven snapped his fingers, a book landing neatly in his upturned palm. Aurelia couldn't keep the smile from her face, even when she knew it would earn her that damned self-satisfied smile in return.

"Impressed?" he asked, raising a dark brow. Clearly gloating that he'd coaxed a smile from her. And something about the fact that he cared enough to try made her smile a little more.

"Hardly," she lied, snatching the book from his hand. Knowing a blush was creeping up her face as she tried to ignore his stare from across the table.

The book's hard leather cover was warm in her hand, embossed with intricate swirls of gold.

His garnet eyes glittered as she cracked the spine open to the first page. "The history of the last human queen ... A record of her life. So that our people would not forget her sacrifice."

She cleared her throat, feigning a casual tone so that he wouldn't see what the act meant to her. Making a point not to look up from the page, she asked, "And is that," she waved a hand at him, "some special power of yours, too?" An effort to lighten the heavy weight of the past that had pressed down on them. For some inexplicable reason, she was desperate to wipe away that haunted look in his eyes.

"Summoning the books?" he drawled. And she was relieved that he'd picked up the offering she'd placed in front of him.

She had a feeling he wanted to make her look at him again. So, she rolled her eyes and sighed. "Yes. The books. A neat little party trick," she said, mimicking his tone as she met his crimson stare, a suggestive smirk curving the corner of his mouth.

It was unnerving. The way he looked at her. Like she might be his next meal ... But she refused to look away. And after a short staring contest, a grin broke across his handsome face.

"No, it's not my power." He sat back in his chair again, propping his boots back up onto the table. "The library allows it," he said with a shrug.

"Allows it?"

He nodded.

"What ... It's haunted?" she asked incredulously.

A dark rumble of laughter escaped his lips, "No. Not haunted. It's ... alive."

She gave him a look of contempt, regretting she'd even asked the question as she pushed herself back into her chair, opening the book in her hands and putting it squarely in front of her eyes to cover his annoyingly perfect face.

"The magick here is so ancient that we don't truly understand how it works. The library was built as a gift from the Allokin thousands of years ago when the first Blood Queen ruled. It was rumored that the Allokin prince was quite taken with her. But they both knew a union of the two kingdoms would never be possible. So instead, he sent her grand gifts to profess his unending love until the day he died." He waved a hand to encompass the library around them.

"I just know that if you have a very specific need, or a particular book in mind, the library hears you. And—" He gave a loud snap of his fingers, earning them a "shush" from a nearby librarian who'd been reshelving books, which sent them both into a silent fit of laughter that seemed all the harder to suppress because they needed to be quiet.

He opened the book in his hands again, "To house so many words ... thoughts. Knowledge. To be a safe haven for all of them." He gave a small shrug. "Is it so crazy that this place might have a soul of some kind?"

It really wasn't crazy at all. The skepticism that clouded her face quickly fell as she took in the beautiful place surrounding her.

No, it wasn't that hard to believe at all.

Aurelia sat back in her chair, feeling properly full for the first time in months. The low table in between her and Ven was littered with the aftermath of another decadent meal that had appeared late into the evening.

For a kingdom of blood-drinkers, the food was some of the best she'd ever tasted. She took another sip of the dark red wine in front of her, savoring the rich taste coating her mouth. No longer as self-conscious about drinking it as she'd been before.

Ven had opened his palm again as she'd been eating, a stream of crimson leaving his clenched fist and trailing into her glass. The first few times, she'd felt a twinge of guilt watching him cut himself open for her. But after he caught her staring, he only said,

"I promise, Love, it doesn't hurt." Opening his palm to show her the wound neatly knitting itself together in front of her eyes.

They'd taken a break from reading, a board game appearing in place of their discarded books. Ven dumped out a bag of small tiles onto the low wooden table before them.

Picking one up in her hand, she ran her finger along the edges, worn smooth from years of use. "I've never seen a game like this ... How old is it?"

"I've had it for at least two centuries. I had to replace it after Nira lost so many times in a row that she started grinding down the tiles between her fingers," he said with a conceited grin.

"Two centuries—how old are you, exactly?"

He plucked tiles from the small bag, lining them up neatly in front of him. "I was still young and naïve when the war started, excited to get my sword bloodied, but I was old enough to fight."

"Then that makes you ... at least 300." She should have guessed with the way he'd described the war. She knew he'd been there to witness it himself, but staring at the male seated across from her, he looked no more than ten years older than herself. And she realized she would remain ageless like that, too.

"Something like that," he replied. "We enjoy celebrating birthdays in this kingdom, but we're not particularly good at remembering anyone's actual age." After two hundred or so, she imagined it would get pedantic counting the rest of them.

After a few rounds, she had gotten the hang of the game. She lost three times in a row, but put up more of a fight with every round they played.

She picked through the tiles in front of her. "You said there were only a few fire wielders left."

"There was a time when the Blood Folk possessed mastery of flame and shadow, thousands of years ago. Long before the war," Ven answered, making his opening move on the board. "Half of them wanted to forge new alliances with the other Kingdoms, the other half wanted to cling to the old ways. Taking power by force, consuming more blood than necessary." His voice had a soothing rhythm. The deep timbre made for storytelling.

"A new kingdom emerged, led by the first Blood Queen. She made allies of kingdoms that had long been enemies. Kingdoms that possessed the magick to help our people evolve. Synthetic blood that sustained our power, binding spells to protect our borders." He waved a hand to encompass the fortress around them.

She'd read as much in one of the books he'd handed her earlier, but it didn't go into detail about the rift that had formed within the kingdom.

"In their never-ending pursuit for more power, the Blood Folk who stayed behind ignored the ancient warnings. Gluttonous for blood magick, their hunger became impossible to satisfy. But as I said—all power comes at a price. And magick will always seek to find balance."

"Their mastery over flame grew to new heights, but their power over shadows dwindled. And they found they could no longer look upon the sun without burning. Even the Blood Queen and her people were affected. Their power over fire lessened year after year, until only shadow magick remained. And so, two kingdoms emerged from the wreckage. The Court of Shadow and the Court of Flame."

"How is it that you possess both?" she asked, placing tiles onto the board, a sinking pit forming in her gut as she guessed at the answer, but wanting to hear it from him all the same.

"The heads of the strongest families thought to reunite the magick that had once belonged to all of us—an experiment," he answered darkly. "And while it worked, the two factions couldn't coexist. Especially once war was upon us. The Court of Flame sided with the King of the Void. The Court of Shadow fought beside the humans."

"But there must have been an entire generation of Blood Folk who could wield both."

"There were ... But we were hunted to extinction during the war," he answered, his deep voice rough with emotion.

She glanced up from the game to see him staring into the red wine in his glass. Guilt and heartache clearly written across his features.

Him.

He was the only one of his kind left, she realized with horror.

"And what became of the Court of Flame?" she finally asked, sadness and anger seething just under her skin with the knowledge that he'd been alone for such a long time. More lifetimes than she could imagine.

"The Nostari retreated deep into the hills, where no sunlight could ever touch them. The humans tell tales of them. Of their ruthlessness. Their violence."

These were the stories she knew. The warnings not to stray too far into the Shades. How many souls had been lost to them?

"And your mother's family was cruel enough that they willingly gave her to this *experiment?*"

He huffed out a laugh, "No. My mother willingly gave herself despite my aunt's warning. She and my father were bound," he said softly. "Their fates intertwined in a way that made them—inevitable."

He glanced up at her. "It's hard to explain." He shook his head. "Something ancient. Elusive, unless you've experienced it for yourself. Rare enough that to deny it would cause catastrophe." He leaned back in his chair, his chin propped on one hand as he ran a finger over his bottom lip. "Her family never would have made her go through with it, but my mother trusted Fate above all else."

"So it's not love at first sight," she said with a faint smile, trying to lighten the tension, worried that she'd asked too much. Dredged up painful memories for him for the sake of satisfying her curiosity.

"Hardly," he chuckled darkly, "it's something much deeper than that. An instinct much harder to ignore." He leaned forward again, studying the tiles in front of him. "I wouldn't have believed it myself if I hadn't seen the bond between Nira and Embra—the small decisions and large actions that led them to find each other."

She was dying to know about his father's side. *The Nostari.* About the brutal folk that accounted for half of his blood magick ... And maybe all of hers. But he'd shared enough for one night, and she didn't want to push him to say more.

The thought still had her trying to adjust to her new reality. Her new identity. Like she'd stepped into a dream and was waiting to wake up. But what was harder to admit, was that for the first time in a long time ... She felt like a burden had lifted off her shoulders.

"So explain to me what the Wraith Commander is doing hunting down stray demons," she asked. They'd read late into the night. Ven never rushed her, only sat silently in the chair next to her with his own stack of books. And finally, when she could barely hold her eyes open, they made the trek back to their rooms. "Shouldn't you be doing something more..."

"Boring?" he laughed.

"I was going to say comfortable, but yes." The Commander of the Blue Guard back in the Capitol wasn't doing nightly patrols along the edge of the Valley with his Captains, she knew that much.

"I don't enjoy politics. Someone needed to lead the Wraiths, and I preferred fighting to sitting around arguing with advisors and emissaries."

She huffed out a commiserating laugh. It was a sentiment she could relate to. The games at court had always exhausted her, and they only got more tiresome as she got older.

They'd fallen into a companionable silence, the halls quiet except for their echoing footsteps. The fortress sprawled across multiple peaks of the Shades, a massive network of corridors and caverns that mostly seemed empty since she'd arrived.

"Are there so few of you left?" she asked quietly.

He gave a somber dip of his chin. "Our people are proud warriors. Fighters, every single one of them. And when war was upon us, anyone old enough to hold a sword went into battle. Not by force—by choice." He let out a weary sigh. "There are some small villages scattered outside of the fortress, but most of our people came to live here after the war. Taking up whatever occupations were essential in the wake of the destruction. Though we are all warriors at heart, whatever else we may do."

You're one of us.

She was finally beginning to understand the gravity of what it meant that he'd somehow stumbled upon her, another one of their kind, in such an unlikely place.

Too soon, they arrived at the door to his chambers, an awkward silence filled the air. She felt like there was more she should be thanking him for, but where could she even begin?

"I—didn't realize I was monopolizing your rooms," she stammered, wanting to buy just a little more time before she'd have to go into those quiet chambers and try to find sleep. Try to dodge every thought that hounded her steps.

"I can have another room ready for you tonight if it's not to your liking." Ven's dark brows raised, but she suspected he saw right through her pathetic attempt to stave off sleep for just a few more minutes.

"No. I'm very comfortable here, it's not that," she laughed. "I just feel bad for depriving you of your bed."

He gestured to the hallway behind them. "There are plenty of other beds in this place," he said casually.

"Are there?" The question slipped out before she could catch herself. She imagined there was no shortage of females who'd volunteer.

He smiled faintly, his crimson eyes glittering in the dark at the insinuation. He pointed toward the door behind them. "*Karro's* chambers are directly across the hall, so if you need anything you'll know where to find me." And it sounded like dark invitation lacing his words, but she couldn't be certain.

Relief smoothed over the strange flare of jealousy that had ignited in her chest for just a second as she opened the door to her chambers—*his* chambers. She clamped her eyes shut in embarrassment. What was she *thinking*?

Her emotions had been a wreck since she'd arrived at Ravenstone. Worse since she'd gone into stasis. Only a week ago she'd thought he was her enemy. Her father's assassin. But it was impossible to ignore the way she felt around him. And with every passing day, she saw a side of him that she never expected.

"You dropped this, by the way," Ven said, grasping her hand before she had the chance to close the door.

Warm metal weighted her palm. She looked down.

The jeweled dagger—just as beautiful as she remembered, the fire rippling under the blade's smooth surface seeming to come alive here. Like it was finally home.

Chapter 30

Ven arrived early the next morning, bringing a large breakfast with him. Buttery eggs and crisp bacon. Rich dark coffee swirled with thick white cream. Gods, how long had it been since she'd been able to enjoy the taste of coffee? She ate plate after plate, enjoying the feeling of being well and truly full.

"There must be more important things for you to be doing than bringing me breakfast," she said around a bite of thick brown bread.

"I'm sure there are." He shrugged, taking a sip of his black coffee. "But they can wait."

It had been nearly a week since she'd gone into stasis, but despite her best efforts to curb her thirst—the raw, gritty feeling in her throat would creep up unbidden until she couldn't stand it anymore. Making her jaw ache and every thought in her head empty out until her only singular focus was on the gnawing craving for blood.

Gripping the stem of the wineglass hard enough to shatter it, she finally worked up the courage to ask, "Will I ever learn to control it? The ... Magick. The thirst."

"You will," he answered with enough conviction that the tension in her shoulders released just a fraction. He grabbed the decanter, refilling her glass. "The bloodlust eases up after the first few weeks. Then you'll only need to feed to replenish your power. Once your body adjusts, you'll be able to drink the synthetic stuff again. But for now, you need the real thing."

"And this feeling under my skin ... Like my blood is trying to pump out of my heart." It was difficult to explain the sensation, the same restless energy that she'd felt crackling along her veins months ago, but tenfold. "Is it normal?"

"Yes," he answered with a knowing smile, "We are a race of warriors. We're born to fight. To hunt. We all get a little twitchy when we have too much downtime." He took another sip. "It's easier to dispel when you use your magick—release some of the power. Training helps." He swirled the dark red wine in his glass. "*Other* physical exertions, too." His mouth curved up in suggestion.

"Shameless," she laughed, trying to contain a smile.

He only shrugged. "You asked."

She cleared her throat, an effort to clear her mind of the image he'd conjured, too. "I don't think..." She began, cutting herself off with a shake of her head.

She'd watched the Wraiths train in the pit on more than a few occasions, but that wasn't a place for *her*. She'd followed her brothers into the training pit like a bothersome shadow, but that was a far cry from anything close to training. Especially what she'd witnessed the Wraiths do.

"Why not?" he asked, and when she gave him an incredulous look, he added, "You'd be welcomed onto the Ledge if you wished."

She hesitated, unable to come up with a good reason *not* to, other than her own pride.

"How will you know what you are capable of unless you test yourself?" he challenged.

She opened her mouth, a protest waiting on her tongue...

What *was* she capable of? For as long as she could remember there had been a strict path for her to follow. Comfortable. Predictable. But something inside of her had always yearned for *more*.

Something beyond the rules and limitations.

Sure, she'd broken a handful of them, but only small indiscretions ... Stolen moments with Bastien because they were the only small ray of light in the monotony of her pre-planned life. If she'd really been bold, she would have run away with him. Found a small temple in the rural hillside where no one would have known her face or his. Found a Nameless Brother to marry them before their families could have intervened.

If she'd really been bold, she wouldn't have taken no for an answer when she'd asked Asher to teach her to fight after their father was killed. She could have learned how to defend herself with or without his instruction, his permission.

But she'd never been that brave.

She was untamed enough to bend the rules, but not strong enough to break them.

And she had herself to blame as much as the rest of them for keeping her in a gilded cage of comfort and ignorance. Years of expectations had worn her down to ... nothing. The woman she was supposed to be. The daughter. The sister. The wife. A shell of who she truly was.

But now that she was here, with no prescribed plan to follow except her own desires...

She took a steadying breath, blurting out the question before she could talk herself out of it, "Then when do we begin?"

He raised a brow, dark invitation in his eyes.

"With the *training*, you ass!" She threw her napkin at him, but he caught it before it could hit him squarely in the face. The gleam in his crimson eyes never leaving.

"It feels like ... heat building under my skin. Like liquid lightning coursing through my veins." She hesitated, not sure exactly how to describe the sensation.

They'd cleared the small table between them. And Aurelia sat on the edge of the bed, Ven facing her from the chair.

"And what emotions have you felt in those moments?"

"Frustration. Fear. Rage ... Despair," she said hesitantly, trying to remember those fleeting moments when her magick had appeared.

He leaned forward. "You and I are the same in that way. The tricky part is recalling the emotions, but separating them from the magick. You need to remain levelheaded enough to wield your power in chaotic situations. Panic and fear can easily smother it, especially at first." His white shirt was unbuttoned at the collar to reveal the black ink spiraling up his neck, and a heavy chain that she hadn't remembered seeing before now.

"For now, try to remember those times, those feelings you had, and focus on bringing your fire to the surface," he gently coached her. And she wished she had the same conviction in herself that he seemed to have.

She thought back to the very first time she'd felt the heat in her veins. The morning after her father had been murdered. It startled her awake with night sweats but never truly went away. Simmering to a boil when her family gathered in her father's study, his maps and his messy bookshelves already being packed away for Wellan's occupation of the space.

And that's when they'd told her and Asher that there would be no investigation. There would be no further search for his killer, because it hadn't really been a discussion. Their mother and Wellan had decided what would happen long before they'd involved her and Asher.

She still remembered how the headache had come on so forcefully that she had to excuse herself to her chambers, the white haze around her fingertips as she splashed cold water onto her face was just a lingering effect of the pounding pain in her temples ... Or at least that's what she'd told herself.

And now ... The rage seemed so misplaced. How could she have ever expected them to track down the beast that was responsible for her father's death? The memory of the fear, the panic she'd felt when the Fengul attacked her came back so viscerally that her heartbeat thudded rapidly in her chest. Loud enough that Ven heard it, too.

"That's it, Aurelia," he whispered.

She glanced down at her hands—

Nothing.

Throwing them down in frustration, she looked to him for any guidance, but he only sat unmoving in the chair across from her. His forearms braced on his long legs as if he planned to be there for a while.

"Be patient. Many of us spend decades learning to control our gifts. You won't master them in an afternoon," he chuckled.

She quirked a brow at the challenge, and when Ven broke into a taunting smile across from her, she couldn't help but smile back.

It took her a moment to school her face into neutral concentration again, closing her eyes, hoping it might help her focus.

An hour passed without her producing so much as a spark. She had nothing to show from her exertion except for the sweat that now dampened the back of her shirt and made her dark waves cling to her neck in curls.

Ven had been patient and encouraging, but he finally cleared his throat. "It might help to stand up. Sometimes having your feet on the floor can help you ground your power." And he held out his hand to help her out of the bed. Catching her by the waist as she tumbled to the floor.

His grip was strong, steady, the warmth from his broad hands seeping into the fabric of the loose shirt and pants she wore. A flush crept up her neck, but she couldn't bring herself to step out of his hold.

He didn't move any closer, but he kept his hands on her waist. Her pulse raced at his proximity. The same feeling she'd had the night she encountered the demon. When he'd found her in the library and she'd still thought him a monster. But even then, she just couldn't bring herself to stay away.

A familiar warmth prickled just under her skin. Building to a heat that simmered in her blood, but now she coaxed it to the surface, allowing the fire to flood her veins. And when she raised her hand between them, bright light danced around her fingertips—just small white embers, like the fireflies she used to catch in the rose gardens with Asher when they were children.

Ven looked at her hand, pride flashing across his face, his crimson eyes glittering as they filled with wonder. "I've known many beings who can manipulate fire ... But I've never seen flame like that."

She was so caught up in the moment—in the feeling of his broad hand still firmly on her waist, the other catching her palm to see the light she had conjured—that she reached up to tuck the dark lock of hair behind his ear that had fallen across his face. An action so intimate, so familiar, it felt as if she'd done it a thousand times.

Ven tilted his head down, his lips so invitingly close to hers—

A loud cough sounded from behind where they stood entangled in each other. And just like that, the sparks evaporated from her fingertips.

"Karro," Ven said in frustrated greeting to the shadow that now filled his doorway. Never taking his eyes off her as she stepped from his grasp and walked to his bookshelves, turning her back to him so that he couldn't see the flush of heat that stained her cheeks.

He finally turned toward Karro, who only raised a singular dark brow from where he stood, looking between the two of them.

"The emissaries from the Allokin Kingdom are here," Karro said, breaking the tense silence that had stretched across the room like a tightrope, before leaving just as quickly as he'd appeared.

Aurelia kept her eyes trained on the bookshelves, not trusting herself to get any closer to where Ven stood. Still waiting for her breath to return to its normal pace, her heart to slow down just a little – even though she knew he could hear its rapid beat from across the room.

"When I return, we'll—pick up where we left off," he said, his voice gravelly. And she wondered if he only meant the training.

Chapter 31

She didn't see him again until the following day, when he pounded on the door, threw her a set of black gear and led her down to that terrifying slab of stone where she'd watched the Wraiths train.

Today it was empty, save for her and Ven. At least here there was a little more space between them now. Since he'd left her yesterday the only thing that had occupied her mind was the feeling of his hands spanning her waist. How his grip had tightened slightly before he'd finally released her.

She purposely walked as far across from him as she could, hoping that he couldn't hear the way her heart pounded in her chest or guess at the heat that flooded her body from more than just her magick surging under the surface of her skin.

"The Ledge," Ven stated, gesturing with a wicked grin to the rock they occupied.

Half of it was covered by the cavern mouth that yawned wide overhead, but the other half was exposed to the elements. Slick with the rain that poured down in the forest beyond.

Ven drew a circle on the slab of stone, dusting her hands in the same white chalk and explaining that he only wanted her to try tapping him, work on her reflexes and her strike responses to an attack. All the while trying to coax forth her reluctant power. How she'd be able to focus on both at the same time...

"Normally, you would have to practice bringing your magick to the surface while avoiding getting your nose broken." Ven shrugged. "But for now, we'll take it slow." He squared up his shoulders, letting her catch a glimpse of the Wraith Commander beneath, and disappeared in a wisp of shadow.

Aurelia glanced around her, letting out a yelp as he crossed the twenty-foot distance between them in the blink of an eye, appearing directly in front of her.

She stumbled back with a string of curses as heat spread between her shoulder blades. He vanished again, appearing behind her left shoulder, his lips so close to her neck that the pale skin on her arms pebbled as he taunted her. Fanning that small spark and making it spread through her blood, flowing down her arms and pooling into her palms by the time he reappeared in front of her again.

A halo spread over her hands, just small sparks between her fingertips, but it was enough that he finally stopped vanishing and reappearing to clasp her palms in his own. "Now find a way to keep it there and hold it for as long as you can," he ordered, before stepping away slowly.

Focusing on trying to keep the white sparks from disappearing, she watched as they danced between her fingers, the white light blinding and beautiful though it was so small ... Not at all like the blast of light she'd emitted in that cavern. So powerful and deadly that she'd burned the golden skin on Ven's arms ... His hands...

And it guttered out.

"Again. Either until you can hold the flame in your hand—or you can mark me," Ven ordered from across the Ledge, his black gear still infuriatingly pristine.

And for the next three hours, that's all she did.

When the small sparks would gasp and sputter, Ven would go back to attacking her, sending her reflexes jumping into action and igniting the fire once more.

By the time she was panting and sweating and he finally let her leave the Ledge, she'd managed to control it for an entire minute. Only one damned minute, but she went back to her chambers with a grin splitting her face from ear to ear.

And so it went for the following week. But even after Ven's prodding and poking at every nerve, she couldn't produce more than small sparks contained in her palms. Making Ven mutter under his breath that he'd pass her off to Nira for training—a threat that so far had proven empty, much to her relief.

Returning to her chambers evening after evening, spent and sweaty, she'd soak in the massive stone tub, easing her aching muscles until the water went tepid. As night fell, she'd make her way to the library, her appetite for the fortress's book collection still insatiable. Seth was the only other person who seemed to stay as late, giving her a nod in acknowledgment before he would go back to his own reading.

Sometimes the raven would find her. Appearing on the windowsill of her chambers or perched on one of the many black balustrades on her now familiar path through the North wing. Croaking until she gave him attention. Usually a few pets on his silky black feathers would be enough to send him away, but she was finding the vain beast preferred compliments.

She put on her black gear for the eighth morning in a row when the flames in the hearth roared to vibrant blue and a speck of white fluttered out to land gently on the thick rug before the hearth.

Balcony.

Glancing at the frosted glass doors across from her, she let out a disbelieving huff of breath at the tall shadow outside. Somehow Ven's demanding tone came through even in his writing.

She stalked outside into the crisp autumn air. "Don't you people believe in boundaries? A little privacy?" She waved the note between her fingers.

"I stayed outside," Ven answered with a shrug. "I've never understood modesty ... And privacy doesn't really exist in the war camps."

"That may be true, but this isn't a war camp." She flung her arm out to encompass the beautiful fortress around them.

He circled behind her, making the hair on her neck raise and the skin on her arms pebble as he dipped his mouth to her ear and whispered, "If you ask nicely, maybe next time I'll cast myself into the bathing chamber."

She let out an annoyed sigh, hoping it masked the way her heartbeat picked up. "And *why* did you choose to grace me with your presence here this morning?"

Another shrug of his massive shoulders as he turned to look down into the forest below, the tops of the pines at eye level with the balcony they stood on. "I thought we could both use a change of scenery."

"Lead the way," she muttered, sweeping a hand toward the chamber behind them.

"We'll take the faster route." He nodded his head toward the expanse of trees below, a mischievous grin on his face. "You've been using your magick, but you acquired a much stronger body when you went into stasis, too."

She didn't realize her mouth had gaped open until he lifted his finger under her chin to close it. He couldn't be serious. It was at least a forty-foot drop from where they stood.

"You're stronger than you think, but you won't know your new limits until you've tested them."

"And testing them means jumping to my death?" she blurted out.

He took a step toward her, his eyes sparkling with mischief, "You'll be perfectly safe," he stated casually, taking one more step that had her pinned against the railing. "I'll be holding your hand the entire time." She had to crane her neck to keep from breaking off the stare.

Without another word, he hopped up onto the wide stone ledge of the balustrade, extending a broad hand to her. He pulled her up easily, but she fought to find her balance with the winds tearing down the mountainside pulling at her.

Damn her—she looked down. Only a split second, but it was enough to make her stomach drop out of her ass, as Asher would have said.

She envied Ven. Unfazed by the reckless drop. Only looking at her with those glittering garnet eyes that felt like a jolt of lightning straight into her chest.

"It's easier if you don't think about it too much," he said, his large palm engulfing hers. And though she hated to admit it, she felt a little more sure of herself with his warm, steady presence next to her. "Tuck your knees." Were the only words he uttered before they jumped.

Her stomach went into her throat as soon as the stone fell away beneath them and then they were plummeting down, down, down into nothing.

The biting autumn air ripped against her face as they fell. She would have screamed, but there was no air left in her lungs as the adrenaline pumped through her body, bracing for the impact that would surely kill her.

This was it.

"Tuck and roll!" Ven roared from beside her.

And through some instinct, her body listened. She tucked her knees up to her chest as the impact jarred her body and she tumbled over and over. Across pine needles and the less forgiving terrain of the mountainside, scraping against rocks and branches as she rolled. Flinging out a hand, she grasped for anything to slow her down. Her hand on a thick root, and grabbing it, she finally came to a halt.

Reluctantly unfolding her body, she braced herself for some unbearable flash of pain, a bone jutting out at an unnatural angle … A gaping wound … But there was only a little soreness in her hip from where her side had taken the brunt of the impact. She sat up, shaking the pine needles from her hair as Ven's footsteps came closer.

He stretched a hand toward her, but she slapped it away, standing up and dusting the dirt from her sleeves. "A little warning?" she hissed.

"I thought I made it pretty clear we were jumping," he replied, crossing his arms over his broad chest, not bothering to hide the smirk forming at the corner of his lips.

"Would a countdown have been too much to ask for?" She threw her arms out in indignation, enraged even further as his deep rumble of laughter filled the forest and he turned toward the clearing ahead, leaving her to stomp after him.

Golden afternoon light filtered through the branches of the ancient pines surrounding them. The rain had finally cleared, but the rich smell of damp earth and moss lingered, filling her nose as she struggled to focus on anything else.

Her heightened senses pummeled her body with sensory input, but something else lingered here, too. The memory of the last time she'd been in the midst of the Shades. A demon deadly enough that it had taken a chunk of flesh from Karro before Ven and the others could put it down.

"You're safe here. We're well behind the wards this time," Ven said, answering her unspoken question in that unnerving way of his. And she tried to believe him, willing her body to relax just a little more.

"Is reading minds a gift of yours too?" she asked, a little scared to know the answer.

"No," he laughed. "But it was written all over your face."

He made a slow circle until he stood across from her. Still not bothering to explain why they were here. He crossed his arms over his broad chest, his tattoos fully displayed in the short-sleeved shirt he wore today. A predatory look on his face as he stared her down.

"I think I know what your problem is." He gestured to the expanse of pines around them. "Space."

He took unhurried steps between the pines, winding his way back until he disappeared behind her. But she didn't give him the satisfaction of turning to look where he went, not taking the bait this time.

His breath caressed her ear, making her skin pebble as it trailed down her spine. "You're too concerned with hurting someone. And the fear is stifling your magick."

She scoffed, shaking her head. "I think you overestimate my abilities."

"And *you* underestimate them. Let your enemies do that... Let it be their demise. Now ground your feet. Close your eyes. And search for the flame."

And she did—whatever that meant. Searching every part of her for that elusive fire. She knew it was there. She'd seen its powerful blast even in her half-conscious state inside that cold stone cavern deep within the heart of the mountain. But the damned thing hadn't answered to her since.

Heat bloomed and she opened her eyes hoping to see a ripple of light—but it was only Ven, a look of impatience forming a crease between his brows.

And so he began poking and prodding her magick. Vanishing into a wisp of shadow only to reappear behind her, his thick arm banded around her shoulders and a dagger placed against her throat. Appearing crouched low on the ground to sweep her feet out from under her until her tailbone was bruised from falling over and over again.

Even though she could finally make the sparks appear at will, the flames were impossible to conjure. Easily snuffed out when she lost focus. And for every failed attempt, he punished her. Making her scramble to the top of the boulders jutting out between the pines and then forcing her to climb back down, an act that was truly humbling since the last time she'd climbed anything had been so long ago she couldn't remember.

"I—thought," she panted, "This was supposed to be—" Sweat dripped off her brow, stinging her eyes as her fingers looked for purchase. "Easy," she gasped, as at last she threw herself onto the flattened surface of the stone.

Annoyingly, Ven had made it to the top with a few leaps, waiting for her to catch up. "I never said it would be easy. Just that you needed to test your new limits."

He dropped effortlessly from the boulder, at least a dozen feet down, and looked up at her expectantly. "You're stronger now, more durable, but you still have to build your muscles. It's practice, just like anything else." He flashed her a merciless grin as she rolled her eyes and began the agonizing descent back down the cluster of rocks.

"That's enough for today." He held out a hand to help her down to the ground, and she clasped it readily this time. And her pride would never let her admit the amount of relief she felt when he swept them up in a whirlwind of shadows and deposited them in front of her chamber door.

"I'll be gone for a few days. Our allies to the North are working to rebuild the wards around the human realm. I need to go check on their progress."

Surprise widened her eyes, a flood of gratitude that caught her off guard as much as the gesture.

The Wraiths that he'd tasked to protect the portal, whoever the people of this other kingdom were—they were making the human realm safer. Even though they'd never hear a word of thanks from the people they protected, people who were ignorant to their existence.

"Take the next few days to rest. As I hope you know by now—you're free to go wherever you'd like, though if you choose to venture outside the wards, you know what roams the in-between. But when I return, I expect you to be ready for more," he said, with the hard edge he used on the Ledge with the Wraiths.

She put a hand on the doorknob, ready to sink into a tub of scalding water and sleep for a very, very long time.

Chapter 32

There was no fist pounding on her door the next morning, or the morning after, but she kept herself busy, flipping through book after book in Ven's extensive collection, walking laps around the North wing. Her body was still sore and stiff in ways she never imagined possible, but she welcomed the scream of protest with every step, breathing through the pain. Anything to avoid having to listen to her own thoughts.

It was late into the evening when she finally returned to her chambers, a quiet pop from the crackling fireplace greeting her as she walked through the door.

A slip of paper fluttered out from the flames, and she retrieved it, a faint smile on her face as she saw the familiar handwriting.

Have you been practicing? Ven wrote.

She didn't want to admit the way her heartbeat picked up just a little at the words.

Padding to the desk, she opened the drawers in search of paper and a pen. Finding them, she wrote back, *Diligently,* with a small amount of guilt. She hadn't even attempted to call on her magick since he'd left. Tomorrow. She would try tomorrow.

Standing in front of the crackling fire, she tossed the folded note into the orange embers, watching with fascination as the flames roared to an unnatural shade of blue and consumed the words, then returned to a glowing amber.

The fire roared again a moment later, and the note that fluttered out said, *I'll know if you're lying, and I'll come up with some very creative punishments.*

Pleasure licked down her spine at the insinuation, and she could picture the exact expression on his face, his dark brow raised in suspicion.

And which one of the Wraiths is a snitch? She wrote back, feeling cheeky.

Seth, obviously. Came the reply after only a few moments, and she shook her head with a laugh.

I promise, Commander, I'll practice. She responded with a large dose of sarcasm that she hoped came through in her words.

Anticipation coiled around her as she waited for an answer.

Careful now, he replied, *Promises are sacred things here. The price for breaking them can be quite steep.*

She read the words, a grin on her face as she got ready for bed and crawled under the heavy covers, the fire in the room banking to glowing embers and the torches dousing themselves one by one.

It wasn't until late that night that the quiet gnawed away at her. She tossed and turned, guilt weighing heavy as lead in her stomach as the thoughts of disgust and self-loathing came creeping back in.

It was only a few weeks ago that she'd been in love with another man. She'd had another life ... Though she couldn't say she was scrambling to return to the path her family had laid out for her. But still—the small snatches of joy she'd found in this place ... The unrestricted library. The freedom to go where she pleased. Even the training with Ven ... It all felt like a betrayal to the people she loved that she'd found a scrap of happiness here.

Sleep eluded her, until the grey haze of dawn crept over the mountains, and she couldn't lay still anymore.

Padding to the center of the room, she dug her toes into the softly worn rug just like Ven had instructed her. Closing her eyes, she took a deep breath, slowing her heartbeat and trying to empty her mind of every thought that had chased her dreams away throughout the night. Searching for the fire that was buried somewhere deep inside her.

The prickling heat began at the base of her neck, flowing through her veins—the warmth spreading through her palms and pooling into her fingertips.

Crackling light sputtered and sparked, but no matter how hard she tried, how sharply she focused— the flame would not come forth from where it wended its way through her body. Utterly and completely out of reach. With a frustrated sigh, she finally threw her hands down in defeat.

Lacing her boots, she barged out of the heavy wooden door and made her way down the corridor, walking past that terrifying slab of stone they called the Ledge.

Some of the Wraiths were training today—if you could call it training. It looked more like they were attempting to kill each other. Nira was with them, fiercely beautiful to behold as she fought two male Wraiths. They were attacking her defense, pressing so hard that she danced inches from the very edge of the black stone where it dropped away into nothing.

Nira's sheet of dark hair whipped across her face with every movement. A wicked looking dagger glinted in her hand as she dodged and whirled gracefully away from them, only to get pushed back over and over again. Until finally, Nira's lithe form tumbled over the edge—

Aurelia gasped, her hands gripping the iron railing and watching with horror as Nira's sheet of raven hair disappeared past the stone.

The two males she'd been sparring with did nothing, only tightening their grips on their daggers, falling back into a fighting stance as they backed away from the cavern mouth.

It was then that Aurelia saw slender fingertips gripping onto the black stone. The only warning before Nira swung herself back onto the Ledge, vaulting over the other Wraiths. She swept the legs out from the one on her left and leveled her dark blade at the other's throat. The two males dropped their daggers in surrender.

A faint smile formed on Aurelia's lips as Nira began barking instructions at the males once more. She turned away as air rushed over her shoulder, and Cog landed beside her a moment later, hopping over to where she stood.

"At least everyone else seems scared of her, too," she whispered to the raven, and he croaked in agreement.

She made her way through the North wing, exploring the tunnels and caverns, the paths that led into the deep emerald green of the Shades, and the bridges that spanned underground springs, as Cog glided along beside her. And even though she didn't have a destination in mind, somehow her feet took her to that corner of the North wing, in front of that familiar set of glass doors.

The warm glow from Embra's greenhouse was so inviting that before she knew it, she'd walked up the wide stone steps, raising a fist to knock on the door.

Thinking better of it, she dropped her hand again. It was silly of her to come here, disrupting Embra's work when she was as much a stranger as the rest of them. What was she expecting to find here, anyway?

But the thought of making her way back to those quiet chambers that weren't hers, past the Ledge full of Wraiths, kept her feet frozen in place.

Shaking her head, she turned to make her way back down the steps just as the door cracked open behind her.

"Aurelia?" Embra said.

Aurelia turned to make her apologies, but before she could get a word out, the slender female opened the door behind her with a warm smile.

"I hoped you'd come back! I have new plants to show you." Embra's gentle tone was like the rustling of leaves on a summer day as she opened the door wider.

Chapter 33

The greenhouse quickly became a second home. Aurelia filled her days in the cozy warmth of the tower, taking Embra up on the offer to come back anytime she liked.

Embra was a patient teacher, and Aurelia was a quick study, finding the tedious work of removing, drying, and crushing petals for Embra's healing salves to be a perfect distraction. Her mind and her hands were occupied for hours in a way that made it easy to forget the thoughts that usually plagued her.

She'd never had the chance to get her hands dirty doing ... anything.

Past the age of ten, her mother had filled her days with dance lessons and etiquette classes that turned into tea and polite social engagements with the other Councilor's families as she'd gotten older. Every second of her days planned and scheduled, but never amounting to anything.

She never could have guessed how rewarding it was to have dirt under her fingernails when she returned to her chambers every evening, or the excitement she had each morning at finding a new leaf unfurled on one of the plants. She never could have imagined the feeling of accomplishment that these small tasks gave her.

Embra's quiet presence was a welcome one. She never made any demands, didn't ask any questions. She only gave gentle corrections when Aurelia pummeled the petals into too fine a powder or added too much oil to the healing salve.

The mornings swiftly gave way to early afternoons in the lush quiet of the tower, and the work kept her busy, making her too tired to think of much by the time her head hit the pillow every night. Thoughts of the home she left. The people who would eventually forget about her. The guilt that still hounded her steps.

The soft glow of Embra's magick emanated around them, and Aurelia watched with fascination as the female coaxed freshly planted seeds into small green sprouts. It had been nearly a week that she'd worked with Embra, watching her use her magick, but it never got old.

"Incredible," Aurelia whispered, a smile of wonder on her face.

"You give me too much credit," Embra chuckled, "This is the most basic magick Green Folk possess." She continued her rounds through the greenhouse, whispering to the plants and doting on them as if they were her children.

"Do you miss them—your people?" Aurelia asked.

"Yes." Embra smiled sadly, "But not enough to go back." She plucked up a brass watering can from the windowsill. "My people long for comfort. Peace. Predictability. I was always a little too wild for my kind. A little too curious. A little too restless."

Aurelia stifled her surprise. She would never have described Embra as wild—she was easily the most calming presence here. Especially compared to Karro's boisterous voice always echoing through the corridors and Nira's intimidating presence, usually barking insults at the males training on the Ledge.

"When the war was upon us, most of my people wanted to remain hidden, as if that might leave us unaffected from the destruction and chaos around us." Embra shook her head. "But I saw a purpose so clearly laid out before me that it was impossible to ignore." Her rich brown eyes flared with a fierce determination that Aurelia had somehow missed until now.

"I put my healing skills to use going into the thick of battle to help. That's where I saw Nira for the first time. Bloodied and half dead on the Valley floor." Embra turned away again, going back to watering the flowers that lined the windows. "I didn't know who she was then, but something in me cried out that I could save her." Her delicate shoulders raised in a shrug. "So, I did. To this day I don't think I've ever produced that kind of magick again."

They were Bound, at least that's what Ven had told her. She didn't really understand the nature of the bond, but she wondered if the magick had been part of that mysterious pull that Ven had spoken of.

"Do you ever regret leaving?" Aurelia asked.

Embra fussed over a small seedling, the dark green braid of hair down her back swaying gracefully with the motion. "The chaos brought out powerful magick in me that I never had reason to call in my peaceful home. I never would have realized my own potential had I stayed."

She turned to face Aurelia again, her eyes shining as she reached for an empty jar on the shelf. "I saw ... horrible things, but I also saw incredible acts of bravery. Selflessness that knew no bounds between kingdoms." She blinked back unshed tears and began gently pinching off pale buds, dropping them one by one into the jar.

"When the war was finally over, Ven offered me a position here if I wanted it. At first, I refused—I didn't think I could ever find a home amongst the Blood Folk. Ven said the offer stood, regardless, if I ever changed my mind." She smiled faintly at the memory, "And when I packed up my things to start on my way back to my village ... I wasn't so certain I had a place back home anymore."

Embra's practiced hands made quick work of filling the jar with buds. "Something changed in me, but I think it changed for the better. I accepted Ven's offer, and I found a purpose that I never would have if I'd gone back to my nice, quiet village."

"And was it because of Nira that you stayed?" Aurelia distractedly reached for a lid, handing it to Embra.

"No," Embra laughed, "No—I pined away for her from a distance for decades after the war." She closed the jar, writing out a label in her delicate script and placing it on the shelf. "You have to understand ... My people are isolated. Closed-off. I was an outcast the moment I decided to leave my home." She shook her head. "The thought of being in love with one of the Blood Folk." A soft smile lit her face, "It felt like too much to admit even to myself."

"Are they enemies? Your people and the Blook Folk?"

"My people worship the Gods of life—Plants, and earth, and everything living. The Blood Folk serve the Goddess of death. My people value peace above all else, which is easy to do when other kingdoms are willing to pay in blood to preserve it. They see the Blood Folk as barbarians. Ruthless and cunning, but not much better than the demons they kill."

Embra put her hands on her hips, the thick green rope of hair down her back shifting as she lowered her head. "I admit I thought the same until I saw for myself on the battlefield what they protected us from, what kind of future a peace-loving people like mine would have if the Blood Folk weren't sacrificing their lives to guarantee it. I witnessed their courage, their capacity to love, and I realized we weren't so different," she said with a faint smile.

Embra's warm gaze fell onto Aurelia. "And your home? Your people?" she asked carefully. Her brown eyes seeming to tell Aurelia that she could have said she didn't want to talk about them and she wouldn't push any further ... But Aurelia found that she *did* want to talk about them. That maybe it would help close the wound that had been festering since she'd arrived here.

"My brother Asher..." Aurelia began, with a smile that stretched across her face as she told Embra of her family, her life—even Bastien. Surprised that it didn't hurt her as much as she'd expected to talk about all of them. And before she realized it, she'd told Embra about her engagement to a man she barely knew. What her life might have looked like had she not stepped through that mirror ... A stranger's bride in an unfamiliar city.

"My life may have appeared beautiful and idyllic from the outside—but it was a cage." Aurelia admitted. And she wasn't sure why she said the thought out loud to this female she barely knew. Maybe she was finally just admitting it to herself. "A beautifully gilded cage. Comfortable. But a cage none the less."

"It sounds like much has changed since the last time I stepped foot into the human realm..." Embra commented darkly. "Odd, how even though they remained protected, safe for so many centuries, they would keep half of their population relegated to—well, what *are* their females allowed to do?"

It took Aurelia a moment to really consider the question. She knew Embra hadn't meant it to be harsh ... But, the reality *was* harsh.

She blew out a breath. "We're allowed to marry. And we're allowed to bear children. And if we're lucky ... it'll be a union with a kind, respectable man."

"A waste," Embra spat. A quiet fury ignited behind her brown eyes, the color of autumn leaves and freshly tilled soil, the anger leaking into her tone taking Aurelia by surprise.

Embra waved a hand impatiently at the look of shock on Aurelia's face. "There are so many more facets to a person than only *those* roles. So much more to offer ... It's not that those pursuits aren't noble. A partner to experience life with, the beauty of creating a family—those are perhaps the most fundamental things any of us can hope for. But they are not the *only* worthy pursuits in life," Embra sighed. "And to not have the freedom to do as you choose..." She shook her head sadly.

And Aurelia understood at once why it affected Embra so deeply. A love like hers wouldn't have been possible in the human realm ... Though she still didn't understand how someone as sweet and nurturing as Embra had fallen in love with Nira, but maybe that was part of what it meant to be Bound? That elusive intertwining of fates that seemed to rise over the din of everything else.

After all, what did it matter if she didn't understand? She could see the look in Embra's eyes when she spoke of her wife ... The admiration. The adoration. It was the same look she had seen in her father's eyes when he had spoken of her mother.

"And when did you finally work up the courage to tell Nira how you felt?" Aurelia asked with a faint smile.

Embra's eyes lit up at the question, the brief frustration that had darkened her expression melting away instantly as the corners of her eyes crinkled. "That—is much too long of a story to tell before dinner, and I'm starving. Will you join us this time?" she asked hopefully.

Embra had made a point of inviting her to meals every evening. But Aurelia always politely declined, seeing the easy manner in which they all interacted. Always feeling a lonely pang in her chest.

An outsider.

She might be one of the Blood Folk, but she'd never be one of *them*. She'd never share the hundreds of years of history they had together. Fighting beside each other. Taking care of each other.

A family.

Something she no longer had.

Aurelia gave a small shake of her head, hating the look of disappointment she saw in Embra's russet eyes. "I'll see you tomorrow though, same time?"

"Of course," Embra answered gently, giving Aurelia's hand a squeeze as she left the greenhouse.

Passing the Ledge on her way back to her room, Aurelia stopped to watch the Wraiths train, fascinated with how they moved. Their graceful, powerful bodies. And she wondered how many more training sessions with Ven she'd have to endure to earn even an ounce of the muscle that layered their bodies.

Seth was training tonight, one of the few places she saw him outside of the library, and when his gaze met hers on the upper level he inclined his head in silent invitation.

Her fingers gripped the railing as she considered it.

Something itched just under her skin. That restless energy that hounded her day and night, making her wonder—*what if?*

But after a heartbeat's hesitation, she shook her head. Ignoring the sour taste of disappointment that filled her mouth as she turned away. And she was glad it was Seth who'd seen her today and not Karro, who was prone to very loudly badgering her from across the Ledge.

Instead, she made her way to the library, taking her meal in the far corner of the second story, the roaring fireplace as her only reading companion. And just like she did every evening, she stayed late into the night until all the candles and torches had extinguished themselves, except for the handful flickering above her head. Only then, when she was too exhausted to walk straight, think straight, did she return to her chambers, falling into the massive bed.

She pulled the heavy covers over her shoulders, catching a whisper of Ven's scent as she laid her head down on the pillow. An ache of loneliness took her by surprise, and she realized that he'd left a small void in his wake.

Chapter 34

The next morning Aurelia returned to her chambers, searching for a change of clothes. Her newfound strength had claimed its latest victim in the form of a test tube in Embra's lab. She'd gripped it just a little too tightly, shattering the delicate glass and sending shards flying across the floor. Embra had been good natured about the accident, but the crisp white button-down shirt that had become Aurelia's uniform of sorts was stained an irredeemable shade of fuchsia.

The braid holding her dark hair out of her face had come loose over the course of the morning's work, and she quickly plaited it over her shoulder again—learning it was the easiest way to avoid getting the errant strands in Embra's more volatile tonics.

There was something refreshing about not being concerned for her appearance. Dressing for her own comfort instead of dressing for someone else's appreciation. No longer feeling limited by the restriction of her clothing. She couldn't imagine doing work in Embra's lab wearing the wide sweeping skirts of her old life.

Shrugging on a fresh shirt, she closed the door and began the walk back to the tower as a breeze whipped her hair over her shoulders. The chilled air so inviting that she stopped to peer over the railing to the Ledge below.

Karro and Seth were the only Wraiths training today. No sharp metallic ring of swords, but the two males were panting regardless from where they grappled on the unforgiving sheet of rock, a tangle of limbs and rippling muscle.

Catching sight of her, they stopped abruptly, two sets of ruby eyes narrowing to where she stood. And before she could duck out of the way, Karro's booming voice echoed across the space.

"Not so fast—" he taunted.

She slowly crept back out from the arch she'd hidden behind, uttering a string of curses. They'd tried to get her onto the Ledge every morning when she walked past. And so far, she'd dodged it, but she was quickly running out of half-decent excuses.

Karro crooked a finger at her, a merciless grin on his rugged face. "If you want to watch, you have to play."

She groaned, crossing her arms over her chest. "I'll only make a fool of myself."

"Nope. Not getting out of it this time," Karro jeered, patting the black stone beside him.

She looked to Seth for a little backup, but he only silently raised a brow at her as if to say, *better to get it over with.*

Aurelia made her way down the stone staircase with a defeated sigh. If she had to make a fool of herself, better to rip the bandage off. Maybe once they realized she was a lost cause they'd leave her alone.

If there had ever been a time when she felt comfortable in her own body, she'd long forgotten it. The extent of her physical activity through her life had been the dance lessons her mother forced her to take.

She'd gained the smallest amount of confidence with Ven's training, surprising herself by pushing past her limits, but scrambling up a boulder was something else completely from the hand to hand combat she watched the Wraiths engage in.

Planting herself far away from the where the edge of the stone dangled into thin air, she crossed her arms, looking expectantly at Karro.

"First—we learn how to fall," he answered.

"I thought the idea was trying to stay upright," she replied dryly, hoping it hid the way her heart hammered in her chest.

"You *will* get knocked on your ass. Everyone does." He grinned in that way of his that could make anyone do any number of things. Unleashing the full extent of his charm on her, his ruby eyes glittered until she finally cracked a smile.

"Even you?" Aurelia asked with a chuckle, finding it hard to believe the solid wall of muscle a few feet in front of her had ever been knocked down.

"Especially him," Seth answered from where he stood to the side.

Karro threw him a glare before smirking at Aurelia again. "And when you do, you want to make sure you fall the right way."

Aurelia didn't expect to be sweaty and out of breath just from falling, but she was. She smudged another layer of grime against her forehead trying to wipe away a bead of sweat, thinking this would have proved useful for that day she spent getting her feet swept from beneath her by Ven out in the Shades.

"Again," Karro commanded.

She fell back for what felt like the hundredth time, trying to focus on dispersing the pressure through her hips, shoulders, and palms as Karro's broad hands patted the areas where he wanted her body to contact the floor—his touch never feeling anything other than respectful, helping her mind connect to her body.

"Enough of that," Karro finally barked, and her shoulders sagged in relief until his grin turned feral. "Let's try something more fun."

"Seth, you're up," he called, as Seth detached his lean figure from where he'd been observing against the wall.

Aurelia found that she liked Seth's quiet presence. At first, she'd been embarrassed to have him watch from the side while she fumbled through Karro's instruction, but he never laughed at her, only encouraging her with gentle pointers while she worked through some basic movements.

"Now try taking Seth down," Karro said flatly.

Aurelia gave him an incredulous look.

"Fighting is all about balance and leverage. I want you to watch how Seth places his feet when he stands and distributes his weight when he falls. Look for openings and take them. If you're up against a male who's taller and heavier than you, your best bet is getting them off balance on your first try, otherwise you'll have a hell of a time getting them onto the ground."

"I thought that's what the sharp things were for," she answered insolently, jerking her chin toward the racks of black-bladed broadswords and daggers.

Karro clicked his tongue. "All in good time—you should learn how to defend yourself *without* a weapon before you learn how to fight *with* one. Besides," He shrugged. "Battles are a messy business. Weapons get lost, blades get knocked from your hand, and often it comes down to hand-to-hand combat."

With a defeated sigh, she turned to Seth, who had the trace of a smile on his lips—as if he had been waiting for Karro to wear her down. He stood a few paces in front of her, his feet braced apart, one foot planted just slightly ahead of the other.

He gave her a nod.

She ran at him, throwing her full force against his body. But it did nothing to budge his footing. She backed up, blew out a breath, and tried again. And again.

And again.

Seth might as well have been a wall of granite for all she moved him. She stood hunched over, bracing her hands on her thighs, her muscles burning and her lungs threatening to burst. Taking a minute to catch her breath, she wiped a hand across her brow.

"Room for one more?" A voice rang out from above.

All three of them looked up to see Nira leaning over the railing twenty feet above. Blood rose into Aurelia's cheeks, wondering how long the dark female been watching her struggle. She hated looking weak, but especially in front of the brutal female.

Karro muttered a curse under his breath as Nira didn't wait for a response, flipping gracefully over the railing and landing without more than a quiet thud in the center of the ledge.

"Show off," Seth laughed as he shook his head.

Nira only sketched a mocking bow as she took up the place beside him. It was only then that Aurelia saw the striking resemblance between the two. Not in the way that they all resembled each other. The dark hair, the dark complexions, deep red eyes. No— with these two it was like looking at two sides of the same coin. The angular, beautiful features almost mirror images of each other.

"You're twins," Aurelia gasped.

"Don't remind me," Seth uttered, earning him a hearty smack on the shoulder from Nira.

"You'll never have more power than them up here," Nira said, grasping Aurelia's arm. "Here." Patting her hip. "This is where our power lies as females. If you can take them down to the ground, you'll have more of an advantage."

Rays of afternoon sun were leaking through the canopy of trees and bathing the stone ledge in golden light as Nira demonstrated a chokehold.

She wrapped her lean legs around Karro's thick torso and held him in place. "Look—I can use Karro's own bulk against him," she added, placing one arm under Karro's chin as she leveraged the other under his armpit and threaded it behind his neck. "His shoulders and arms are at a disadvantage to him here. He doesn't have the flexibility to break my grasp." She smirked as Karro tried, and failed, to reach her. And somehow even his considerable strength wasn't a match for the position Nira had taken up behind him.

Someone leaned over the railing above them as Nira explained the mechanics of the grip, and Aurelia glanced over to see Embra watching them with an amused look. "So that's where my assistant disappeared to."

"Just teaching her a few basics, darling," Nira answered with an adoring smile, reinforcing her grip around Karro's neck as his eyelids drooped, his mouth going slack. "Shit," Nira uttered, giving Karro a smack that had his eyes rolling back into place. "You're supposed to tap, idiot."

"Never surrender," Karro sputtered as Seth just shook his head from where he stood off to the side, Embra rolling her eyes with a laugh as she walked back in the direction of her tower.

"That's payback for Embra," Nira hissed, as she released Karro and his back hit the floor again.

Aurelia turned away to hide her chuckle.

"Really?" Karro shook his head, trying to clear the fog she'd put him in. "How long am I going to be apologizing for that?"

Nira stalked toward the staircase. "I wagered seventy-five years," she shot over her shoulder.

"Seventy-five!" Karro bellowed.

"I said eighty," Seth answered dryly from where he leaned against the wall.

Karro's eyes widened with a look of betrayal. "You too, Seth?" he grumbled, shaking his head.

Seth shrugged. "I won the last time," he said with a grin. "What was it again? Eleven years, three months, and four days—not that anyone was counting."

Chapter 35

Hobbling back to her room, Aurelia pushed the door shut and headed for the bathing chamber. She turned the faucets on with a crack and watched the steam billow out from the deep stone tub. Pouring out a healthy dose of citrus scented oil into the water, she stripped off her sweat-soaked shirt and pants, catching a glimpse of herself in the large mirror above the wash basin.

It was the first time she'd really taken a moment to look at herself since she'd settled in here, since she'd ... changed.

It had only been a few weeks, but already she'd lost the gaunt look on her face, some color coming back into her skin after her appetite returned. Something about the food and wine here was exquisite, and she couldn't be certain if it was the cooks or her heightened senses. The purple smudges under her eyes from all her restless nights back at the Capitol were completely gone, thanks to the deep slumber she'd fallen into every night since being here.

Training on the Ledge had been added into her daily routine, rather unwillingly, if she had to admit, but she gained a little more confidence with every passing day. There was a little muscle on her, too. Nothing like the hard-won muscle Nira flaunted, but enough to fill out her curves and make her arms and legs look strong and capable. It was impossible to ignore that she looked ... healthy. Better than she had in months—maybe ever.

Her mother had always been so concerned with keeping her waist and arms as delicate as possible that Aurelia never considered that she might be strong if she tested her body, found its limits, and chose to push past them anyway.

And she realized with a sharp clarity that's what she'd been doing since she arrived—pushing past the discomfort of training her magick, her body. And ignoring that voice in the back of her head that said she didn't have a place here. Easier to drown out when she spent quiet mornings with Embra, hidden away amongst the leaves and growing things.

It had given her a sense of purpose when she woke up in the morning. And Aurelia was ravenous for the work that Embra delegated to her. The female had become a friend, filling an empty spot in Aurelia's soul that she hadn't realized was there. Always happy to answer her questions, never making her feel like a burden in the well-oiled machine of her laboratory.

Even the rest of them had relentlessly included her in everything they did, whether it was Seth quietly walking up to her corner in the library and leaving a book on the table because he thought it would interest her, or Karro playfully hounding her to train with them day after day. She'd even had a breakthrough with Nira when she'd successfully hooked a leg around Karro's ankle and brought the mountain of a male crashing down onto the Ledge, earning a rare smirk of approval on Nira's face.

The endless banter between all of them was endearing. How at ease they were with each other. With their place in this world. And some part of her wondered if maybe she could find that here, too.

There was comfort in the predictable routine she'd made for herself—a schedule completely dictated by her own desires. None of the pressure that had come with her family name back in the Capitol. None of the expectations that had weighed so heavily on her before.

She was … content.

But that was a harder thing to admit. Because admitting that tasted bitterly of betrayal. Betrayal of her family. Betrayal of the man she loved and the life she'd left behind.

Her *real* life.

She swallowed hard as another wave of emotion washed over her.

Not hers. Not anymore.

Aurelia slipped beneath the surface, letting her mind focus on the sting of the scalding water against her skin. A welcome distraction as it melted away the knots in her sore muscles. And when the water finally grew tepid, she reluctantly got out, toweling off her damp hair and throwing on the nearest set of clean clothes.

The warm glow of candles in the library felt a little lonelier tonight as she pushed through the large doors, even though she had her place marked in a book she'd had trouble putting down the night before.

She climbed the spiral staircase to the second floor, rounding the row of bookshelves that took her back to that tucked away corner that she'd come to love so much in such a short time. But instead of the usual quiet she'd expected, the soft rumble of conversation greeted her ears along with the gentle clink of silverware against dishes, and the delicious aroma of food.

And as she rounded the bookshelves, where there were normally two leather armchairs by the fire, an assortment of seats had been crowded in.

Karro's large frame overwhelmed a footstool that she'd guess the librarians were missing. Embra and Nira shared a bench that belonged to one of the first-floor desks. Seth sat in a wooden chair squeezed between the shelves, a dozen different platters of food littering the low table between them. And sitting in the leather armchair directly in front of her—

Ven.

His face was lit up in an uninhibited smile, the sharp points of his fangs visible, still laughing at something Karro had said before she walked in. And her heart gave an unexpected leap at seeing he'd returned. His crimson eyes glanced to where she stood, his smile lingering as he patted the seat next to him in invitation, and she didn't hesitate to join them. Feeling like that place was meant just for her.

Ven leaned toward her. "We thought we'd bring dinner to you tonight," his voice rumbled over the din of conversation.

Across the table, Nira tucked a stray lock of emerald hair that had escaped Embra's thick braid behind her ear, and Embra gave her cheek a peck in return. It felt so intimate that Aurelia cast her eyes to the floor, a little embarrassed to have witnessed something so gentle from someone so fierce.

Karro was retelling some tale with such vigor that he knocked over his glass of wine, Seth catching it before it could stain the wooden floor.

Ven handed her a plate, already piled high with her favorite dishes, and she tucked into the food eagerly, perfectly content to be in the midst of them.

Ven leaned toward her again. "The Allokin have made quick progress on rebuilding the wards around the human realm. They're almost finished," he said quietly.

Something constricted in her chest. The taste of relief and dread indistinguishable on her tongue. She nodded, to let him know she heard, she understood.

Ven had already returned to the human realm the night after he'd convinced her to stay. He'd done as she had asked, left her family with the story imbedded in their minds that she had given herself over to the Faceless Sisters.

She didn't doubt his word or his abilities, but he'd left the door open to her that she could still return to see them one last time before the wards were completely sealed. She couldn't bring herself to consider it right now—not when this moment felt so ... right.

She chewed a bite of food, taking a sip of the rich wine Ven poured for her. "So, what *exactly* did you do this time to get banned from Embra's lab?" she asked, barely containing her smile as she watched the color drain from Karro's face.

His eyes snapped to where Embra sat just a few seats away, as if the slight female might turn into a viper at any moment. Seth dropped his fork, letting it clatter onto his plate while he silently shook his head as the uproar around them began.

She glanced at Ven, a rare unrestrained smile on his face as he took another bite of food.

Chapter 36

"Yes, Aurelia! That's it!" Ven encouraged her, as another series of sparks ringed her fingertips.

A smile burst forth on her face where her lips had only been a thin line of concentration before. Her eyes left her hands long enough to catch the huge grin on Ven's face only a few feet away from her.

"Now ... reign it back in," he instructed.

This was the part she hated. She had worked so hard to finally coax out some small bit of her magick. And even though it was barely a flicker of sparks at her fingertips, she was able to control their appearance at will, holding them steady in her palms. Then Ven would get that gleam in his eye, making her struggle to cut off the fire that flowed into her hands. Something she had *not* figured out how to control yet. Leaving him to resort to—unorthodox tactics.

"I swear to the Unnamed. If you throw one more pitcher of ice water at me..." she threatened.

"You'll do—what exactly?" he taunted, raising his dark brows.

Ignoring him, she clamped her eyes shut, practicing the breathing techniques he'd taught her to calm her heart rate and staunch the flow of magick.

After a few moments, she felt the power ebb away from her fingertips, receding back into her palms, up through the veins in her wrist, and disappearing again inside her blood. When she opened her eyes again to look down at her hands, the sparks had vanished.

She turned to look at Ven, a self-satisfied smile on her face.

"Good work," he said, pride in his voice. "You're a fast learner." He clicked his tongue. "Shame though. I was really hoping I'd have to throw you into one of the ice springs—"

Aurelia followed Ven's gaze as his voice trailed off.

Seth had silently appeared in the open doorway. He was so unnervingly still and quiet, even for their kind, that it seemed she never knew where he was or how long he'd been there.

"The Allokin have sent word," he said without preamble.

"And?" Ven replied, pouring himself a glass out of the pitcher of ice water he'd been threatening Aurelia with.

"They await our arrival."

Ven put the glass down. "Good." Something that wasn't quite relief flickered across the sharp planes of his face.

Aurelia looked to the doorway again, only to see Seth had already disappeared.

Ven crossed his arms over his broad chest and Aurelia had to catch herself from looking too closely at the way his shirt hugged his body, clinging to the cuts of hard muscle beneath.

This unspoken thing between them had remained that way. His teasing and taunting during their training always bordering on flirtatious, but never going further. And she'd found herself a little disappointed, and maybe a bit relieved, too. She tore her eyes away, but a smirk was already on his face.

Heat flooded her cheeks knowing she'd been caught staring. Again. But he didn't comment on it. Just as she never called him out when she caught him looking at her.

She knew what those looks meant, but Ven always kept himself just out of reach for a reason she couldn't decipher. It was better that way ... She had too much to focus on as it was.

He poured another glass of water and handed it to her. "I've asked an old friend for his help. Finding out exactly how the demons managed to escape their wards and gain access to the human realm, He's somewhat of an expert on wards and containment spells. I imagine if he's sending us an invitation it means he has something to tell us."

He turned to the wardrobe, getting out a fresh set of clothing. "We should prepare to leave shortly. The Allokin don't give invitations freely and we'd be foolish to keep them waiting."

"Us?" she asked, a little surprised.

"You should be there with us. Your perspective is valuable," he said over his shoulder as he left the room, leaving her a little stunned as she began toweling off her hair.

She headed for the bathing chamber, quickly rinsing off. When she returned, an assortment of clothing had appeared on the bed. She picked up the heavy cloak that had arrived, a thick fur trim lining the hood. Wherever they were going must be cold.

A set of black gear was folded next to it. The strange fabric feeling like a smoother version of leather. She always envied how Nira made the outfit look—she owned it. Owned the way it molded to her body without any self-consciousness. But it would still take a little time for Aurelia to get used to having her ass on display. Not a single curve hidden.

A new sheath laid on the bed, the leather supple and soft. And as she buckled it into place against her thigh, she realized it had been made to fit her measurements, much like the clothing. Not the borrowed pieces she'd grown accustomed to.

Your perspective is valuable.

No one had ever said that to her. And until this moment, she had never considered that it might be.

Ven and Karro were ready and waiting when she opened the chamber door. Lean lines of muscle were apparent even under the dark gear they wore, and she wondered how many years of training it had taken for them to look like that.

Centuries, she thought, a little dejectedly.

Karro was all brute strength. A formidable wall of muscle mass and towering height as he turned to lead them down the corridor. But Ven had a predatory grace about him, his stance as he waited for her in the hallway seeming like he carefully watched her, even now.

He bent his head close to hers. "I see I got your measurements right," he uttered once Karro was well ahead of them. He lowered his voice even further as he added, "The shadowskin suits you." Making heat rush up the back of her neck.

"Years of practice sizing up females, I suppose?" she threw back.

"Only one. And I still don't think I'm any match for her," he chuckled lightly, making Aurelia's steps falter.

Thankfully she was saved from having to look at him as they stopped outside a set of doors. So tall that she had to crane her neck to see where they ended. Iron hinges braced either side, the heavy lock at the center etched into an intricate maze of patterns.

"I see the stories were wrong about iron, too," she muttered under her breath.

"Depends what you're hunting," Ven answered, as he rotated a small iron disk buried in the design of the lock, imperceptible to her eyes until he'd pointed it out.

A sharp point lay underneath the surface, and as Ven pressed the pad of his finger to it, a small bead of blood welled onto the metal, rolling down the carved channels of the lock. A moment later, the latch gave way with a heavy thunk. The series of locks and latches rotating and falling away with clicks and whirs until at last the doors opened inward, welcoming them inside.

"The Armory," Ven stated, as Aurelia tried not to let her mouth hang open.

Gleaming metal covered every surface of the torchlit cavern. Black blades of every shape and size lining the walls. Smaller weapons in glistening rows on shelves and some ominous looking objects inside glass cases.

She turned in a slow circle to take in the room. "Are we expecting a fight?"

"No, but better to be prepared," Ven answered, stopping in front of a set of drawers and opening them one after the other to reveal small knives, larger daggers, and wickedly curved blades.

"What kind of metal is this, anyway?" she asked, reverently touching one of the daggers that looked like a larger version of the one already strapped to her thigh.

"It's not—it's Black Tourmaline. Mined from this very mountain."

She lifted it from the shelf, studying the glossy blade. And sure enough, when she looked closely, she saw the ripples of gold and bronze woven throughout the dagger.

Iron.

Aurelia remembered how one sure strike into the heart of the Fengul had made the beast disintegrate into dust, when no normal blade would have been capable of that.

"Take what you like," Ven said, nodding to the blade she held in her hands. "Anything here is yours should you wish it," he added, holding her gaze for just a little too long before he finally turned away.

Seth had appeared without so much as a sound, gracefully flipping blades as he plucked them from the wall and sheathed them against his thigh, his biceps. Slipping a smaller one into his boot and strapping a large broadsword down the column of his back. Pausing briefly to consider the row of gleaming metal in front of him before he chose one of the curved blades Aurelia had spotted when they'd first walked in, slipping it into the baldrick across his chest. For his quiet, studious nature—she suspected he might be the most dangerous of them all.

She picked out a narrow blade, the handle on it well-balanced but nothing like the ornate work on the dagger against her body. Feeling like an imposter, she strapped the small dagger to her arm. She wasn't a warrior like them. She was just dressing up in a costume like a child. But still, its weight against her body made her feel a little more dangerous, and that had to count for something.

Ven's deft fingers were cinching the leather and buckling it into place before Aurelia even had the chance to ask for help. Her eyes wandered the glass cases as he tightened the straps, a small distraction from the feel of his hands on her legs. Gentle, despite the strength she knew they possessed.

Her gaze landed on a set of iron coins, an intricate pattern stamped into the metal.

"Those," Ven answered as he followed her gaze, "are very precious."

"What are they?"

He glanced up from where he knelt in front of her. "Coins of Atonement—a gift from our closest allies."

"The Allokin?"

"No, a far older kingdom. One that no longer exists, which is partly what makes the coins so valuable," he said with a hint of sadness.

"What do they do?"

"They can banish a demon prince back to the Void. Something even a Ravenstone blade is not capable of doing," Ven answered, running a finger underneath the leather strap on Aurelia's arm, the heat from his hand branding her even through the shadowskin gear.

"Karro and Seth will go ahead of us." He nodded to where the two Wraiths stood, ready and waiting.

Nira stood off to the side, her mouth tightening into a thinner line than usual as she studied the row of weapons behind her twin.

"You're not coming with us?" Aurelia asked.

"I won't step foot into that place unless it's absolutely necessary." Nira glowered darkly, her tone not inviting any further explanation. And Aurelia wondered what, exactly, she was walking into. The dark female's sensuous lips tipped into a vicious grin. "I prefer my women with curves and my men … a little less pretty. Plus, someone needs to stay here and keep an eye on things," she added with a shrug.

"Can't imagine the poor bastard who tries to pull something while you're in charge." Karro grinned, his crimson eyes flashing with grim excitement.

"Does anyone else know where we're headed?" Aurelia asked, wondering if it was infighting that concerned them, or an outside threat.

"No, but we're always being watched, or at least they're always *trying* to watch us," Nira answered vaguely.

Seth stepped into the center of the room, his body gleaming with weapons. "The Court of Flame still likes to send out spies and scouts from time to time. They usually don't get the chance to return with anything useful," Seth supplied, his soft-spoken voice making the words sound even more menacing.

The Court of Flame.

That mysterious place on the map. The other half of their kind—the Nostari.

Had the other court suffered as many losses as this one? Had their people also been diminished to a fraction of what they'd once been? It was only the second time she'd heard any of them speak of the place, and it made her bite back the questions forming on her tongue.

Ven spoke from where he still checked the weapons strapped to her body. "For now—it's best if we keep our reasons for being there to ourselves. The Triarchy have been made aware of the breach in the human realm's wards, a few select others." He glanced around the room to where Karro and Seth stood. "If anyone asks, we're there to restock the armory. We aren't expecting a warm welcome anyway, so I doubt anyone will get too friendly."

"I thought the Allokin were your allies," she questioned.

"They are, but our relations have been strained since the war." Seth interjected from where he stood across the room, "The Allokin lost many of their people. They chose to isolate themselves. Some of them believed they never should have fought with the humans, that they should have barricaded themselves inside their Crystal City and let the rest of us fight it out, deal with whoever was left standing."

Ven cinched a final buckle into place against her arm. "Many Allokin have always felt the Blood Folk are beneath them. Good enough to protect the realms against demons—"

"But uncultured brutes all the same," Karro finished with a feral grin, as if he took it as a compliment. "They tolerate our visits to their realm because of our longstanding loyalty—better the devil you know." He winked.

"Ready?" Seth asked.

Ven looked to Aurelia, and she gave a nod, though not sure at all if she was ready.

Within moments, Karro's large form and Seth's lean figure disappeared in wisps of shadow. Ven extended a broad hand to Aurelia. His calluses a reassuring feeling under her fingertips as his shadows pooled and swirled around them and they plunged into weightlessness.

Chapter 37

Her boots landed on brittle pine needles. It took a moment for her balance to catch up, and when the ground righted itself, she saw they were at the base of the highest peaks in the Shades. So far up that the chill of winter was already here.

The heavy beat of wings broke the silence of the forest around them as Cog appeared, landing on Ven's shoulder.

"Sorry friend, you'll have to stay here—you make the Allokin uneasy," Ven murmured as Cog launched himself back into the air again with a disgruntled croak, finding a branch above them to perch instead, ruffling his feathers in irritation.

"Are they superstitious as well?" Aurelia asked as she drew up her hood, grateful for the thick fur that shielded her face from the harsh gusts of biting wind that snapped at their cloaks.

"He's gained a—reputation," Ven said with a faint smirk.

Her gaze slid sideways, not entirely certain that she wanted to know why the raven was so feared amongst another kingdom of immortals, but morbid curiosity getting the better of her.

Ven's crimson eyes glittered darkly. "For taking the left eye of his enemies—my enemies. Some eternal retribution that he seeks for the one he lost."

She gave a small nod, looking straight ahead to the rugged trail cut into the mountainside. "And did they deserve it?" she asked, the trace of a smile on her lips.

A small amount of tension seemed to leak out of Ven's shoulders at the question. "Every single one," he answered without hesitation as his eyes snagged on hers for just a moment.

Karro's footprints in the hard-packed trail swallowed up the imprint of her own boots as they ascended the steep climb up the mountain. She found herself grateful for the small amount of training she'd done at Ravenstone, her thighs protesting with every step.

Karro's broad back disappeared at regular intervals, scouting ahead on the trail before he would jog back to them. The three Wraiths looked like they could have trekked all day, and she wondered how much they'd slowed their usual pace to accommodate her.

"How did he lose his eye?" she panted, hoping that talking might help her catch her breath.

Ven walked beside her, his long legs eating up the trail effortlessly as he scanned the boulders and pines crowding the rough-cut path. "That—is only a story that Cog knows. It happened long before he came into my possession."

But that could only mean Cog was ... ancient. Somehow older than the rest of them. Aurelia whipped her head to face him.

Catching the look of incredulousness in her eyes, he added, "He was my mother's—well, as much as it's possible for a creature like Cog to *belong* to anyone. He was her companion for as long as I can remember ... And when she died—he chose me." His tone was full of reverence. Something underlying his deep voice that resembled unworthiness.

Karro paused at a stretch of forest where the pines began to thin out as the climb steeply angled toward the peak. He reached out his hand, touching the air in front of him. The space shimmered and rippled like quicksilver.

He took a step forward, and just like that, he was gone. His powerful shoulders completely disappeared through the mercurial surface of the portal. A second later, his large hand shot out from the space, open and waiting.

The memory of that night when she'd walked through the mirror was dredged up as Aurelia passed through the portal. The same icy fingers gripping her neck and shoulders. Resisting her entrance as she passed through to the other side.

The wind instantly subsided. The same crisp air surrounded them, but without the hounding gusts it was tolerable, the sunlight much brighter now that the trees had thinned out around them. The glistening sheen of early winter crusted some of the more stubborn leaves. The trunks encased in crystal as they glittered in the fading afternoon sun.

She turned to see that Ven and Seth were behind her again, and they'd been transported up to the very peak of the mountain. A trek, that if they'd attempted on foot, would have easily taken them a few days.

Her eyes followed the trail worn into the rugged mountainside, up, up, up, until it landed on the sprawling city above them.

Crystal towers reflected the sunlight like cut glass, and narrow spires jutted up to disappear into the clouds like icicles attempting to reach the heavens. Even from this distance, Aurelia could see the web of bridges seemingly suspended in mid-air between the buildings, the architecture of the city severe and sharp like the climate it inhabited.

"Eisenea," Ven said from where he stood next to her.

The view was breathtaking, partially because it seemed utterly impossible. A beautiful city built in the midst of the harsh landscape surrounding them. Ven's hand closed around hers again, his touch familiar now as his shadows carried them away.

Ven's wisps of shadow deposited them at the wide bridge that passed under the towering gates of the city, the crystal floor beneath their feet shimmering with light.

Sweeping toward them were three slender figures, appearing to hover just above the crystalline bridge. Their silvery white robes were similar to the ones that she'd seen the librarians wearing at Ravenstone, but much finer, the metallic threads casting an ethereal glow over the trio.

Two blonde males approached with a female, her hair the same shade of red as the tulips that bloomed on the Valley floor in springtime.

Ven fell to one knee, Karro and Seth doing the same as Aurelia dropped into a curtsy, her eyes trained on the silvery rainbow veins of the bridge.

The three Allokin came to a halt in front of them, their icy gazes landing on Ven. The taller male at the center stretched out a hand the color of ash. "Prince Ven."

"King Osmius, Queen Irid, King Galan." Ven dipped his chin to each of them, clasping the male's outstretched hand in return with an uneasy smile. "I renounced that title long ago. *Ven*, is sufficient."

"Blood titles are not so easily cast aside," the blonde king replied a bit coldly, turning to lead them across the bridge and into the heart of the city.

Aurelia glanced to where Ven walked beside her, but he stared straight ahead, clearly avoiding her gaze as they followed the Triarchy. Whatever had just passed between him and the King didn't seem to be something he cared to discuss.

The Blood Folk didn't seem to have a ruler—there were so few of them left that they seemed content to have Ven as their commander and leave it at that.

The rumble of the swiftly moving water was enough to drown out the footsteps of their procession. The deep blue river a shade of dark sapphire as it swept over the falls and churned down the mountainside in an unstoppable torrent. This must be the Kesh, but it was hard to believe the same muddy water that ran through the Capitol could originate from something so majestic.

Silver banners lined each side of the wide bridge, snapping in the crisp winter air, three white stars emblazoned on each of them. A glacial palace sprawled on the other side like a great slumbering beast, the stones polished and gleaming in the fading sunlight. Darkly veined white marble towered into the sky. Verandas jutted out from every floor, trailing into terraced winter gardens that tumbled down to the banks of the river. Arched walkways spanned the smaller brooks and waterfalls feeding into the raging river that cascaded through the rest of the city.

Statues stood guard at every entrance; crystal broadswords grasped in their cold hands as they were led up the wide sweeping steps into the Triarchy's glittering palace. The glistening entryway opened into a courtyard, burbling fountains and lush plants betraying the winter chill just outside the doors.

Pale blue-grey faces turned to watch them from the paths in the gardens, sparkling quartz eyes peering over the balconies above.

The Allokin were breathtaking, their graceful bodies seeming to float over the ground when they walked. The females' lithe figures were draped in silky fabric that clung to their delicate shoulders and narrow hips. The males were lean and tall. Hair of varying shades of blonde and red—not like Asher's coppery hair or her mother's beautiful auburn, but shades of deep rust and vermilion.

It made her thankful for the towering presence of the three Wraiths hiding her from view, the males surrounding her taking the full brunt of the curious looks. Earning appraising glances from more than a few of the females that were taking strolls through the gardens.

"I do hope you'll partake in the festivities tonight," The red-haired queen said with a tight smile. "We've prepared rooms for you and your... guests." Her eyes flitted to Aurelia.

"Thank you for your hospitality," Ven replied, and as the three Allokin parted ways from them, they were led away to their rooms.

As soon as the Triarchy were out of sight, Karro clapped his hands together. The thundering sound making the servant carrying their bags flinch. "Just in time for Nevedin!" his voice boomed.

"Best you lay low, brother. I doubt they've forgotten the incident from the last one we attended." Ven said.

"There's no proof I started that," Karro replied with a mischievous smile and a wink at Aurelia.

"So the brawl during the Allokin's sacred celebration of the First Snowfall just happened on its own?" Seth muttered from behind her, sending Aurelia into a fit of laughter that she had to muffle in the echoing hallways.

"I didn't realize the female was married ... It didn't exactly come up." Karro shrugged his broad shoulders. "I offered for her husband to join us."

Ven cleared his throat. "Regardless—let's all be on our best behavior."

The male in front of them stopped in the corridor, gesturing to the rooms on either side and with a shallow bow he left them.

"There must be at least twenty empty rooms in this place at any given time, and they still make us bunk together," Karro muttered with a shake of his head once the servant was out of earshot.

Color flooded Aurelia's face. There were only two rooms for the four of them...

Karro glanced over to where Ven and Aurelia stood near the other guest chamber door, quickly covering a smirk as he coughed into his hand. "Right, guess I'll have to deal with your snoring, Seth."

Seth ducked his head without a reply and followed Karro into the room across the hall without further discussion, the door clicking shut before Aurelia had a chance to protest.

She turned on a heel toward the other room. Ven was leaning in the doorway, his mouth curved in a suggestive smirk.

Gods, she was a grown female for fuck's sake. It shouldn't unsettle her so much to share a room with him. She'd shared her bed with Bastien plenty of times.

"I thought the three of you were used to sharing quarters—war camps and all that," she remarked, but somehow the words didn't drip with the sarcasm she'd intended.

"You're not staying in a room alone—not here," Ven answered, crossing his muscled arms over his chest, a booted heel hooking over his ankle, suggesting he had no intention of going anywhere else.

"What could possibly happen to me here?" She swept a hand to encompass their grand surroundings, a palace filled with people so beautiful they didn't seem real. And it was obvious that the most dangerous individuals in the city were directly across the hall from her.

"I'm not taking any chances," he replied sharply. "The Allokin may be vain and aloof, but they can be entitled pricks if given half a chance. End of discussion. If you'd prefer Karro or Seth stay with you, now's the time to speak up," he said with forced calm, the hard-set line between his brows daring her to argue. His eyes were like chips of garnet as they stared her down, seeming to glitter with anticipation at the prospect of a fight.

She broke off first, rolling her eyes as she let out a defeated sigh.

He held the door to their chamber open. "Shall we, Love?" he drawled.

She avoided looking at him as she stepped into the room, not wanting to see the triumph that was no doubt on his face. The room was high up. She didn't remember exactly how many floors they'd climbed, but enough that her thighs still burned from it. Their trunks had arrived by some magick she still didn't understand, stacked neatly against the bench at the end of the bed.

The bed.

She walked towards the window to take in the view. But mostly it was to avoid looking at Ven, who was already making himself at home. Unpacking his clothing and removing the less obvious blades from his body.

The large window faced the glittering city below. An unobstructed view of the grand bridge and the rapids now turning into molten gold in the early evening sunlight.

Ven's reflection appeared in the glass next to hers. "The city is quite beautiful," he remarked.

The pale pinks and lavenders of the sunset painted the crystal buildings the most beautiful pastels, and she couldn't have said how many minutes they stood side by side watching them deepen into saturated magentas and violets. If she dared to admit it to herself, he was easy to be around. That same familiarity she'd felt between them that first night she'd met him. How easy it had been to talk to him, to banter with him even though he was still mostly a stranger. She didn't feel that usual pressure to make small talk, and he didn't seem to feel the need to fill the silence with words as they watched the sunset slowly fade into dusk.

"Our meeting with Lanthius isn't until tomorrow morning," he finally said, and a little disappointment filled her chest.

She'd come here for answers, and every second they waited to piece together how the demons had been entering the human realm was another second the people she'd left behind were in peril. Impatience tugged at her as Ven turned away from the window.

"The Triarchy will expect our presence at the Nevedin ball tonight—don't be fooled by their indifference, they're very easily offended," He began removing his black gear without warning.

Aurelia crossed her arms, her gaze dropping to the floor, to the walls, to the bed... But it kept roaming back to where Ven stood shirtless, cuts of thick muscle shifting under the black whorls of ink that covered his chest. The pink staining her cheeks would have been evident from a dozen feet away.

When she glanced up again, Ven was shrugging on a fresh shirt and fastening the buttons. "Plus, their food and drink are renowned. I don't know about you, but I'm starving." Aurelia's stomach grumbled in response.

He removed an item from his trunk, a perfectly tailored jacket that looked nearly black. The charcoal grey of the fabric brought out the deep crimson of his eyes and his onyx hair, the cut of the collar following the sharp line of his jaw.

"I—I don't know if I have anything appropriate to wear for the celebration."

"You do," he replied smugly. When she raised her eyebrows in question, he only nodded toward the second trunk.

Opening the lid, she found a stack of neatly folded clothing. Picking up the items one by one, she felt the texture of thick sweaters and comfortably tapered pants like the ones she'd grown accustomed to wearing since being at Ravenstone. There were slips of silky material in the trunk as well. Beautifully sewn gowns and more practical clothing for the cold climate.

She plucked out a lacy scrap of fabric, realizing with a rush of heat to her face that it was the smallest set of undergarments she'd ever seen. The shirts she wore every day were so large that she hadn't needed to worry about corsets and underpinnings, though what she held up in the light could hardly be considered restrictive.

The intricate details of the lace were buttery soft, and she considered what they might feel like against her skin. Even with all of the beautiful clothing she'd had back in the Capitol, nothing could compare to these. *These* were clearly meant to be seen.

"I'll leave you to get ready then," Ven said, ripping her from where her thoughts had headed. She didn't dare turn around until she heard the door latch into place behind him.

The dress she'd found in her trunk was of slippery silk. Deep charcoal like the jacket Ven wore, but with an undertone of indigo that made her pale skin glow like cream and the deep russet of her hair gleam with strands of copper and burnished gold. Simple compared to the complex puzzle of laces and corsets that were in fashion in the human realm. But the gown was anything but plain.

The fabric felt like sin, clinging to her curves and cascading down her body, pooling in a slight train that flowed behind her as she walked. The smooth silk draped down to expose her back. Delicate chains held the dress in place over her shoulders, the sweep of fabric at the front dropping just low enough to expose the swell of her breasts. A little daring, but still elegant. Regal.

It made her feel confident ... Beautiful.

Chapter 38

The door across the hall was propped open as she left her room. Ven was leaning against the doorframe, his hands in his pockets as he spoke to Seth.

"I'll catch up with you later," Seth said, casting a glance over his shoulder.

That's when Aurelia noticed Karro's large body sprawled across the bed. The male grumbling as he put a washcloth over his face. "What's wrong with him?" she asked.

"The damn altitude," Karro mumbled from the bed.

Ven looked over his shoulder and gave her an approving rake of his eyes before adding, "He gets a little nauseous and a case of the spins every time we visit. It always hits him a few hours after we arrive. He'll be fine by tomorrow."

She shook her head as they left Seth to tend to Karro. "I watched him nearly bleed out on the table in your room from a demon wound and still manage to crack a joke, and all it takes is a little elevation."

"Does it inspire confidence to know he's probably the toughest of us?" Ven laughed.

A servant led them through the opulent floors of the Allokin palace to a glittering ballroom that would have put all her mother's parties to shame.

Stalactites made of pure, sparkling crystal hung from the ceiling high above their heads. Ice sculptures bubbled with pale wine, and the tables were laid out with decadent food. Every surface seeming to be inlaid with precious metals and gemstones that reflected and refracted the candlelight, but they were nothing compared to the people here—

Stunningly, impossibly beautiful in a way that seemed so far removed from anything human. Their bodies made up of graceful lines, their movements fluid. There was no mistaking these beings for anything but immortal.

"Enjoy yourself, but take care—" Ven whispered, "They like beautiful things." The low rumble of his voice trailed like fingertips down her spine.

Surely that wasn't possessiveness that laced his words. They flirted, they trained together—but there seemed to be an invisible line he'd drawn, never crossing it.

He brought her a glass of pale wine, and dozens of quartz-colored eyes watched him walk through the crowd. He received more than a few lingering looks from the females, a few of the males, too. Most were only fleeting glances, but some were brazen stares.

Ven's golden skin and ebony hair were only part of the reason, he was gorgeous after all, and it wasn't just the way he looked. It was the way he carried himself, the crowds parting easily for his graceful, unhurried stride. Well aware he was the biggest threat here. A Shadecat taking a leisurely stroll through the forest.

She felt the burn of eyes watching her as well, but after weeks of wearing nothing but oversized shirts, it felt good to wear something that flaunted her curves, made her feel beautiful even here in this kingdom of exquisite creatures.

She'd been content with her existence at Ravenstone, training with the Wraiths and helping Embra in her lab, and she loved that the males treated her like one of them. But she couldn't deny the flush of pleasure she had at receiving appreciative glances from the beautiful males here. It was nice to be seen—to be noticed. Though if she were honest with herself, it was only one set of eyes that she cared about, and even in her periphery, their unflinching attention branded her skin, making her feel raw and exposed.

A handsome blonde male crossed the ballroom, angling his body ever so slightly in front of where Ven stood next to her as he extended a slender, pale grey hand.

"Could I have this dance?" he asked, blocking her view of Ven as he took her hand in his own.

It was only as he led her through the crowd that she saw the way Ven silently glared at him over the rim of his wineglass, his gaze still burning down her spine even though she couldn't see him.

The male drew her into the center of the ballroom. "Celius. Prince Celius," he said with a faint smile, bending at the waist as the music picked up.

"Aurelia," she replied, following the other females and curtseying. Soon enough she'd picked up the steps of the unfamiliar dance. Thankful, maybe for the first time, for all the lessons her mother put her through.

"They've been hiding you away in that dreary castle." The prince grinned, his ice blue eyes sparkling as their palms met. The exact color of Bastien's. The thought hit her like a punch to the gut, the breath leaving her lungs.

Would she ever look into those eyes again? Was he still searching for her ... while she was here, safe, content.

The prince's perfectly soft hands snagged against her newly formed calluses, bringing her back from her thoughts. "You've never seen the splendor of the Crystal City, I take it."

Shaking her head, she fought to regain her composure.

A conceited smile curved his mouth. "I would have remembered if you'd been here before with the rest of them. That dreadful female that came last time had the disposition of a viper." He could only be talking about Nira, and she had to choke back her laughter. "You're much more pleasant to look at," he simpered.

The compliment was debatable, but she could only guess what Nira's response would have been to the prince's preening. She'd known plenty of men just like him in the Capitol, arrogant, self-obsessed, and utterly boring.

"I find Ravenstone to be quite beautiful, though a bit rugged if you've grown accustomed to comfort," she added with a bland smile.

"The landscape is beautiful, I must agree. But the company is rather lacking." He sneered, before he spun her away, his tone making a flare of irritation prickle her neck, but she only smiled indulgently. Better to keep him talking—the less he'd expect her to say about herself. "And do you find yourself lonely in the Blood Kingdom that you finally ventured here?" he asked, his lip curling in suggestion.

"Lonely—no. But there's an entire world out there, and I intend to see it all," she replied, keeping a well-trained smile on her face.

"Indeed. Well, I do hope our beautiful city does not disappoint." Suggestion laced his words. "Our evenings have many diversions to offer, and I'd be happy to show you."

She knew exactly what kind of diversions he had in mind, but thankfully the end of the song saved her from giving a response. Curtseying, she turned to leave, but the prince caught her wrist. A familiar look in his eye that sent a warning tingle along her spine.

"May I cut in?" a deep voice rumbled from over her shoulder.

Ven stood behind them, his dark hair falling just below the sharp line of his jaw, his crimson eyes focused on her.

And she was instantly transported back to that first night she'd met him, the first time she'd laid eyes on him, heard his deep, rich voice... Even then, there had been *something* about him that made her heart beat faster.

"We're not done here—" Prince Celius snapped at Ven.

But Ven only smiled at Aurelia, holding out his hand to her without so much as glancing in the prince's direction. The tips of his fangs exposed as he replied quietly, "I was asking the lady."

She grasped his outstretched hand, the familiar map of his calluses meeting her fingertips as the orchestra picked up again.

"I won't say I told you so," Ven purred in her ear before stepping away and bending at the waist.

"But you'll imply it," she laughed, raising her brows. "Jealous?" she asked, dropping into a curtsey.

"Of him?" His dark brows furrowed. He twirled her expertly across the dancefloor, his palm spanning the small of her back as he pulled her close. "Everyone knows the pretty ones are all talk..." His breath caressed her ear, all playfulness gone from his voice as it sent a lick of fire down her spine. The invitation unmistakable this time.

His movements were graceful and practiced, surprising her just a little. "I didn't realize the Wraiths had time for dance lessons." A smile tugged at her lips. "Seems frivolous when you could be training or killing something."

He smiled faintly, a solemn look darkening his features, and she was confused by the sudden change in his disposition.

"There was a time when the kingdom of the Blood Folk was like any other," he replied quietly.

Before the war had taken so much from them.

She wondered what it would be like if she returned to her home to find most of its people gone ... And she bit her tongue, cursing herself for saying something so careless.

"And are these—*diversions* something you miss?" he asked, his voice still low, the question catching her off guard.

She glanced around the ballroom. Gilded and glittering in the candlelight that bobbed overhead. The beautiful beings that surrounded them on the dance floor, elegant and proud.

"I thought maybe I did."

But as she looked closer, she noticed slender, grey-skinned Allokin tilting their heads to whisper. Sneering at whatever perceived slight or social infraction one of their beautiful peers had committed. So much about this place felt foreign, but so much of it felt familiar, too ... Funny how immortality didn't change much.

A stark contrast to the rough, guarded nature of the Blood Folk. Maybe not elegant and refined in the way the Allokin seemed to be, but brutal and honest in a way that had become familiar in a short span of time.

No ... she didn't miss it much at all.

Their palms met, the steps of the dance bringing the planes of their body flush with one another, and Ven tilted his head slightly, his lips brushing against her temple. "You are stunning ... In case I haven't said that out loud already."

A rush of heat flooded her face as her breath caught, and she was spun away again into a stranger's arms before circling back to Ven. Waiting like a pillar of dark stone, towering above the rest of the males on the dancefloor.

He deftly caught her waist in his broad hand on the final note of the song. And once the music died away completely, he still made no move to release her. His gaze dipped to hers with such intensity that she had to force herself not to look away. And she would have stayed trapped in that moment forever—

The crowded ballroom began emptying out into the chilled night air, the current of people tugging them along through the opened doors and onto the large veranda. Marble statues stood watch as the entire palace filtered out onto the stone balcony that overlooked the palace's winter gardens, and beyond, the banks of the Kesh.

Eisenea had been beautiful in the daylight, but it was drab compared to how it looked at nighttime. The city must have been protected by some sorcery that kept the howling wind they'd felt on their trek to the mountain peak at bay. Still, she wrapped her arms around herself, admiring the glittering lights below, reflecting like cut glass on the towering buildings and endless spires of the Crystal City.

"Are you cold?" Ven asked, moving to shuck off his jacket as concern creased his brow.

"No," Aurelia protested with a laugh, putting out a hand to stop him. "I'm perfectly fine, thank you." Her hand lingered on his chest for a little too long, but she couldn't bring herself to pull it away. She cleared her throat, finally dropping it back to her side. "Thank you for the clothing. It's beautiful."

He gave her a roguish grin. "Unfortunately, I can't take credit for that. But I'll be sure to pass along your thanks to Embra. She has much better taste than I do."

A small smirk tugged at the corner of her mouth, and she wondered if her friend's intentions had been entirely innocent when she'd packed the beautiful gown and the lacy undergarments for this trip.

"Look," he whispered, taking her hand into his own and pointing up at the sky just as a hush fell over the crowd.

A single speck of white floated down toward them. Quickly joined by another, and another, and another. Until a soft murmur of awe rose up from the crowd and she looked around to see the Allokin surrounding them were just as enamored with the falling snowflakes.

The hushed quiet stretched on for minutes. Every person in the kingdom seeming to enjoy the simple beauty of the first snowfall. The flecks of white gently swirled and eddied around them as Ven's hand closed around hers.

A singular, perfect note pierced the silence. A chorus of voices joining in from the balconies lining every floor of the palace, the sound wrapping and layering with harmonies in some ancient language that nearly brought Aurelia to tears. The singers stepped forward from where they were scattered throughout the crowds, dressed in shimmering silvery blue robes, each of them holding a large glass orb glowing with warm light. And as the song ended on one beautiful note, they released the orbs into the air, letting them hover and mingle with the snowflakes in a slow, peaceful descent into the river.

Silence enveloped the palace once more, only the echo of the final note lingering in the air, and finally, the rumble of conversation picked up again. But it wasn't until that moment that Aurelia realized one thing was missing.

No laughter of children. No high-pitched squeals of excitement as soft white powder dusted the ground and fell from the skies in gentle flurries.

"There are no children here," Aurelia murmured, almost to herself. Not even gangly adolescents, she noticed, looking through the crowds in the glittering palace. But she didn't hear them far below in the city, either—a sound that had become synonymous with every snowfall in the Captiol, children having snowball fights, trying to be the first to catch a snowflake on their tongue.

"No. There aren't." Ven rested his forearms against the railing, so close to her that she felt the delicious warmth of him seeping through her dress. "When our magick started dwindling, it was so gradual that it was easy to ignore it. But then all the kingdoms quickly realized it wasn't only the existing magick that had been affected—it was the creation of new magick as well."

A sad look crossed his handsome face, softening the sharp features for a moment. "Our bodies are different from humans. Pregnancy has always been longer and more grueling for our females, but—" He shook his head, "none of them have been able to bear children for centuries. We noticed it first in our kingdom, but soon we reached out to our allies and they confirmed they were experiencing the same thing."

And she considered then what the war had taken from them. Not only the Blood Folk and their depleted numbers, the loved ones they'd lost who had sacrificed themselves. But the Allokin, too. And no doubt the Green Folk as well. All of the kingdoms left without a future.

Even for races that possessed near immortality, it was a bleak thought. And somehow—after centuries—he'd found *her*.

Ven's profile was in stark relief against the night sky, his dark hair catching small glittering flecks of snow as he leaned against the railing, the top button of his shirt undone, exposing the black ink that crept up his chest and onto the side of his neck. A heavy metal chain glinted at his throat.

She'd seen it around his neck from the moment he'd brought her to Ravenstone, but whatever hung at the center always remained hidden just beneath the collar of his shirt, and she hadn't been bold enough to ask.

She placed her palm on top of where his large hand rested. Meaning to only keep it there for a moment. An acknowledgement that she didn't blame him for what happened to her. She meant to thank him—for inviting her into his world, his home, his family, when she might not have had anywhere else to go. For finding her before she'd had the chance to become one of the monsters she'd been taught to fear as a child.

But none of the words could escape her lips—not with the way he was looking at her now.

The sound of footsteps behind them made Ven's posture shift instantly, his hand going to the dagger hidden beneath his jacket as he shoved her behind him.

"The night is young!" Karro crowed as he skidded to a halt, slinging one arm over Aurelia's shoulders and the other around Ven's. Seth reached them a moment later, throwing an apologetic look their way.

"I see you're feeling better," Ven muttered, his stance relaxing.

"Turns out—there is a cure for altitude sickness." Karro leaned heavily between them. "Allokin Ale," he said thickly. "And Allokin females." He turned to wink at two red-haired Allokin nearby who gave him inviting smiles in return.

Ven let out a weary sigh as he braced an arm behind Karro's back, shifting his substantial bulk off Aurelia's shoulders.

"You look radiant, Ari," Karro slurred. "The climate really suits you," he added, his compliment so sincere that Aurelia laughed and patted the arm still hooked over her shoulder. "I can call you Ari, right?" he hiccuped.

"Of course, you can," she laughed as Ven let out a sigh. "So, where's this ale you spoke of?" she asked, turning to see Seth silently shaking his head and lifting his eyes to the heavens as the four of them made their way back toward the glittering lights of the party. The snow gently drifting down in lazy flakes as it dusted the city.

Chapter 39

For all their warnings about the Allokin, the Wraiths seemed to have no shortage of admirers here. And before long, a handful of Allokin females were batting their eyelashes at the three males, swaying their slender hips past the table where they sat.

After Karro griped for a full hour about the tiny finger foods circulating the party, he finally stood up. "I'm going in search of some real food," he bellowed. Tipping back the dregs of his ale, he slammed his mug down on the table before following a blonde that had been trying to get his attention all evening.

Seth stood up with a weary sigh, clearly used to Karro's drunk antics. "I'll make sure he doesn't get into too much trouble."

"It seems trouble is looking for him," Aurelia laughed, watching Karro's large body get drug into a dark corner by a slender blue-grey arm.

"Some more wine, I think," Ven said, clearing his throat and heading toward one of the bubbling ice sculptures spouting the pale sparkling wine.

A blonde-haired couple sidled up next to him as he was filling their glasses, the female placing a delicate hand on his muscled arm as she whispered something into his ear with a seductive smile. An unexpected flare of jealousy rose in Aurelia's chest, quickly doused as Ven gently removed the female's hand from his bicep, leaving the couple to stare after him in disbelief as he walked away.

Turning away to hide her laughter, a lean figure blocked Aurelia's view of the party, cutting her off from the crowd.

"I was hoping I might find you out here," Prince Celius drawled, extending a glass of wine to her. "Blood Folk males are so…"

"Intimidating?" she supplied with a bland smile.

He scoffed, "Hardly—I was going to say unrefined."

His pale gaze scanned the crowd around them, his slender shoulders seeming to relax a little when he didn't see any of the dark-haired males nearby.

Taking a step closer to her, he lowered his voice. "But if you'd really like to have some fun, I know of more than a few places where we won't be disturbed again." He smirked, the look of a male who didn't get turned down often.

Aurelia smothered the urge to roll her eyes. "Thank you, but I'm enjoying myself here." She took a sip of her wine, glancing around the prince, looking for any sign of Ven. Realizing now how far away they were from the rest of the crowd.

Prince Celius took another step closer to her, too close, catching a strand of her hair between his fingers. "Such an unusual color for your kind." He rubbed his fingertips over her lock of hair in a way that made her nauseous before dropping it again. "No need to be ashamed of it—bastards have more fun, or so I've heard ... No family name to uphold." He thought she was a bastard—

The prince leaned in, making the hair on the back of her neck stand up. "And the black hair and red eyes get so boring after a while ... Once you've had one—" he whispered into her ear, making her skin crawl as his body pressed hers into the unforgiving stone wall behind her.

"I'm not interested in whatever it is you have to offer," she said with icy calm.

She'd spent enough hours training on the Ledge with the Wraiths to feel capable of putting this prick on his ass, but she just needed to make it to tomorrow morning without incident. She *needed* to know how the demons had found their way into the human realm, and Ven's friend here in the Allokin kingdom seemed to be their only chance. They'd get their answers, and they'd leave—

His hand found the curve of her hip, the uninvited touch of his fingers sending bile into her throat. His pale eyes found the curve of her breasts, brazen as he ran a thumb across her collarbone, and she willed her pulse to slow, not daring to give the prince the satisfaction of thinking he'd affected her. Hating herself for enjoying the attention when she'd walked into the ballroom earlier.

"Come now, don't you want to go back to that dark, dank mountain keep and tell your friends about how you fucked an

Allokin prince?" His lip curled up into an oily smile as he pressed his hips into hers, and it took all of her self-control not to punch him in his perfectly straight, white teeth.

The inuendo, the outright propositioning she could have handled, but it was the continued insults to the Wraiths and their home that made fire lick across her shoulders as her temper heated.

Willing it to recede, she caressed the heat back into her veins. She couldn't do something that would compromise the reason they were here, the information they needed was too important. And nothing could get in the way of that meeting. Not even the urge to break the hand that lingered at her hip.

"Prince Celius," a deep voice rumbled.

"Commander," the prince drawled, as Ven stepped beside her. "I was just telling your ... friend, of all the pleasures Eisenea has to offer." Celius smirked at Aurelia as if they had some shared jest, and she had to swallow back the rage that was threatening to choke her.

Ven's eyes were liquid fire as he took a step between them, bringing his chest only a few inches from the prince's chin—forcing the other male to look up and meet his gaze. "I'm aware of *exactly* what you told the lady, and I'll remind you that she is a member of the Court of Shadow and will be given the respect due to her as an emissary of the Blood Kingdom."

The prince laughed, attracting the attention of a few Allokin standing nearby. They drew closer to the scene, morbid curiosity in their glittering crystal eyes. Hungry for entertainment. Haughty and distant.

And she finally saw the looks for what they really were. She understood now—the appraising stares that hid thinly veiled contempt.

The Blood Folk were a curiosity. An exotic delicacy to sample, but not equals. Something *other*.

Ven's posture relaxed beside her, but Aurelia knew it was an act. "You will apologize," he said with deathly quiet.

Shadows slithered along the balcony, snaking between the feet of the males and along the hemlines of the females. Unnoticed as they waited like sentinels for their master's command.

Karro and Seth had appeared at the front of the crowd. Nothing except sharp focus in Karro's red eyes, the threat of a fight sobering him up instantly. Seth's lean frame was coiled tightly, waiting.

The prince scoffed, making the lethal mistake of taking his eyes off Ven for even a second.

And the shadows struck like vipers, silently wrapping around the prince's throat, and choking off his laughter.

Gasps of shock perforated the low murmur of voices as the Allokin nearby backed up, looking toward the three dark males that had eaten up every square inch of the wide veranda.

Ven put a hand in his pocket, the other raising his glass to his lips and taking another sip of the pale wine as he waited for the prince to apologize. Anger flared in the prince's pale blue eyes but quickly gave way to panic as Ven's shadows tightened around his neck just a fraction.

The sound of grating stone filled the air, the veranda trembling as the crowds parted and scurried toward the palace—

The marble statues posted at every doorway were crawling from their perches high above the balcony, down the stone façade of the building, and lining up in formation around the Wraiths. Their crystal swords drawn with the sound of a blade against a whetstone to level at Ven.

Ven's mouth curved up into a wicked smirk, taking another sip of wine as the prince's eyes grew wild. Hands clawing at his throat frantically—finding nothing to grasp but wisps of air. All the outrage and arrogance draining from his face, his already pale skin leeching to ghastly white as two pale-haired males pushed past the ring of marble guards.

"What is the meaning of this?" King Osmius demanded, storming toward them.

"Indeed," Ven stated with deadly calm. "I was under the impression that we were welcomed guests here. Your closest allies—" He tipped his glass toward where the prince still stood paralyzed in front of him, completely at his mercy. "And yet one of your princes finds it acceptable to dishonor a member of our court."

"He forgets himself—" The king threw a scathing look at the prince, thinly veiled fear in his quartz eyes as he addressed Ven. "I'm sure it was a misunderstanding." His gaze landed on Aurelia for only a second as he lowered his voice. "Surely we would not throw away millennia of friendship between our two great kingdoms over a lack of manners."

"Of course not," Ven drawled, releasing the shadows that wrapped around the prince's throat without lifting a finger.

The prince fell to his knees in front of Aurelia, taking a great wheezing breath.

"But our emissary is still owed an apology," Ven added with a benevolent smile, as his shadows slithered away again to gasps and strangled shock from the crowd.

Prince Celius' pale eyes glittered with rage as he glanced up to where she stood. A snarl of contempt contorting his face until the King shoved a booted foot into his back.

"I apologize—my lady," the prince choked out, before he stumbled back to his feet. He shoved past the ring of marble guards, not daring to look back before disappearing through the crowd.

King Osmius offered a small dip of his chin to Ven before he barked, "Enough."

The stone guards dropped their swords back to their sides. The sound of grating rock filled the air once more as they climbed back to their posts above the walls and alongside the doors, retreating to the palace's façade.

The remaining crowd dispersed around them, casting wary glances at the Wraiths, and giving Aurelia a wide berth as they went back to their drinks.

"So much for being on our best behavior." Karro grinned.

"I expect we'll be hearing from mommy dearest before our visit is over," Seth murmured into his glass with a reassuring wink at Aurelia.

Ven drained his wine. "They were overdue for a reminder."

Chapter 40

They didn't speak as they made their way back to their rooms. Ven only gave a nod to Karro and Seth as they parted ways in the corridor. The pleasantly warm buzz from the glasses of dark brown ale Aurelia had shared with Karro melted away entirely after the evening's events, the prince's words making bile rise in her throat even now that they were safely back in their rooms.

If Ven hadn't overheard the disgusting comments, she would have swallowed them. She'd known enough men exactly like the prince over her lifetime to know that they were usually all talk. And if you stayed quiet and boring, they'd move on. Men who viewed her as an object. A possession. A conquest. Most of them respected her family's name enough to cover their desires in flowery language and romantic proposals—but some thought themselves powerful enough not to bother. Ones like the prince.

Seeing Ven's response to him ... No one had ever done something like that for her. No one had ever stepped in on her behalf. Not even when she'd been a mere child.

"You should get changed into your gear," Ven urged as he closed the door, his voice hushed as he put the latch into place.

It left her to wonder what the repercussions might be, and if it had been worth it. If *she* was worth it.

"You didn't have you do that," she said quietly as she stepped into the darkened bathing chamber.

"Yes. I did," Ven answered from the other side of the cracked door. There was silence as he paused, only the sound of her dress slithering to the floor of the bathroom.

"The Allokin nobles have been overstepping boundaries for too long." he finally said. And she thought back to the couple that had approached him at the party... wondering how many centuries he'd been dodging indecent proposals. "The prince was out of line," he muttered darkly. "Though you're strong enough to kick his ass yourself, you know," he added.

"I think he's learned his lesson," she laughed.

He huffed out a breath. "Prince Celius is not one to suffer a blow to his ego quietly—he'll be looking for revenge."

She heard him lean against the heavy door to their room as she quickly pulled on her gear in the dark, stepping into the bed chamber again. Ven shifted against the wooden door, hooking a booted foot across his ankle, dark gear covering his powerful body now.

So, they *were* expecting a fight.

Throwing her garments into her trunk, she reached for her boots. "If you're worried about the prince—we should leave."

He gave a singular shake of his head. "This meeting is too important. We've waited weeks for them to extend the invitation ... I would have done this sooner if I could have sliced through all their damned protocols and made the meeting with Lanthius directly ... But it would have stretched our already precariously thin alliance to a breaking point if I'd ignored the usual channels."

He rolled his muscled shoulders, shaking off the tension that he was trying to hide from her. "And if we leave now in the dark of night after such a public dispute—that opportunity will be closed to us. So we will wait. And we will act as if the matter is finished—handled. And we will hope that the Prince found even a drop of sense in the ocean of idiocy that usually dictates his decisions, and doesn't do anything *else* until we've seen to our matters and have left the city," he said decidedly, a quiet rage simmering beneath his words.

She looked up to where he stood, his dark silhouette eating up most of the door as his glittering crimson eyes found hers. "You shouldn't have done that..." she repeated quietly.

"He insulted you," Ven answered darkly, his voice laced with venom.

Casting her eyes to the floor, she uttered, "Other men have said worse."

His dark eyes snapped up to her face, biting back whatever words were on his tongue. "You're one of us," he replied with fire burning in his gaze.

She scoffed. *One of them.*

She lived with them, trained with them, but she couldn't come close to matching their skill. She'd still only managed to produce a few sparks at her fingertips after weeks of one-on-one training with their commander.

Someone who had a list that probably spanned the mountainside of things more important than defending her honor. More important than trying to coax whatever small amount of power she possessed into existence. More important than making sure she'd settled into her new life. And yet, he'd never made her feel unworthy of his time.

Whatever he saw in her—she was blind to it.

His voice was hushed in the dark silence of the room. "Do you know how the Wraiths were chosen?"

She knew it was a distraction to keep her nerves from fraying while they waited for dawn, but she played along, shaking her head.

"Hundreds of new recruits volunteered when I took over as Commander during the war. It was a prestigious honor to fight in the Blood Queen's elite force—still is." He crossed his arms over his chest.

"Months of training would weed out the ones who only wanted to be there for the title, but it was the final task that decided who was worthy of being called a Wraith." The edge of his mouth curved up. "They had to beat Seth in combat. No weapons. Only shadow magick and their wits." A breathless laugh escaped her as he added, "I allowed them limitless chances." Shrugging his shoulders, as if it that made it a reasonable request.

"Who could possibly beat Seth?" she asked incredulously.

A grin spread across his face. "No one. That's the point. The biggest and strongest always thought they could, but their egos usually got in the way, and after a few tries, most would give up." He leaned his broad back against the door, watching as she laced up her boots.

"It was the ones who tried again and again. The ones who never expected to beat him, because they'd been watching him. They knew exactly how dangerous he was, but they tried anyway. Knowing if they trained with him long enough, he would teach them where their weaknesses were and make them stronger, better—even if they never became a Wraith."

He moved to help her tighten the leather straps on her gear, handing her the jeweled dagger she'd left on the bed and moving back to the table to secure his own.

"They didn't become Wraiths because they beat him … But because they had their asses handed to them over and over and over, and they never stopped coming back for more," he said, tucking a knife into his boot and sheathing a set of daggers in the baldrick across his chest. "Because battles are not won by the biggest or strongest. They're won by the fiercest. They're won by those who know what they're fighting for and are willing to die defending it. Who fight to the brink of death and beg the Goddess for another taste."

Silence enveloped the room as she let his words sink in. Conscious of his gaze still on her.

The deep rumble of his voice was no louder than a whisper. "How many times have you sparred with Seth on the Ledge?"

A smile tugged at her lips, because he already knew the answer, but he wanted her to say it out loud. "I stopped counting."

"So did I," he replied with a grin.

And she wondered if he knew what he did for her in that moment.

She'd only just left the shambles of her old life and a man that she loved, the memory of that woman feeling so distant now that she couldn't be certain what she'd felt for Bastien.

At the time, it had been love … Or what she knew of it. But now, she wondered with no small amount of guilt, if maybe he'd just been the only thing she'd chosen for herself in her old life. The only thing that hadn't been dictated to her. Selected for her. Forced on her.

And maybe Bastien deserved someone who would look at him with more than just a hunger for distraction … He deserved someone who would truly love him. Someone that could offer him more than stolen minutes in the dark hours of night.

And how long would she punish herself? Months? Years?

She didn't choose this. She didn't choose the life that she'd fallen into, but the moments when her guilt was forgotten, maybe—just maybe—she was enjoying it.

She liked the way it felt to help Embra in her laboratory—needed, essential. She liked the way it felt to train on the Ledge, to be in control of her body in a way she never had before. She liked the way the males treated her, too. Like she was one of them, not a trophy, not something to be possessed—like she was an equal. Like she might be capable of anything. She even liked Nira, though the female still scared the shit out of her. She liked the quiet solitude of the cozy library at Ravenstone, where she could come and go as she pleased. Where candles were always left burning for *her*.

And maybe the hardest thing to admit, was that she noticed the way Ven looked at her—the same way he was looking at her right now—and she liked that, too.

He stood across the room, his usually perfect composure seeming to slip for a moment when his eyes snagged on hers.

She took a step toward him, and he matched her with prowling strides, until there was only a hand's breadth of space between them. Until she could feel the heat from his body seep through her gear and into her skin. So close that she could have plucked the heavy silver chain he wore around his neck from under his shirt, finally seeing whatever talisman hung on the end of it, next to his heart.

"Would you really have let one of the others keep watch over me?" she whispered, wondering how she managed to keep her voice even, with her heart threatening to pound its way out of her chest.

"If that's what you wanted," he said quietly, "They are honorable males."

But she didn't believe a word of it.

"And you're not?" she asked, swallowing hard as he took another step closer, towering above her until he was the only thing she could see.

"An honorable male would tell you that there's no future for us." One of his hands spanned the small of her back as he pulled her closer, a small gasp escaping her lips as the soft curves of her body met the hard planes of his.

And in a heartbeat, he spun her around and pushed her back against the door, hinting at the tightly controlled power in his body, poised like a cage around her. "An honorable male wouldn't kiss you right now," he whispered against her lips, tilting his head down, his crimson eyes dark and half hidden beneath the lock of black hair that had fallen across his face. His other hand warm against her cheek, his rough calluses sending a tingle down her spine as his fingers traced her jaw and tangled into her hair.

And just when she thought she might combust from standing still, his lips brushed hers. Soft and gentle. Somehow exactly as she'd imagined.

He pulled away, his hands still holding onto her as if she might slip away at any moment.

She glanced up to see him gazing down at her. "Do you feel it, too?" she whispered into the dark.

It was all she could bear to say ... The inexplicable pull she'd felt towards him since the first night she'd seen him. One that she had only just now admitted to herself. A feeling so terrifying that she nearly wished she could have taken the words back—but it wouldn't make them any less true.

"Yes," he breathed without hesitation, like a sigh of relief.

And then his mouth was on hers again, not as gentle this time, but with tightly coiled control that she was dying to snap. Hungrier. Harder with longing as he abruptly pulled away, his hands still wrapped around her waist, not daring to let her go entirely. His breath hard and uneven, his eyes liquid crimson.

Her skin felt feverish for his touch, her gear feeling unbearable as he kissed her again. Ravenous, matching the way she felt. The hard length of him pressing against her—

An urgent knock against the door had him reluctantly breaking off his lips from hers. A silent apology filled his eyes as he opened it a fraction.

Seth's voice murmured from the other side, "The Silver Guard are on the bottom floor of the palace. We need to leave."

Ven closed the door again with a soft click, muttering a string of curses as she stepped away to let Seth and Karro inside, but before she could move Ven caught her chin between his fingers—gentle, but unyielding until she looked up into his eyes.

"If you still want this when we return—I'll gladly oblige," he whispered wickedly into her ear. His breath sent a fresh wave of goosebumps across her skin at the promise in his voice. "I give you my word."

Chapter 41

Karro and Seth slipped into the room, still securing blades to their bodies as she tried to remember how to breathe. She had a feeling both males knew what they'd walked in on, studiously focusing on anything but her and Ven as they entered.

Seth palmed one of his smaller blades. "The wards protecting the palace stifle transporting magick—we won't be able to cast ourselves until we've made it past the border of the city."

Karro secured the heavy latch on the inside of the door. "I could use a little exercise anyway." He grinned darkly.

Ven walked to the window, judging the distance to the street. "The jump won't be too bad; it's trying not to hit every balcony on the way down that might be tricky. But it's our best option."

"Only option," Seth added as the sound of heavy footsteps echoed beyond the door.

A moment later the wood reverberated with pounding fists.

Seth threw open the window and climbed out, offering his hand to help Aurelia onto the marble ledge. Karro and Ven followed closely behind.

Seth grasped Aurelia's hand again, pointing silently to a balcony twenty feet below them, and without any other warning—leapt into the air, taking her with him.

The fall was nothing compared to what Ven had made her do in the Shades, and despite the danger they were in, a thrill of exhilaration shot through her blood as she tumbled through the air and onto the stone, soft thuds behind her telling her that Ven and Karro had safely made it out of the room, too.

The sound of splintering wood rent the night air above them and Ven yanked her back against the exterior wall of the Triarchy's palace, his body flattening hers. Heavy footsteps pounded above them as she held her breath.

The Wraiths were completely silent as they listened for the muffled voices above them, the tails of silver cloaks snapping just over the balcony's edge overhead. But soon the footsteps receded back into the chambers, and she took a gasping breath.

With one nod toward where Karro and Seth melted into the shadows of the balcony, Ven grabbed her hand, and they jumped again. At last, the wide veranda that had been crowded with Allokin nobility only a few hours ago was underneath them.

The marble terrace was dark and quiet now as Karro gripped the railing of the balcony and dropped soundlessly onto the stone. He held his arms wide as Aurelia lowered herself down next, his large hands gripping her waist and gently setting her feet. Seth and

Ven silently dropped onto the ground beside her, scanning the space.

Karro and Ven rounded the corner first, checking for a clear path through the palace's bottom floor, but the sound of grating stone made Aurelia stop short—

Behind her, the marble statues were leaving their posts beside the doors, a dozen more crawling down the marble façade of the palace. Seth was weaving between them to reach the other side of the terrace as they circled him.

He'd managed to dodge the first line of them, but a massive crystal broadsword swung low to block his path further down the veranda. The circle of marble guards tightened further, trapping Seth between them.

As panic flooded Aurelia's throat, shadows whipped out from behind her, coiling around the crystal blade blocking Seth's escape. The shadows lashed so tightly, that with one mighty heave the broadsword shattered into thousands of sparkling shards, scattering crystal across the marble veranda.

Seth slid underneath the statues' outstretched arms and grabbed Aurelia's hand, hauling her along into a full sprint as the heavy rumble of stone footsteps grew louder behind them. A dozen feet ahead, Ven and Karro held the palace doors wide for them, and they dashed through.

They flew through the empty ballroom, down the cavernous hallway that led into the lush gardens of the courtyard. Their feet pounded, eating up the distance between the Allokin palace and the crystal bridge leading out of Eisenea.

Under the grand entrance they sprinted, up the cobblestone road that gently curved to follow the Kesh and would lead them straight to the bridge—

As the bridge came into view, so did the wall of guards stretched from one side of the raging Kesh to the other.

Karro skidded to a halt first, letting out a hollow laugh. "I'm not sure if we should feel insulted or relieved he brought so few," he said, flipping a black-bladed dagger in his hand.

"Don't escalate this," Aurelia panted from beside him. She threw a glance toward where Ven had stepped beside her. "Not on my account."

The line of guards remained where they were, blocking their only path out of the city, their silver cloaks snapping in the night air the only sound as the Wraiths stood their ground. Each side waiting for the other to make a move.

A fiery-haired male broke the line, stepping forward to walk the distance between the guards and the Wraiths. Ven prowled forward to meet him.

"I'm sorry I have to do this…" the male uttered, his genuine apology catching Aurelia by surprise.

"So don't. Let us leave and we'll be on our way," Ven replied, sizing up the two dozen guards blocking their path out of the city. "And you won't be left with another one of your brother's messes to clean up."

"You threatened an Allokin prince," the male replied tightly, a jeweled crest pinning the richly embroidered silver cloak to his shoulder. His tone suggesting that he'd rather be doing anything else right now.

"We both know he deserved it, Agius," Ven answered.

"It doesn't change my orders," the male replied dispassionately.

Chapter 42

The cell door slammed shut with a metallic clink. More of the enchanted marble statues stood guard at intervals through the dark tunnels leading back out to the palace courtyard—to freedom. Although as far as dungeons went, Aurelia supposed this wasn't too bad. She'd heard stories about the ones underneath the Capitol, reserved for only the worst offenders. Dank and dark. A place where people were brought to rot away their lives. To be forgotten.

At least it was dry here.

Seth stood nearly as still as the stone guardians while Karro paced. Ven kept his eyes on the marble statues, testing them with bits of straw that he dropped from between the cell bars—seeing exactly how quickly they struck with their crystal broadswords to cut the pieces in two before they floated down to the floor.

The footsteps of the living guards had echoed into silence, a heavy door slamming shut somewhere far away.

"There must be something we can do to get out of here," Aurelia whispered, looking down at her hands and feeling useless.

"Allokin metal—" Seth tapped the silver bars of the cell. "Stifles all forms of magick."

"Even if we could, it's not worth the risk," Ven answered. "We'd have at least twenty of those to contend with before we made it out of here." He nodded toward the stoic, featureless face of the marble statue across from them. "And probably a few dozen breathing guards, too. And while I don't mind a challenge—I'd like to leave Eisensea on a less conspicuous note."

"What happened to sharing food and not coming to harm inside your host's walls?" she muttered dejectedly.

Ven crossed his arms over his chest, the movement bunching the muscles in his biceps, dragging her thoughts back to what it had felt like to have those arms braced on either side of her body…

Ven let out a weary sigh, bringing her back to their bleak circumstances. "They haven't *harmed* us … They'll just leave us here until Lanthius sends word to the Queen that we never arrived for our meeting."

"So we'll just rot down here?" she demanded, throwing her hands down in frustration as she began pacing behind Karro.

"I doubt we'll rot—it's just a show to quell Prince Celius' tantrum. His mother will come down and release us in a day or so as a show of good will," Seth answered from where he'd slid down onto the floor. "I doubt the Triarchy are even aware that the prince sicced the royal guard on us—they never would have sanctioned it. But it will be the public lashing the prince desires as the Silver Guard escorts us from the dungeons and out of the kingdom."

Aurelia looked to Ven, "What about the one on the bridge? He almost seemed to like you," she asked hopefully.

"Agius is a respectable male. If he weren't the half-brother and right hand of Prince Celius, I might even consider him a friend—but he'd never go against his brother's wishes."

She shook her head, letting it fall back against the cell wall and squeezing her eyes shut. If she hadn't come here, if she'd just given in to the prince's whims—

"Don't," Ven murmured from beside her. "I know what you're thinking. If anything, you should blame me for putting the prick in his place, and I won't apologize for that."

Hours dragged on before Karro finally stopped his pacing. Aurelia tried to sleep, but there was no getting comfortable here. Guards checked their cells at regular intervals, passing underneath the marble statues that stood watch through the night.

Watery light bled through the grate high above their heads, telling them dawn was nearing as another set of footsteps came past their cell.

A tall pale-haired guard stopped in front of their door. His broad smile was so out of place that Aurelia took a small step back as the set of keys in his hands clinked against the bars. The cell door swung open on rusty hinges, and the male stepped into a pool of torchlight.

Ven lifted his head, his eyes flaring with recognition. "Lanthius," he whispered, grasping the male's forearm and embracing him. "Aurelia, this is an old friend..." he chuckled in disbelief, "I wasn't expecting to see *you* here."

"Quite old, indeed," the male replied, grasping Aurelia's hand in his, his eyes the color of shattered glass. "I heard some Wraiths started trouble at the Nevedin ball," he laughed, letting himself into the cell and closing the door behind him, making the already tight space feel even smaller. "Pardon me," he apologized to Aurelia as he squeezed past her.

She glanced over to Ven who only shrugged his shoulders with a look that said, *I've no idea what he has in mind either.*

Lanthius raised a pale blue hand toward one wall of the cell, muttering a few unintelligible words under his breath as his palm flattened against the cinderblock. "You may want to take a step back, my lady," he said to Aurelia as a muffled rumble filled the small confines of the cell.

Seth and Karro leaned against the bars of the cell watching for any sign of guards while Aurelia stood awestruck as the large stone blocks collapsed in on each other. A lowly arched doorway appeared where only the wall had been moments before. And behind it, a staircase spiraled down into darkness just beyond the newly made threshold.

"Of course, if you prefer to make a mess—" Lanthius shrugged. "I wouldn't mind watching the prince get his ass handed to him."

"Glad to see my efforts in being a bad influence on you all those centuries ago haven't gone to waste." Karro clapped Lanthius on the shoulder, making the other male stumble just a step before regaining his footing.

"Come!" Lanthius whispered urgently, distractedly ushering them into the passageway. "We have much to discuss."

Seth and Karro went first, Ven taking up the place behind her as Aurelia descended into the darkened stairway, her heightened vision adjusting quickly.

Lanthius followed, sealing the doorway behind him with another wave of his hands. "I built it myself," he whispered to Aurelia, taking up a torch from the wall and removing a bit of rock from a pocket in his robe. "A secret, of course, in case I had to evacuate my apprentices during the war."

He placed the bit of dusty blue rock on the torch base, gently blowing on it until a flame sprung to life. "It comes in handy when someone's looking for me and I'd rather not be disturbed." He smiled mischievously, his eyes crinkling at the corners. She could see why the Wraiths liked him so much.

Lanthius's mannerisms were similar to the rest of the Allokin, the way they seemed to effortlessly float across the ground, the ethereal grace they all seemed to possess. But there was a frenetic energy to him that seemed so out of place here, a warmth about him—not the haughty, cold demeanor she'd come to expect from this kingdom.

"It's a left ahead," Lanthius whispered, careful of the echoing sound that bounced along the stone.

"No one will suspect you had a hand in helping us flee the city?" Seth asked.

"No, on the contrary, I have a feeling the Triarchy will be relieved that they won't have a mess to clean up tomorrow morning." Lanthius smiled ruefully, "Prince Celius may be in a state when he discovers you're gone, but the Kings and Queen will keep him in check. And no one will suspect a scholar who was locked in this study all night long—we're quite boring you know." He turned to wink at Aurelia.

They were careful with their footing, listening closely for Lanthius' directions, until at last the tunnel seemed to open up, and the Allokin scholar's posture relaxed slightly.

"We came to know Lanthius during the war. A master scholar in wards and spells," Ven said, clapping Lanthius on the shoulder.

"The least I could do," Lanthius deflected, "A small effort in keeping the realms safe." Aurelia already found herself liking him. Something about his disposition reminding her so much of her father.

"This isn't how I would have preferred to do things, but since you'll be remarkably absent for our meeting tomorrow, it's best

I tell you everything I can now," Lanthius said, directing them through a section of the tunnel that rumbled with the sound of rushing water, and she suspected they must be underneath the riverbed. "But first—" Lanthius' pale brows were drawn together with severity as he looked between the three males, "I need to know that you are quite certain you saw one of the Fengul in the Human realm."

Ven only gave a nod in Aurelia's direction. "You'll have you ask her. She was the one who killed it."

Lanthius turned his quartz-colored eyes on her with thinly veiled awe. "Tell me everything."

It felt like recalling a dream as she recounted the journey that brought her to this moment, but Lanthius never balked at any detail, only furrowing his pale brows as she told him of the demon she killed.

"For the Fengul to escape the lower levels of the Void—" Lanthius muttered. "Layers of wards guard every level," he explained to Aurelia, "Each level more and more difficult to break through, so as to contain the worst of its creatures." He stopped abruptly. "I know what power it would take to escape, because I was the one who built the wards."

Aurelia remembered the strange feeling of passing through the mirror from the human realm into the kingdom of the Blood Folk.

How the surface had resisted her passage, trying to pull her back. And that was with the wards broken, she could only imagine what it would do if fully intact.

"It wasn't only demons that were able to get out," Ven murmured. "One of the princes found his way into the human realm as well."

Lanthius' blue skin paled even further. "Which one?"

"Asmodeus," Ven answered.

The tall male's spine seemed to relax just a fraction. "He's powerful enough to pull his way out of the first level, especially if demons like the Fengul have managed to escape," Lanthius replied, guiding them through a series of forks in the tunnels below the glittering city.

Faint ringing sounded in the distance—so soft, that they all stopped, waiting in the dark silence as the chime sounded again somewhere far away in the city above them.

Aurelia turned to Lanthius, her eyes wide. "Alarm bells? Have they noticed we've escaped?"

"No—" the male replied, a look of disbelief clouding his eyes as he listened intently for the next chime. "I have not heard those bells ring in an age..." he whispered, his voice tinged with awe before he picked up his pace.

"We still don't know the full extent of the wards that were severed, is it possible the fracture could reach to the lower levels?" Seth asked.

"Possible?" Lanthius stopped. "At this moment ... anything feels possible," he said, more to himself. "But I don't think it's likely. We haven't been overrun by demons or the other princes, and they would have taken the first chance they had at freedom."

He turned to Ven. "You went to see the wards for yourself, they weren't damaged enough for demons to enter on their own, even before we began repairing them." He paused for a moment as a thought struck him, his crystal eyes widening as they met Ven's. "But there are other ways for a demon to escape the confines of the Void."

"You don't mean someone summoned one," Karro interjected. "Who would risk that?"

Silence enveloped the tunnel again, Aurelia lost as to whatever passed unspoken between the Wraiths and the Allokin scholar, until finally Ven's voice rumbled through the passageway.

"Someone who does not remember what they are. What their master is capable of..."

And it struck her.

"Someone in the human realm?" Aurelia whispered. "But how?"

Seth spoke from where he walked behind her. "The humans used to wield residual magick once, is there a spell that could widen the crack enough to call forth a greater demon?"

"There are few records." Lanthius answered, ushering them across a narrow bridge. "Most never lived to tell the tale of how they did it. But with the wards in place, even severed as they are … A spell couldn't produce nearly enough magick on its own to summon a greater demon. And definitely not one of the Fengul—they only answer to one master," Lanthius muttered to himself as the rest of them could only guess where his mind was going. "Unless the Fengul thought they were being called by him."

"If the King of the Void had escaped his confines, we wouldn't be here to discuss it," Karro replied grimly.

"No, that much is true," Lanthius contemplated.

"But what if a drop of his power made them mistake the call?" Aurelia asked, making Lanthius and the Wraiths pause, four immortal pairs of eyes turning to look at her. "The relics that were separated after the War—they harnessed his power," she continued hesitantly, trying to remember the exact details she'd read in the book at Ravenstone.

Silence echoed so loudly through the tunnel that she nearly questioned whether she'd said the thought out loud.

But it was Seth that finally spoke, glancing to where Ven stood, "Two were never recovered after the war."

"And maybe one has been found," Ven replied, his voice a low rumble.

They'd been following the same stretch of tunnel for the better part of an hour before daylight glowed softly into the passageway.

Lanthius waved a grey hand toward what looked like a dead end in the tunnel, revealing snow-dusted ground sloping steeply down the mountain peak. Aurelia moved to follow Seth out into the Shades, where the passageway had deposited them well outside of the city.

Lanthius put a pale grey hand on her forearm to stop her. "The Fengul never could have entered the human realm without assistance. And the Dark King never would have let someone else have control of his pets unless he was getting something in return." His crystal eyes narrowed sharply on her, seeming to see through the shallow details of the story she'd given him. "Tread carefully, my lady," he uttered, giving her hand a parting squeeze. "Send word to me if you find anything else, I'll do my best to research any other possibilities," he murmured to the others.

"Stay safe, old friend. And thank you," Seth said, grasping Lanthius' arm.

Karro wrapped the male in a bear hug, Lanthius' eyes bulging slightly as the Wraith crushed him against his broad chest.

Ven fell back, the murmured conversation between him and Lanthius too soft for her ears to distinguish as she followed Seth and Karro down the mountain, only dark smudges against the white peaks where they'd walked through the wards of the Allokin Kingdom.

She turned to glance behind her, but the glittering beauty of the Crystal City above them had dulled. And not only because she'd seen the darker side of the beautiful, brilliant kingdom...

Someone in the human realm was responsible for opening the doors for demons to come crawling through. The same person responsible for her father's death. For threatening the entire human realm.

Why would someone do this? *Who* could be capable of something like this? She didn't know where to begin, but one thing was certain.

She had to go back.

Chapter 43

They landed softly on the floor of the Shades, now coated in a thin dusting of snow. The forest was silent around them as the shadows dispersed.

Aurelia went to take a step, but Ven's arm snaked around her waist before she could move, his other hand clamping over her mouth as he scanned the tree line, gently releasing her to unsheathe one of the daggers strapped across his chest.

Twilight fell over the Shades, distorting the shadows until they seemed to separate from the trees surrounding them, slinking across the forest floor in a disjointed march. But Aurelia realized too late that they weren't shadows...

Karro stepped beside them, his stance subtly shifting in front of her. Seth silently removed the blade strapped across his chest as Ven pressed into her back. The scent of sulfur burned her lungs. Demons.

They crept closer, dozens of them, even more grotesque than the Fengul or the Arachnadae. They almost looked like—

People.

Their faces were stretched and contorted as they trudged closer to where Aurelia stood hidden between the Wraiths.

Dark flame erupted from her left. Ear-splitting screams pierced the night as a handful of the demons in front of Ven went up in smoke, scorched earth where they'd been standing a moment before. But the other demons didn't seem to notice, or they didn't care, still herding toward them.

Shadows pooled along the ground to meet the demons at the front, and Aurelia glanced to her side to see Seth's hands raised, sending dark tendrils coiling tightly along their limbs, making them stumble and fall to the ground.

Karro stepped forward to deliver the killing blows with his gleaming black blade. "Winner claims a weapon of choice," he grunted.

"If you've had your eye on my hexes, you'll be sorely disappointed," Seth said from the other side of her.

Aurelia drew the jeweled dagger at her thigh, gripping it so tightly that her knuckles turned white.

"I won't make you give up all of them, just a few." Karro slashed his blade through another demon, gutting it, as it burst into a cloud of ash.

Aurelia stood frozen between them, watching them take down demon after demon. Their movements synchronized, aware of each other at all times without taking their eyes from the advancing enemy.

A dark streak moved across the sky, cutting through the trees silently as it shot past. But Ven only spared it a glance, continuing to cut down the demons around them.

"Reminds me of Skyhelm," Karro barked, as his blade gracefully arched to detach two demons' heads from their bodies.

"Except you'd joined the fray to avoid the wrath of that Gandrian commander, if I recall," Ven gritted out through his teeth as he lashed out with fire from one hand and tendrils of shadow from the other.

"Well how was I supposed to know it was his daughter?" Karro panted, letting his blade drop for a moment to catch his breath as another demon shambled forward.

Seth gave a flick of his wrist and something dark whipped past Aurelia's head, curving to hit the demon squarely in the neck. The thin circle of ravenstone carved into six wicked points protruded from the demon's neck for only a moment before the creature tumbled into a pile of ash.

"Because she dined at the head table next to him the night before—you'd been introduced multiple times," Seth said.

"No." Karro wiped his face, a dark streak smudged across the handsome features. "I think I would have remembered that," he replied with a roguish grin.

"Not eight ales deep," Ven grunted, dispatching the last remaining demon with a well-placed dagger.

Karro's boisterous laugh filled the empty forest. "That feels like his fault for providing *very* good ale." He bent to pick up the nasty looking throwing blade, handing it back to Seth. "Besides, she approached me," he said with a shrug and a wicked grin.

"You always did like the assertive ones." Seth smiled faintly, shaking his head. "By my count, I'll be keeping my hexes," he added, fastening the gleaming black disk to his gear, just as another flash of movement caught their eyes.

More.

The sight made Aurelia's heart leap into her throat again. She knew the Wraiths were experienced, capable of handling this. But there were so many. A seemingly endless amount of those awful looking creatures. So similar and yet so completely unrecognizable as people.

A chill crept down her spine as Ven's words replayed in her mind.

All his demons were something else before—something alive. Until he got a hold of them.

She watched, entranced, as the three dark males surrounding her engaged in a deadly dance with the horde of demons. Ven lashing out with fire, Seth sending tendrils of dark shadow to restrain the creatures while Karro made short work of dispatching them with his blade. No quips or banter this time, just the sound of death.

She saw it now—the terrifying beauty of them all. Graceful and sure with their strikes. The hard-won muscle covering their bodies put to use doing what they were born to do.

Kill.

She'd only ever seen Karro's boisterous laughter, his easy smiles, the hearty slaps on his brothers' shoulders. She knew he was dangerous from his instruction on the Ledge—but to see it in action…

All of the jests they made were accurate it seemed. Seth was the one to fear despite his quiet demeanor. The lean cords of muscle down his arms and across his shoulders every bit as dangerous as the hulking mass of Karro's.

And Ven.

Gods, he was beautiful to watch, his body all hard lines and swells of muscle, gracefully moving as he coiled shadows around the demons throats with one hand and threw spears of flame with the other. Beads of sweat were forming at his brow and dampening the strands of hair at his neck. An avenging god delivering death as dark flames erupted from his fingertips. If she learned to possess even an ounce of that control one day…

Over and over the demons fell, but still they came. The Wraiths lashed out with their shadows and their blades, relying more and more on the weapons as the flood of demons continued. She wondered if it was because they'd drained their magick.

How much longer they could keep this up?

She held her blade out in front of her. Not as lethal as them certainly, but not useless either.

Heat had been building under her skin since the very first prickle of fear, slowly flooding her veins, ready and waiting, but it felt wilder now—the fear and adrenaline making it surge and recede. Her fingertips glowed white, crackling softly with barely controlled energy as she watched the Wraiths fight off demon after demon.

Thunder rumbled somewhere in the distance, a storm approaching over the mountains as Ven stepped out into a circle of demons, trying to move away from where Seth and Karro were fighting. And it happened in a split second—

One of them crawled across the ground, grasping Ven's calf with a clawed hand that sliced through his gear, enough of a distraction that three more descended on him.

Panic rose in Aurelia's chest. She held her breath, waiting for his hand to emerge from the pile of demons on top of him. She glanced to where Karro and Seth were busy fighting off a dozen more. There was no way they could help Ven without putting themselves in a worse position.

Her magick crackled and sizzled along her nerves with restless energy, begging to be let loose. And Ven had been right about her. She was scared. But not of hurting *someone*.

Scared of hurting *him*.

The memory that came unbidden to her every time she trained with him, every time he prodded and poked her into exposing her magick, or at night when she was on the edge of sleep ... The angry red blisters that had marred his perfect golden skin, the fabric of his shirt singed away to burnt scraps as he held her.

More demons shambled over toward the frenzy, the scent of blood seeming to draw them in. Too many to count, emerging from the thickly wooded forest, one after the other.

The reckless, wild magick that was hidden inside of her was dangerous—but it was *hers*.

Hers to control. *Hers* to command.

And rage unfurled from Aurelia.

Everything went silent, every movement in slow motion as a blast of light shot from her fingertips. White heat crackling and surging toward the demons that had overtaken Ven. But it wasn't fire that enveloped them...

Her magick arched gracefully, the blinding white tendrils branching over the demons crowding around Ven, throwing them into the air with its force. Splitting off again to strike another dozen nearby, blasting black holes into their chests and leaving only charred husks behind.

Aurelia held her breath in the aching silence, struck frozen with horror as she looked at the pile of scorched demons that slowly began to disintegrate into grey ash.

At last, from under the rubble and charred bodies, Ven emerged. Covered in ash and grime, but alive. And Aurelia finally let herself breathe a sigh of relief.

Shock widened Ven's crimson eyes just a heartbeat before a flare of pain lanced through her shoulder.

The stench of sulfur suffocated her moments before she was being drug backwards. Her boots scrabbled for purchase against the hard ground. Her gear tore against the rocks and dirt as she fought the demon digging its claws into her back, trying to drag her away from the clearing where the Wraiths were busy fighting off at least ten more of them.

A spear of flame shot out, passing so close to her face that it kissed her cheek with its heat.

The claws latched into her shoulder immediately loosened, and the sulfuric ash stung her eyes and coated her mouth. She heard Seth shout out in panic through her coughing and sputtering, trying to wipe away the grime coating her face.

A shadow hit the ground beside her, and lightning crackled at her fingertips, ready and waiting as she whirled to fight off another attack.

Black boots crunched the dry pine straw next to her head, and she looked up to see Nira's fierce eyes staring down at her.

The dark female only glanced at Aurelia before she sent out dark whips of shadow to coil around two demons that had managed to get Seth on the ground. Slashing her arms down, the movement ripped their torsos in two, the top halves of the demons crumbling into dust before they even hit the ground.

"Get her out of here!" Ven roared, helping Seth back to his feet as more demons attacked.

"No!" Aurelia screamed, just as Nira's hand grasped her own. Her feet were firmly planted on the ground, the crackling lighting at her fingertips ready to be released again—but it didn't matter.

In seconds they were ripped away by Nira's shadows, thrown to the ground outside of Ravenstone's black gates.

Aurelia whirled around to face Nira. "Take me back!" she raged.

Nira planted her feet in a wide stance, crossing her arms over her chest. "I can't do that," she ground out firmly, gazing down the narrow bridge of her nose at Aurelia, unmoving as the marble faces of the Unnamed.

"Take. Me. Back!" Aurelia shouted again, taking a step forward until her chest was level with Nira's, even though she knew it was suicide.

Nira's crimson eyes met Aurelia's golden ones as her face remained impassive. "You'll only put them in more danger."

She didn't say anything else, letting the words sink in. And they stung because it was the truth.

Her power was unpredictable. Still unwieldy. The Wraiths were like a well-oiled machine. Fine-tuned in fighting together. She was more likely to get one of them hurt.

After a few moments of silence, Nira finally said with surprising gentleness, "They've done this a thousand times—you need to trust them."

The fight leaked out of Aurelia as she nodded her head, following Nira across the bridge into the black fortress.

Chapter 44

The shaking began only a few minutes after they'd made it through the doors. Uncontrollable spasms that rattled her bones and her teeth despite every effort to sit still.

Nira had been ready with a glass of the synthetic blood, extending it to Aurelia and saying, "You're going into shock."

But it was just another bitter reminder that she wasn't one of them. She wasn't battle hardened. She couldn't fight like them. She was a liability, and that's why she'd been brought back *here*.

Embra silently tended to the wounds in her shoulder, the burn of the demon venom much easier to tolerate now that she'd gone into stasis. But that had been what felt like hours ago, and now that the shaking had subsided, the stillness was worse somehow, leaving her to pace the floor while she chewed her nails to the quick. But she had to do *something*.

The door creaked open behind her.

Ven's black hair was clinging to his neck in damp ebony waves, a constellation of dark specks splattered his face and hands. The smell of sulfur was laced with a sharp unpleasant metallic scent that stung her nostrils as he took two long strides to where she stood.

He raised his hands to cup her face, his crimson eyes taking in every inch of her as if to reassure himself that she was alive. Unharmed. Safe.

He looked like he'd been through hell, but the deeply furrowed crease between his brows softened as her eyes raked over his body, searching him for any signs of injury, any hint of pain. Something loosened when she found none, making her dizzy with relief. And the swelling emotion in her chest caught her off guard.

He was alright ... He was safe...

And that's when her relief quickly bled into outrage.

"Don't ever order me away from a fight again!" she fumed. Her venomous anger turning her words into a hiss. "I had every right to be there with you. Fighting beside you!"

Ven balked, his eyes narrowing at her tone. "You can't control your power yet—it's still wild." He raised his forearm, displaying the singed fabric of his gear where her magick had burned a hole through the sleeve.

"I'm sorry..." she choked out, bringing a hand to her mouth.

He shook his head, scrubbing a hand over his face. "I don't give a shit about that!" He grasped her hands in his. "Don't you understand?" he pleaded, "I can't have you out there putting yourself in danger ... You're a distraction. I wasn't watching Seth's back because I was worried about you ... I needed you here." He stabbed a finger at the black stone floor beneath their feet. "Safe."

Rage bubbled to the surface again. "And let all of you put yourselves in danger?"

She knew she needed training. Her stronger body still remained untested, but keeping her sheltered in the fortress would do nothing to remedy that, and she'd be damned if she sat idly on the sidelines in her life here, too.

"Don't ask me to stand aside," she uttered.

The molten fire in Ven's eyes receded into something so vulnerable that she had to look away.

Strong fingers grasped her chin, and he lifted her eyes to meet his. "Do not ask me to forfeit your safety," he whispered.

Their breath mingled in the small space between them.

It took her right back to the night before, to that room in Eisenea ... The promise he'd made still fresh in her mind. But admitting that she wanted him was dangerous. Even to herself. And she saw the same understanding in his eyes as he finally released her.

She walked to the bathing chamber, returning a few moments later with a clean cloth and a small wash basin filled with warm water. She held it out to him.

Ven took the cloth from her. "Thank you," he said, his crimson eyes never leaving her face as he scrubbed it over his hands. Rinsing it methodically before scrubbing it over his face, like a ritual he'd done hundreds of times.

Caked demon blood sloughed off, tinting the water grey.

"Are you alright?" she asked, feeling the heat of his gaze still on her body.

He turned away, tugging off his bandolier, heavy with black-bladed daggers. "Yes."

"Karro? Seth?"

"They're fine too, only a few scratches." He unbuckled the straps securing knives to his legs and arms with practiced hands, dropping them onto the table nearby. Muscles shifting across his broad back as he peeled away the outer layer of his gear.

The urge to touch him—make herself believe that he was truly alright, was overwhelming, but she stopped herself. The conversation she'd been dreading since they'd left the Allokin kingdom ... The realization that had been left unspoken between the two of them hung heavy in the air.

"I have to go back," she whispered.

He straightened slightly, though he didn't turn to face her. "I know," he answered, removing the chain from around his neck and tucking it into the pocket of his discarded gear.

The Blood Folk didn't strike her as the kind to be superstitious, but clearly whatever was suspended from the heavy silver chain was something very dear. Maybe a token from a past lover ... or a current one.

Was that why he'd said there was no future for them? They'd made no promises to each other, and she couldn't put a name to what she felt toward him.

He removed his shirt next, the dark fabric clinging to the swells of muscle along his stomach in a way that made her breath hitch—not all of the blood was demon blood. A set of claw marks were sunk down deep into his skin, fresh blood still leaking from the wound. He winced, peeling away the fabric.

"Let me get Embra," she said, starting toward the door, but his hand shot out and wrapped around her arm before she could even make it a step.

The movement opened the ragged gashes further. "Don't—I'll be alright," he answered with a tight grimace.

He pressed the cloth to his side trying to staunch the bleeding, but even she knew that it wasn't enough.

She held out her wrist to him. "Here—"

"I'll be fine," he replied gently, falling into the chair, his head tipping back in exhaustion.

"You've been offering me your blood since I went into stasis. Drink," she demanded, wondering why he refused her.

"You don't understand what you're offering," he answered. "I do." His eyes glazed over just a little.

"Then explain it to me and be done with it." She crossed her arms over her chest, resisting the urge to pace again.

"It's like a window into someone's power. It's a vulnerability to let someone tap the well of your magick—intimate," he mumbled. "Like an exposed nerve…" he trailed off, the words no longer making sense.

Whatever he was mumbling about was a conversation they could have later, when his eyes didn't have that half-unconscious look to them. "It doesn't matter, drink for fuck's sake!" she shouted.

His eyelids closed for just a breath too long and she gave his cheek a light smack just to make sure he hadn't lost consciousness. He gave her a sleepy smile as they fluttered back open.

"Later ... We'll have to talk about that mouth of yours," he drawled, his speech garbled in a way that made her nervous.

"I think it's too late to be a good influence," she retorted, grabbing one of the newly cleaned blades from the table and pressing it to her skin like she'd watched him do for her dozens of times.

"Oh, you misunderstand me," he answered with a dazed grin. "I'd like to discuss how utterly undoing it is to hear those dirty words from your beautiful lips."

She rolled her eyes, heat blooming in her cheeks as his head lolled to the side.

The slight sting of the blade cutting into her wrist was nothing compared to the flare of panic she felt. Blood welled up along the black edge of the dagger and Aurelia pressed her wrist to Ven's mouth, holding his head in place until she felt the feather-light touch of his tongue against her skin. Stronger with every sweep he made. After a few moments, his hands raised to grip her arm in place, and he lifted his head again.

Then she felt it.

A fleeting sting as his fangs pierced her skin, sinking into her. Delicious pain giving way to dizzying exhilaration. The sensation flushing her body with liquid heat just as Ven's eyes opened, focused once more.

He released himself from her just as suddenly.

"You shouldn't have done that," he panted, wiping a hand across his mouth. And she watched as the deep claw marks across his abdomen knitted themselves back together.

Frustration boiled up in her throat. How dare he stop her from giving him what he had offered freely since she'd arrived. She'd give him every drop of her blood if she damn well pleased—

"Lightning," he whispered in disbelief. He looked at her with such awe that her mouth clamped shut again. "Karro told me you called down lightning from the skies to kill those demons that attacked me, but I—I didn't quite believe it." A misty-eyed look clouded his expression as he watched her intently.

"Is it so different from your flame?" she asked, trying to mask the rising panic in her chest as she turned away from his searing gaze.

She looked down, watching the two neat puncture marks in her wrist seal up instantly. If it wasn't flame that she wielded … what did that make her?

"It makes sense why we weren't getting very far in our training up to that point," he answered, his voice rough. "How could you call your power forth when you did not know its name?"

"What does it mean?" she asked hesitantly, not really wanting to know the answer. Not wanting to hear that she didn't actually belong here—with them. With *him*.

"I'm not sure," he said softly, like he was trying to make sense of it all, trying to make sense of *her*.

He leaned forward again in the chair, dropping his head into his hands to rub his temples. "There was one other request I made of Lanthius before we left," he whispered quietly. "I asked him if it was possible to create a spell that would let you pass through the wards without resistance when they seal off the human realm."

Pushing himself to his feet, he turned away to collect his things from the desk, his voice low. "So that if you choose to return for good ... You would have access to blood when you need it. It would only be a short window of time every month, but it should be enough to sustain your magick and still keep the wards intact."

The words seemed to pain him, even with his back to her, the knot of dark hair at the nape of his neck coming loose in a way that made her want to run her fingers through the onyx tangles.

"I didn't want to say anything before I knew it could be done. I didn't want to give you hope of returning to your ... life, until I knew it was possible."

His words struck her so hard that she couldn't breathe for a moment. Taking in the sharp profile of his face in the darkened room, the broad shoulders and spiraling bands of black ink that had become so familiar to her.

She swallowed hard as he made his way to the door.

"Thank you, Ven," she whispered.

He turned to face her, his crimson eyes holding her hostage along with her ability to breathe before he slipped out of the door, shadows trailing after him.

Chapter 45

Go back.

And not just to see her family one last time. She knew she needed to return to track down whoever had been summoning demons, but Ven presented her with the choice to *stay*. To go back to her family. Her home. For good.

It was what she had so desperately wanted since she'd ended up here.

But would her family love her still, once they knew what she was?

She could keep up appearances for a while. Years, decades maybe. But eventually they'd find out what she was when she didn't age like the rest of them. Maybe she'd learn to control her power enough to hide it, but she knew if there was ever a threat to any of them, she wouldn't hesitate to use it ... And then what? She couldn't pretend she was the helpless thing she'd been when she left.

And Bastien...

She'd let him go already in her heart, thinking she'd never see him again.

Ripping off the covers, she threw on the closest pair of pants and hastily buttoned her shirt as she left the chambers. She couldn't stand to lie in bed with her thoughts any longer.

Padding through the now familiar maze of caverns and corridors, she pushed open the heavy doors of the library to find candles already burning upstairs. Each floating torch along the stairway flared to life as she made her way to the second level.

When she found herself in her usual corner, Ven was already occupying one of the chairs, a cup of black coffee in front of him along with a stack of books.

He glanced up to where she stood, snapping his fingers as she wordlessly took the chair beside him. A cup of coffee appeared, swirled with cream—exactly how she preferred. He inclined his head to her without lifting his eyes from the page, and her shoulders dropped in relief that he didn't bring up where they'd left the conversation in her chambers.

They were both treading carefully. The things she wanted to say to him—things she almost didn't dare admit to herself—would only make leaving here that much harder. But he'd been clear with her that night in Eisenea. There was no future with him.

But even if there wasn't, she would miss *this*.

Ravenstone. Karro and Embra and Seth. Even Nira.

She wasn't sure what to call them—*friends* wasn't enough to describe what they had come to mean to her, but family felt like a word she couldn't claim.

Ven handed her a familiar book from the stack on the low table between them, a welcomed distraction from her thoughts. She'd only flipped a few of the worn pages when large sketches stopped her. The relics.

He tapped the picture in front of her, finally breaking the tension that had filled the air between them. A rendering of a brutally beautiful crown filled the page, its edges crafted into sharp spikes.

"The Allokin have kept safe watch over this relic since the war. Warded and guarded so well that even Lanthius doesn't know where it's kept."

A large broadsword was on the next page. Something akin to the ones the blue cloaks strapped down their backs before they left on patrols near the Shades. But this looked... monstrous. She couldn't imagine the strength and size of the male capable of wielding it.

Even mere drawings of the objects felt wrong. *Off*, somehow in a way that made the hair on her arms stand up, fighting to keep her gaze on the pages even though her body was begging her to look away.

"The sword remains in our possession." Ven turned a few more pages, shifting his body just a little closer to hers so that their knees nearly touched, holding the book between them. "Which leaves the scythe and the ring..." he uttered, flipping further, revealing a wickedly curved blade much like the ones used in the fields this time of year nearing the harvest. But it was the last sketch that made her take a sharp inhale.

Her hand landed on top of his, ignoring the jolt of electricity that passed between them.

"I've seen this ring before," she whispered.

After pouring over books into the wee hours of the morning, she and Ven finally left the library.

She studied the ring for most of the night, trying to dredge her memory. The relic felt familiar, but she couldn't place it. It was simple, and that was the problem, really. It could have been *any* ring. Just a large square cut stone centered on an otherwise unremarkable setting.

Determined to commit every detail to memory before she went back to the human realm, she poured over the illustration. But when her eyelids drooped and her head nodded for the second time, Ven gently took her arm and led her down the spiral staircase and back toward their chambers, the candles dousing themselves one by one as they left.

Only the sound of their echoing footsteps in synch with one another, and the quiet flickering of the torches accompanied them. They finally reached the large door to her chambers—*his* chambers, she reminded herself.

She turned the heavy knob, pushing the door open into the quiet room beyond, her footsteps feeling heavy from something more than exhaustion.

Ven's large hand gently caught hers, spinning her around to face him. He took a single step toward her, their bodies so close that she had to crane her neck to meet his eyes, her chin brushing against his chest. Gods, he was handsome.

No—handsome didn't do him justice. He was breathtaking. Impossibly beautiful. She'd thought so the first time she laid eyes on him in the Capitol, and it hadn't changed since, try as she might to fight the feelings she had for him with every ounce of self-control she possessed.

She breathed in his scent, pine and citrus, and stood perfectly still as his hand slowly swept up the side of her face to tuck a stray lock of her dark waves behind her ear. He quickly took his hand back, as if the gesture had been unconscious. Irresistible.

He glanced down at the item in his hand. The book about the last queen of the Human Realm.

Ven held it out to her. "Keep it," he said quietly.

"I can't. It ... belongs here," she whispered, trying to keep the longing from her voice. Her eyes dipping to the swirls of black ink visible under the collar of his partially unbuttoned shirt.

"Just ... take it."

She blew out a breath. "What if I don't have the chance to return it?" she asked, shaking her head at the thought that she might never see this place again. Trying to chase away the ache she already felt in her chest at knowing this place existed but would be out of her reach once she returned.

"Then keep it," Ven whispered. His large hand engulfing most of the leather-bound tome as he gently pressed it into her hands. He couldn't possibly understand the gift he had offered her.

Their eyes met for a moment, her golden fire meeting his crimson flame.

Without another word, he bent his dark head over the inside of her wrist, placing a featherlight kiss on her heated skin. Tendrils of shadow caressed her skin as he left.

Chapter 46

He had to talk himself into leaving the room. *His* room. But if she'd told him she wanted to stay here for the rest of her life, he would have gladly told her it was hers. All of it. He would have given her everything—*anything*—to stay.

But he would never burden her with that.

He closed his eyes, leaning back against the heavy wooden door that now separated them, silently seething at the life she was willingly returning to. If you could call it a life. An existence, maybe.

But it was her choice, and he'd realized sitting across from her in the library weeks ago, watching the fire next to them turn her dark strands of hair golden, then crimson, and back to that lovely deep rich brown ... Her amber eyes fully absorbed in a book, completely voracious for more knowledge, more life, more of *everything*—it was then, he knew he would do anything for her. Anything she asked.

And she'd asked to return.

A shaky breath escaped his lips. It wasn't safe for him to stay here, knowing she was just on the other side of that fucking door.

Every scrap of self-control he possessed funneled into convincing himself to leave. It was cleaner this way, she could leave this place, go back to her life, and he would go on with his existence.

He'd lived a handful of lifetimes without her, he could live another handful with the knowledge that once they removed the threat from the Human realm, she would be there—safe, happy...

An arm slammed him back against the corridor wall like an iron band.

Karro's face appeared before his own, their matching eyes nearly level with each other. Ven grinned, trying to shake off the defeat he felt. But the stern line of Karro's mouth made his smile falter.

"Were you going to tell me? Tell the others?" Karro demanded.

He was confused by Karro's sudden seriousness. "Tell you what?" he asked.

Karro looked at him like he was a fucking idiot, rolling his eyes in exasperation. "What she *means* to you. Who she *is* to you," Karro ground out.

Ven let out a breath. He should have known Karro, of all people, would see straight through him.

Silence stretched thinly between them.

"It was one thing when you helped her through her stasis," Karro began. Ven tried to push himself off the wall, letting out an irritated sigh at being lectured. Karro slammed him back into the unforgiving stone. "As fucking *dangerous* and *stupid* as it might have been." Karro's red eyes bored into him, unrelenting. "She could have easily killed you—and you know it."

The Blood Folk were a harsh people. He still remembered going through his own stasis and how he'd been shoved into the cave alone until his magick had subsided. Suffering through it had been terrifying, even when he'd grown up among his own people and knew what to expect. For her—he couldn't imagine leaving her to bear that alone, regardless of the danger.

He moved to push off the wall again, but Karro's thick arm only shoved him back against the black stone, and Ven gritted his teeth. "I smelled you on her … When was the last time you offered your blood to *anyone*?" Karro prodded, clearly not willing to let this go.

"You should know," Ven answered, meeting Karro's stare, both sets of red eyes flaring with emotion in the silence that followed.

"I do," Karro whispered. His voice rough and raw. "And I should have died … Split from groin to shoulder and lying in a puddle of my own blood and shit. I remember, brother. And that is why I know that you do not give it lightly." He cleared his throat, his voice even again as he said, "And *that* is why, if she is important to you, I deserve to know. Nira and Seth and Embra deserve to know, so that we can keep a close watch on her, too."

Ven dropped his head. "She's going back," he murmured.

Karro released the pressure from his chest, giving him a sideways glance that asked, *and you'd let her?*

"It's not my decision to make. This is her fight, too," he uttered. Grateful that for once, Karro kept his mouth shut.

Chapter 47

Aurelia splashed cold water onto her face. The woman that stared back in the mirror was a stark contrast to the girl she'd been when she'd first arrived. The black shadowskin covering her body felt familiar now. It was what she'd chosen to wear in case they encountered anything on their way back to the human realm and she needed to run.

No—she wouldn't run, she'd fight beside them. Even if it was a pathetic attempt. Even if Ven commanded one of the others to get her away from harm again. Regardless, she was wearing the damn pants.

They were so form-fitting that she felt nearly naked wearing them. But she was starting to own her body with confidence. Enough time spent around the Wraiths had worn off on her, apparently. Always in a partial state of undress, especially Nira. And always well-aware of the hard-earned muscle that covered them.

Lean muscle had begun to take shape on her too, along with the hearty meals, giving her curves that she'd never had before. No longer the delicate, dainty thing her mother had shaped her to be.

But she couldn't remember a time when she felt more comfortable in her own skin or more confident in what she was capable of.

She tucked the leather book Ven had given her into the pouch belted across her hips. Rechecked that the sheath was cinched tightly around her thigh before she slid the jeweled black dagger into it, realizing there was nothing else for her to take back ... home.

Pressing the pad of her thumb against the lock on the Armory doors, she watched her blood bead and trickle into the intricate ironwork.

Ven received word from Lanthius that the wards would be nearing the final stages of completion within a day. Surprisingly, Ven agreed that the best course of action was for her to go back into the human realm while the Wraiths guarded the entrance. Though he'd made it clear he wouldn't let her leave without every weapon at her disposal.

The Wraiths were already gathered when she pushed the doors open.

Karro's thick arms were crossed over his chest, the look on his face telling her that she'd walked in on a disagreement. "Tell me this isn't your plan!" he bellowed in her direction.

"It is."

Karro threw his hands up in frustration. "I can't believe you're going along with this." He looked at Ven in disbelief. Seth leaned against one of the glass cases, his eyes trained on the floor.

Karro paced the floor of the Armory. "Let's go into the human realm, hunt down the stupid bastard that's been using the ring and be done with it!"

"No," Aurelia ground out. Karro stopped his pacing, surprise flashing across his expression at the steel in her voice. "Whoever did this doesn't deserve a clean death."

"We never said it would be clean." Nira replied darkly, throwing a grim smile at her as she flipped a black-bladed knife in her hand.

Aurelia braced her feet apart. "They need to be held accountable for their crimes," she began. "If they're found dead—"

"They'd never be found," Seth interrupted flatly, clearly not a fan of her plan either.

"It'll only be labeled an assassination—just like the others. The Council needs to know who's responsible for all of it," she finished, her fists clenched at her sides as she brazenly met three pairs of ruby eyes.

Ven stepped beside her from where he'd been leaning against the shelves, and her resolve was bolstered. "Regardless, we can't just go into the human realm and kill one of them. Demons are Wraith business, but dealing out justice to a human should be left to the humans. We may need them as allies again before this is all over." Ven looked directly at Karro as he said, "She's right—we need to play the long game. Find out what—exactly—this person has been doing, beyond using death hounds as their own personal attack dogs."

He glanced to where she stood beside him, "We need to be outside the wards to make sure nothing can come through, to buy her time to find out who's responsible."

Her eyes flicked to him, and she gave him an imperceptible dip of her chin. For backing her up. For not forcing her to the periphery. This was her fight. Her father had been the first victim. Her home invaded. And she would find the person who did this and bring them to justice. No matter how dangerous it might be for her to return.

She was the only one who might have a chance at finding the ring without turning the human realm inside out.

Karro shook his head, but seemed to accept the order from his Commander as he began loading up on gear, grumbling under his breath. If Seth and Nira still had reservations, they didn't protest any further as they went back to arming themselves.

Seth opened one of the glass cabinets and removed two small pouches. "Salt," he said, tossing one to Aurelia. "If you find yourself backed into a corner, demons can't cross it."

She tied it to her belt, feeling a little better with the weight of it against her side just as a streak of green came running at her from the open Armory door.

Embra, small though she might be, sent Aurelia tumbling to the ground with her hug. "You didn't think you could leave without saying goodbye did you?" Embra said through muffled sobs.

"Of course not," Aurelia responded, clasping her friend tighter as tears pooled in her eyes.

"You can always come with me when we meet every month," Ven offered softly from where he leaned against the door.

"It's not the same," Embra howled, which only sent her into another fit of tears until Nira finally interrupted with an assuring arm around her shoulders.

Aurelia gave a squeeze of Embra's pale green hand, before letting go and looking back to where Ven stood.

Karro was still glowering from across the room, but he didn't protest any more about their plan as he and Seth disappeared into wisps of shadow.

"Ready?" Ven asked.

And with a nod, she gripped his outstretched palm. Inky darkness pooled out from the corners of the room to where they stood, the shadows collecting at their feet, gathering at his command. He pulled her in closer, tucking her tight against his body as his scent filled her lungs.

And too soon, he gently released her again, setting her feet onto the brittle pine needles blanketing the Shades. When she finally got her bearings, she almost didn't recognize the place where she'd tumbled through the mirror.

When she'd left the human realm, it had been the final days of summer, the air still thick and warm. Now the chilled autumn wind had reached its hand even into the Valley. A shadow dropped to the ground a moment later and Nira emerged, making her way toward the small group of silver-robed Allokin. Wraiths surrounded them, standing guard as they poured their magick into rebuilding the wards.

A familiar face broke out from the group closest to them, and Lanthius stepped forward, talking with Seth as they made their way over to where Ven and Aurelia stood. Karro gave a quick nod of his head to a handful of Wraiths as they dispersed back into the pines to take up their positions further out into the Shades.

"Quiet, I hope?" Ven asked.

"Nothing," Karro replied, eyes wary as if he didn't trust the lull.

"Good." Ven turned to Lanthius. "How much time can you give her?" he asked, as the pale-haired Allokin stepped forward.

"The wards are almost complete—I'd say a few more days before we'll be ready for the final thread. They'll be at their most vulnerable while I weave in the spell to allow you to cross them," Lanthius said, looking to Aurelia now. "I'll need a drop of your blood at the exact moment the wards are sealed."

"We'll make sure you have it," Ven answered from beside her.

"Thank you, Lanthius," she said, grasping the male's hand in her own before following Ven toward the shimmering circle of light in the middle of the Grey Wood.

She hadn't noticed it that night so long ago when she'd tumbled through, but now she saw it, like a reflection pool in mid-air hovering just a few feet above the ground. Similar to the one they'd stepped through at the edge of the Allokin realm.

Ven's eyes scanned the forest around them. "Ready?" he asked quietly.

She squared her shoulders, and she knew somewhere deep in her gut that if she said no, he would have taken her back to Ravenstone in an instant—no questions asked. But she didn't hesitate as she gave him a nod.

He placed the flat of his palm against the surface of the portal and it broke around his hand like molten metal, swallowing up his forearm, then the rest of his body as he took a step through the shimmering oval and disappeared. A moment later, his hand broke through the other side, outstretched and waiting for hers.

They were only in the abandoned room for a moment before his shadows curled around them once more. She caught the briefest glimpse of deep claw marks gouged into the stone floor, the only evidence of the demon that had attacked her.

And then they were back in her chambers. The room exactly as she'd left it...

The weight in the air felt palpable. So heavy with unspoken words, feelings, emotions that it was like a mist covering every polished surface of her old life. Returning here after so much...

There was nothing familiar about this place anymore—like she was a stranger to her own life here. Pushing down the ache in her chest, she turned toward Ven, wondering if he felt it, too. But whatever unspoken words lay hidden behind those eyes remained there. His expression betraying nothing as he silently watched her.

One long stride brought him a hand's breadth away from her. His palm hovering just above her arm before he dropped it again.

They'd gone over the plan dozens of times before they left Ravenstone. Lanthius had made it clear that the longer he kept the wards open for her, the weaker the threads of the spell became. The Wraiths were ready for whatever demons might wander through, but the night they'd left Eisenea was still fresh in her mind. And she knew that every minute they bought her was another minute they might spend fighting off a horde of those monsters to protect the human realm.

She would find the ring-bearer and put an end to this.

The hardest part had been figuring out a way for her to return that wouldn't raise too many questions at court, or disrupt the compulsion that Ven had placed on her family. She still didn't quite understand how Ven's magick worked, but he'd reassured her that he had left the story vague enough that they wouldn't ask questions when she returned.

She would be able to slip back into her old life as if she'd never left.

"I'll see you at midnight," Ven whispered as the shadow of large wings passed over the white marble of her balcony and Cog perched like a gargoyle outside of the glass doors to her chambers. "Keep your guard up ... Stay safe," he said, his breath kissing her cheek as a wisp of shadow curled around where he'd stood just a moment before.

"You, too," she replied to the breaking dawn light that leaked through her windows.

Chapter 48

Aurelia stood still for a few seconds, wondering if this whole thing had been some fever dream, and she'd woken up to find herself safely back in her chambers. Her life remarkably unchanged.

Then she looked down.

Black gear and boots still clad her body. It was enough to startle her back into action, and she hurriedly removed the clothing, rifling through her dresser for a nightgown and stuffing the shadowskin into a drawer.

She folded back the covers on her neatly made bed just as the soft click of the door sounded behind her.

She spun around to see the petite silhouette of a woman.

"Ari?" her mother breathed, green eyes wide like she was seeing a ghost. "Thank the gods!" her mother exclaimed, rushing over to where she stood and wrapping her in a tight hug.

It had been months since she'd vanished without a word, following what everyone believed was the assassination of a second Councilor. Ven's magick was powerful, but how well would his compulsion hold up now that she was back in the Capitol?

"You came back—but you couldn't have made the journey by yourself," Lady Norrick exclaimed, turning Aurelia's face from side to side until she was satisfied that she was unharmed. "It doesn't matter."

Her mother hugged her again fiercely, making her wonder if this was indeed the same woman who would do anything to avoid a scandal, upholding the Norrick name above all else. But somehow, the anger that she'd been expecting upon her arrival back at court didn't seem to be there behind the glowing warmth of her mother's eyes. Only unrestrained relief.

"I understand why you ran away..." Lady Norrick said softly, tucking a strand of Aurelia's hair behind her ear. The look on her mother's face was one of remorse as she asked, "Can you ever forgive me?" Glistening tears lined her veridian eyes.

Forgive *her*?

All the anger she'd felt toward Wellan and her mother had long since dissipated. It had evaporated like water in that cavern beneath Ravenstone when she'd realized she was something *other*. It seemed so inconsequential now, given everything that she'd gone through. Given everything she still needed to do ... So trivial compared to her reasons for returning.

Stepping forward, she wrapped her mother's small body against her own, burying her face in her auburn hair and smelling her familiar rose scented perfume. The one thing she'd thought about doing the entire time she'd been at Ravenstone.

Her mother finally pulled away again. "Gods—I should have told you when you were old enough to understand." She grasped Aurelia's hands in her own, "But it never mattered to me—and I didn't want it to matter to you, either. You were *mine*, blood or not. *My* daughter."

Her family thought she'd run away after realizing she wasn't truly a Norrick—

"Tell me," Aurelia urged gently, so relieved to hear her mother's voice again that she would have listened to her say anything.

Lady Norrick sat on the corner of the bed, and after swallowing thickly a handful of times, she patted the place beside her for Aurelia to sit.

It was so strange to see her mother anything but perfectly elegant and polished. So ... human.

Her mother began smoothing her skirts nervously, looking down at her hands, a hesitancy in her voice that Aurelia had never heard in her twenty-five years of life. "We'd been visiting my sister in Hillsdeep, near the Valley edge." Her green eyes glanced up toward the ceiling. "You see, there was a baby after Asher ... One that we never had the chance to meet," her mother said quietly, wiping away a single tear from her cheek. "I could barely get out of bed—and your poor brothers, they were too young to understand—"

Her mother broke off for a moment, unable to find her voice. Aurelia placed a hand over hers, grasping it between her own.

"But I was a ghost—a shell of myself. It was why your father took us out into the hills, back to my home. He hoped it might help." Her mother's green eyes were pleading as they met hers. "He went into the Shades one morning, thinking he heard a mewling kitten stuck in a thicket. And there you were ... Alone, with no one to look after you." Sadness clouded her mother's lovely face as she recalled the story. "And then your father walked into the house with this little scrawny thing, wrapped in a blanket, needing someone to take care of her."

Her mother wiped away another tear. "We knew some of the townsfolk still believed in faeries and wood nymphs, and I thought maybe some poor young mother left you as a gift—hoping you might have a better life with them than what she could provide." She smiled sadly, squeezing Aurelia's hands. "You got me out of bed in the morning, and you gave me light in the dark hours of the night when it was only you and I awake while the whole world slept."

More tears trailed down her mother's beautiful face, but her voice wasn't weak as she said, "And when we returned to the Capitol, we claimed you as our own. We didn't know where you came from, and we didn't care—because you were *ours*. You were *mine*. A gift from the Unnamed."

Aurelia felt warm drops running down her own face now, too, but she didn't dare take her hands from where they were clasped around her mother's to wipe away the tears. She'd guessed most of the story when she discovered what she truly was, but it was something else entirely to hear it from her mother.

And when she finally felt she could get the words out without her voice breaking, she whispered, "I forgive you."

Both of them let the tears fall freely now, grasping each other. Aurelia knew deep down that her mother loved her, but it was so hidden beneath the layers of expectations and hardened shells of appearances that she couldn't remember a time either of them had been this vulnerable with each other.

"Please don't ever scare me like that again," her mother laughed, wiping at her face. "I never meant for you to find out this way, but for all of Wellan's scheming, I'm secretly happy things have worked out."

The confusion must have shown on Aurelia's face, because her mother paused, clapping a hand to her mouth. "Of course—when Wellan changed his mind, you'd already left. Gods, it was all my fault." Lady Norrick shook her head. "He's broken off your engagement with the Governor of Tidesrift. He was worried that Tidesrift would cause a scene once he knew you weren't a Norrick by blood."

But Aurelia had only come to that realization days after she'd left. Days after she'd been at Ravenstone, when she'd gone into stasis and couldn't deny what she truly was anymore ... Why would her mother have thought it was the cause for her disappearance?

"But who else would have known?" Aurelia whispered.

Chapter 49

Walking the corridor to the Councilors' private quarters, Aurelia took a steadying breath. She'd only left this place months ago, but it might as well have been a lifetime for all that had changed.

Blue cloaks patrolled the hallways and stood guard at every door. If they only knew what they were trying to protect the Councilors from ... They'd be torn to shreds in seconds if they encountered the real threat. Then again, somehow she'd walked away alive.

The two guards at the chamber doors were known to her, men who had served in the Blue Guard since Asher had joined. Both of them gave her a dip of their chins, trying to stifle their surprise at her sudden reappearance.

"Lady Norrick, it's good to see you again," Dodge answered stiffly, his heavy fist pounding twice on the door.

She waited, choosing to stare down at her pale hands rather than try to make small talk with them. Her heart was racing, pounding through her chest at the fact that she was here. She was *home*.

The door opened, and the irritated crease between Bastien's brows slowly flattened out as his eyes took her in.

"Aurelia?" He took a hesitant step toward her, dismissing the guards before wrapping his arms around her, lifting her feet from the ground. Pulling her into his chambers, he hauled her against him before crushing his lips to hers.

And she tried—she tried to remember what it was like to kiss him. But another memory invaded her thoughts ... Another pair of lips, sensuous and unrelenting.

She pulled away, looking into his ice blue eyes, the tawny mess of curls falling over his forehead. She must have tangled her hands in his hair hundreds of times, but the gesture felt foreign now.

"Where have you been?" he breathed.

"I was with the Faceless Sisters," she lied smoothly, hating that her voice sounded so convincing. "I just returned late last night, and I needed to see you." That much was true. After so many nights thinking she'd never lay her eyes on his face again, she needed to see him, needed to know that he was alright.

"I've been so worried about you." Bastien stammered. He gave her an appraising rake of his eyes. "But you look..."

Different.

But whatever changes he discerned didn't seem to be enough to put his finger on. He shook his head in disbelief, a wide grin spreading across his face, reminding her so much of the lanky teenage boy she'd fallen head over heels for a decade ago.

"Why didn't you send word? Why didn't your family say anything?" he demanded.

"They wanted to give me space … Let things simmer after Wellan broke off my engagement with Tidesrift. They wanted to make sure nothing appeared questionable for why the arrangement ended."

That seemed to quell his curiosity because his shoulders relaxed a little. The crease between his golden brows releasing. Not the set of dark brows she'd grown accustomed to looking at, the pair of crimson eyes that had become so familiar.

"You don't seem surprised," she hedged.

"Circumstances have changed," he deflected, something out of place in his tone as he turned away from her. "I told you I could convince Wellan to accept my proposal now that I'm on the council. My title holds as much weight as his."

The glint of gold caught her eye as he grasped her hand and led her to his opulent new sitting room. A far cry from the humble Captain's chambers he'd occupied only a few months ago. But as he took a seat on the stiff-backed divan, he looked comfortable here. Like he belonged.

Eyes landing on the ring that now occupied his finger, the constriction in her chest loosened … A blue sapphire. The Veron crest was inlaid in gold across the large oval stone. Wellan had one, too, with the Norrick family crest. All the Councilors possessed something similar, a token of their title passed through the seven original families.

He leaned in close to her again. "You're back now ... And that's what matters," he whispered against her lips, trying to smooth over the snag. "And everything we dreamt of, everything we wanted, is within reach."

And she tried—she tried to dredge up the memory of those feelings she'd had for him just a few months ago as his lips parted hers in silent invitation. But he must have sensed her hesitation because he broke away from her with a look of confusion in his eyes.

This isn't at all how she'd imagined their reunion. The pit that formed in her stomach only got deeper as the silence stretched between them, but she needed rest, she needed time to be alone.

Forcing a smile to her lips, she wondered how someone who had known her for so long could have been so easily fooled by it.

Chapter 50

The gold flecks in her eyes looked dull in the mirror as she tugged at the tight bodice of her gown, digging into her hips, and cutting into her chest. The restrictive boning in the corset only allowed her shallow breaths, pushing her breasts up to an unnatural height. Her small amount of freedom from them had been enough to forget how uncomfortable they were.

A new set of lady's maids helped her into the dark lavender gown for dinner tonight, a night of celebrations, she'd been told; her return to the Capitol, and her engagement to the newest Councilor. But it also meant she'd have to face her brothers, and she wasn't sure she was ready for that.

Thanks to her mother and the Norrick family name, no one questioned her prolonged absence from court—at least publicly. Only nodded and smiled as she passed them in the hallways, saying they were glad to see her back while they whispered behind their hands once they thought she was out of earshot. But her ears picked up everything now, a curse as much as a blessing, she'd realized.

The rumors ranged from petty to diabolical, but she didn't care, she was too busy searching relentlessly for the ring. A large task, given that the palace was full of nobles flaunting their wealth in jewelry. But she'd studied the drawing of the relic so many times that she knew none of them were the one she searched for.

She could only manage a few bites of food over the course of dinner. Her appetite had been fine, but the corset she wore was laced so tightly that she was in pain already from sitting so stiffly in the chair.

Wellan had only kissed her on the cheek in greeting when she'd taken her place at the table, his eyes distant and unreadable. If he had any lingering anger over the botched arrangement with Tidesrift, he hadn't shown even a glimmer of it.

But Asher—she evaded eye contact with him all evening. Quite a feat, considering he sat across from her as she studiously sliced tiny pieces of venison on her plate to avoid looking up. Christian sat to his left, doting on the recently widowed Lady Veron.

"Governor Caspane has extended his stay, I see," she whispered to Bastien. Casting a glance across the table, Christian had coaxed a small smile from the pretty young wife of Bastien's late uncle, looking radiant even in her mourning black. Her cheeks pink with color from the undivided attention Christian was bestowing on her.

"Indeed…" Bastien answered. "He's been quite helpful during my aunt's mourning."

Asher threw an annoyed glance toward Christian at whatever he'd whispered to Lady Veron. He'd been in a sour mood all evening, and she didn't want to consider that she might have been the reason for it. She needed to trust that the compulsion Ven had used on them would hold.

To her right sat the eldest Councilor's wife, trying to engage her in talk of the upcoming events for the winter season, but Aurelia couldn't focus on the conversation, her eyes glancing to every hand in the room.

There was plenty of glittering jewelry at the table, but none matched the drawing from the book. And every minute she spent making small talk with the Councilors' wives about the upcoming parties was another minute that the killer was loose. Another minute wasted.

At least Ven and the other Wraiths were keeping watch over the portal in the meantime, but she felt a sense of urgency all the same. Lanthius' spell was close to being complete, but if he sealed the wards before she found the ring bearer, the Wraiths wouldn't be able to cross over and help her. So instead, he was holding them open for her—buying her time to find her father's murderer.

Bastien gave her a gentle nudge in the ribs. "Lady Fost is talking to you."

The older woman smiled widely. "Did you enjoy your visit to the coast? The sea air always does wonders for my health,"

So that was the lie her mother had told everyone at court. It was believable enough that no one would question it, private enough that no one would press for details.

"Yes, how was your stay on the coast?" Asher drawled from where he was seated down the table, his eyes narrowed at her.

She cleared her throat. "Lovely. Refreshing," she answered brightly, taking a large gulp of the wine in front of her and choking it down. The taste like vinegar compared to what she'd been used to at Ravenstone.

"And the wedding plans?" Lady Fost beamed, gesturing to the large ring that now occupied Aurelia's left hand.

She wasn't quite sure how to answer. Her mother had already taken over the preparations, which was all for the best since she couldn't bring herself to focus on any of the details.

"Coming along." Was all she could think to say before her heart began a steady pounding in her chest, heat spreading along her shoulders with the thought of what still stood between her and her future with Bastien. "Excuse me," she said, standing up abruptly from her chair. Air—she needed air. Anything to distract her.

The corridor was chilled, but she hoped it might take the edge off the restless magick that had been crackling under her skin since she'd been back. Humming relentlessly in her veins, looking for an outlet.

Training on the Ledge for hours every day had helped keep her magick in check, but now that she spent her days in her chambers or sitting rooms, there was nowhere for the pent-up energy to go. No outlet to work off the power that roiled through her blood.

Quiet footsteps approached behind her, and she had to remind herself to act startled. Had to remind herself that the old Aurelia wouldn't have been able to smell the cedar scented soap that her brother preferred from this far away. Or that she wouldn't have been able to know it was Asher simply from hearing the way he ground his teeth as he walked toward her.

"Where were you really, Aurelia," Asher demanded, his voice low.

It was a moment before she turned to face him. "You know where I was," she replied tightly, turning to go back to the crowded dining room where her brother wouldn't dare cause a scene.

Asher blocked her path, his green eyes dancing with irritation. She fought the urge to hook a foot around his ankle and bring him crashing down onto the floor. Frustration flashed across his face, as if Ven's compulsion worked, but some part of Asher's mind fought the block that had wiped away his memories and replaced them with something else. And she hated the irritation she saw lingering in his eyes. The confusion. As if he knew something was amiss.

But it was necessary, she reminded herself.

"Lie to *them*, I don't care ... You know I'd keep any secret for you," Asher spat out. "But when did you start lying to me, Ari?" And the hurt in his eyes almost made her come clean about everything. Tell him absolutely every single thing that had happened to her since she'd gone looking for answers in the library that night months ago.

"Aurelia?"

They both turned to see Bastien had come out into the hallway, concern creasing his brows at the anger still storming across Asher's features.

"Coming," she answered, not able to bring herself to look into Asher's eyes. And she wondered if there would ever be a time when she wouldn't have to lie to the people she loved.

Bastien's chambers were sprawling. The space luxurious and echoing now that Bastien had dismissed the small armada of servants waiting to fulfill any request of the newest Councilor.

There had been a time not so long ago when they'd only ever dreamed of this. Whispered about a future together in stolen minutes and hours under the cover of darkness, always hiding, always afraid of being caught.

He'd held her hand the entire walk back through the palace to his door, blatantly leading her into his chambers in front of the two guards who stood watch. His title protected him, protected both of them, from the ruthless rumors that would have destroyed their reputations only months ago. And it was such a sudden change, that Aurelia found herself still walking on eggshells. Wondering who would begin whispering that she was here after dark, unescorted.

But they were engaged now. They'd be married in just a few weeks, and her mother—*her mother*—had said, *to hell with anyone who has anything to say about the short engagement.*

Her gaze still took in the details of the massive chambers around them when Bastien's broad hand caressed the small of her back. "They'll be your chambers, soon," he said, the thought making her chest tight.

Everything from the sitting room to the bathing chamber felt … sterile. All of it for show, to host visitors and the other Councilors. Meant to be tidy and perfect. A display of wealth and power. And she wondered if it would ever feel like home. Feel like *theirs. Hers.*

When his voice finally broke through her thoughts, his mouth was set in a thin line. "No more sneaking off, Aurelia."

She froze in place, effortless now, thanks to these strange new abilities her body possessed, holding her breath.

"Dodge told me he saw you wandering the palace late the night you left, and I doubt Wellan sanctioned your stay with the Faceless Sisters and made you leave in the dead of night." His tone was gentle but chiding. A father scolding his child.

She blew out the breath she'd been holding, mild irritation taking its place. It all felt so ridiculous now, so trivial compared to everything she'd been through ... The task that was still ahead of her. But all the small freedoms she'd grown accustomed to at Ravenstone were gone now that she'd returned. And now that she didn't have them anymore—they didn't feel small.

Bastien let out a weary sigh. "I was a member of the Blue Guard just a few weeks ago if you remember, I know all of them, they still keep me informed." He waved his hand towards her. "You're lucky it was only Dodge who saw you and not someone prone to gossip," he added, his brows raised in disapproval.

"I was at the library," she answered abruptly. Might as well give him one small truth in the middle of all the lies she would have to tell him, and since spending every night in the library at Ravenstone, it just seemed so inconsequential now.

"The library? Why would you need to go in there?" His dismissive tone was enough to shatter the thin amount of control she kept in place.

"Why does anyone? To *read*, to *learn*, to experience the world outside of this tiny bubble we live in!" she replied with a humorless laugh.

His expression was incredulous. "Only the Nameless Brothers have access to the records in there, you know that," he responded, his voice rising with impatience.

"And why is that?" she demanded, her temper emboldening her.

He threw his hands down in frustration, standing up again to pace in front of her, crossing his arms over his chest. "Why does it matter? Stop behaving like a child, Aurelia! You're a grown woman—you shouldn't be sneaking into restricted areas in the dead of night!" he lectured, his steps coming to a halt in front of where she sat. "I won't allow it."

The air in the room sang with his anger. His ice blue eyes fixed on her golden ones in a silent battle.

"Won't *allow* it?" she asked with lethal quiet, daring him to repeat himself.

He had the decency to balk. "That's not what I meant." He raised his hands in placation. "Just think how it would appear, Aurelia—I'm a Councilor now, and soon you'll be my wife. Appearances are important. Propriety needs to be upheld."

"Maybe with you and Wellan on the council now, some of those things can change," she replied, trying to smooth over the sharp edge in her voice. Bastien gave her a blank look. "Everyone could have access to the library. To an education. Knowledge," she said in exasperation.

He shook his head in disbelief, as if he couldn't understand how naïve she was. "Ari ... I'm the newest Councilor, the youngest. Your brother has only held the title a few months longer. We don't have that kind of sway over the established members."

He took a step closer to her, tucking a strand of her dark waves behind her ear, and she had to stop herself from recoiling at the intimate gesture. Letting him trail his fingertips down the side of her face.

"Maybe one day, in the future, I can change things," he said, planting a kiss on her forehead. "But in the meantime, please..."

Behave.

The word hung unspoken in the air between the two of them.

It was late when she finally returned to her chambers. The spat had been smoothed over with a few well-placed words and better placed kisses.

It made sense that they'd disagree after being apart for so long ... That was to be expected.

Bastien had plied her with chaste kisses, whispering promises against her lips that had quickly dissolved into desperate touches, and greedily tearing at each other's clothing ... But then the hunger had hit her so suddenly, so viciously, that she had to physically pull away from him and leave his chambers.

Her gums ached where her fangs were barely hidden beneath the corners of her mouth, the tight smiles something she'd quickly gotten used to since returning. But what she hadn't been expecting was the lingering feeling when Bastien had touched her. Something that felt a little too close to disgust. Unfamiliar and unwanted once the thirst finally left her.

She hadn't realized exactly how late it was until she entered her darkened chambers, a large silhouette standing at the glass doors of her balcony.

Ven stared out into the night sky, turning as she closed the door, his gaze snagging on the low-cut bodice of her gown.

"What news?" she murmured, trying to ignore the heat that flared to life inside her.

"Nothing," he answered with a shake of his head. The look on his face saying he didn't trust the quiet. "Anything here?"

Giving a shake of her head, she twirled the large ring from Bastien absentmindedly on her finger. The blue stone at the center a reminder of the obstacles that still remained.

There had been no activity since she'd returned. And now that the Allokin were nearing completion of the wards, it seemed all was going according to plan.

"Then I'll see you tomorrow," Ven said. Relief and disappointment mingled in Aurelia's chest that he always kept their meetings short and to the point. "Send Cog if you find anything before then."

He turned to leave, stopping short, his nostrils flaring slightly as his eyes narrowed in her direction. And he crossed the distance between them in the blink of an eye, appearing mere inches in front of her.

His eyes were fire made liquid as they gazed down from where he towered over her. And she realized what he'd scented on her ... *Who* he'd scented on her.

Her heart thundered in her chest, but not out of fear. And she knew he heard it, expecting an arrogant smirk at the fact that he could elicit that response from her, but it never appeared.

Her cheeks burned, but she wouldn't be ashamed of it. Bastien was her future now. And the whispered promises Ven had made in Eisenea seemed null and void given everything that had happened ... And the things that hadn't.

A better male would tell you there's no future for us.

He'd never expanded on that—and she wasn't desperate enough to beg him to tell her why. There would be no groveling from her.

"You should be careful." Was all he said, his crimson eyes piercing into her.

She let out a breathless laugh, looking away first. Not exactly sure what response she'd hoped for.

"I'm sure I don't have to remind you what kinds of activities can trigger the thirst for blood," he added quietly, his gaze burning a trail down her spine as she turned away.

"I can handle myself." Was all she said, because she didn't care to explain herself.

"I'm well aware of that," he replied before shadows coiled around him and he disappeared again, leaving her staring at the white patch of marble where he'd been standing only seconds before.

Breathing rapidly, she hadn't realized she'd been preparing for a fight until she looked down at her feet, braced apart just the way Karro and Seth had taught her. Her magick crackling softly underneath her skin with nowhere to go.

Chapter 51

Cerulean blue banners snapped in the autumn breeze. The seven interlocking circles embroidered in silver thread were set ablaze in the afternoon light.

Not so long ago, Aurelia wondered if she'd ever see this place again—home. And now here she was…

Bastian covered her hand with his, where it rested on his arm, giving it a small squeeze before he led her to the bottom of the sweeping stone steps of the temple.

His appointment to Councilor had happened the very night of his uncle's death, a speedy and efficient transition of power, but he'd held off on the pomp and circumstance indefinitely, waiting the long months that she'd been gone. Optimistic that when Aurelia finally returned, she would be at his side while his induction onto the High Council was made public.

Glancing up at his handsome profile beside her, she wondered if she would have had the same resolve had the situation been reversed … Guilt tightly coiled around her. She'd been so certain that her fate was sealed—her return to the human realm so impossible, that she'd completely let go of a future with Bastien.

Horns blared inside the glistening white walls of the temple, muted by the mass of people who had gathered. Crowds poured out from the opened doors to collect on the wide stone steps, trailing as far back as the gardens.

The sheer sleeves of her sky-blue gown ruffled gracefully in the cool breeze, her heart-shaped bodice just a shade darker to match Bastien's ornately embroidered jacket. They looked like royalty as they walked up the steps of the temple and made their way inside, the crowds parting effortlessly for them.

Bastien left her at the seat next to her family before stepping up toward the dais, kneeling before the row of Nameless Brothers that lined the front of the temple. And as the ceremony droned on—the same words that had been spoken over her brother less than a year ago when he'd taken the family seat on the council—her mind wandered back to another future. Another set of possibilities.

Back to that cozy corner of the second floor in Ravenstone's library. Back to Embra's greenhouse. Back to the Ledge. Back to Ven's perfectly unkempt chambers. That darkened room in Eisenea...

But it was desperation that formed some attachment to Ven, wasn't it? Or maybe just finding someone who was more like her than she cared to admit ... Someone who was lonely and different, too. Here in the human realm she was one of a kind, but even in the kingdom of the Blood Folk, Ven was a rarity. And maybe that connection between them had been enough to make her think there was something more.

Her skin still burned where his lips had brushed the inside of her wrist. It had been days, and still she felt the tingle across her skin.

Relief and longing were a bitter mixture on her tongue. Ven was beyond the wards, protecting this realm and buying her time to find the ring. To find the killer. Their interactions since she'd returned had been short and to the point. She was grateful for that, less of a distraction from what she'd come back to do. And less of a distraction from her future...

Bastien stood, and the crowd knelt before him.

Aurelia's dark waves were piled on top of her head, braided and curled, held in place by a dozen glittering pins weighed down with heavy sapphires that matched the cerulean blue banners hanging from the temple walls. The pins stabbed and pulled along her scalp as she dropped to her knees, she'd yank the things free as soon as she was back in the privacy of her own chambers. Her neck barked with the effort of holding her head upright as she bowed before Bastien. She may be his future wife, but she would always be expected to bend the knee for her husband.

Bastien glanced down at her, his blue eyes so ... normal. Everything about him so unchanged. Did he see the same woman looking up at him?

That person felt so removed from who she was now that she couldn't quite remember how the old Aurelia would have acted, would have looked at him, what she would have said. But she'd find her again. She'd remember what things had been like between them with enough time, and soon—soon, everything would go back to normal.

Heat sang under her skin. The humming energy was more bearable with every passing day, but it would still creep up on her without warning. But maybe without her calling on it, her magick would dry up entirely.

Lightning.

Not flame. Not shadow. And yet somehow her magick demanded the same price as the Blood Folk. Ven had seemed unsettled by that realization, but she'd never gotten the chance to ask him why. And now, it seemed it didn't matter. Soon everything would go back to its rightful place. Her magick would have no reason to surface, and she could live out a relatively normal life here, without the burden of it.

Light blinded her briefly from the tall windows in the temple, and as she blinked the flash of gold drew her attention back to the dais.

To a blood red stone sitting on the First Brother's finger. The ring.

One of the relics, right here under her nose. The sensation of dread and gloom pressed so heavily on her that she couldn't understand how no one else felt it.

How many years, decades, had they all been forced to kiss that damned ring. It was much too large for the Brother's hand, she noticed now, as he spun it around his finger, fidgeting with the heavy trinket. The First Brother steepled his fingers under his chin, the cold glint of the metal making the magick in her blood crackle in response.

The feast and the following celebration were a haze. A singular focus occupied her mind through the entirety of it as she tried not to draw any attention to herself. She needed to find out exactly how he was doing it—how the First Brother was using the ring to control the demons.

As the evening finally drew to a close, tightly wound fury kept her silent until her chamber door had closed behind Bastien.

She looked over to where he sat, sipping a glass of sparkling wine, fighting down the voice in her head telling her that it was best to leave him out of this. He was a Councilor now, and if anyone should deal out justice to the man who'd killed her father, his uncle, it should be him.

Dealing out justice to a human should be left to the humans.

And she wasn't one of them anymore.

"I know who killed them…" she said quietly, expecting the look of confusion that he gave her, but she trudged on, knowing if she stopped now, she might never work up the nerve to tell him. "And if we don't stop him, more people will die."

Bastien set his glass down. "What are you talking about?" he asked slowly.

She held up a palm when he moved to stand up. "You have to promise me that you'll listen. Just— listen."

He nodded his head, the crease only deepening between his brows as she paced in front of him, telling him what she knew. Not the entire truth, that was still too much for her to admit. But she told him of the demon that had attacked her, the same one that had been responsible for the deaths of her father and his uncle. That magick was alive in this world and that the First Brother had been using it for his own gain.

She told him what she could, and left out the details that didn't seem relevant to what they needed to do ... The details that pained her to skim over. But her time at Ravenstone, her time with *them* ... It was something that she needed to remain hers, and hers alone. Things that would stay locked and kept in her heart but didn't have a place in her life here.

True to his word, Bastien hadn't interrupted, sitting silently on the divan across from her as she paced.

When she finally stopped talking, she took a shaky breath and looked up. His face had drained of color, but after a few heartbeats he finally looked up at her.

Standing slowly, he placed a gentle hand on her shoulder. "Aurelia…"

And at that exact moment—she knew he didn't believe a word of it.

Bitter disappointment coated her mouth, but she'd been expecting this reaction, so she squared her shoulders, bracing her feet apart. The act alone was enough to bolster her resolve.

"It's true, Bastien. He's responsible for my father's death. Your uncle's," she repeated more forcefully.

"Demons…" He shook his head, his blue eyes wide with disbelief. "Aurelia, you sound mad," he whispered frantically, as if he was trying to shake her out of fever dream.

She took a breath, trying to reign in her frustration. Trying to keep a leash on the heat that was winding its way down her shoulders and flooding into her fingertips. "There are many things that should not be possible, Bastien."

It was reckless, but she didn't know what other choice she had, she needed an ally, and if she couldn't trust her future husband, who *could* she trust? So she loosened the tether on that small bit of magick, letting the heat trickle into her fingers.

"Magick is alive, Bastien," she said, lifting her hand as small white sparks danced between her fingertips.

Bastien stumbled back as if she'd struck him in the chest. "What—" His eyes wild with fear.

She held her hand between them, letting the small bit of magick dance in her palm. Bastien shook his head, disbelief clouding his expression, the acrid tang of terror drenched his scent.

Something cold froze over the blue of his eyes as he gained his footing again, still keeping a healthy distance between her and himself as he stood up. "We can fix this, Aurelia—I can fix you," he uttered.

Fix her.

As if she were a problem to be solved.

"He is a complicated man, but he will know how to help." Bastien began pacing her chambers, newfound resolve in his expression.

Dawning horror made the sparks at her fingertips evaporate. "What?" she asked quietly, not wanting to believe that she'd heard his words correctly, but her heightened hearing only made the blade twist in her gut. "That man will let dark magick enter this realm." She stabbed a finger at the floor as Bastien continued pacing. And for a moment, she thought maybe he hadn't heard her.

He stopped pacing abruptly, warily glancing to where she stood. "It's already here," Bastien uttered, his eyes fixed on her. "But the First Brother will know a solution."

"His solutions have put the entire realm in danger," she shouted. "Do you know what lurks outside the wards? What creatures he has helped escape from their confines?"

She took a step toward Bastien, and he stumbled back from her. A mixture of fear and contempt on his face as he left her room without turning his back to her, as if she were some feral beast ... A monster.

Chapter 52

If Bastien got to the First Brother before she did, there was no telling what the man might do.

Yanking the dresser drawer open, she rifled through her clothing, finding the gear she'd hidden. She tugged on the shadowskin, buckling the leather sheath around her thigh, and sliding the jeweled dagger home. The actions were second-nature now. Lifting the latch on her door, she turned the knob, but it didn't budge.

She pushed harder—but still nothing. Throwing her full weight against the door, she gritted her teeth as her shoulder made contact with the heavy wood. It shuddered in its frame against the impact of her new strength, but it clearly wasn't stuck.

It had been locked from the outside.

Pressing her ear to the door, she listened ... Two sets of heartbeats thudded on the other side, ratcheting up as she threw her body against the thick wood once more. Blue cloaks—Bastien had stationed guards outside her door.

A scream ripped through her lungs, feral and sounding more beast than human. But even if anyone could hear her, no one would come to help. Not with blue cloaks guarding her chambers at the command of a Councilor.

She gave one final blow to the door, both hands landing against the wood, so hard that the heavy door reverberated in its frame. She might be able to break down the door. She was strong enough now that the hinges might give after a few more attempts. But it wouldn't serve her purpose to make every guard in the palace rush to her chambers. And there would be no hiding what she was if she fought them all. There was another way out of here—

Throwing open the glass doors, she scanned the night sky. The whoosh of heavy wings greeted her ears as Cog landed lightly on the white stone. Yanking open the drawer of her vanity, she reached for her father's journal. Tearing off a corner of the last page, she quickly scrawled a note and ran out onto the balcony. She handed the scrap of paper to the raven, who took it in his beak and was in the air again, his black wings melting into the sky as he disappeared once more.

There wasn't enough time. Even if the message reached Ven, every one of the Wraiths were needed to protect the wards until they were sealed completely. But at least it might give them some warning.

No one would be coming to rescue her.

She ran the length of the balcony, looking down to the dark courtyard far below. She'd jumped from higher when Ven had pushed her into the Shades, it was no different than when they'd been running from the Silver Guard in Eisenea... She paced the length of white marble, the chilled air biting into her skin with every step.

Fucking coward, she silently cursed herself.

And before she could talk herself out of it, she ran toward the ledge, leaping up onto the railing with her newly honed strength, and plunging into the air.

Cold wind whipped against her face as she tucked her knees, bracing for the impact. The ground rose up to meet her.

The fall hadn't been nearly as bad as the first one, and rolling once, she braced her feet wide, coming to a stop. She stifled the shout of triumph that threatened to burst from her, taking off at a run. Her legs swiftly carried her through the courtyard, up the stone steps of the temple.

Silently unsheathing the black blade from where it was strapped to her thigh, Aurelia pressed her body against the wall.

Cold fingers trailed down her spine as she made her way down the steps that crept beneath the temple floor. And she was grateful for her heightened senses as she felt her way along the darkened corridors in this unfamiliar place. She'd heard that dungeons from centuries past had been carved beneath the temple's foundation, and though it seemed an odd place to keep prisoners, she believed it now that she was here.

Her footsteps were light and soft in the silent corridor, her ears waiting to pick up any sound beneath the thick stone. She began to wonder if her instincts had been wrong to lead her down here— that nagging pull toward this place, something deep in her gut telling her that the First Brother was here.

And just then, she saw the faint glow of light ahead. A room far at the end of the dank hallway.

The First Brother stood hunched over a dirty table, some discarded remnant from when the dungeons had still been in use long ago. Her gaze sharpened to the paper spread out in front of him, a map of the Crescent Valley. A dagger lay on the table next to his age weathered hand as he studied the map, muttering to himself.

There was still time to stop him before he could do any more damage, but she needed proof to hand over to the Council if she was going to convince them of his guilt. With the way Bastien had responded, it hadn't given her hope that her brother or the other Councilors would be any more receptive.

The First Brother muttered a string of words. His voice was guttural, an ancient, wicked tongue that made the hair on her neck stand up as the oily words seemed to coat the air beneath the temple. Raising the dagger, he sliced his palm deeply, his blood welling up and pooling in his hand.

Clenching his fist over the map, he let fat red drops of his blood spatter the paper beneath, marking out a pattern that ringed the outside of the Valley. Some of his blood pooled over large cities, other drops speckled the rural villages. The ruby on his finger glowed dully in the torchlight, seeming to pulse as the air grew oppressively thick, pressing in on her ears and her temples. And then, just as suddenly—it evaporated. She hadn't realized how difficult it had become to breathe, until she'd taken a silent gasp to fill her lungs again with the musty air.

The First Brother wiped his hand against his robe, the gesture agitated, frustrated, as if whatever he'd wanted to accomplish hadn't gone as planned. Whatever she had witnessed him attempt, had failed.

Grim relief washed over her. It had failed because the Wraiths had been on the other side, waiting.

The room was littered with evidence of dark magick, rings of salt and old, dried blood. How long had the First Brother been performing forbidden spells in this forgotten part of the temple? Would it be enough to bring him to justice? Would it be enough to prove that he'd been trying to summon demons?

If it wasn't ... Karro would get his wish after all. But right now, she needed to get the ring. And better that she be the one to do it here and now, rather than have the Wraiths turn the human realm inside out to collect it.

The First Brother turned suddenly toward where she hid, his shoulders relaxing. "It's good that you came," he called out.

The dagger was still firmly in her hand as she held her breath, keeping to the shadows. Was he expecting someone else? An accomplice?

"I know you're there, Lady Norrick. You might as well come out."

Her breath hitched. He didn't know what she was or what she was capable of. She could kill him quickly and be done with it ... But this man didn't deserve a quick death. He deserved to be dragged in front of the Council for the entire Valley to see. He had blood on his hands, and he would pay for it.

She took a step into the room. "I know it was you," she said quietly, but there was no weakness in her voice. Only cold, sharply honed vengeance as she emerged. "Why?"

He didn't bother feigning ignorance, clasping his hands behind his back as she circled him.

"The Council strayed too far from the wishes of the Unnamed—for decades, pulling further and further away from their wisdom, their guidance." He shook his head sadly. "There was a time when the First Brother sat at the head of the table, but slowly ... We have been relegated to ceremonies, solstice celebrations. Dusted off and taken out twice a year for a performance."

"You murdered my father over a seat?" she hissed with deadly quiet.

"An unfortunate necessity. Younger councilors will be more—agreeable to guidance." He nodded, as though the matter was settled. "Though it did burden me. Your father was a good man."

He leisurely walked around the table, but she kept her eyes on the ring—waiting for her moment to strike.

"I can't say the same of Veron, but he held sway on the Council because he always managed to keep Tidesrift in check, so with him out of the picture—" He shook his head. "Then your brother ... I underestimated him. I thought he might gain Tidesrift's support permanently with you as the offer."

But that had been Bastien's intervention—

The First Brother read the look on her face, chuckling to himself. "Who do you think whispered into his ear that you were the adoptive daughter of the Norrick family? That the vain, arrogant Governor of Tidesrift would be so outraged if he found out his bride wasn't actually a Norrick?"

Heat began branching out from her shoulders, flooding through her arms and pooling into her hands. She only needed to command it—

"Aurelia." The voice broke off her concentration, the liquid lightning receding back into her body even though she called it forth. She didn't need to turn around to know who it belonged to.

"What have you done, Bastien?" she asked sadly.

Chapter 53

Bastien stepped in front of her, blocking her path to the Brother. "My uncle was a monster, you said so yourself. How many times did you ask me to intervene? And how could I? He was a Councilor, and I was just the forgotten nephew. What could I have done?"

"Anything," she uttered.

Bastien gripped her shoulders. "Now I can take his place. Be a better man. A better leader," he pleaded.

"Only when it suited your own circumstances!" she shouted, tearing herself free of his grasp. "Only when it gave you everything you wanted," she spat in rage. "Did you ever love me? Or only my family name."

"Aurelia, please," Bastien implored.

"Chain her here," the Brother said impatiently. "I need her safe and unharmed until this is done," he ordered, jerking his head toward a set of iron chains that bolted into the stone. And dread pooled in her gut...

Bastien swiveled around, caught by surprise. "What? That was never the agreement—"

"The agreement?" The First Brother's eyes narrowed. "You mean the deal we made that when your uncle was visiting one of his whores late at night, you'd make certain he was alone and unguarded? That in return you'd be given information and a title that would give you everything you wanted?" The First Brother's veneer of composure cracked, impatience making his voice reedy and thin. "You mean *that* agreement?"

Bastien's head dropped in defeat, his hands balled into useless fists at his side.

The Brother turned away distractedly. "When this is over, you can marry her, put a child in her for all I care. But when he comes to claim his price, you would be foolish to stand in his way."

There is always a price.

She lifted her eyes to the First Brother with harsh clarity. *She'd* been the price.

All focus funneled onto the ring that sat proudly on the Brother's middle finger as Bastien stoically dragged her back toward the wall. She was strong enough now to fight him, but she didn't want it to end this way. There must be a shred of the man she thought she knew still dwelling inside him.

"Don't do this, Bastien," she whispered, but Bastien only pushed her up against the wall, pinning her in place. He refused to meet her eyes as the lock clinked, and one iron manacle circled her wrist.

"I'm sorry, but it's for the best," he whispered back, finally glancing down at her.

"Don't do this—" she repeated.

His ice blue eyes went wide, his pupils dilating slightly as a dazed look came over his features.

"I won't do this," he mumbled, dropping her hand, and going back to unlock the one that was shackled. As if he was under some influence...

Compulsion.

The rare gift Ven possessed. This must be what he'd spoken of. The lifeless look of utter obedience in Bastien's eyes made bile rise up in her throat, but she didn't have time to feel guilt over it now.

"Leave—tell the others what this man has done," she breathed, watching his pupils widen as the command sunk into his subconscious.

She didn't hesitate, shoving Bastien out of her path and calling her lightning forth to crackle at her fingertips as he fled back through the tunnel, stumbling as he ran into something on his way through the door.

Not something. *Someone.*

Aurelia's stomach plummeted as she looked at the doorway.

Asher stepped into the room, leaving the restless crackling nowhere to go but stay hidden beneath her skin. She didn't trust herself enough to kill the First brother without harming him in the process.

"Get out of here!" she shouted at Asher. If she could just get him to look into her eyes for a moment, she could compel him to go, but Asher's venomous green stare was focused solely on the First Brother.

"What are you doing with my sister?" he asked in a low threat.

And the First Brother moved quicker than she would have thought possible, yanking Asher in front of him with strength he shouldn't have been capable of possessing—the dagger poised in front of Asher's throat.

"She's part of the bargain."

"What bargain?" Asher demanded, gritting his teeth against the blade's edge digging into his neck. Seeming to be just as shocked at the First Brother's newfound strength.

"Let him go!" Aurelia ordered the First Brother, hoping that her compulsion would take hold, but his eyes remained unchanged. Another hidden gift from his master's ring if she had to guess.

She circled closer, trying to find an opening so that she could send him to whatever afterlife awaited him.

The First Brother let out a bark of cruel laughter as he dragged Asher back into the dank corner of the room. "Put the shackles back on," he growled, eyes narrowed in rage as he pressed the blade harder against her brother's throat.

"Don't listen to him, Ari," Asher gritted out through his teeth, a bead of blood welling at where the blade pressed in.

But she had no choice. There was no opening to attack the First Brother without harming Asher.

Backing slowly toward the wall again, she cuffed one hand into a manacle, never letting her eyes leave the First Brother's face. "The Council will execute you for what you've done," she hissed.

The First Brother gave her a sickeningly sweet smile, "Not after I save the Capitol," he uttered. He laughed at the look of confusion on her face.

"You didn't see it—locked away in the palace. Safe and sheltered." Her blood ran cold at the way the First Brother's smile sharpened. "The people have been swarming the temples since your father died. The rumors coming from the edges of the Valley were enough to drive some of the peasants back, but with the death of two of the most prominent Councilors… Even the nobility have renewed their devotion to the Unnamed Gods."

Asher's eyes widened in understanding as they met hers from across the room.

"All it will take is one final act to plunge the Republic into chaos. Sacrifices must be made for the greater good," the First Brother said dispassionately. "But it won't take long before panic takes hold through the Valley and people are rushing to their temples to cling to the Gods they abandoned."

Sharp clarity tore through her. The bloody marks on the map—

He was going to tear open new rifts in the wards.

Laughter bubbled out from her lips, "You're so concerned with faith? And yet you intend to release a flood of demons on the very people you swore to protect?" It was impossible for her to know how much of the Dark King's power he was channeling, if it was even possible. But if he managed to open dozens of rifts around the border of the Valley, call on masses of demons...

"They won't make it far before I use the power granted to me by the Unnamed to turn them to dust," the First Brother answered with righteous purpose.

Disbelief clouded Asher's expression as he listened to their conversation. She hoped that for his own sake he believed all of it and would run as soon as he had the chance.

"Their power in this world has grown weak without the devotion of the people, but this—" the First Brother held his hand up, the ring on his finger flashing ominously. "This gift has given them a tether. Another chance to return our world to its former glory," his voice quivered with fervor.

An irreverent huff of breath escaped her, "You think it's been the voice of the Unnamed whispering orders to you?" she uttered. "It's the King of the Void, you fool! He's the only one capable of commanding the beasts you wield!" she shouted, trying to make the man see sense. But he was blinded by his own lust for power. Blinded by his own self-righteous cause.

His look of unquestioning devotion fell away into a cruel smile. "How long do you think it will take before the people revolt against the Council and demand that I rule in their stead?" he asked, seeming to savor the look of panic that flared in her eyes. "The High Council may still rule the people ... But I will be their guardian against the Dark King and his demons. Their savior." He cocked his head to the side, looking at her.

Her stomach turned to lead. The Wraiths were fierce, strong ... But even they couldn't stop an onslaught like this. She'd seen the map of the Crescent Valley herself, the dozens of bloody marks smeared across the paper where he planned to create fissures in the wards protecting their borders. How many innocent people would die before his deception was over?

"Let my brother go," she pleaded, hating the panic leaking into her voice. "Please, I did what you asked." She raised her shackled hands. "I'll stay here—just let him go."

If she could just get Asher out of the way, she'd have an opening. She could kill the First Brother where he stood.

"No, Ari!" Asher managed to shout before the Brother choked off his words again.

The First Brother smiled at her then. The same benevolent smile he used in front of the crowded temple when he preached messages of the Unnamed Gods' unending wisdom and compassion.

"He's a loose end," he uttered.

The flash of metal was so sudden that Aurelia gasped from where she was still chained against the wall.

Asher arched his back, his face twisting in agony as he looked at Aurelia. His green eyes glittered as he slumped to the dirty floor, the dagger in the Brother's hand now wet with his blood.

"No!" Aurelia screamed.

A wild blast of magick left her fingertips, striking the wall behind the First Brother. A cloud of dust and debris fell as the brick crumbled, but before she could strike again he stumbled and ran from the room.

She strained against the chains that bound her, reaching for Asher. He was slumped over just a few feet away, but out of her reach.

Metal groaned as she pulled harder, but the chains wouldn't give.

Closing her eyes, she dug deep into that well of power that Ven had spoken of. A well that she'd been too frightened to explore until now. Too timid.

She pushed past the wall of doubt in her mind, that hardened shell around her of the words she'd spoken to herself over and over all of her life. That she was weak. That she was powerless. That she was inconsequential.

And brick by fucking brick, she brought it crashing down.

The metal chains screamed in protest as they finally gave, breaking free from where they were bolted into the stone wall.

She was thrown to the ground, and she crawled across the floor to Asher, the color steadily draining from his face.

"Stay with me!" she shouted, slapping his face. She gripped his shoulders, shaking him as tears pooled at her lashes. There was so much blood, too much.

His green eyes were unfocused as he looked up into her face.

She choked out a sob of relief, but even as she looked down at him, she knew from the scent alone that it was too late.

"Damn it, Asher ... Why did you have to follow me here." Her voice broke around the words.

He coughed, wet and thick before his lips moved, and she had to lean in to hear him. "Because you came back ... different," he whispered. "Do you think I care so little that I wouldn't notice?" he rasped. "I thought ... You knew me better than that," he said heavily, his breath shallow and uneven as his eyes closed, the tension in his body melting away beneath her hands.

She pressed her forehead to his, blinking away the tears that were lining her eyes.

Shadows pounded down onto the floor beside her. The stench of demon blood overtook the smell of Asher's as Ven ran to where she cradled her brother's head.

"Please—" she begged, "There must be something."

Another shadow hit the floor and Seth emerged from the dark tendrils.

"Take him back to Ravenstone. Embra might be able to help," Ven ordered, and without a word Seth lifted Asher into his arms and vanished again.

Ven towered above her, his hair was tied back, and black blood speckled his face and neck. "What happened to waiting for backup?" he growled, helping her to her feet.

"I couldn't just sit and wait while the rest of you were defending *my* people. *My* home," she snarled.

He gripped her shoulder, spinning her around to look at him. His hands lifted to cup her face, and she was surprised to see worry etched between his brows. "I would ask that of any Wraith. It's not because I don't believe you are capable—but because we do not leave one another to fight alone."

She's part of the bargain.

The words came crashing down on her once more in the musty silence of the cell.

"It's me," she whispered to him, nearly unable to get the words out as his shadows enveloped them in velvet midnight, casting them out into the darkened courtyard. "I'm the price the King of the Void demanded."

She turned to see his jaw was set in a rigid line. His crimson eyes darkened as they met hers.

He knew.

"Your power called to mine even before I realized you were one of us." The tension that thrummed through her body loosened a little at his words. "It's blood magick you wield, that much is clear, but your power is something I've never seen before…" Ven uttered, as if he didn't quite believe it himself.

All the centuries that he'd witnessed, and *she* was something he hadn't seen before.

"You were the surge in magick, Aurelia," he whispered, pressing on when she didn't say anything. "The shattered wards…" He paused. "Lanthius told me what the bells meant before we left Eisenea." His crimson eyes branded her as if there was some hidden truth beneath her own. "A child has been conceived in the kingdom," he said quietly. Reverently. "Magick is returning."

Centuries … It had been centuries since a child had been born to any of the magickal kingdoms. He'd told her as much on that glittering balcony in the Crystal City … The evidence was clear in the vacant halls of Ravenstone.

"Me?" The word tumbled out of her mouth. "But that means…" She couldn't finish the sentence. Her voice giving out with dawning horror. Tense silence stretched between them as the words sank in.

She had shattered the wards protecting the human realm.

Her breath turned ragged as the other pieces started falling into place. Her vision tunneling … The King of the Void wanted *her*…

"It was because of me," she whispered, a tear welling in her eye and rolling down her cheek. "All of this was because of me…"

The First Brother had said he needed to keep her somewhere safe until the Dark King called in his favor. Now it made sense how she'd managed to escape the Fengul alive, how the demons had found them as they left the wards of the Allokin Kingdom. Why the attacks on the Captiol had stopped and nothing had tried to come through the portal since she'd been gone—the demons had never meant to kill her.

They were tracking her.

They'd been coming into the human realm to find her, and she'd put everyone she'd ever loved in danger because of it. Her power had led them straight to the Capitol. Straight to her family. Her father—Asher.

"Look at me," Ven commanded, his voice resonating in the darkened gardens. Fresh tears lined her eyes as she met his gaze.

"None of this was your fault," he said quietly.

Swallowing down the constriction in her throat, she scrubbed away the tears stinging her eyes. There was no time left for them. If they didn't get the ring from the First Brother and seal the wards soon, the human realm would be overrun—and she'd die before she let that happen.

"Promise me one thing," she uttered.

"His death belongs to you." Ven gripped her chin, his cold stare meeting hers. "I give you my word."

Chapter 54

She told Ven everything the First Brother had done, what he still hoped to accomplish, as they crossed the night-darkened courtyard.

"The border is being overrun, the demons that the First Brother summoned are targeting the Allokin. Lanthius is buying us time by keeping the wards held open, but he wouldn't risk his apprentice's lives. He sent them back. He's closing up the gaps as quickly as he can find them, but whatever spell the First Brother used is threatening to bring the entire border crashing down."

"Then let's not waste the time he's given us," she uttered, coming to a halt in the middle of the gardens and glancing around at the palace grounds. "The First Brother is a coward," she ground out between her teeth, "He'll be somewhere safe. Somewhere a stray demon wouldn't be able to touch him," she panted, grateful now for the torturous training sessions Ven had put her through.

"Someplace he could ward with rudimentary magick…" Ven muttered, "Or someplace that was built to withstand an attack like this. Are there any parts of the palace that predate the Council?"

"One," Aurelia gasped, sprinting across the courtyard.

Ven's jaw was set into a stubborn line as she worked out the plan for them. He opened and closed his mouth a dozen times, but shockingly, remained quiet until she had laid out every detail.

"I have a right to fight for you, too," she said, resolve hardening her voice.

He glanced at her, narrowing his eyes like he might argue one last time.

"You gave me your word," she said fiercely.

His mouth remained a tight line as his crimson eyes met hers, conveying with one look what a thousand words would never manage to express. The aching sadness that was there was almost enough to make her abandon her plan.

With a dip of his chin, Ven disappeared into a wisp of shadow mid-stride.

Aurelia pounded her way up the palace steps and flew down the corridors leading to the library. She didn't know if she would survive the night, but she would gladly die if it meant severing that ring from the First Brother's cold, dead hand—what she should have done the first time she'd had him alone.

Skidding to a halt in front of the towering wooden doors, Aurelia placed a hand on the knob, recoiling at the bite of cold metal. And she wondered how the First Brother could have gone so long without realizing the kind of dark magick he'd been harnessing. Or maybe he did, and he just didn't care.

The door swung open without resistance, and she placed feather-light steps along the perimeter of the darkened library.

She could find her way in this place blindly, but her new eyes adjusted quickly to the darkness. It made sense that he'd be here—where he had the protection of the elements around him. The library's bricks had been laced with salt and threaded with iron if the tales were to be believed. And she knew well enough by now that there was a seed of truth to every story.

Torchlight flickered at the back corner. Something in her screamed to run, all senses on high alert, but she couldn't leave until she saw the man dead. The man who'd killed her father. Asher ... She couldn't let herself think about what had become of Asher right now. Her mind needed to be here.

Standing outside a circle of dark powder on the stone floor, the First Brother was hunched over the map, a dagger in his hand, muttering that cold, sinister, lost language under his breath. The large ruby from his ring glinted threateningly in the torchlight.

A shot of white light exploded from her hand, the branch of lightning unfocused and wild, but she only needed to disrupt the spell and distract him.

Her magick struck the First Brother on the shoulder, the force of it throwing him back against the wall, but the heat glanced off of some invisible shield, leaving him unharmed.

He covered his face from the blinding light, and she tightened her grip on the black dagger in her hand, running for where he was hunched against the bookshelves. She'd never killed anyone. Not a person, at least … But she felt no hesitation at what she needed to do to save her family, the human realm … Even Bastien.

She lunged for him, testing the immortal strength of her body, but he swatted her away like a fly, throwing her into the stacks and watching them teeter and fall on top of her.

He went back to his spell, speaking the ancient language rapidly now, every syllable clipped and cut. But she sensed the darkness they called forth. Felt it in her very bones as she heaved the broken bookshelf off of her, clawing her way through the pile of heavy tomes.

Lightning crackled at her fingertips as the First Brother continued his chanting, surging through her body and erupting.

She struck him again and again, each blast of magick more untamed than the last, but each strike harmlessly bounced off his robes.

It was enough of a disruption that there was frustration written across his features. He whirled around again to face her, seeming to battle with himself over harming her. Good—angry was good. They circled each other slowly, like two predators sizing each other up.

The ring had given him twice the strength of a normal man but sparring with Karro and Nira had prepared her for this. She attacked low, hooking a boot around his ankle and sending him sprawling to the floor. She dug into her well of magick for another bolt of lightning, hoping this might be the one to shatter the shield around him—

Her magick sputtered, rising just to the surface but fizzling out. She called it forth once more, waiting for the familiar heat to flood through her veins and overflow her senses—but nothing came.

So be it. She'd only tested her newfound strength a little, it was time to see what she was *really* capable of. She stepped forward, hitting an invisible force, the sensation like running into a glass door.

The First Brother's oily laughter echoed through the library as he leisurely pushed himself back to his feet, seeming to be in no hurry now. "As tempting as it is to kill you, *he* wants you safe until he comes to claim you." He glanced down to the floor near her feet, and she followed his gaze.

To the ring of black powder encircling her.

Fear skittered down her spine as she beat her fist against the transparent walls that surrounded her.

She was trapped.

Chapter 55

Every instinct in his body was fighting against him. Millenia of evolution or maybe that cold bitch, Fate— He wasn't sure which was responsible for the physical ache in his chest that tore into a gaping hole as he left the human realm and went back into the fray just outside the shattered wards.

Chaos had descended around them. The stench of sulfur and blood was thick in the air. The mist covering the ground seemed denser, somehow.

Karro grunted as shadows flew from his left hand and the heavy blade in his right sliced through demon after demon. The putrid bodies were swarming closer to where Lanthius was frantically working to weave his spell. The pale golden light emitted from his fingertips like a beacon in the dark night of the Shades, though the mist that hovered around them seemed to disorient the demons and work in their favor.

Nira was at Lanthius' back, slicing through three rows of demons with whips of midnight and onyx, turning them into ash before they could get within a dozen feet of the Allokin spellmaster. And Lanthius, true to the male he'd remembered in the thick of battle centuries ago, didn't even flinch from his work as the dark creatures crept forward.

Demons were gathering along the entire border of the Valley, but this portal, this one section of the wards was the weakest link, and if even one thread was pulled—it could unravel entirely.

Nira paused from her death-dealing only long enough to give him a dip of her chin in acknowledgement, surprise flaring in her dark eyes.

"Do it!" he shouted to Lanthius, over the deafening sound of battle.

Karro glanced over his shoulder as Ven took up his position beside him. Heavy understanding in his scarlet eyes as he looked to where Ven stood. Alone.

Without hesitation, Lanthius laced the gold threads of magick tighter and tighter. Weaving a silken spell that threaded its way across the portal ... One that would seal it shut.

Putting fingers to his lips, Ven let out a whistle that pierced the night air of the Shades.

Glowing green eyes focused on him from every direction. He dug his feet into the earth, swinging the sword in his hand and lighting it aflame with his black fire.

A beacon.

A distraction.

A grim smile curved his lips at the blur of black that went screaming past him, unnoticed.

Chapter 56

The First Brother turned around again, confident that he wouldn't be disturbed anymore. Aurelia pounded her fists against the hard wall of air surrounding her, the sound muffled along with her shouts of rage.

The air turned thick and heavy as his chanting resumed, just like it had in the tunnel beneath the temple, and suddenly his voice broke off, leaving the library stagnant and silent.

The air grew still around them. Deathly still. Like a great gasp before a plunge.

Dread pooled in her stomach as a sound rent the air around them, like the very fabric of their world had been torn in two. And though she saw no visible change, she could feel the rift in … something.

Reedy laughter echoed across the room as the First Brother straightened up again and turned to face her. "It's done," he uttered.

Rage unfurled under her skin, bringing the blistering heat to the surface as her magick answered her call, only to be smothered by whatever spell he was using to contain her. White heat flashed in her eyes, blazing behind the gold of her irises. For a fleeting moment, there was fear in the First Brother's eyes—and she savored that. Rolling it around on her tongue so that she could remember the flavor of his terror when she finally killed him.

"What does he want with me?" Her voice was flat with resolve.

The First Brother offered her an eel-like smile in return. "That is for him to tell you."

She gave a breathless laugh, "You don't know."

"Their plans are beyond human comprehension," the Brother answered with pious indignation.

She kicked at the air encasing her, testing the boundaries over and over again, searching for any weakness. Reaching deep into her well of power, she tried to dredge forth anything that might answer the call.

Her lightning hissed in frustration, the crackling, restless energy smothered by some dark magick.

A clever trick, but eventually … eventually it wouldn't hold. And whether it took hours or weeks— when she was finally free—there would be nowhere for the First Brother to hide from her wrath.

The First Brother laughed, nervous and unsettled, not daring to take a step closer to where he'd contained her inside the ring of dark powder. "No one is coming for you," he spat, a cold gleam in his eyes.

But what he didn't realize, is that had been the point.

She replayed the last thing she'd said to Ven over and over in her mind. If only to hear the deep rumble of his voice as he argued with her for the last time.

She could have gone with him, but the cost would have been letting the First Brother live to see another day, live to try and bring the wards crashing down again ... And that was something she could not abide.

So she'd told him to seal her inside. Knowing that it meant Ven, Karro, Nira ... None of them could cross the wards to help her, but if it kept the demons outside, too, then the cost was worth it. She only hoped that she'd given them enough time to accomplish the task.

She looked at the small silhouette of the man in front of her. He'd gone quiet and still, waiting for something. Waiting for the sounds of the Capitol descending into chaos, she realized. Waiting for his moment to be the shining savior of the human realm.

And indeed, there was the sound of something—

Even her newly immortal ears strained to listen for it...

A deep, rhythmic, beating.

Air rushed above her, a dark shadow falling over the First Brother's face, but she kept her eyes trained on him as she finally said, "We do not fight alone."

The only thing that had tipped the scales for Ven to willingly leave her behind.

Black wings descended silently.

Gleaming onyx talons lashed out at the First Brother's face. And as he tried to fight off the large bird, he didn't notice that the rush of air from the massive wings had broken the sharp line of black powder on the floor.

Barely a smudge in the perimeter, but enough that Aurelia stepped over the line, no longer contained by his spell.

The First Brother's back was on the ground, limbs flailing as he fought the heavy raven who had settled on his chest, his hysterical screams filling the vaulted ceilings of the library.

Aurelia put a booted foot on his arm, picking up the hand that bore the too large ring. And palming the jeweled hilt of her dagger, she sawed through his finger, ignoring the slick blood that coated the heavy ring as it fell into her palm. She recoiled at the cold bite of the metal as she pocketed the relic before glancing down to the First Brother writhing on the floor.

Blood sprayed across the white marble as Cog ripped his own token from the First Brother's head. The man's screams turned into muffled sobs as the raven circled the room with his trophy before his weight settled on Aurelia's shoulder.

"I called for backup," she uttered.

She drank in the pure panic on the First Brother's face like a finely aged wine. Terror and fear drenched the air in the library and she savored that, too.

A thick branch of lightning arched from her fingertips straight into his chest, the flood of pent-up power begging for release. Aurelia watched as the white fire consumed him entirely.

Chapter 57

She sprinted out into the gardens, her ears straining for screaming or chaos breaking out in the Capitol. But there was ... nothing.

Silence greeted her. Peaceful, undisturbed silence. The slumbering palace loomed over her, and she breathed a sigh of relief at the quiet.

Lanthius had sealed the wards—she'd stalled the First Brother long enough to protect the human realm, and that's what mattered.

A cold, heavy weight sat over her chest, and she lifted a hand—touching the ring in her pocket. A reminder that even though the King of the Void was banished to his own realm, he still had reach. And he wanted her.

A dark blot flew past in the night sky.

Cog—going back to whatever fight was still waging outside of the wards. The raven could come and go as he pleased, the beast belonging to something far older than the magick that built the wards, or so Ven had explained to her—

And before the thought had fully formed, she was sprinting back inside the palace walls, past the library's open doors that still stank of sulfur and burnt flesh.

Voices rang out through the hallways, the heavy sound of boots hitting hard stone. If her compulsion on Bastien held... what would they think when they found the First Brother, or whatever was left of him?

She looked down to the ring in her palm, trying to ignore the bite of the metal. The Dark King still wielded control even locked away in his realm. And maybe she'd cut off one knuckle of his power tonight, but there would be more. There would always be more. And if she stayed here, she'd only ensure that he would search for another foothold to rip the wards open again.

Her mother, Wellan, they were safe.

She clenched the ring in her fist so hard that her palm sang with the bitter cold burning a brand into her skin.

The commotion herded her into the old wing of the palace. The place where all of this had begun.

She couldn't stay here—not when her magick was a beacon, drawing the Dark King and his creatures to wherever she was. Her father and Asher had already paid the price for that, and she would only bring more death and destruction with her. And somewhere buried inside her was a deeper truth...

One that had been echoing in her head since she'd returned, never really feeling like she'd come back.

Stepping into the last room at the end of the corridor, she walked over the deep gouges on the floor.

She turned to face the gilded mirror. An answer to a question. And as her fingertips were swallowed up by the quicksilver surface of the glass, she knew it was time to go ... home.

Epilogue

Five Nights Earlier

Bound.

The word hung heavy in the air. Ven toyed with the heavy chain around his neck, dropping it under the collar of his shirt again.

"It would explain why you felt her magick awaken," Seth offered.

He knew Seth well enough not to question it. The male used his words sparingly, so when he spoke—it was worth listening. Seth didn't say anything else, allowing Ven to digest the information in silence.

There had been a time when he'd been envious of Seth's gift. When he was younger, naïve. Before he'd watched with dawning horror as his friend showed no amount of surprise at the people they'd lost. The loved ones and the lifelong friends. Warriors who had been killing demons for centuries before they'd walked the earth beside them. Males and females much more deserving of life than he was.

And Seth witnessed their deaths twice. Once in his premonitions. Again, when they fell in battle at his side.

He wasn't certain how the knowledge came to Seth. Whether it was in thoughts or came in visions. He didn't have the balls to ask.

Ven dropped his head into his palms, scrubbing his hands over his face before he picked up the glass of Red on the oiled wood table next to him.

"Nira and Embra are bound," Seth reminded him.

"And so was my mother," Ven replied dryly.

"But you are not your father," Seth answered quietly, never one to be fooled by Ven's dismissive humor.

The words touched an exposed nerve. Because as much as Ven did to prove otherwise—it was the constant fear that dogged his steps. His every waking moment. That the blood from his father's side would one day win out, devouring everything good he'd received from his mother and her people. Spitting him out into someone he didn't recognize. Tearing him away entirely from the family he'd fought so hard to forge.

"She is honored to have her fate bound to yours," Seth said barely above a whisper, but there was no uncertainty in his words as Ven met his stare. "Will you tell her?"

"She deserves to know," Ven answered flatly. "Even if I am to curse her existence."

Acknowledgements

To my love, my soulmate, my everything, Thomas. Thank you for believing in me. Thank you for the countless nights lying in bed discussing what to do with this jumble of words. Thank you for supporting me not only in this crazy dream, but in everything else too. Even if no one else reads this thing, it means the world that you did.

To the woman who gave me my love of reading and fantasy worlds, thank you for always being my biggest cheerleader, Mom.

To my friend, Ashley, who supported me throughout this entire endeavor—when this book was just a few pages of writing to almost two years later when it was a fully-fledged novel. Thank you for being with me through this journey.

To my friend, Carolyn. My one-woman hype team. From frantic phone calls about cover designs to the nitty-gritty details of the book. Thank you for being as excited about these characters as I am and getting me through the final stages of editing.

To my fellow author and dear friend, Stacey Reynolds, thank you for answering every single question about the publishing process. From coffee dates to formatting meetings, thank you for holding my hand and showing me that I could see this thing through to the end.

To my dedicated beta readers, Clara, Katelynn, and Kathrine. Thank you for your invaluable input, your time, and your enthusiasm that led me to the final stretch of releasing this book.

About the Author

Kate Cunningham grew up in northwest Ohio, but as a military spouse has called many places home; including Virginia, Japan, New Jersey, and North Carolina. She has a love of black cats and home renovation projects, and spends her time raising her growing family with her wonderful husband on the NC coast.

Printed in Great Britain
by Amazon